Harken

KALEB NATION

HARKEN

First Print Edition

ISBN-13: 978-0-615-79929-2
ISBN-10: 0-615-79929-9

WWW.READHARKEN.COM

TO MY MOM
*for raising me on a steady diet
of herbs and conspiracy theories.*

AND DAD
*because he should get
another book dedicated to him.*

CONTENTS

1

THE MIDNIGHT CLIENT

There are some places in the world so empty you could scream and hear your voice echo a hundred times, like an entire village crying out at once. Almost everywhere else in Los Angeles, even in the vacant hours before dawn, there are distant rumblings of cars over concrete bridges, screaming jets flying from the LAX airport over shingled apartments, a nearby husband and wife arguing in Spanish over the credit card bill.

But not where I waited. The deserted street had been long forgotten by municipal workers, its pavement speckled with potholes and gleaming lines of tar left behind from shoddy repairs. Even the grass barely swayed as the soundless wind crept through the ends of my hair like fingers. You never notice the crickets until their hum has died.

I stood on a thin strip of gravel beside the road, surrounded on all sides by trees and boulders tall enough to block my sight of the San Fernando Valley of California. The road was swept gently by the glow from a single streetlamp a few paces away, only bright enough to stroke my face and the body of my silver BMW, its usually-sparkling paint now dusty from our drive up the hills. I sniffed with wry amusement. That was the terrible truth about nice cars: you might pay a fortune, but you still drive the same dirty roads as everyone else. Funny how roads were the great equalizer.

I leaned my back against its door, checking the time on my phone then glancing down the street in both directions. The client had told me midnight; he was ten minutes late. Every second I was gone was another chance my mom might get up and do a check through my door, or my little sister might have a nightmare and run into my room for consolation.

Rule Two: No clients on school nights, I could hear my mom's voice saying.

For a hundred-twenty an hour, I think it's worth the risk, I'd murmur back. That came out to two dollars a minute. She'd just grin and remind me of Rule Three: if I was caught, all the money I made that night and from my next two clients would go to my sister's college fund.

For the risk, I added a surcharge.

I finally saw the blue-tinged headlights of a car appear around the bend of a hill in the distance. I grumbled and stood straighter, hoping it was really the client and not some random guy out for a joyride. I always had late-night clients meet me here, where I could get a good look at them as they approached. Late clients made me suspicious. A few extra minutes were easily enough time to check a soundproof basement's padlocks, mix up more chloroform, and test the sharpness of some butcher knives.

But again, I couldn't complain: tardiness brought another surcharge.

The car inched to a park behind mine but the windows were too tinted for me to see who was inside, its lights nearly blinding me. It was regal and as silver as the moon above us, fresh-from-the-factory and polished on every beveled edge—the three-pronged Maserati emblem on its front like a miniature trident. A GranTurismo. Wealthy clients were not uncommon purchasers of my skills, but I still had trouble acting unimpressed. I opened my hands in greeting as the driver's door opened and my client stepped out.

"Mr. Sharpe?" I said, finally getting my first look at his face: a nearly square chin, tanned complexion, blonde hair cropped short with the stubble of a matching beard. Even in the faint glow his eyes narrowed toward me like scalpels. This wasn't out of the ordinary either. My new clients were usually startled when they saw I was only sixteen.

"Michael Asher?" he checked, a hand still holding on to his door. I nodded.

"One and only, at your service," I replied. "At least, for the next fifty minutes. The contract *does* stipulate your hour started at midnight, I'm afraid, and it's…"

I pulled my phone out to find the new time, but Mr. Sharpe had already slammed his door and locked it with the remote. He glanced up and down the road, which had resumed its deathly state, and approached me with his hands in the pockets of his jacket.

"Where's the target?" I asked.

"*My wife* is down the road a bit," he said with sharp correction. "She's meeting him over by the lookout I think."

"Your email said this has been happening all year," I pointed out. "You could have contacted me earlier and fixed things before it got this bad." *Lies*, of course—my practiced marketing spiel.

"It's probably been more than a year," he replied, brow furrowing. "Likely not even all the same man, knowing how *she* is. Who knows how many she's—?"

He cut himself off and his eyes dropped from mine, suddenly unable to continue what had spiraled into a spitting rant. I shrugged.

"I'd figure at least four or five men by now," I proposed, which was rather solid math in my client experience. He looked at me with dismay. I was never good at the sympathy part. It was impossible to feel for him, not after being mentally numbed by a hundred overburdened businessmen all suddenly anxious to keep up with their wives as their marriages crumbled from years of neglect. This was likely the most attention Mr. Sharpe had paid Mrs. Sharpe since their wedding day.

But my job wasn't to solve his romantic problems. I gestured to my car.

"Climb in," I told him. "I'll drive. Just tell me where I can watch from."

He strolled around stiffly and huffed as he looked over my BMW. "Work must be good."

"A lot of people like to know the truth," I replied. This was why the car was worth the money: it left an impression that I was successful, that I was right, that my gift was true enough for me to be paid well. And in business, impressions are everything. One good word from a client to his friends and soon I might have thirty more jobs.

Mr. Sharpe sat crammed against the armrest and door with his long legs uncomfortably bent. His clothes were too fancy for being out on this type of work: a bold jacket over dark slacks, hair trimmed perfectly and skin that showed no flaw. He wore a misty white ring on his right hand that was undecorated except for a single vertical line cut in its center. He could have been a movie star, but I wasn't supposed to ask questions like that.

My headlights divided the night from the road ahead as he pointed me to turn another corner, going deeper into trees and mountains. As we drove, I crept glances his way, but his eyes told me nothing—he was too determined or distracted to betray himself.

"So you're absolutely certain you can read their thoughts," he asked as I drove.

"Not their thoughts," I reminded him.

"You know what I mean."

"All I need is a photo," I replied. "Get me a direct shot, you go up and talk to her, I'll snap my photo and we'll be done. I'll have your answer."

"Have you ever been wrong?"

"I am always right," I told him firmly. That ended it. After all, I was Michael Asher: *the Eye Guy*, some called me. I'd read more eyes by my sixteenth birthday than an optometrist would in their entire career. It was why this man, and so many countless people before him, travelled for miles to see me.

Mr. Sharpe squeezed his hands together, glancing at me then back to the road again. We came to a crossing and he pointed left. The minutes began to tick by in silence, which was odd to me. Usually when I was dealing with a client who thought his spouse was cheating on him, he would continue to babble and make excuses and eventually start to defend her. He'd proclaim dozens of times that perhaps we should turn around because he was being stupid, only for us to continue driving without pause, because the truth was simply too tempting to ignore.

The trees got thicker, and the numbers on the dash clock continued to roll higher. I wondered if we would even make it to this secret rendezvous point before he'd have to start paying for overtime. I really just wanted to get this one done. I could get home and rest before school, and use the cash to pick up the camera lens I'd been eyeing for weeks at the photography shop.

"How old are you again?" he asked. Even though they always wondered, it wasn't the usual type of question from clients—an unwritten rule that the less we knew about each other, the less trouble we would be in if we were caught.

"Five days until I turn seventeen," I said. "I accept tips for my birthday."

He gave a low and yet not amused laugh, and I gave up trying to make him lighten up.

"We're almost there," he said. "The lights."

I slowed down and switched the beams off. Darkness enveloped us once again, this time unbroken by anything besides the moonlight. At first it appeared that we had stopped in the middle of a long stretch of road winding up the canyon, but when I followed Mr. Sharpe's gaze, I saw that there was a thin dirt path leading into the trees to our right.

He nodded toward it.

"They're down there?" I said.

"No," he replied. "But we'll be able to see them. There's a clear view of the cabin."

I sighed and considered my car's underbelly, but in the end left the road. I'd done bizarre things for clients so many times before that this wasn't strange. I'd once had a teenage girl as a client who was convinced her father wasn't really biologically related to her, even thinking he'd kidnapped her at birth. She'd led me all the way out of town to grab my photograph of him when she confronted him at his office, only to find out that yes, he was her father, and no, he was not at all amused by her bizarre accusations.

There was a bump as my tires left the pavement and sank into the loose dirt. The woods glowed with a dim haze. Finally, when the road had disappeared entirely from my rear-view mirror, he held a hand up.

"Here," he whispered. I put the car in park, turned off the engine, and bathed in silence.

We sat still for a minute, just listening for anyone who might have discovered our presence. My eyes scanned the forest. I couldn't detect any motion or life between the leaves and branches and gnarly trunks. It was a place even deader than the road I'd been on before, and would have been frightening if I hadn't developed an immense disregard for fear by then.

I grabbed my binoculars and camera from the back seat as Mr. Sharpe pointed out my window. I switched on the night vision so that I could scan the trees in its exposing green hue. *A cabin*, I reminded myself. *That should be easy to find out here.*

But even as I scanned the area, I couldn't see any building breaking the endless tangle of trees. I pressed the binoculars harder against my eyes, trying to spot anything unnatural at all, to no avail. All I saw was more brush, tangled even thicker off the path.

"You're sure it's this side?" I asked, looking at Mr. Sharpe. He nodded so I tried again. Still nothing. I breathed out with irritation. There wasn't a building anywhere in those woods, and if there was, the cabin was far too invisible for me to spot anyone's eyes. *All I needed was one photo.*

"Why don't you look?" I proposed, turning to toss the binoculars to Mr. Sharpe. He hadn't been ready to catch it and the binoculars dropped heavily into his lap.

I opened my mouth to apologize but stopped in that same split second. The moment the falling binoculars surprised Mr. Sharpe, the camouflage that he had so masterfully held over his gaze vanished, and I saw *the Glimpse.*

It was gone a half-second later. But that was all I ever needed.

I felt so stupid for not seeing it before.

I'd studied killers, mostly from afar through history textbooks and documentaries. Usually they were nervous, balancing their barely-restrained aggression against the aching of their almost-stifled conscience. But sociopaths had no conscience. In Mr. Sharpe's eyes, there was no fear for what he was about to do because life simply meant less to him than a blade of grass.

He unbuckled his seat belt and leaned forward, pretending to study the empty woods—as he'd been doing the entire time. All of it had been an act. There were no lovers in the woods, there was no cabin, and there was no reason for this man to have brought me this far into the middle of nowhere, except for one. I tightened my hands into fists, hoping that this one time, I had read someone wrong.

Unfortunately, I was never wrong.

"I was sure they'd be here," he said with false lament. "It's a pity I brought you all the way out."

Then, with a swift and practiced motion devoid of feeling, Mr. Sharpe jerked his hand from the inside of his jacket, tearing a hidden seam as the handle and blade of a long and thick knife broke free. The knife swung at my shoulder and would have pinned my corpse to my own seat if I hadn't been ready, sliding down in one swift motion with my head under the steering wheel, my foot flying up and slamming hard into the man's unsuspecting chest.

Air exploded from his lungs but I wasn't finished, catching the handle of his door next so that it flew open. He shouted at me, teeth ground together in rage, ripping his blade from the seat and tearing the cushion and material out in the process. His voice came as a maniacal shriek, striking within inches of my heart, scraping the skin on my arm as I dodged the knife.

I shouted, though I knew that no one would hear it, as the man turning into a beast of thrashing and striking and stabbing.

"Curse you!" he yelled. He swung the knife but in his momentum I kicked him again and he tumbled backward, half inside my car and half on the dirt, his knife still splattered with red.

In a flash of motion, I turned the keys in the ignition and threw all my weight onto the gas pedal, heart racing as the car flew into reverse. I missed him only by inches as he dove out of the way. With the passenger door still flapping against brush and grass, I rocketed backwards, the murderous gaze of the madman still chasing me through the woods.

My arm stung like a thousand teeth had bitten it. Blood ran over the gray material of my seat, its split-open insides an image of what my chest would have been if I'd acted a second later. But still, the man continued to chase me, shouting, clinging the torn bits of his clothes as he ran, diving to reach the passenger door.

I pressed the pedal harder, shaking as I flew back onto the main road again, brakes screeching as the car whirled around and my headlights grazed the trees in all directions. The momentum threw my door to slam shut. I hit the locks as the man burst out of the woods a few steps behind. I scrambled to switch the gears just as he hit the opposite window, pounding the glass with his sweaty face behind it, his hands grabbing for the handle. I shot off, throwing him from his feet again.

Always, always check for weapons, you idiot! I mentally yelled at myself, breathing so fast that I was dizzy, my heart racing and every inch of me trembling with the foreign feeling of terror. I'd had crazy ones before, but nothing like this maniac. I shouted just because it boiled up inside me, trying to hold my arm against my shirt so the blood wouldn't run everywhere.

Mr. Sharpe refused to give up even as I pushed my car to its limits. He'd appear in the mirror then fall back into the trees, only to dive back out closer to me again. I cursed at him, sweaty hands slipping on the steering wheel. I glanced at the speedometer but noticed something else instead.

Holy hell, no… I thought. The gas was nearly on empty. If this car died, so would I.

I checked the mirror, but suddenly the man was gone. I hit the steering wheel. This was exactly why I never met clients at my house. I had a website and a special email address for them to reach me. I didn't want any of them knowing where I slept at night. But that insane gaze behind his eyes—that Glimpse I still hadn't had a chance to fully process—had been so intent on my death that I knew he'd find a way to track me down.

My car engine whirred in protest. I checked the mirrors for him again.

In answer, there came a gigantic slam on the roof of my car that nearly threw me swerving off the road. The ceiling had dented above me from being struck, the hand of Mr. Sharpe clinging to the top of my car outside the front window. I wrenched the steering wheel to the left to get back on the road, sending him sliding over the side of my roof. His face stared at me wide eyed again, punching the glass with the rounded handle of the knife, breaking a hole in it and spraying me with shards of glass..

"Why won't you give up?" I shouted. He tucked the knife under his arm and reached through the hole to grab me with his free hand as the road and trees sped on behind him. I pushed myself against my door. He swung his hand further, catching the end of my shirt, seizing it and pulling me toward his growling face.

The pull on my arm caused my hand to slip, sending the car flying over the edge of the road and into the grass. My right headlight exploded when I bounced off a tree—the same tree that threw Mr. Sharpe from my car as I careened into the woods.

I couldn't regain control as I sped over sticks and brush, tires rumbling against pointed rocks as the bottom of my car rattled from being beaten. My head hit the ceiling painfully, my hands struggling to turn the car away from the trees as my feet tried to find the brakes. I could see a clearing ahead, coming so swiftly that I knew it was the mountain's edge.

Suddenly, there was a pair of trees too close together for me to pass between. My car slammed into one and then the other, shoving me into the airbag from the steering wheel as I came to a stop.

I waved the bag out of my face, breathing heavily and looking up. There was nothing out my front window but the glittering landscape of the San Fernando Valley, houses and cars and streetlights sprawling for miles. The car had come to a stop with its front wheels over the cliff's edge, the car's body sandwiched between a pair of tree trunks and tilting dangerously forward.

Somehow I managed to regain control of myself, diving into the back seat and wrestling the door open. I slid to the ground and crawled away on all fours as the grass and sticks cut my palms, and I collapsed behind a thick bush with my head buried in leaves. Dizzy, breathless… I had to force myself not to pass out as my vision faded in and out of black.

No more than two seconds later, I heard something tearing through the woods, branches being knocked aside like a ferocious animal approaching. The terror brought back my wits, and I buried myself deeper into the bushes, just as Mr. Sharpe appeared from the path my car had created.

Gone were his decorous jacket and his perfectly styled hair: now, his clothes were tattered from thorns and covered with tree bark, his hair a wild fray above his head. But even more shocking than his frenzied state was the leap that Mr. Sharpe suddenly took, taking to the air like he was weightless. He was lifted with a shriek of anger, slamming feet-first onto the top of my car, fingers curled open.

To my shock, ten pointed blades sprouted from the ends of his fingers, emerging from his skin like a cat's claws. The razors were long like a lizard's though, six inches at least, flashing and gleaming as if they were silver implants. They struck the roof of my car, embedding into the metal so powerfully that they split through the roof like blades against paper; claws aligned exactly where my skull had been moments before.

But they hadn't struck anything. I couldn't restrain my gasp, unable to believe my own eyes. Mr. Sharpe heard me and looked up, catching my gaze.

He jerked to stand; tiny sparks flying where the claws of his right hand scraped my car. But unexpectedly, he slipped when he found that his left arm was still stuck in the metal, the jagged edges drawing deep lines down his arm. I couldn't move. He pounded the roof with his other fist and pulled harder, but this only served to upset the already unbalanced vehicle. My car began to tilt forward.

Mr. Sharpe struggled to pull his arm free, digging his free claws into the roof. But it did nothing: no matter how hard he pulled, he was held tight. With a sudden scraping and crumbling of rocks, my car fell over the edge.

I heard a single crunch of metal against rocks, against skin and bones.

Everything went silent again. I trembled in the bushes, too terrified to move, the grass shaking against me. When he didn't reappear, I managed to stand, fingers tearing into the bark as I breathed in dizzy gasps. My mind was so shaken that I was in a daze, so I stumbled uneasily to the edge and looked over.

My car—my beautiful, gleaming car, whose mere down payment had taken me months to afford—was not far below, upside-down with its now-beaten underside showing. One of the wheels was still turning leisurely. The car had fallen against a tall part of the mountainous rocks, spiked in the middle so abruptly that it had been smashed almost flat. It was between this rock and my car that I saw what was left of Mr. Sharpe: two feet, one arm still stuck in my roof, and the other hand sprawled open in death's weakness, its silver claws gleaming like daggers in the moonlight.

2

DELIRIUM

Fear was usually a foreign sensation to me. In my mind, being afraid of something was little more than a waste of time, and at my hourly rate that meant quite a big waste of money. No matter whom I was meeting, or how dangerous my job became, I was *always* in control.

But this time, I wasn't. This time, I ran.

My pounding footsteps carried me out of the woods—carried is a fitting term, because I was hardly controlling my movements as I darted in one direction and then another. When I had no more breath to drive me, I found myself far away from my car, stumbling across the yellow line in the middle of the road, in the middle of nowhere, so deep in the middle of the night that I could barely see my own hands. My mind told me this was a nightmare, but that wasn't possible—not with the very real pain that stung from the knife's gash down my arm.

The firmness of the gravel against my shoes was a strange security that nursed my senses back. I remembered all of a sudden that I still had my cell phone in my pocket. But it had no service. *Typical Los Angeles.* I kicked the grass so hard that some of the tall blades went flying, and I wanted to throw my phone at the nearest tree, but that wouldn't have helped anything.

So I started running again, every hit of my shoes against the ground clicking into the woods like a steadily beating snare.

I am always in control... I told myself, over and over. This lie wasn't its usual comfort.

Somehow—I wasn't sure how long it took me—I found a spot in the hills with service for my phone and dialed 911. What followed was a dizzying rush of sirens, people in uniforms collecting me, an ambulance appearing and lights, lights...a cacophony of flashing, headache-inducing lights that burned my eyes and sent me reeling again.

Thankfully it was those same lights that broke me back into my senses. *What had just happened to me?* I expected for people with cameras to come running out and say that this was all part of a prank television show. That never happened.

Two officers sat me down at the back door of the ambulance, asking questions. I hesitated at first, because I knew how unbelievable my story was, but I also knew the proof was far too concrete. They just needed to go to the edge, to look at the corpse of the man with the silver claws, and they would be just as amazed and terrified as I was. Maybe they—professionals, no less—could drag the body up and find some explanation, some mechanical device that the madman had strung together that'd allowed him to soar through the air.

I only became more concerned, though, when the officers kept asking about the body, and kept forgetting about the silver claws. It was almost like they weren't even surprised...or worse, I soon realized, they didn't even believe me.

"Just go get the body!" I protested irritably, when they went back to asking about Mr. Sharpe for a third time. It was obvious I was tired of cooperating, so the paramedic shooed the officers away, saying I wasn't in the right state of mind for questions anymore.

The police had done a solid job of putting me in a bad mood. I saw my mom's minivan driving up. I was still sitting on the back of the ambulance, parked at the edge of the same forest I'd barely escaped from. Officers were spread out in the woods with flashlights, studying tire tracks and scratches and tears of paint from my car that marked the trees. The sirens were off but the lights still flashed in my face, a red and blue dissonance that illuminated my mom as she ran for me.

"Michael!" she shouted, voice cracking as its volume neared a scream. At the sight of me, she pressed her hands together in shock, face falling. This wasn't her usual reaction—she'd seen me in spots like this before and was a pro at the "you'll-suffer-for-this-later-Michael" shrug. Her brown eyes were marred with horror, slightly-over-forty wrinkles on her face and unkempt blonde hair evenly graying. I was probably helping speed the graying process along.

"Are you the mother?" the paramedic asked, his boots dangling inches from the ground as he sat beside me on the ambulance bumper. He was wrapping up the wound on my arm. My mom didn't answer and moved to examine the cuts, but the paramedic put up a hand to stop her, holding the bandage together between two of his fingers.

"He's alright," he assured her. "Only a cut and some bruises. And some...head trauma, maybe."

"The car's in worse shape," said another officer as she approached. She had DELANEY pinned to her shirt, one of the two officers who'd questioned me. She was dressed in full uniform, heavyset and a head taller than me even if I'd been standing, with large boots crushing the damp leaves under her steps as she tilted her flashlight out of our faces. Her radio buzzed as an officer checked in from another part of the woods. I was relieved—they'd finally found the crash. It'd taken them long enough.

"You're lucky he's still alive," she went on gruffly, hardly directing any sympathies in my direction. Her glance to me could have been a glare.

"Looks like he lost control of the car from driving too fast," Officer Delaney said, lifting her flashlight to wave at somewhere in the dirt, then into the trees. She was so disinterested she wasn't really pointing out anything.

"These are some winding roads and it's easy to lose control, especially when joyriding in the dark," she said. "The car is absolutely totaled too."

My mom opened her mouth to say something, but I broke in before she could.

"*Joyriding?*" I protested. "What are you talking about? Didn't you see my car?"

19

The officer looked at me and pressed her lips together. "Yeah, we found it, over the hill where you told us it'd be. Upside down and smashed."

My mom's mouth dropped further open in disbelief. I moved to stand but the paramedic tugged me back down, winding more bandage around my arm as I winced in pain.

"What about the man?" I burst. "I told you, he tried to kill me!"

"What the hell is going on?" my mom erupted. "A man? What man, Michael?"

Good thing so many paramedics were around because I was afraid she was about to have a heart attack. The officer, though, seemed far too unconcerned for my comfort. She just huffed, clicking her flashlight off.

"Come on," she said. "You crashed your car. Don't make this harder on yourself."

"Because he was trying to *kill me!*" I shouted with dismay. "Didn't you see… did you even go look for the body out there? Did you find the knife he nearly stuck me with?"

"Michael," Officer Delaney sighed, "there's no dead man by your car. We shone down lights and everything. You just drove too fast. Don't make up some murder story to—"

I'd had enough. My rage at her insinuations reawakened me. I jumped to my feet and tore through the circle before anyone could react.

"Michael, stop!" the paramedic shouted, but I continued to run, holding the torn white wrapping against the cut on my arm as I pushed through the tangled limbs. I could hear their frantic footsteps behind me, my mom calling my name and the officer barking something sharp into her radio.

I crashed through a pair of trees and was back on the familiar cliff edge. In the moonlight I could see the tracks from where my car had skidded through the dirt, the places where the trees had been scraped from hitting my doors, and the underbrush that I'd dived into to hide from my ruthless pursuer. I could even see the spot where Mr. Sharpe had leapt into the air and crashed onto my car's roof, tree branches cracked in his wake. There was no way I'd made any of this up, because I could still recognize the ground beneath me as the same that I'd dashed madly away from, shocked that I was still alive. I rushed to the edge, knowing that what I'd seen would still be down below, just as gruesome as I remembered.

But when I got there, shoes scratching to stop me, I was greeted with an even more appalling sight than the corpse that had been left behind. Now, there was no man, no long knife, and no silver claws—nothing at all beneath my car, not even a trace of blood to show that a corpse had ever been there. The only thing that rested over the edge of the cliff was my own BMW, smashed beyond repair. At that moment, the car didn't even matter to me anymore.

My throat felt like it'd become a runaway elevator, dropping deep into my stomach as my eyes studied every inch, hoping the dark concealed the body. But nothing could have hidden those claws, not their reflective edges shining like mirrors. I continued searching though, even as the group appeared out of the woods and my mom pulled me back abruptly.

"Michael Asher!" she shouted in my face, as I stood like a wax figure. I *had* seen the man. I *knew* he'd been down there!

"We've got him now," the officer said into her radio, pointing her flashlight straight into my face, not even trying to mask her disgust or how out of breath she was.

"When I tell you to stop, you *stop*," she ordered me. She waved the beam of her flashlight at the edge.

"I know there was a man!" I insisted. "I promise, I saw him!"

I looked at my mom. "He was a client. I'm sorry. But it's true: he was a client who wanted me to meet him to check on his wife, so we drove out into the woods and then he tried to kill me. But I kicked him out of the car and... and..."

I couldn't continue, because my story was beginning to crumble even as I told it. I knew what I'd seen, and yet every rational, reasonable part of my brain knew that most of my story was something I'd have laughed at yesterday, the banter of a crazy person on the sidewalks. *What had even happened? Flying and claws?* I couldn't say that again, not with the officer's face staring incredulously at me, like I was a five-year-old saying I'd met a unicorn.

"And *what?*" my mom said, shaking me, still listening fixedly. Our trio was immediately left to silence, the officer's face saying she already thought me to be a lying delinquent, while my mother's intense stare told me the opposite. She believed me, or at least she wanted to.

"He was there," I said, forging on. "Over the edge. He got stuck under my car."

I waved to it. The officer shook her head.

"Look," she said. She pointed her flashlight over. I wasn't going to oblige her mockery.

"Go on," she told me. "Go, look again. There's nobody—"

"Shut up!" my mom burst, so harshly that the officer gave a small jump. My mom let go of me and snatched the flashlight from the officer, glaring up at her as she did. She was a kitten compared to the buffalo of Officer Delaney, but I saw the officer shrink back an inch.

"I don't pay taxes for you to badger my son," my mom hissed.

She went to the cliff's end, swinging the light in front of her. The officer and I stared after her, neither of us able to say or do anything as we watched the light go side to side, my mom's head looking down at the tire tracks then over the edge.

She studied the rocks below for far longer than anyone could have been compelled, even someone who truly wanted to believe me. Though I hoped that she would spot even a hint that a dead man had been there, in the end her eyes just continued searching. My shoulders fell when I saw her blink and a dejected expression overtake her face.

She turned to us, appearing exhausted.

The flashlight was handed back to the officer without another word. In the silence I heard volumes of defeat. My throat went dry, and I didn't even feel the pain in my arm anymore.

"He...*was*..." I said. My mom didn't reply, only starting back through the woods toward the road. The officer, smirking slightly at us, nodded for me to go ahead.

I followed my mom, buried in devastation. The beam of the flashlight lit the way from the officer behind me, who was likely taking up the rear in case I decided to run again. When we reached the road, the paramedic greeted me with crossed arms. Everyone had his or her arms crossed at me now: Michael Asher, the boy who'd made up the story of nearly being killed to cover for wrecking his car. That was the type of thing a normal person would do—the same type of normal idiot I'd always tried to never be.

My mom stopped near her minivan, running her fingers through her hair.

"Do I need to fill out anything?" she asked, now timid. There was nothing left for us to do. The paramedics deemed me well enough to skip a hospital visit, probably because they were tired of dealing with me. The police told us that my car would be collected and scrapped. I winced, because as inappropriate a time to think of it was, I remembered my $2,500 camera was still somewhere in the car, soon to be smashed and shredded and melted.

My mom and I got into the minivan, but she didn't start to drive. She stared straight ahead at the scene before us as the officers began packing up. The road, tired now of all the action, had fallen asleep again.

"Really, Michael," she said.

I didn't reply.

"Really?"

"I know what happened," I insisted.

"Shut up about the man!"

There it was. I was finally going to hear it now.

"Seriously!" she said. "You could have sneaked out *without* getting caught. I've been awake the past three hours waiting to hear you get home, and instead I get a call from the police!"

I blinked. That was not at all what I'd been expecting to hear. She'd been awake all this time? Then she knew I'd been going out... *she knew?*

I opened my mouth to splutter a protest but she held up her hand.

"No, I've had enough," she told me. "You've made this impossible on me. Last week, I completely ignored you sneaking out at two in the morning, pretty much making an earthquake of noise on the stairs. Not to mention the night before that, when your keys were louder than my alarm clock."

I'd made noise with my keys? All of this was jaw-dropping news to me. How in the world was I such a miserable failure at sneaking out? And she'd known all this time!

"You go out the door at midnight and forget to lock it," she went on. "And I can't just leave it that way—not in Arleta—so I have to lock it behind you, and stay awake watching out the window for you to come back so I can unlock it again before you notice. And all this time, I'm like—*Cheryl, don't say a word. Don't get on to him. He's spreading his wings like teenagers do.* Except my teenager meets adults in the middle of the night and brings home money for it."

Crime after crime was being piled onto me at once. All this time that I'd thought I'd been cleverly getting out under her nose, she'd been two steps ahead of me. She'd practically been covering up my tracks *for* me.

She sighed. "I've done so well at this for years now. But the car...I just can't ignore the car. *You crashed a car.* You ran a car *over* the edge of a *cliff*, and now it's just impossible for me to act like that didn't happen. Why, Michael? *Why* would you do that?"

She lifted her shoulders in exasperation and any words I might have prepared in my defense raced out of my open mouth. One of the officers glanced toward the minivan, but seeing the pantomime of what appeared to be my mother's fiery wrath, he grinned and continued his work.

"I... I don't know," I stammered.

"You don't know?" she said. She laughed, like my reply was absurd.

"You're a genius, and you don't know why you crashed your car," she said. "I don't think I've ever heard you say you didn't know something before."

"I know it *happened*," I said, trying to pick up the pieces of my story that her revelation had shattered to bits. She rubbed her temples, trying to squeeze the tension out.

"I know the man tried to kill me," I continued. "I know exactly what I saw. I didn't make that up. And that's how the car crashed."

She sighed, releasing her fury and confusion. At least she'd gotten all of her yelling out. Even though she couldn't read eyes like I could, she had a way of telling things from my face. I wished I could have just told her what she wanted to hear, and she knew that, which was why I saw her expression soften.

"Come on," she said. "I want to believe you. So you better not be lying to me."

She studied my face for a few seconds. Her lips twisted up.

"Maybe," she said, "you just *think* it happened. Maybe you hit your head and now you've imagined all that stuff when really, it's all from delirium."

A weak response, especially from her—mental alarms shouted at me to protest. I knew that if I did she would believe me, and might even jump right out of the van that very minute and go with me to look for clues the police had missed. That was the way my mom was. She'd figure it out based on my word, and ask for evidence later.

But the last officer was driving off, and my mom and I were the only ones left. It was late. So I chose to lie.

"Maybe so," I resigned. She saw past it immediately but we both knew that rationally, her theory was the more solid one. After all, I had hit my head pretty hard while careening through the woods. Maybe I'd left the client behind hours ago, and all the extra parts were made up in my head during the aimless wandering after the crash?

Without anything left to say, my mom turned the key and started to drive.

Part of me hoped she was right.

∗   ∗   ∗

The night's ordeal had exhausted me, so as soon as we got home I went straight to bed. I heard my mom's key ring rattle as she hung it onto the tack on the kitchen wall, and suddenly I was aware of just how much keys echoed in the house. It was funny and bitter at the same time—how long had I thought I'd been making it out undiscovered when my mom had been patiently locking doors and closing windows behind me? I felt like the world's most bumbling spy.

This is going to make work ten times harder now, I caught myself thinking. But it was true. I needed to figure out entirely new escape plans.

And like that, I was already thinking of work again. I'd nearly been murdered—or at least thought I'd been nearly murdered—and already work was back on my mind. I was an addict.

I heard my mom's steps as she laboriously climbed back up the same stairs she had likely dashed down a few hours earlier. Of course I'd had no scruples about sneaking out for work. But that guiltlessness only lasted until I realized how many hours of rest my mom had missed for me. She didn't need anything else to add to her current list of reasons to lose sleep.

My head pounded wickedly, the heartbeat in my ears overtaking the silence my house soon fell into. I wanted to pore over all that'd happened between the two times I'd gone to bed, but I forced myself to leave it alone. I was starting to feel sore, probably from the swerving I'd done in my car. Sleep crept up slowly, though just as I became certain I'd never get any rest before morning, I was gone.

The moment I drifted off I found myself awakening again—this time, somewhere other than my room. *Dreaming.*

I was falling backward. Not the typical type of dream where I was simply dropping through the air but more of a steady plunge into darkness behind me. It was like I was being carried on a feather through a black mist, until the invisible ship on which I floated entered into a place of whirling gray. This gray soon became watery colors, then formed shapes, then all of a sudden I was back in the woods.

I was running through the trees, this time without the protection of my car. Where the branches and sticks had once torn paint from the car's doors and sides, they now ripped into my skin, forcing tears from my eyes.

And my finger...there was now a heavy, silver ring around the third finger from my thumb on my right hand, just like the white ring I'd seen on Mr. Sharpe, with three vertical cuts instead of one. It was throbbing and bleeding so terribly that I held it in my left fist to stop the flow of red liquid, like the band itself was digging into my skin. Still, even as it dripped across my shirt, I couldn't stop.

Every few seconds, I looked back, seeing something moving between the gray towers of trees that stood like prison fence posts—a flash of muted blonde hair, a gleam of silver. It made a rustling noise, diving from side-to-side, its breath even louder than my own. I could hear it against leaves, my steps heavy but my pursuer's nearly silent.

I was vulnerable without my car's layer of metal between the relentless man and me. So I continued to run, not daring to stop even though I spotted countless tree trunks I could dive behind. My pursuer was always four steps behind me—just far enough so he couldn't reach me, but always so close I could hear him and the torn spots in his coat that fluttered in the wind.

"We're almost there," I heard him say, voice like a whisper beside my ear. "The lights."

I slid to a stop because I'd reached the edge of the cliff. It was hazy this time, darker than it had been in real life, but I could tell where the edge dropped into nothing. In my sudden halt, I'd skidded against rocks, and they clattered over the edge against the metal wreckage of an upside-down car. Its wheel was still spinning.

I whirled around. Mr. Sharpe had stopped at the edge of the trees. His fingers were spread open, long claws in a brilliant array. There was little emotion on his face, no reaction or feeling for what he was about to do, like I was merely an item for him to cross off a list.

He stepped forward. My feet slid back an inch and I could already feel where the rock ended. Mr. Sharpe didn't grin, didn't acknowledge that he had cornered me.

No words. No warning or threat. He just moved forward, fingers twitching and curling with anticipation.

I stepped back again but my foot slipped against the dusty edge. Before I could catch myself, I heard my shoes scrape, the gasp of my own breath, and then I stumbled into nothing.

3

BIRTHMARK

I expected to feel my spine colliding with the rocks, to be flipped over as I slammed into the stones...even the man's dagger-like fingers pricking my skin, if only for a moment. But the only thing I felt was my own pillow, pulled from under my head and slammed against my nose a second later.

"Zombie attack!" came the yell of my sister Alli, battering me with the pillow as I rolled over and shouted at her. She beat me again but I managed to grab the pillow, throwing it across the room where it crashed with a line of tripods and sent them flying.

"Are you insane?" I burst, freeing myself from under the sheets and raising my hands in defense. She held my other pillow as a shield.

"That's what you get when you don't turn on your alarm," she said between laughs. Alli was eleven, a mirror of my mom with messy blonde hair and brown eyes. She was very awake, even though my mind was still hopping back and forth from my nightmare to the oh-so-thankfully-opposite world I was in now.

"Why didn't you at least knock?" I protested.

"I *did* knock," she replied. I glared at her.

"Knocked very *softly*," she corrected. I threw a pillow at her but she was a good dodger. My heart was still beating rapidly beneath skin drenched in sweat—I could still hear the horrible breathing of

Mr. Sharpe as he chased me. I rolled over miserably, wishing the entire night could have all been one long nightmare. The white bandage still wrapped around my arm told me I wasn't so lucky.

"You're up, finally," my mom said, appearing in the doorway with a cordless phone in hand, her palm over the receiver.

"Phone call, for you," she told me. Her voice didn't sound *too* sharp—at least not as bad as was to be expected the night after I'd crashed my car, though she did regard me with a gaze of slight dissatisfaction. Why was she even letting me take clients today? It seemed odd, until I realized that she was so entirely convinced that Mr. Sharpe had been my imagination that she wasn't worried about more murderous clients. I put a hand out to take the phone but she kept it out of reach.

"We're not gonna talk about what happened last night," she said, looking at the gash on my arm. "But don't think just because you paid for that car that I'm driving you to clients or to school."

I would have argued but she obviously wasn't in the mood for me to defend myself.

"So we're skipping The Rules at least?" I said, hopeful.

"You are absolutely *incorrect*," she said.

"After all I've been through?" I protested. We both knew I'd need money to replace the car; luckily I had plenty of other, cheaper cameras. But there was really no use in trying to get around it. I knew The Rules. Alli knew The Rules too, especially the third one about my pay going to her college fund. She giggled lightly and rubbed her fingers together like she was shuffling through a stack of cash. My mom shot her a glare and the little troll darted out.

"So yeah," my mom said. "*Tammy* is waiting. Your sister might afford Harvard after all."

"It's not Tammy, it's Mrs. Milo." I spat. "She's the only one with our house number."

"Either way, take care of it." She shrugged. "*Eye Guy*."

She tossed the phone to me and started to leave, but turned back to glance around the room again. Perhaps a quick eyeball of my stuff for weapons of mass destruction was enough to make her feel like she was doing a better job of parenting. There were stacks of lights with cubical diffusers, tripods freshly knocked over, two or three cameras and a shelf holding lenses lined up like a cabinet of drinking glasses. This was where most of my birthday and client money went: that shelf of glass and tubes I used to take pictures.

These, however, were hardly noticeable when placed against the most obviously unnatural part of the room. Almost every inch of every wall was covered with photographs, going along the edges of the furniture and even onto the ceiling around the wobbling fan. They were pasted up carefully with double-sided tape; their edges lined up as perfectly as a ruler—my best photos from my countless albums and computer folders. The crinkled edges of the papers made it look like the old house was peeling, and the splattering of color and black-and-white rectangles sometimes took the form of a mural.

Every picture was of a person: men and women and children, old and young, of every ethnicity I'd come across in LA, captured through the lens of my camera. They were all portraits but none had names, because the names didn't matter to me, most of them cropped from the neck up. I didn't really care about their faces so much either; what was important were their eyes. Most people might have easily thought it was just an art project, something I did to convince myself that I was unique and creative. But it was far more than that. This was my life of study: my *Great Work*.

Or maybe they were more proof to the world that I really was a fine, budding psychopath. The phone beeped to remind us someone was on hold. My mom lingered but I refused to answer the phone while she was still there. She huffed.

"On my way out." She disappeared and I swung the phone up to my ear.

"It's Michael." I got to my feet and nearly tripped over my blanket that had fallen to the floor in my sister's mini-skirmish. The aged house creaked under my feet.

"Michael!" came the voice of Mrs. Milo. I sighed—of course it was her. She'd been my teacher in fifth grade, but now she worked in the office at my high school. Like the game Duck Duck Goose, there were many things I wished I could have left back then.

"Have you done something to Tammy?" I asked.

"Listen, there's no Tammy," she whispered, words racing in her native Alabama drawl. "I didn't want your mother to get suspicious or anything, so I faked an accent."

"She knows who you are," I said. "You call here a lot. It's getting creepy."

I glanced at the caller ID. "You're calling from a Tammy's number. Please tell me—"

"It's my cousin's phone," she said. "I figured when you didn't return my calls you might have accidentally blocked my number."

"That feature *is* commonly activated by accident." I wrestled with my jammed dresser drawers. "Now I've got to get ready for school, and I'm sore from a car crash, so—"

"I need you to do one more check of my husband," she whispered frantically. "He didn't come home until three AM last night. Lately he isn't home at all. Like he's avoiding me."

"No idea why anyone'd do that," I thought aloud.

"I have a bad feeling," she burst. "I think he's running off with some other woman."

"I already told you he isn't," I replied. "We did this last month, right? Remember?"

"But it's worse now," she insisted. "He's going out for golf Thursday evening. I want you to come with me. I'm gonna go surprise him. You can snap a picture of him from the car when he sees me. I've got it all planned out."

"I'm busy Thursday."

"With what?" she asked wildly.

"I'm recording snail sounds," I said, exasperated. "Come on, you've already gotten me to look at eight photographs and I've met him three times. I'm sick of seeing the man."

"I'll pay more," she said. "I'll double your rate."

"No." Doubling the rate wouldn't help when it ended up as my sister's money.

"I'll...I'll get you a new camera," she begged. This offer stood for 0.03 seconds and I hadn't declined it. She leapt onto it as her chance.

"The one with the most megapixels!" she blurted. "I know you love megapixels!"

Her bribes weren't swaying me, though they were tempting. It wasn't money, so that was a loophole in the The Rules, right? She sounded so distraught I knew she'd soon be selling her house to pay private investigators if I didn't put her mind to rest.

"Fine," I relented, slamming the drawer shut. "Don't bother me after then."

"Not once," she said. "And if he's cheating, I swear I'll do it quick, with a tire iron or—"

I hung up before she could incriminate me any further. Adults—that was still a strange type of work. It wasn't like I

31

advertised. Word of mouth had just gotten around with the people at school, and then that had spread to me needing a website so people didn't show up at my house. My reputation of being right was too solid for them to resist knowing the truth. Not long ago, I'd only been approached by classmates at my school. But adults? Their secrets wrecked more than just social lives.

My confidence was sturdy. There were no mistakes, ever. I'd lived with it long enough that it didn't feel odd—it was just a part of me, the same way that some people could pull a train with their teeth or others could gauge distances miles away down to the inch. I knew eyes. I didn't know the parts—the lenses from the pupils from the zonular fibers. I *knew* eyes. Girls would bring me photographs of their boyfriends and I could see if he loved the person who took it, or secretly hated her, or had secretly cheated on her and didn't regret it and was planning to break up with her that afternoon. Business owners would have me lurk at an opposite table in a coffee shop while they met with potential investors so I could detect any hints of treachery.

And that was the true nature of my Great Work. The photos on my walls weren't just pictures of people's faces lined up in no particular order. If everyone could read eyes as I did, they'd see just how plainly sorted they were. In those eyes—every single one of them—I could see exactly what the person had been thinking and feeling at that moment, printing their Glimpse on paper. With the careful attention of a scientist, I had divided emotions onto my walls. *Joy*, next to my bed. *Sadness*, going around the door so people couldn't see them when they first walked in. On the wall with my desk were pictures of eyes showing *Anger*, and across from that were photos of *Fear*—those faces had a way of disguising themselves, but I could see straight through that. My ceiling, patchiest from missing the most pieces, had photos of faces showing *Love*. Eyes of love are the hardest to find. Love is the emotion most-often faked.

One day, when my walls were finally covered, I planned to take all of them down and turn them into a book. I'd have every human emotion ever expressed in it, and show the world just how many shades there were between them. Like primary colors mixing, joy and surprise might be *relief*, or sadness and love could be *bittersweet*. Maybe then my obsession wouldn't seem so crazy.

But that was years away. For now, my skills were just a gift; when it came to people like Mrs. Milo or Mr. Sharpe, sometimes I wished I'd unwrapped this one in secret.

I tossed the phone onto my bed and scooped up my clothes. A shower sounded perfect.

"Girlfriend?" my sister asked in the hall.

"Mistress," I replied, swinging into the bathroom.

"It's not a mistress if you don't already have a girlfriend!" she hollered at me through the door. I pulled the shower knob to wash her voice away.

Water stung the gash on my arm but the pain was becoming easier to ignore. A cloud of steam hit me from the shower. I choked at the door, struggling for air that didn't reek of old and damp metal. Even under the shower, I sweat faster than the water washed me off.

"This heat is killing me!" I shouted through the wall. Arleta is in the San Fernando Valley, which by some measurements is the hottest place in all of California. But my mom was on an electrical bill craze. Her patients never showed until 11 AM, so the air stayed off until 30 minutes to the hour—long after I'd left.

Mrs. Milo had effectively distracted me from my nightmare, but for some reason it hadn't departed entirely. I tried to scrub it out of my mind with fervent scratches of shampoo onto my scalp, realizing that I hadn't showered the night before and there were still bits of leaves attached to me. I happily washed it all down the drain.

I dried my hair, a mess of brown that was just a shade lighter than my eyes, but the room's humidity made it fall flat again.

"This is all very attractive," I grumbled, trying to brush it in the mirror. My hand stopped.

The mirror reflected my single birthmark: a circle of black going around the third finger from my thumb on my right hand, almost like a ring tattoo. In fact, as I thought back to the dream, it was far *too* much like a ring for my comfort. The doctor had said years ago that the pigment in that part of my finger was different for some reason, but not to worry. I never thought much about it before. It was strange how my dream had changed it into something else entirely.

I decided not to think about it. I'd been hung up on the previous night for far too long already.

In my haste, the shirt I had grabbed was a stomach-turning cacophony of orange and red. But it masked my tall and skinny frame, so I pulled it on and hurried down the stairs.

"Humans *have* invented devices that reduce the sun's effects upon temperature," I told my mom irritably, falling to sit across from Alli at the table—it was cheap and old, like almost everything else in the house, and the whole town. Downstairs stank of my mom's herbal concoctions, some liquefied in plastic bottles on shelves, some dangling as plants from string in the window. Each threw off its own prickly smell, and these mixed together into an odor more sickening than whatever they supposedly cured.

"You'll be out of here in five minutes," my mom said, dropping one of her organic toaster pastries in front of me. "I'll turn it on later. Nobody's in here all morning. It's a money sucker."

"Funny how the patients get the mercy of air and your own family doesn't," I grumbled. My mom was officially known as a homeopath, which despite phonetic similarities is not a gay serial killer. It meant she worked with some type of natural medicine and herbs—I didn't understand it, but whatever it was, people with far too much money drove in to see her.

I bit down on my food. It scalded my tongue so I spit it out. My mom smirked in a you-deserved-it way. *Revenge for crashing the car...* I actually hoped it was that. If she got it out now there was less chance of her blowing up again later, and all of the night before might gently fade away.

"I'm going to Meg's birthday on Saturday," my sister proclaimed. She stuffed her mouth with toast.

"Is that the costume party?" my mom asked. "I don't have anything for you."

"I've still got stuff from Halloween."

"Zombie again? Aren't you sick of zombies?" I said.

"You'll be the only zombie in a house of mermaids and princesses," my mom agreed.

"Then I'll be a zombie, and eat the princesses for snacks," Alli ended it.

There was no arguing with that. I dropped my dishes into the sink as I left for school.

*　　　　　*　　　　　*

34

Every house on Hogan Lane was built of wood and brick in shanty designs entrenched in the 1980s, unmowed square yards protected by iron fences. Towering mountains partially encircled the city like a wall hidden behind treetops. Our house had a white metal gate around it with brick supports and decorative spikes at the top, which was a very polite and middle-class-American way of telling burglars they were unwelcome. I had to click the lock to get through, and then stopped in my tracks when I reached the curb.

No car, I remembered. The car that had been parked outside my house for almost half a year was probably being pulped into a baby-food consistency at that very moment. I was like a king dethroned. So I walked.

Hunter High was a behemoth of beige and tan brick with rectangular blue windows and red and black flags hanging from the corners. It bore a sweeping glass entrance that made it look a little more like a space museum than a school. From the outside, it was one of those pleasant little places that old donors adored, with its own football team, a basketball team, a volleyball team, a wrestling team, and even a chess club.

But like peeling away at an onion, there were only a few layers between the outside and a more depressing core. Bars were behind the glass windows and metal detectors sat stoically inside the doorway, a groggy officer standing watch as I walked in. The only decoration on the white walls was a solid red stripe in the center, going all the way down, around the corner, and continuing on throughout the entire institution. If suddenly there were a shortage of students and funding, my school would make a fine prison.

I got to my first class and sat in my usual spot three chairs back and three from the wall. I could see everyone as they came in. I was accustomed to them avoiding my gaze—they didn't know what I'd do if I got a good look. Could I read their secrets? Would I suck out their souls? The rumors about me had grown far from my actual intuition. In a way, I was both revered, and feared.

The reminders of how different I was came so constantly that I almost didn't notice them anymore. A girl walked in to the classroom and, by accident, looked straight at me, and upon our eyes meeting she got enough shock to reveal a Glimpse. It was ironic how that worked. I read fear, disgust, and a little intrigue... but not in a good way, in the way that someone looked through the glass in a zoo at an anaconda.

Strangely enough, that didn't bother me, nor did it bother me that the seats surrounding my chair were the last to be filled. This was all usual. Why should I care, really? They'd all end up coming to me one day or another, meeting in an abandoned hall or beside the school, eyes watching in case their friends saw them near me. Hands full of money. Desperation in their eyes. And I'd just smile and do my job for them anyway.

Mr. Candas wheeled in an ancient television, its black and brown case sporting dials so old that the dust wedged between them had probably been there since before I was born. He was a short man of Indian descent, from Chicago, always wearing a sporty blazer over his jeans, never a tie. He loathed the principal with all his heart, but that was between his Glimpse and me.

"Who followed the earthquake in Japan yesterday?" he asked loudly, positive hope lurking in his voice. A few people raised wearied hands, though half of them were probably lying to get on his good side. My hand stayed down; I'd been busy, as usual.

"Well that's what we're studying today," he declared, searching for the end of the power cord. "I taped some of the news coverage and we're going to watch."

Watching a video...the day was getting slightly better already. Everyone's collective sigh of relief could be heard across the walls. Mr. Candas lifted a hand.

"But you'll take notes," he added. Grumbling sounded throughout the room. I reluctantly retrieved the notebook I'd started to stow, plopping it open onto my desk.

"I'm not sure if what happened *yesterday* counts as *history* yet..." I said under my breath. Mr. Candas, ever vigilant, sent a glare my direction.

"It's part of your worldviews. Some important people died in that," he said. "I say it counts."

That really didn't make much difference to me but I wasn't in the mood for fighting back. So Mr. Candas plugged the screen in amidst the shuffles of our papers and pens.

The tape began but there was no sound. A cable was unhooked somewhere, so Mr. Candas jumped behind the TV as the video continued to play. It was a newscast from the day before, showing a helicopter view of a wrecked city. Buildings were toppled like blocks, all the fancy windows and decorations now like the ruins of old Grecian temples. *Earthquake rubble.* Cars were knocked aside like a giant had played golf with them.

The report didn't stick on that for long though, switching almost immediately to an older bit of archive footage showing a tall man in a navy blue suit, being pulled by the arm through a crowd of reporters. Under his face was the chyron: *HAROLD WOLF, CEO of DREYCORP.* The graininess of the footage betrayed how old the video was, likely sometime in the 1980s if I could gauge the hairstyles right. It switched to a photograph overlay on the screen.

Finally, something I found interesting. I could see his Glimpse as clear as the day outside our windows, lurking behind his youthful, overconfident smile and the still-outdated, slicked-back hair. *Assurance. Absolute, total control over everything around him. Pride.* These were signatures of people who had money, but even stronger in the super-wealthy: those who'd taken the leap from millionaire to billionaire. No matter what they did, no one could hurt or stop them. They could circumvent any law, cover up any crime, and have any misdeed go unseen. They were almost like gods that walked among us, unfettered by our lowly restrictions.

I enjoyed reading eyes of people like that: people who I didn't see in the ordinary places. Their Glimpses were like exotic pets that I could mentally collect, rarities I could never find in a park with a bunch of ordinary people. Luckily, I didn't need to get close to Harold Wolf to read his eyes because a photograph did the trick.

I'd never tried to figure out the full mechanics of my ability, even though I wondered sometimes. How was it that a camera could uncover the Glimpse for me, when I would never see Harold Wolf in my life? Was it the momentary click of the shutter that forced it from a subject's eyes? Something else? Either way, a photograph brought down the mental walls, exposing the insides to me.

Mr. Candas found the cable. The volume exploded through the twin speakers, everyone jumping to cover their ears.

"*... seen here in 1979, when he was named head of Dreycorp and began what could be the largest about-face in corporate history for a company on the brink of bankruptcy...*" The TV anchor's calm voice came out as a scream. Mr. Candas stumbled to turn it down, instead slamming the pause button with the photograph frozen on screen.

"This is Harold Wolf," Mr. Candas said far too loudly, probably because he'd been deafened.

"Do you know who that is?" he said, pointing both hands at the screen.

"Harold...Wolf...?" the class stated the obvious in slow, disjointed unison. Mr. Candas looked ready to jump off a roof.

"Thank you, Captains Obvious," he murmured. He turned his back to us while shaking his head, the marker squeaking against the white board.

"You're right, but *who* is he," Mr. Candas said with a sigh. "Why was Mr. Wolf so important in the world?"

No one raised a hand. The marker continued to scribble—Mr. Candas didn't even check if anyone had tried to answer. He was familiar with our inherent laziness by now.

"Mr. Wolf," he said, "was CEO of the company Dreycorp."

He looked over his shoulder. Our faces were like a collection of mannequins.

"Do you buy sandwiches?" he asked. There was a bunch of nodding.

"Then you should know what Dreycorp is, because you've paid them lots of money," he said. "Every piece of your sandwich was likely Dreycorp made or contains some Dreycorp ingredient. That makes him a billionaire."

He scratched the back of his head. "I don't have time to go into it. You'll learn this in college. But basically..."

He scribbled a word onto the board: *DREYCORP INDUSTRIES*.

"Everything in the world boils down to which companies make the things we need to live and work," he said, cupping his hands in insistence. "Energy, oil, technology. Food most of all."

He shrugged. "And when a corporation controls a good part of one of those industries, they almost become a world power in themselves. It's not like we can simply tell them we don't want food."

"We could grow it ourselves," a girl in the front of class said.

"What if they own all the seeds?" Mr. Candas countered. "It's all about who controls the supply. Food is essential to life. It's how Harold Wolf became so wealthy. Because we *all* need what his company provides."

Mr. Candas punched the play button, and immediately the tape began again. The reporter picked up where she'd been cut off, describing the business of Dreycorp, the camera panning across rows of crops swaying in the wind, farm animals and giant barns with the heads of cows sticking through while they were milked by machines underneath their fat stomachs. It switched to the snow-covered door of a giant vault buried in the ground—a vault of seeds, she said, to protect copies of every plant in the world. *A seed bank.*

Then it changed to another picture of Harold Wolf. He was much older than he'd appeared in the previous, hair beginning to lighten and lines now creasing around his eyes, which had begun to look sallower with age. He was pale, with eyes of green and a beard covering his chin.

The Glimpse had changed. Harold Wolf was working hard to hide his emotions, but not even that could get past me. Behind the oh-so-well disguised smile, I saw that fear had entered into his gaze. At first I thought it was fear of death, which I would have expected for a man of his age. But when I studied it deeper, I saw that Harold Wolf was actually terrified of something different, something that loomed in his future. I detected a fear of a secret being found out, like a debt that he owed or a misstep he'd made and couldn't remedy.

Crime money? I wondered. I was already almost sure of it. Somehow he'd gotten in debt to someone even bigger, and he knew that they were coming after him. A man who feared nothing had learned the meaning of terror.

"Everyone watch and take notes. Concentrate on how this affects industries!" Mr. Candas commanded. Inside, I wanted to shake my head. Harold Wolf had probably felt relieved in that crumbling building, knowing that the earthquake was quicker than the death he'd have faced at the hands of whomever he was afraid of. How many years before some so-called investigation would uncover what he'd been hiding?

I suppose I could have made a good living in government work. But that was only if they could match my current hourly rate.

My classes continued, slithering by in minutes that felt like weeks. As the lessons became tedious, disturbing reminders of the night before distracted me. Someone's chair slid against the wall and the metallic cry brought me back to the screeching of my car against trees. The edge of someone's shirt got caught on the metal end of the desk and ripped, a sound far too much like the tear of

Mr. Sharpe's jacket. It became a struggle just to keep the memories away.

I escaped into the cafeteria for lunch, simultaneously catching up on Ovid's *Metamorphoses* and eating the abysmal food that only appeared worse under the fluorescent lights. In this babbling crowd of people, habit demanded I get my camera out and take pictures. High schools were wrought with drama and students' faces were always showing emotions I loved to pick apart. But the principal and I had been through this before: no photos of students on school property. Being prohibited from my usual occupation left me in a restless state.

"Don't dress in that bright color," a familiar voice interrupted my thoughts. "Drunk people will think you're a piñata and hit you with sticks."

"Hello to you too, Spud," I said without looking up.

"I mean it," he insisted. "Big sticks and bats. It's happened to me twice. They think 'cause I'm fat I'm full of candy."

"Or did they do it because you hacked their passwords?" I mused. He grunted—guiltily enough for me to know I was right— and heaved his backpack onto the table. Spud looked much like his vegetable namesake: not overly obese but with bits of pudge sticking out in his cheeks and in odd places up and down his short, lightly brown stature. His damp mess of curly spaghetti hair was as deep black as his Polo shirt, face already showing the beginnings of a moustache like a smudge of charcoal above his lip, even though he'd likely shaved that morning.

"So you crashed your car?" he said. He had his laptop open already, typing in a password as he unrolled the aluminum foil that held his lunch: cold scrambled eggs, three sausage patties, and a dried piece of toast.

"Word got around fast." I grunted.

"People talk," he said. "Actually—" he took a bite, "my aunt's an officer, and—"

He didn't even try finishing, his mouth so full his tongue couldn't move up or down anymore. I hoped his aunt wasn't the policewoman I'd forced to chase me down. That'd be awkward if we both showed up at Spud's family Christmas party that year.

"I don't understand how you can eat that," I tried to change the subject.

"You want me to be a normal Mexican and eat a taco and some guacamole?" he accused, diving into an exaggerated Spanish accent. "Don't try to get me off topic, man. I want to hear about your big fiery crash everyone's talking about."

"Are they really talking about it?" I asked, surprised. My eyes swept over the room, unexpectedly elated at the idea I'd turned into a topic of conversation. Spud shook his head.

"Actually, no," he corrected. "Not even a car crash can make us popular, man. I mean for a little bit this morning it was buzzing around, but that was when the rumor went that you were dead."

"I feel so loved," I said, clearing my throat.

"I'd have called you if I thought it was bad," he said. "But I figured it wasn't. I saw you walking in earlier, so at worst your car was gone."

"And a $2,500 camera," I said with a sniff.

"Yeah, that," he said, disinterested. "My aunt was pretty mad about it because she told my mom this morning when she found out you went to my school. Then she really popped when she found out I knew you. So here."

He lifted a hand and lightly thwacked my cheek. "That's from her. She said to do that if I saw you, for that murder story."

I sighed. This was Arleta—if there was any confidentiality in my police report, it was long gone once the officers went home. One of the most popular pastimes in Arleta was gossiping. Spud took another bite.

"So did you make that up or did you hit your head or what?" Spud pressed. "You know, that part about the guy trying to kill you."

"I actually don't remember," I said. He narrowed his eyes. *You salty liar*, they accused.

"Don't start," I told him. "I'm not even sure what happened anyway. Maybe I did just hit my head really hard."

Part of me hoped it'd eventually become something Spud and I would laugh about. Now that it was midday and the cloak of night had disappeared, even considering what I had seen felt silly.

"Well, that's nice," Spud said with a shrug. "It's good you're in one piece, because I need your help with something, and that'd be really difficult if you were in a hospital bed."

"I can't help you crack any more codes or unsolvable puzzles," I said. "You'll have to hack it yourself."

"What?" he stammered. "No, I figured that out. I need you to tell me if this girl likes me."

"I said no unsolvable puzzles," I reminded him.

"Listen," he leaned closer. "I need this. I need to know. You're the only person in the world who can help me. Literally, you are."

He nodded his head to the side. "It's Tiffany Dawson. She's in a green shirt. It says 'West Is Best.' Beside the table. You see?"

"Yeah, I do," I said with a halfhearted sigh. Tiffany was one of those girls who fell three rings outside of our socially mandated circle, with naturally blonde hair and glittery blue eyes. She also had an inclination toward any male whose arm muscle circumference neared the size of my head.

She picked up her tray and began to leave the cafeteria line, weaving in and out of the jostling students, hair brushing around her face like a magical gust of wind had entered the room to dance around her. Was her glow real or from her bleach-white teeth? She remained unaware of our reconnaissance: an easy thing to do when she was unaware of our existence entirely.

"Just curious about which alternate universe you met her in," I said, tearing my gaze away sourly. "I'd like to visit it one day."

"She totally looked *at me* in English earlier," he protested. "And her eyes lingered. They *lingered*, Michael. Against mine."

"In horror?" I said.

"In wild, uncontainable love," he replied. "I'm gonna go up to her, and you watch her, alright?"

"Please," I said, "stick to romancing computers. You won't like this, I promise."

"Michael," he insisted.

"She's far away."

"Don't give me that," he said. "You're the boy genius, Eye Guy."

He was gone. I wasn't in the mood for this but I tried to keep my gaze on her so I wouldn't miss it. Staring at Tiffany Dawson...*such a chore, Michael.* I guess my job had some perks.

There were actually two ways that I could read someone's emotions. Looking at a photograph was one, the other was a bit more complicated. In person, there was one specific moment I could read in someone's eyes, a certain look of surprise when their guard was let down. It was hard to pin what it was exactly: it was usually that split second when someone made eye contact for the first time or when they were surprised abruptly. That was why I called it the Glimpse.

Spud was just a step away from her already but then clumsily tripped beside her and into a table, causing her to spin around at the sound. I winced as I saw his cheeks go red. Their eyes met for a fleeting moment, he spluttered out in apology, then he was gone again. He dove back into the chair across from me.

"Please tell me you saw it, I can't do that again," he said, out of breath.

"I'm sorry Spud," I replied. "It's just no."

"No?" he echoed, his face falling. "But...didn't you see? She smiled, for a second."

"Tiffany is always smiling," I replied, taking a bite of food.

"You gotta be wrong."

I didn't need to reply. He was very quiet for a while, then he huffed.

"But every psycho-prodigy messes up once in a while."

"No."

"Really, there's a chance."

"*No*."

He sighed. It was an unfortunate fact that neither of us got dates. I was frightening enough, and Spud, my only friend, was exclusively intimate with computer programming languages.

"Do I owe you anything?" he murmured.

"Nah," I replied. "But you could show me some fun secret government files if you want."

He grabbed his laptop far too eagerly for my comfort.

"I wasn't serious," I stopped him. He leaned back dejectedly, nibbling on his toast.

The day did not get any more interesting, but only got worse when the yawning math teacher Mr. Chex twirled his moustache and assigned us a massive test, during which time he took a nap. I was all too happy when school was over, only to walk out to my usual parking spot and be greeted by someone else's car in place of mine. I cursed the crash again and started the long trip home on foot.

A mild breeze brushed the grass on the roadside. Every step away from the school and from my lifeless day lifted tiny weights off my shoulder. Alli's school wasn't far from mine, and when I started to pass it on the sidewalk, I saw her hovering around a group. I strolled up, pushing my fingers through the chain links.

"Get in my van, I have candy," I growled at her in my best creepy voice, and she turned from her friends, who all looked at me with expressions of horror.

"Get in my van instead," she replied, "I've got a jar of punch-you-in-the-face."

Her expression betrayed her words though, because she had lit up when I'd appeared. I usually drove myself home so I never showed up to see her. Her friends' started breathing again, but I'd probably upset Alli's chances of getting them to come to our house for a while.

"Where's Spud?" Alli asked. I nodded my head back in the direction of school.

"In the library," I said. "I'm here walking home all alone and lonely."

"Mom said I could go with Kate and Sammy," Alli said apologetically. Her friends continued to eye me suspiciously.

"I get it," I said, shrugging. "I'll just walk home, and probably get run over by a car, or mauled by a bear coming out of the trees—"

"Fine." Alli sighed in defeat. Both of her friends looked at her wildly, but she paid them no heed. Sometimes I wondered if she could read my emotions too. She had changed from their side to mine and I hadn't even gotten to my good begging yet.

She ran around the gate and joined me, waving to her friends as she disappeared.

"They're not gonna be mad at you, right?" I asked.

"They'll get over it," she replied. "Hungry?"

She held out a remaining half of a sandwich. I shook my head. We walked in silence for a while, the March sun throwing pinks and yellows across the horizon that bordered the high canyon sides of the Valley. Multilayered clouds hovered above us like the fluffy shreds of a torn pillow littered across the sky. Cars drove slowly by us in the school zone, kids babbling as they traveled in packs down a crosswalk.

"Did you do anything today?" Alli asked, since I wasn't talking.

"Not much," I replied. "Lame stuff mostly. Math. I hate math."

"I hate math too," she agreed.

"You'll die when you get to mine." I elbowed her. "They use letters as numbers."

"I'm already doing that," she huffed. "X plus one equals four. What is X?"

"X needs to die in a fire," I replied, and my sister chuckled. She always did that, at every crazy joke I made. That was probably why I'd gone to get her that evening. Which reminded me...

Without warning, I whipped my pocket camera out, and Alli dodged to get out of the lens. I was faster though, and rattled off a few snapshots as she struggled to hide her face.

"Stop it!" she demanded. This was our game. Alli hated me taking photographs of her. She wouldn't take her hands from her face until I put the camera away.

"I got at least ten this time," I gloated.

"And you'll have none when I break that camera with a tennis racket," she said.

Neighborhoods went by on both sides separated by the road we were following, the smell of damp grass coming from the vigilantly watered lawns. Some people were home from work and in their yards, babbling from terraces, blue fluorescent fly zappers hanging from the porches and armed for the attack of flying beasts. It was all a blur to me, because I'd seen this route every day for years now, even if it was from a car window. My steps became an autopilot.

"You're not listening, are you?" Alli said, slapping my arm.

"What?" I looked at her quickly. "Of course I'm listening."

"What did I just say?" she demanded.

"Something about death? Destruction?" I tried. She hit me again.

"I don't know why you wanted me to walk home with you if you're not listening."

"I'm sorry," I apologized. "Look, I was in a car crash last night—I'm not in the best condition."

I waved at my gauze-covered arm. "You can't blame me. Then on top of that I had a really weird dream last night."

"Were you chained to a chair and fed maggots?" she asked. My eyes widened in horror.

"What? No?" I coughed. "Where did you read that?" *Holy hell, she's only eleven.*

"It was on TV," she said. "I watched a show on a serial killer."

"How do you even know what a serial killer is?" I said with dismay. "You're supposed to still think that's somebody who murders Cap'n Crunch."

"I don't even eat Cap'n Crunch."

I gave in. "It was a dream about…running, from somebody." I didn't know if I should mention he'd been my client.

"Was he really ugly?" Alli said. "I dreamed of an old ugly man last week. But when he tried to get me into the gas chamber, I sprayed him with acid."

I stared at her blankly. My sister stared back.

"I don't really know how to respond to that," I said, blinking. "But I think you might want to schedule something with mom when we get home."

"I don't need a therapist," Alli said adamantly. "I'm eleven."

I was about to retort but we were crossing another busy street and the cars covered my voice. We got onto the sidewalk again, passing into our neighborhood.

"Mom said I wasn't supposed to ask you about nearly getting murdered," Alli stated. I tried not to look at her suspiciously. She had a clever way of getting her intentions across.

"You know I *do* enjoy a good almost-murder story," she said.

"Didn't mom rule that out?" I replied. "I was just delirious, right?" Part of me wanted to know what my mom was saying about it.

"But still," she insisted, "you remember *something*."

I debated whether continuing with this conversation was a good idea. My sister's head was disturbed enough. In the end, I decided I probably wouldn't make things any worse up there.

So I told her everything that I could remember, from sneaking out of the house and quietly driving to meet Mr. Sharpe. My story followed what'd happened step-by-step, but I left out the silver claws and the flying. Even she would find that unbelievable, I thought. When I came to the end, we were nearly home, and Alli was quiet for a long time.

"Mom really swore at you?" Alli finally asked, and I burst out laughing. That *would* be the one part of the story that Alli got hung up on. We'd reached Hogan Lane—thanks to Alli, I'd returned to this street in much higher spirits than I'd left it. *I knew it'd be a good idea to get her.*

"So what do you think?" she said. "You sure it's in your head, or maybe it happened and it was a good cover-up."

"There wasn't a body," I replied. "I can see where mom and the police are coming from."

"Yeah," Alli agreed, and I could hear that even she was slowly becoming convinced. "And honestly, if Mr. Sharpe *was* real, wouldn't his car still be parked on the side of the road right now?"

It took all of my mental power to keep myself from gasping out loud, though I couldn't disguise the sudden shuffle of my steps.

His car! I realized. Mr. Sharpe had driven up to meet me…and…if he'd been killed on the rocks, his car would still be out there!

All of a sudden, a way of definitely proving my story—true or otherwise—had appeared. In my shaken state the night before, I had completely forgotten that detail, and now that it had showed up, every cell in my consciousness focused on it at once.

Luckily, we had just reached our driveway and Alli was distracted. She went into the house without paying me any more regard, clueless that she had caused me to have a breakthrough.

I remained in this nearly frozen state through dinner, my body like a discarded exoskeleton. There were few questions over dinner: *how was the day, what did you learn Alli, did you remember to ask if your sister could help at the bake sale, is Michael listening to us speaking…hello, Michael, are you there?* Alli's hand waved in front of my face and broke me from my thoughts, and I robotically rolled out answers to them. Luckily they ignored my mental absence, probably thinking that regret over my car crash was sinking in.

After my mom disappeared into her office and my sister took over the living room television, I headed for my room and switched on my computer screen. That was my habit. I'd sit at the screen and edit photos all night, or study the gazes of politicians who'd been on the news, or the eyes of celebrities just so that I could mentally predict the tabloid headlines that'd be out months later.

That night, though, I couldn't even touch the mouse. I sat in the center of my face-covered walls, Alli's revelation rolling through my head. *The car…*that silver Maserati with the blue headlights.

I know it's there…

Now that everything had blown over for the most part, did I even want to know the truth?

I was unable to banish it. Finding truth was too much a part of me to simply disregard. If I found it, then I could tell the police and my story would be proven true, and they'd go hunting for this man who'd somehow escaped. My mom wouldn't be angry with me anymore and my name would be cleared.

And if there was no car in the first place? It was an option I didn't want to think of, because that meant I'd truly been having hallucinations. But it would put my mind to rest. Because if there was no car, then there had been no man. And if there was no man, there had been no murderous gaze or silver claws, and all of this was a mere overreaction.

I glanced at the clock. It was almost time for bed.

Or time for work? my treacherous mind countered.

My cell phone was in my grasp a second later, dialing Spud.

"What's up?" he answered. "Crash another car?"

"Not yet," I replied.

4

EVIDENCE

The last time I'd sneaked out of the house, I'd nearly been turned into human rotisserie. Sometimes I wondered just how dangerous I could get if I didn't constantly keep myself in check. Maybe if I'd tried to be more normal, I wouldn't have found myself climbing out my window at midnight again, careful of even the slightest noise this time. Maybe then I wouldn't have scraped my palms by scooting across the shingles until I reached the roof of our garage, dangling from the edge until the ground was close enough to let go. Maybe then I'd just stay at home and sleep at night, and surround myself with insignificant pains like how to get a hotter girlfriend or how to keep my boss from yelling at me for being late to work.

A girlfriend and a real job wouldn't be that bad, would it? I thought. As if I had time for either. I stole across the grass that was still damp from the light shower that had appeared early in the night, and slipped through the gate.

The emptiness of the street squeezed in. There were no lights in the houses, no cars pulling into the driveways. One might have found more life in a taxidermist's freezer.

I hurried down the sidewalk with furtive glances back at my house, its wooden panels appearing gray in the glow that covered the dismal street. My mom was probably (and hopefully) catching up on sleep, now that I didn't have a car to escape with. No lights switched on as I walked with my hands in the pockets of my jeans. There were only the empty echoes of the city far away, and the ever-present blue fly zapper someone had forgotten to unplug before going in to sleep.

To be safe though, I'd told Spud to park at the end of the street. I could see the outline of his beaten brown Chevy pickup around the corner, the lights off but the engine rumbling low into the night.

"I knew I kept you around for something," I told him as I climbed into the passenger side, the bench seats covered with an old mat stitched over its original material. Spud huffed as I closed the door.

"You owe me a good bunch of things for this," he said, though his tone betrayed his phony annoyance.

"What about the free work I gave you yesterday?" I countered. "I think we'll be even."

Spud pushed on the gas to shut me up. The engine was far louder than my BMW's had been—the sound made me wince, but there was nothing to be done about it. Most of his truck's original pieces weren't even there anymore, the radio from sometime in the 1990s but the steering wheel at least two decades older. A new sound system had been wired in messily with cables poking up from under the seat, and every time Spud slowed for a stop I had to push a speaker back under the chair with my foot. I only relaxed when we were a good half-mile from my house and Spud turned the headlights on.

The closer we came to the meeting spot, the more the anticipation inside me grew. What if the car was where I remembered? I hadn't planned through what I would do next. If I found no car, the least it would do was convince me that my mom was right, and all of this had been my imagination. I wasn't sure which I wanted more.

The truck wheezed as we crawled up the canyon road, everywhere around us still deserted and far too familiar for my own comfort. I stared out the side window as the trees and rocks passed, recalling my own quiet drive out. I'd left my house early so I was there on time, barely thinking about what I was about to do because it came so naturally. That job wasn't supposed to be out of the ordinary.

Now the woods bore a sinister feeling. My eyes kept imagining things darting amongst the trees: the glint of an animal's eyes, the face of someone watching us when it was only the withered side of a dying bush. I could smell the woods through the crack in Spud's broken passenger window that didn't shut all the way—branches still damp from rain, like the sharp scent in December when people started putting up their Christmas trees.

If I'd died out there, it might have taken weeks for anyone to find my corpse. It made me wonder how many other sets of bones might be spread out in those gloomy trees, never to be found again.

"Hey man?" Spud broke the silence. "You see something up there?"

I sat up straight. Spud's headlights were weak and their flashlight-level radiance hardly penetrated much of what was in front of us. But far in the distance, around the bend we were taking, I could see a gravelly spot on the side of the road. And parked there, like a lonely hitchhiker resting for the night, was a silver Maserati.

"Holy..." I couldn't finish. The closer we got, the more the lights shone on the car's gleaming sides. When Spud's headlights brushed with those of the car, the bulbs reflected like giant eyes, and all at once my fears were confirmed.

Like the flipping of a switch, I immediately returned to all of my original beliefs that the officers and my mom had done a good job of burying. Spud, so much in shock that his face had gone paler, pulled his truck onto the side of the road and faced the car, wrestling the stick shift into park.

Both of us sat wordlessly, the truck's engine buzzing against our pounding heartbeats.

"Is that it?" Spud said. I nodded.

"I think so." Part of me still didn't want to believe it.

"So what's that mean?" he said. "The whole murder thing? You didn't hallucinate all that up after all?"

"I... I'm not sure," I said. All along, I hadn't expected to see the car there. But now that it was sitting in front of me—a real, three-dimensional proof of the things that'd happened...

I jolted out of my thoughts and pushed the door open, the sound of my footsteps against the rocky ground bringing back memories of twenty-four hours earlier. I hurried to the car, walking around the side as my reflection appeared in its tinted windows. It was the same car, no mistake. No one would have left something this expensive sitting this far in the middle of nowhere, not if they didn't want it stolen. Not if they were still alive.

Spud appeared beside me, cupping his hands around his eyes so that he could see through the glass. I did the same. It was hard to see much. The seats inside were leather and the beige material had tightened back into shape long ago, since its driver had never returned. There was a briefcase in the passenger seat and a half-full bottle of water in the cup holder. I slid to the back window but the other seats were empty.

"Your clients are filthy rich," Spud exclaimed.

"That reminds me," I said. "He never paid before he tried to kill me."

"Priorities, Scrooge," Spud reminded me. He circled around the back of the car and to the other side, trying all the doors with his hands wrapped in the edge of his shirt. The doors were locked though. Adrenaline pumped through me so strongly that I didn't care about making a proper entry. So I walked back to Spud's truck, picked a long baseball bat from the assorted junk in the bed, and returned.

"Wait, what are you—!" Spud started to protest, but I swung the bat without letting him finish. Its heavy end cracked hard against the window glass but didn't break through. Spud dashed to stop me but I slammed it again, and this time it worked, the entire panel crumbling like an eggshell.

"Are you insane?!" Spud shouted. It looked like he was about to pass out. "People can hear that!"

"No they can't," I told him, passing the bat into his hands.

"You're lucky the alarm isn't armed," Spud hissed. "That's all we need. W-what are you doing now?"

I'd gone back to Spud's truck and retrieved a pair of work gloves from the tool compartment, which I slipped on. Careful to leave no fingerprints, I held my arm steady through the glass of the car window. My fingers found the lock and I pulled the door open, while Spud watched with a dumbfounded face.

Even the inside of the car smelled new, the scent of the leather having overtaken the enclosed space under the beating sun all day. I couldn't slide to sit into the seat though, because now it was covered in glass. So I leaned my arm against the headrest, managing to snatch up the briefcase.

"I knew I was right," I insisted, a thrill driving me as I dug through the glove compartment, finding nothing but a flashlight and the car's owner manual. I lifted myself out and dropped the briefcase hard onto the car's hood.

"Do you take diabolical joy in ruining precious cars?" Spud asked, waving his hands. I didn't reply, snapping both of the already-set combination locks. I clicked on the flashlight I'd taken and shone its beam down as I lifted the lid.

The briefcase's meager contents were painstakingly organized: two pens hooked on a leather pocket and a single file folder encompassing crumpled papers. I accidentally picked the folder up by the wrong edge and a mishmash of printouts and photographs fell out.

Something immediately caught my attention. I passed the light to Spud.

"That's you," he said, aghast. On the top of the pile had fallen a sharp color photograph of me, in the motion of getting into my former car. It was bright daylight outside and I was in front of my house, the photo taken from far down my street.

"It sure is…" I confirmed sourly. I lifted the photo only to find another like it below, this one of me walking from the parking lot to school, and then another beneath that of me at the Santa Monica Pier, camera in hand. There was an entire album of photos of me, all from the past two days. Mr. Sharpe hadn't simply been a deranged lunatic: he'd been stalking me.

Under normal circumstances, I should have felt violated. But I was far past feeling like someone had invaded my personal life. Too many other disturbing things surrounded this man, so that I only slid the photos aside and started to brush through the other papers.

I found a map of the Valley, showing a path in red marker that I suspected to be the drive I'd taken from home to school, then another tracing a path to the lot on which I stood. I found another scrap beneath that, the scrawled notes illegible to me. Then finally, a large strip of paper.

It didn't belong with the others, a clipping from a San Francisco newspaper not sturdy enough to stand straight without me holding it at both ends. The page had been cut to show part of a single headline, ink faded and smudged at the ends. There was a row of four photographs in the middle, showing a middle-aged man and a woman, and beside them two nearly-identical boys with matching hair and gray eyes, much younger than my sister. They were obviously a family, all blonde except the father, who had black hair and a thin, graying beard.

But above the four, there was a distracting picture that almost leapt out at me the moment my eyes met the page. The face of a girl. She was about my age, with dark chocolate-colored hair that hung over her forehead, the rest pulled back behind her ears, skin lightly browned like most of the people at school who lived close to the Pacific coast. Her eyes were a shining blue, saturated like a photo editor had enhanced them unrealistically, a center of flaring gray that raced out in a bursting star. They should have been nearly indiscernible in the cheap newspaper ink, but they flashed with an almost unearthly vibrancy. She stared into my soul from the paper, through the camera lens... *the Glimpse.*

Ten thousand thoughts lay behind her eyes, but no words could describe them. It threw me off. With that much clarity, I should have been able to read her emotions precisely, but somehow I'd become too boggled to do it. I managed to pick out a few: *amusement* and *happiness* and *joy.* But there were thousands more hidden inside her. I could have studied them for hours.

It belonged on my wall. I *needed* her eyes on my wall.

"Who's that?" Spud asked from beside me. I swallowed, having forgotten he was there.

"I don't know," I replied.

"That's really sad," he told me, with far too much lament in his voice. "She was hot."

For a moment I couldn't figure out why he sounded so down, but then I noticed the headline at the top of the page: SAN FRANCISCO FAMILY DEAD, BURNED IN HOME.

I'd had the breath knocked out of me before. When I was nine, my neighbor Andrew Roscolli had lost twelve Pokémon cards to me in a bet, and in a rage he'd hit me with a baseball bat. That was the feeling that overcame me the second I read that headline. Instantly I was lightheaded, blinking, my throat dry as dizziness forced me to lean against the car's side to steady myself. The cold metal brought me back, squeezing the edges of the newspaper so tightly that I crumpled it.

"Calm down, man," Spud told me. What was wrong with me? I unfolded the bottom of the paper only to find that the article wasn't a part of the clipping. There were names, though, in the caption: THE STEWART FAMILY. Steve and Margaret, with their twin sons Bobby and Steve Jr. And the girl: *Callista*.

My heart was beating faster now. I glanced to the top of the newspaper. It was dated five days ago. She'd been alive so recently. Barely gone. Freshly dead.

"You think he killed them too?" Spud said, voicing what I was too shaken to say.

"That would…make sense," I agreed, gesturing emptily at the briefcase and then rubbing my forehead to ease the pounding headache that had arisen. *Why?* How could there be any reason to kill this family? Then go after me but leave my family unharmed?

Those thoughts made my insides reel. *What are you doing, Michael?* I didn't know these people and there was no logical reason for me to act like I cared.

I folded the newspaper up immediately, not wanting to think about it anymore. Moving it revealed that there was actually one final paper in the bottom of the briefcase: an index card. I reached for it.

There was a scribbled note on the front, written in pen and smudged slightly by the writer's hand. My name was written and circled with my business email address below it.

But to the right of my name was something else: a website address, also circled, with an arrow from my name pointing toward it.

"I'm on that!" Spud jumped to reach for his phone, but I was faster, pulling mine out of my pocket. I started my web browser. No connection at first. I held my phone up high, begging for it to work, until finally I managed to grab a strand of Internet through the trees.

It was difficult to type the long website address with my hands trembling and my sweaty thumbs sliding on the screen. Spud's head pressed close to mine so that we could both see, the webpage loading slowly, every second feeling like forever. First came the black background, then some of the text, then lastly the subtitle at the top:

Only those who listen can hear what is true.

The website was arranged simply and had little design or flourish: only a plain black background, a long row of text for content and a sidebar on the right with links to archives. As I zoomed in on my tiny screen I saw that the archive dates went back for years, hyperlinks to hundreds of old posts. *A blog.*

The articles on the front page were truncated and showed only their titles and the first paragraph before having a link to read more. I scrolled down with my thumb and read the titles, most of them not making much sense to me. I saw one called THE FINANCIAL AND INDUSTRIAL CHIEFS OF INFLUENCE, and another THE AQUAFUEL TECHNOLOGY, and further down the page one called POST DEMOCRATIC PLAN OF ACTION.

Photographs broke up the page in several spots, and I paused on one of a pencil illustration of a coastline's side view and deep under the sea that surrounded it. The picture showed a giant wave approaching the coastal city, but far away under the water was a long torpedo-shaped submarine. The title read, *THE TSUNAMI DEVICE*, and below that the beginning text:

Harken, all seekers of truth. I received this most recent correspondence and illustration from Anon this weekend, who reveals in it not only the further malicious intent of the Society, but their absolute disregard for the lives of those their procedures affect. For while even guilty offenders receive a trial, the humans who are in the path of these technologies fall to the side like slaughtered cattle, as witnessed by the ...

And it cut off there, with a link for me to read more below the fold.

"It's like a conspiracy theory..." Spud said under his breath. I looked at him, and he pointed to the page.

"These are all about secret government things," he said. "Look at the titles: "Post Democratic Plan Of Action"? That's like some sort of end-of-the-world theory I'd guess: what they'll do when democracy falls apart. Like the black helicopters and Area 51."

He gestured toward the illustration of the coastline. "This is about the tsunami that hit Indonesia a few months ago—see the date? It looks like whoever-this-is... this Anon person... he's trying to say that it was a cover-up, and leaked it to this blog."

"How do you know so much about this?" I asked with surprise.

"Don't you ever listen to AM radio after midnight?" Spud asked, looking a little shocked that I didn't. "I'm telling you, this is one of those sites. They pull out all this proof about a *New World*

Order and aliens space ships and stuff. At least…what they *call* proof."

He scratched his neck. "You wouldn't believe how many of these things go through torrent sites. According to them, pretty much everything out there is a hoax by the government."

"And you've read this site?" I said. He shook his head.

"No, never seen this one," he replied. "I don't really read much of it, just when I'm bored at night. Most of it's on the radio. People call in all the time saying they know something. But you can't take it seriously."

Of course I can take it seriously. Because if the car was there, then I'd really met Mr. Sharpe. And if Mr. Sharpe existed, then he had tried to kill me. And if I was still alive, that meant he had failed, and the silver claws that I'd seen smashed through the roof of my car hadn't been a delusion at all.

These thoughts caused everything I'd believed to be turned over. Many of my clients might have thought that my abilities were paranormal, and if it drove up sales I didn't mind perpetuating that belief. But now that I felt I had seen something concrete, I didn't know what was up or down anymore.

"What does this even have to do with me?" I asked aloud. It wasn't like I knew anything about this stuff—no obvious reason for Mr. Sharpe to connect this site to me and come to the conclusion that I needed to be dead. Spud and I exchanged glances but neither of us had a good answer.

All this time, my thumb had been scrolling the webpage, and suddenly when my eyes turned back to the screen, my finger stopped abruptly. In the sidebar were links under a subheading labeled *Introductory,* bolded in cobalt blue with titles like FEDERAL RESERVE CARTEL and DIVISION OF EARTHLY POWERS. One in particular had caught my attention: THE SILVER-CLAWED GUARDIANS.

I clicked the link in the same instant I spotted it. However, I was greeted by a screen that required me to log in.

"What's this?" I told Spud, gesturing. "Break through this."

Spud snatched my phone and started to type quickly. However, his face showed from the start that he wouldn't get far trying to break in. He tried a few logins and passwords but gave up without much of a fight.

"Are you serious?" I said with disbelief. "Just hack it."

"You must watch too much TV," he snarled. "I can't just '*beep*! *boop*! *beep*! I think I'm into their mainframe, officer!'"

He looked at me resentfully. I wasn't taking that answer.

"I mean, I *can* do it," he went on with confidence. "I just can't do it on a phone. I've got to be at my house. All my stuff is on that computer."

I wanted to protest but I knew it would be no use. I clicked *back* and then tried the link again, even trying some usernames like ADMIN and easy passwords I knew were common. But Spud had already been on top of that. The tiny mention of silver claws had set off alarms in my mind. It meant I hadn't imagined those either; someone else out there had an answer.

"Can you find out who runs this?" I asked. Spud didn't look certain but there still appeared to be hope in there. So I tore off the edge of one of the photographs and scribbled the web address onto it, giving it to him.

"Can you do this first thing tonight?" I insisted. Spud winced. I could read him like a book: *Not all of us can stay up all night working, Michael.*

"Early tomorrow then? It's Saturday." I relented. He nodded.

"Don't tell anyone," I added. The hesitation returned to Spud's gaze.

"Do you even know what this is?" he said. "I mean…we really just found out that there *was* a man who tried to kill you. Aren't you worried about telling the police?"

I hadn't even thought about it. I'd forgotten all about the terror I'd experienced the night before because all my thoughts had become enveloped in the embrace of the mystery that'd come up. It was like the murder attempt was suddenly just a small piece of something so much larger that the original fear had been scared right out of me.

"Let's keep it to us for now," I told him. "I just… I want to find out why he wanted to kill me. And they might not even believe me just because I found a car."

"But if there was one guy, what if someone else tries to finish what he started?" Spud asked. He sounded far more afraid for me than I was.

"Now you're the one talking conspiracy theories," I said, putting on a reassuring smile.

I was good at acting confident. It was enough to convince Spud to stuff the note into his pocket without any more protest.

Still, the racing feeling that shot through every vein in my body told a different story. A simple murder attempt against me was too large for me to comprehend—but now there was more. Unintentionally, my hands had unfolded the newspaper clipping one more time. I was greeted by the girl's face again and the mysteries that it bore.

Who are you? Maybe if she'd been alive, she could have told me what was going on.

When Spud wasn't looking, I stuffed the newspaper clipping into my pocket. I couldn't help but glance back over my shoulder as we left the car behind, the folder of photographs in my hand. With its window broken, the car didn't appear nearly as prestigious as it had before. Now it was like a lonely, injured beast staring after us, warning me that I should stop now…that I was venturing deep into something that I shouldn't.

*　　　　*　　　　*

Spud didn't say a single word during our drive home. I could feel his anxiety from across the truck. He remembered to leave me at the corner and I let him go without trying to diffuse the anxious air. I knew if I said anything, it'd do little but frighten us both even more.

Getting back into my room proved to be much more difficult than getting out had been. My mom knew all my tricks now, and it'd be a shame for me to be found when I was nearly able to hang a "1" on the mental <u>X</u> *DAYS SINCE MICHAEL WAS CAUGHT* sign.

Luckily, we kept a long aluminum ladder stored between our house and the neighbor's. But if I used it to get onto the garage, I wouldn't be able to hide the ladder once I was up. Since I couldn't go back in through my room, I lifted the ladder onto the side of the house and climbed toward my sister's bedroom window instead.

The window was unlocked, as usual. That was our deal. My sister knew that I sneaked out sometimes to do work for clients, and it was her unspoken vote of support to give me a way back in again. She didn't care about the college money she could've gained; she wanted to be a screenwriter fresh out of high school anyway. If she'd been anyone else's sister she probably would have turned me in long ago, but she was Alli.

I crept inside and eased the ladder away, so that it went across the space between our houses and tapped the roof of our neighbor's. I stood like Dracula over the bed, arms frozen out as I listened for any stirring from my mom's bedroom. Nothing. In the morning I would take the ladder down, but this was just in case she happened to walk outside before I could.

I checked on Alli briefly but she was still sound asleep, so I hurried out. I closed my bedroom door behind me but even then I didn't think it wise to turn on a light. With careful steps I went to my desk, emptying my pockets onto it and crawling under the sheets.

I didn't even try to sleep. Minute after minute, I lay staring up at my photographs and the ceiling fan, mind racing faster than its rotating blades. There were no answers for the host of mysteries that bombarded me, and I knew even though Spud had told me he'd work on it in the morning, he was probably at his house already trying to break into the website. I wondered if I had dragged him into something I should have left him out of. But I needed someone I could trust, and there was no one better than Spud.

When I was certain that the creaks of our house were not my mom coming to check on me, I rolled over and reached for the newspaper article again, looking at it in the light from my cell phone screen. I stared at the photograph of the girl.

Did you really have to die? I wondered. Spud was right: it was a shame. A waste, even, when you got down to the gritty technicalities. This girl—*Callista*—she would have had an amazing life. Just looking at her, surrounded by that family—she'd have gotten some degree in a nice college whose air I'd never afford to breathe, and probably marry some genius guy who was starting up a million dollar company.

The girl in the newspaper certainly looked like she had everything together, yet I didn't get a feeling of any arrogance that should have gone along with it. She'd been heading nowhere but up, and she'd actually deserved it.

Stop thinking about that stupid girl. She was dead, and I'd almost been dead with her. I tossed the paper back. I wondered if it was even a good idea to keep it anymore.

Sleep refused to come easily. I wanted to forget everything. But my brain wouldn't allow that. It was for that reason I was taken by surprise when I finally drifted to sleep, and felt my skin brush with icy air.

I was running again.

5

NEAR-DEATH EXPERIENCES

My legs moved frantically, winding up a circular stairway in a thin tower-like space walled by gray stone. I saw everything as if it were through my eyes, but as cognitive as I was for being in a dream, I had no control over my muscles.

There was little light around me, only that which came from the old metal flashlight I clutched in my right hand. It was like the inside of a refrigerator. The steps rang like deep metal bells but I continued without stumbling once, hearing others chasing behind me.

My pursuers were only a step or two away but I never paused to look back, only continuing to run, the surrounding chill clouding my frantic breath into a mist. The end of the steps came suddenly when I arrived at a doorway, the passage already open and waiting for me. My body raced out and then turned to close the door, but to my surprise I waited for the other two to pass with me. I realized they were not chasing me after all, but were my companions.

I barely caught a glance of their features. One was a guy who appeared to be close to my age. He had long, black hair that went past his shoulders and hung over his ears but was free from his forehead, and green eyes with irises nearly unperceivable from his pupils in the low light. The other was a girl shorter than me, but I didn't get to see her face before I turned, pressing something in the wall with my palm.

Immediately, a massive wall began to move across heavy railings, closing over the doorway and sealing flat, now making it appear like there was no opening at all.

"Hurry!" the girl said. Then I was running again. We had exited into a room with a low ceiling, only a few inches higher than my head—if I'd been claustrophobic I might have been petrified. We dashed up a set of stairs and around a corner that my subconscious didn't even take the time to illustrate, and shot though another door into the cold night.

There was a vintage Oldsmobile waiting under the moonlight outside, and I leapt into the driver's seat. I turned the key in the ignition without hesitation. It rumbled to life, the old radio bursting out music as it did, and we roared away without taking a second to turn the sound off.

My heart raced even though I still had no control over anything that was happening. My clothing felt odd: the design of my shirt was old, my jacket stitched tighter than I was accustomed to. On my right hand was a silver ring that glimmered in the lamps that hung outside of the buildings' doors. We shot out of the alley and into a giant parking lot surrounded by buildings and a chain-link fence, racing toward an opening on the other side.

But suddenly from all directions, a multitude of other cars appeared, and my foot slammed on the brakes. Tires squealed as the cars blocked our escape. But my dream self wasn't giving up, switching gears into reverse and pulling around the other way, only to find that we were trapped in a corner.

None of the cars moved, no doors popped open. I switched gears but saw that I was boxed in no matter which way I turned. There was nowhere to go.

I turned my head to look at the girl who was in the passenger seat, as she searched our surroundings for a way out. But there wasn't any. So she turned to me, and for the first time I saw her face.

I had seen her before.

But where? It was like time had slowed to nothing. The dark hair, the blue eyes... Somehow I knew her eyes microscopically well, down to every fleck and line in her iris. I always remembered a pair of eyes.

Callista.

She didn't say anything. She only stared deep into me as if she could read my thoughts.

I heard doors popping open from the cars outside our windows, men in suits emerging. The song continued to play. None of us moved.

A man appeared through the front window of the car, unhesitating steps as he moved to stand an inch from the center of the hood. He was thin and tall and wearing a long coat with no tie, arms nearly enveloped in his sleeves, his breath blowing mist. His chin was sharp and his gray eyes studied us through the window— no smile, just a dry and dutiful stare. His eyebrows were completely white in contrast to his deeply black hair. He held a pistol with a long barrel, which he lifted with no emotion and pointed straight at the side of my head. On one of the fingers he had wrapped around the gun's handle, he wore a red metal ring.

All of this had faded into the background. I was unable to tear myself from my deep entrenchment in Callista's merciless gaze.

A burst of noise.

A vicious crack.

A shattering of glass.

My bedroom ceiling fan whirred above my head like a cage of hornets was caught in its motor. I found myself staring at the fan blades going around and around before my eyes had fully focused on them, hypnotizing me, as I lay motionless in wide-eyed terror, my bed drenched in sweat. The heavy click of the gun would not leave the recesses of my eardrums, even though it—and the stairs, the car, the girl—had never been real at all.

I was scratching my hand furiously so I forced myself to stop, trying to slow my breathing before I hyperventilated. The darkness of night still surrounded me. I managed to turn my head to look at the alarm clock. *5:31 AM.*

Again, I had to stop myself from scratching my hand. The sweat was causing me to itch all over, and this only added to my growing misery as I forced myself to sit up.

This is your own fault, I told myself. It was because I'd spent so much time concentrating on her picture before falling asleep. There is nothing more to the dream than what was caught in my subconscious.

Yet I'd dreamed of running again, for a second time. Now I'd been running with the girl I'd never met—who was dead—and a boy I'd never seen before in my life. I couldn't make the horrible images in my head disappear.

"Crazy dream," I grumbled, standing up but refusing to turn on a light. I wiped my forehead with the back of my arm, hair damp. When I couldn't take the ferocious itching any longer, I walked quietly down the hall to the bathroom, closing the door so I wouldn't wake anyone as I switched on the dim shower light.

I went to the sink and tossed a rag into it, wiping my wearied face with the cool water. It was such a relief against the heat. I held the rag up against my neck.

I dropped it in fright.

In the reflection of the mirror, I saw that the black birthmark on my right hand was now surrounded by red. The line was still dark but now swelled to the size of my knuckle, and the skin surrounding it was vibrantly inflamed, worse than any rash I'd ever seen.

Startled, I touched my birthmark, drawing my hand back at the sting. The skin was hard. I scrambled to turn the water on and ran my finger under the cold, but it didn't help.

What is happening to me...? I thought, breathless. Poison ivy? Something that'd been in the work gloves I'd gotten from Spud's truck? That was all I needed, something else to add on top of the gloom of this week. I rubbed the mark, struggling to numb it.

The burning!

I ground my teeth together, fighting back a sharp scream as it struggled to exit. A massive tremor of pain shook throughout me, heat seeming to radiate from the spot I had touched. The skin had come loose, sliding, peeling...

My eyes had closed in the grimace but I forced them open, breathing heavily, looking down. Between my own two fingers, stuck to their tips by my own blood, was a thin strip of my skin that had fallen off.

From my birthmark, a trickle of liquid started to run down my hand, staining the white porcelain of the sink with red.

I found gauze in the cabinet above the toilet, wrapping it so tightly around my finger that it forced the flow of blood to stop and hid the wretched sight. The spot of skin looked mangled like a burn victim's, so I covered my entire hand in ointment to be safe, making me wince even more. My finger continued to throb. I scrubbed the sink until it was clean again, and hid the rag in the trash under a wad of tissues.

I didn't sleep any more that night, mulling over the most horrible thoughts I could collect under the watchful eyes of the photographs on my walls. Maybe the briefcase had been booby-trapped with a chemical defense, and somehow I'd caught a skin-degenerating disease. Now there was nothing too supernatural, nothing too otherworldly that I could simply dismiss as impossible.

I tried to forget the girl and the dreams. I didn't need the distraction. The only real lead I had was whatever Spud could find.

Now with a wrapped-up finger to add to my already wrapped-up knife wound on my arm, avoiding attention seemed impossible. I went downstairs and nonchalantly poured a bowl of cereal. Alli sat cross-legged on the couch with her own bowl, watching TV.

"Trying out as a mummy?" she asked, spotting the new gauze immediately. There was no getting past her. I tried to give her a sliver of a smile so she wouldn't think anything was wrong. My acting skills were deteriorating though.

"You look like a mess," she told me.

"Why thank you, Miss Positivity," I replied, pouring the milk. "Anything else I need to know about myself?"

"You eat little kid cereal," she said, stirring hers and taking a bite.

"I prefer my breakfast to have cinnamon, not just raisins and flakes," I retorted and began to shovel food into my mouth. This proved to be a bit more difficult than usual with gauze wrapped around my finger, but I managed.

"Any more dreams?" Alli asked without warning, and at first I had trouble swallowing down the food in my mouth. I debated not telling her, but I knew she'd see right through that.

"Yeah, maybe," I told her without commitment to elaborate.

"And you said *I* need a therapist," she said, grinning. She shook her head.

"Same stuff as last time?" she asked. I did a small nod-and-shrug combination.

"Somewhat," I said. "Running again, at least. But this time there was a girl."

I knew that would set Alli off. I heard her legs scratching across the couch cushions as she pulled them under her, turning to face me, completely ignoring whatever was on the TV now. I grinned because I couldn't help it.

"A *real* girl?" Alli said, sounding out a fake gasp. "She must have been coming to kill you."

"Can't I be around a girl and you not think she has ulterior motives?" I protested. Alli shook her head. She had a point. I bit into my food with a sense of vengeance.

"No," I told Alli. "She was actually running *with* me. Are you a dream expert now?"

Alli gave me an unamused look. "Well everyone knows dreams reflect what you obsess over in real life." She shrugged. "Creeper."

I certainly wasn't about to tell her that the girl who'd been in my dream had been dead for nearly a week. So I sniffed at her and washed my bowl out, and left.

I started on foot in the direction of Spud's house. His was only a short distance from mine, a left on the corner of Hogan Lane then a few blocks of sidewalk, the streets still lonely due to the weekend's late-sleepers. He lived in one of Arleta's rare two-story places, painted dark blue with fake white shutters. In contrast to my mom's small and progressively dying garden, his mother's covered about half of their front yard, with nearly-bursting tomatoes and an assortment of vegetables. His parents were invested in being energy efficient: skylights and solar panels cut into a roof of temperature-reflective metal. Spud's truck was parked across the street, a distance he'd probably been hoping would get him indoors undetected the night before. I envied him having parents who slept like rocks.

I knocked softly on the front door. He was there in seconds.

"You're up early," I said.

"I don't know if I even slept last night," he returned, but he didn't look entirely defeated and that gave me hope. He led me upstairs through upholstered couches and traffic-flattened orange carpet, a finger to his lips as we passed the rooms shared by his seven siblings, then his parents' door, then his grandmother's door, and finally to his.

Spud's bedroom was even more of a wreck than my own. Instead of camera equipment, though, his was packed to every wall with parts of computers and old video game consoles. If any collector were to creep about—if they could, seeing as there were very few places to step—they would have been greeted by countless

67

old Ataris, Segas in color and monochrome, Game Boys, and tons of other gaming systems and circuit boards I couldn't identify. In the corner was an old arcade system with a busted screen, the sides advertising a fighting game whose image was defaced in marker and pen from years of abuse by teenagers. For a moment, I wasn't watching where I was going and nearly tripped over a pizza box that had wires coming out of it.

"Careful!" Spud warned in a whisper. He produced a folding chair from against the wall and slid things aside with his foot until there was a space for it. I sat next to him in front of a computer monitor—it was one screen in a row of five, the others dormant.

"So," he began, "I don't have the news I was hoping for. But I do have something good."

He clicked on a window he'd lowered, bringing up a web browser with at least twenty tabs open. He shuffled through them until he found the site we'd discovered the night before. It appeared different when it wasn't on the tiny screen of my phone, but still bore its scant decoration and barely-understandable pieces of text. He clicked a link and brought up the login screen that had denied us before.

"I couldn't break through it after all," he said. "They've got some federal-banking level encryption in there—the stuff governments use. Nothing I have can smash through it. I even tried—" he paused, seeing my blank expression, and sighed. "Never mind, you won't understand it. But basically, we're not getting in."

"I thought you had good news," I said.

He held up a finger to silence me. "I couldn't get in, but you also asked me to find out who's running the site," he continued. "It's this guy here."

He pointed to a line that appeared in dark gray beneath the post titles. I hadn't noticed it before because my screen had been so small. In tiny letters it said *"POSTED BY: THE EXPOSITOR"*.

"That's not much help," I said with a hint of dissatisfaction. Again, Spud waved his finger.

"Take a hint from this site," he said gruffly. He pointed to the words at the top of the website. *"Only. Those. Who. Listen. Shall. Hear. What. Is. True.* It's telling you to shut up."

"You're way too smug to have not cracked anything," I said, lifting an eyebrow. He nodded. He enjoyed feeling like a genius.

"I couldn't get through the passwords, and I couldn't find out who owned the site—all the domain ownership information was private. But I found something while digging in the pages."

He scrolled to the bottom, clicking a link to go back a page of posts. He did this again, three more times, until he reached blogs that had been posted two months before we'd visited. He stopped the scrollbar halfway down the page, showing the beginning of a post, titled *INERTIAL PROPULSION*, and a photograph before the thin paragraph of text.

"Some of these posts," Spud said, "have a picture uploaded and embedded into the top of the article. Since they show up before it cuts off and forces the login, I can actually see some of these pictures. Look really close."

I leaned in toward the screen. The photograph was plain, simply a snapshot of a piece of paper with words typed on it, the stationary sitting unfolded on a desk against a blue wall. I couldn't read the words because the picture was too small to see the miniature typeface.

"I don't understand what it is," I told Spud.

"It's one of the letters," Spud said excitedly. "Look, this guy— the Expositor—he keeps mentioning up and down this site that he's getting letters from someone called Anon. That's his informant. Someone who knows about all this secret government stuff and keeps mailing the blogger info about it."

He tapped his computer monitor. "But obviously, the readers who follow this site don't always believe him. So he posts photographs of some of the letters he gets. That's what this is."

"Does that help us?" I asked. It wasn't like I could simply go searching the world for someone called Anon—short for Anonymous, I figured.

Spud shook his head quickly.

"This is why you're lucky to have a friend like me," he said. "And more importantly, why I'm lucky to have my granny."

He was smiling with victory. "Because when I first saw this, I thought I saw something familiar in the picture. And it's hardly even in the picture at all. It's *behind* the letter."

His finger moved from the letter to the blue wall that was at the back it. Only a sliver was visible before being cut off: an energetic hue decorated with an unusual pattern of swirls, tiny angels sitting in the curves like they were in a pillow of clouds. The angels had hair and skin hand-painted in a metallic yellow so it appeared they were gold, though it was obvious the wall behind them was merely cheap plaster.

"That wall," Spud said, "reminds me of my granny. My granny reminds me of going to church. And going to church reminds me of my Uncle Richard's funeral, where the walls were decorated with gold angels on a blue wall that my little sister wanted to draw moustaches on."

"Wait…" I jumped in with shock. "You're saying you—"

Spud nodded. "This wall is from Saint Lita's church, just down the road from here."

I jumped forward, grabbing the mouse from Spud. My fingers drummed across the keyboard, typing SAINT LITA'S CHURCH ARLETA into a search engine. A website for the church had service schedules, contact information, and photos in a line. One of the pictures showed two priests and a deacon posing in religious garb beside a row of old pews. Over the shoulder of the priest furthest to the left was a blue wall with golden angels.

Spud hit the desk triumphantly. I was aghast.

"You're actually brilliant," I told him, unable to form any other words. He nodded like he'd known this already.

"So," he said, "chances are the person who's getting these letters attends this church, maybe even one of the cleaning crew or someone in the office who spends a lot of time alone there."

"What time is the next service?" I blurted out. Spud checked the site's schedule.

"It's Catholic," he said. "So Saturday evening mass starts at 4:30. But then you have 7:30 AM tomorrow, and 9 AM, and 11, and…"

He paused for a moment. "What, are you going to go down to the church and see if you can just spot someone who looks like they enjoy conspiracy theories?"

"I don't know," I said. "But it's all I have. Maybe if someone overhears me asking questions I'll catch a Glimpse…"

My voice trailed off. The chances of that happening were very thin, and both of us knew it. Spud didn't look too enthusiastic about the idea. But when he didn't answer, I entered the church's address into my phone, heart racing.

*   *   *

Spud's family started moving around downstairs, and once his younger brothers and sisters discovered I was there, the whole place turned into a zoo of screaming voices. I was nearly knocked backward when they all ran into me at once, and it took half an hour before I managed to get outside and head home. Spud offered to come with me, but his mother forced him to stay because they'd already planned a family trip to the beach.

So I went alone through the slowly-awakening neighborhood again, now interspersed by cars and trucks heading out for the weekend. Some of the daze-like feeling still lingered over me. I guessed that was my mental defense: continue to believe there was some reasonable explanation to all this so that I wouldn't lose my sanity.

I walked quickly—the church service didn't start for hours but I was eager to be home. My birthmark itched furiously so I unwrapped the gauze with caution. It was even redder than before, though the outside air helped to relieve the pain.

Seeing that the redness hadn't subsided since I'd awoken only made me more concerned. There was one person in the world that would know how to fix it. So when I got home, I headed straight for the back of the house.

To call my mom's workspace an "office" was far too conformist of a term, a word that implied organization and efficiency and maybe even a sturdy chair, none of which my mom had. The previous owners had converted a section of the back porch into a storage space. My mom, ever resourceful, had painted the place cream and redone the wooden flooring herself, tacking up thin, colorful cloths to make it cozier. She had a desk and a stool in the corner that she'd gotten from a secondhand shop, two couches for her and clients, and bookshelves stuffed with old records and bottles on the far wall.

It was the strongest smelling room in the house, on account of the herbal invasion spread upon her desk, but I knew for every awful scent there was some ailment she could cure. Alli and I were sick the least out of everyone in our schools, and we'd never gotten a single shot from a doctor in our lives.

"I only work by appointment!" my mom said loudly to me, not looking from the tall notebook she was scribbling in, glasses over her eyes. "Walk-ins not welcome!"

"You're supposed to heal me, you Hippocratic hypocrite," I said, falling onto one of her torn couches, from the same secondhand store as the rest of the room.

"I didn't take any Hippocratic Oath," she growled, turning a page in one of the thick books open on her desk. "I'm not your doctor."

This was the game we played—she would be researching something for a patient and I'd come in, and she'd act like it bothered her when it really didn't. Half the time I wondered how Alli and I hadn't driven her to get a job away from the house. I rolled over onto my back, looking up at the walls. She had a guitar hanging on one side, from back when she was part of a girl band called Fruity Joos. They'd never really gone anywhere, except for the time the trio had opened for Aerosmith—she'd told that story to me dozens of times, and I guess it made her cool enough.

Next to that, like a stop sign that signaled the end of her guitar age, was her framed college degree. She'd studied zoology at UCSB. When I was old enough to know what that was, I'd asked her why she wasn't working with penguins and lions and elephants, and she'd just said she had enough wild animals living in her home to suffice.

"I have an appointment in half an hour," she told me when I didn't leave. She looked up, blinking at me expectantly through her glasses.

"I'm hurt," I told her with a whimper. She scrunched her mouth together. I held my hand out where she could see it, and she nearly jumped.

"What in the world, Michael…" she said with a gasp. "What have you been doing to that?"

She took me by the wrist and I was forced to sit up as she pulled my mangled finger closer to the lamp. The heat from the bulb made my finger burn harshly so I tried to pull away.

"Did you hit it in the car wreck?" she asked, not letting me go.

"No, I think it's a rash," I said.

"The skin is peeling bad." She examined it closer, touching lightly. I winced and my hand trembled from the intense burning.

"Take this first," she said, producing a slim blue cylinder labeled *Arnica* from one of the desk drawers. She popped the lid and a pile of tiny white pebbles tumbled into my other hand. They tasted like sugar.

"What witchery is this?" I said.

"It'll make the ache go away," she replied, stretching up to rearrange glass bottles on her shelf, pulling two and setting them on her desk. Each was labeled but I couldn't read the scribbled handwriting, glass droppers were exposed when my mom unscrewed the caps.

"This will help heal it," she said, filling the dropper then hovering it over my hand. "Hold still, it'll burn a—"

I nearly screamed, jerking my hand back. The first drip, no larger than a raindrop, had fallen onto my finger.

"THAT. BURNS." I exploded, flinging my hand back and forth to drive the pain away.

"That means it's *working!*" my mom insisted. "Put your hand down NOW."

I whined and whimpered, but in the end she had more power over me than any doctor, so I had to obey. She leaned her elbow lightly against my arm, but to me it was like a vice holding me down.

"While I'm doing this," she said, "tell me about those dreams."

I looked at her with a hint of alarm but she didn't register my reaction as she dripped more solution onto my finger.

"Alli," I said sharply.

"Don't hate her," my mom said in warning. "She told me because she's scared for you."

"Alli, scared?" I said with disbelief, wincing at the medicine again. "She's in there watching a movie about killers right now."

"And her brother was nearly killed two nights ago," my mom said. It cut me off. Was that her silent voicing of confidence in my story about Mr. Sharpe? Certainly not. If she thought that the murder had been real, she'd be out in front of the police station picketing right then for an investigation. Was she making fun of me? I wasn't detecting that either.

The car crash, I remembered. Even with Mr. Sharpe out of the picture, I'd still nearly died in that wreck. She'd already crossed the possibility of Mr. Sharpe's existence out.

Would she cross him out so easily now that I had proof of something different?

I could have told her then. I could have blurted out everything I'd found: the car, the briefcase, and the girl's face on the newspaper. My life would have taken a dramatic turn in the space of a few seconds.

But my mouth remained shut. I didn't need the police—not yet.

"They're just dreams," I told her.

"Do you normally dream of dying?" she pressed. *Stupid Alli.* Were there no secrets in this house anymore?

"No," I replied slowly, but one look from my mom caused the gates to break. That, or the fresh droplet of burning herbal concoction that sent pain racing through my nervous system.

"Alright, they're dreams of me dying," I admitted. "It's happened twice. They feel real when I'm in them, but I know I'm dreaming, so it's even weirder."

Was that enough of the truth for her without giving too much? I was already uncomfortable and in pain, I didn't need her to think that I was losing my mind on top of it. Or any more evidence to that fact, at least.

If she thought that, she surely didn't show it through her face. She shrugged.

"You're the kid who keeps getting into strange trouble," she said. "It only makes sense it happens in your dreams too."

That got a wry smile out of me, one that became more genuine when she let go of my arm and I knew the evil drops were over. She threw the gauze away before I could wrap my finger up again—she was a firm believer in the healing powers of outside air.

"You've been doing that all your life, you know," my mom went on. "You remember when you were ten and I almost ran you over?"

"You're supposed to *look* before backing up," I said.

"If I remember correctly, you were playing hide-and-seek *under* the car," she reminded me. "Before that you were eight and I found you under your Aunt Bama's sink, the cap already off the bleach and a straw in your hands," she said. "And you almost died before you were born too."

I shifted on the couch. I'd heard these stories so many times; I'd usually disregarded them as unimportant family folklore that only got brought up at birthday parties. They felt a little bit different this time though, as if my most recent incident called for a reminder of all the times I'd flirted brazenly with Death.

"I got pregnant with you at twenty, and just a few months in I got really sick," my mom said. "I went in and they told me there was some complication, and you were taking more of my body's resources than you should have. Which sounds small, but at the rate you were going, you were actually killing me, they said."

She'd told me this story many years before but I didn't remember much of it. I listened enraptured, my mom's gaze turning up to the wall behind me.

"They told me I should get rid of you, because otherwise I'd die for sure," she said. "They were very convincing too. They made you sound like a leech. Five percent chance you'd make it, and even less that I would. But you think I was about to give you up?"

"Obviously not," I said. She grinned.

"Yeah. I told the doctors to screw off," she said, crinkling her nose with some degree of delight. "And I've been telling them that ever since," she snorted. "Them and the whole bonkers medical system. And after I left them, I endured six more months of miserable torture hoping for some reward at the end," she looked back down at me. "But unfortunately, all I got was you."

She knocked me on the side of the head with the back of her hand.

"And that is why, Michael, you can never complain about chores, ever," she said. Then her face softened up. She leaned her elbow against the edge of the couch, brushing the hair from my forehead.

"You really wanted to live," she said. "You weren't supposed to. I think even G wanted to listen to the doctors. Then Alli came along. Then G left for Megan McSluttus, and now we're a happy family of the Asher Trio, which thanks to you, often seems close to becoming the Asher Duo."

G was what we called my invisible father, George, because we'd come to a consensus that he wasn't worth the time of pronouncing all six letters. I shook my head, making the hairs she'd pushed away fall back into place. I knew she was thinking about the car crash.

"You're good at not dying, Michael. Keep that up," she said. It was gently, lovingly…so unreserved that even without a moment of surprise, I could read the Glimpse behind her gaze, the gate opening without the walls being broken down. I'd hardly ever read my mother, probably because it felt weird to know what she was thinking. But seeing the warmth behind her, that real and genuine care for me was almost like an unspoken renewal of what I already knew. No matter what else the world would do, she actually cared.

I could have told her everything. I *wanted* to tell her. I should have told her. But I didn't.

When the silence wore off, she drew back to her desk.

"What are your plans for this evening?" she asked me. I sat up straighter, stretching my arms. I debated what to say.

"Church," I replied. She gave me an odd look but didn't ask. So I stood up, left the room, and closed the door between us.

6

THE EXPOSITOR

Exhausted from another night of little sleep, I tried to take a nap to pass the time, but only ended up lying still for hours. The closed blinds let in a mild glow between long shadows across the pictures on my walls.

Maybe I needed something new up there? I had too much time to kill until leaving again. So I rolled over and went to my desk, turning my music player to a low buzz of electronic-fused sounds as I dug through my files. All of my digital photographs were organized into folders, sorted by day and on some, the location. There were so many places to photograph people in California. I could go down to The Grove and watch shoppers. Or I could venture down Hollywood Boulevard and capture tourists wandering through the attractions, pressing their hands into that of celebrities at Grauman's Chinese Theatre.

I didn't only use my talent for the money that clients would pay me. It was an addiction. I *had* to keep watching people, *had* to keep studying their faces for ones that would fit my walls. I clicked through photos one after the other, checking a face and then the next, hundreds flashing by.

I'd been searching for Callista's face without even knowing it. My mind was fixed on how close San Francisco was and how she might have been down in LA at some point, maybe even in the background of one of my photos. But I wasn't going to let myself go further down that path. I clicked my monitor off and hid the newspaper again.

When 3:45 came around, I dug through my closet for a button-up shirt then ventured downstairs. Alli was in the living room and I passed by the TV screen just as a tentacle speared a screaming woman.

"Keep watching all that joy and positivity," I told her. She looked over my formal wear and lifted an eyebrow.

"Have...fun," she said. On screen, tiny octopus-shaped babies started to slither out of the woman's head. Alli rolled back over again.

I hadn't ridden my bike in months so it was a bit difficult finding it in the garage. By the time I had it, I was already so dusty and sweaty that I wondered why I'd even bothered to dress up at all. Nothing was going to stop me now though. The author of the blog was the only clue I had left.

I pedaled down the road and followed the crossing street to the right, avoiding pedestrians out for an evening walk. Everywhere I turned, there were people I already felt I knew, either from school or from my venturing all over the town while hunting for good photographs. Arleta was like that: you knew one, you knew them all.

Most of the houses that I passed were rickety and uneven, the old wooden panels held together by boards added for support, concrete foundations crumbled after years of age. There were chain-link covered yards holding back snapping dogs, trucks jacked up on giant tires half as tall as I was, uneven sidewalks that made my bike bounce and swerve. Scrap vendors had tall strips of tin wired up as makeshift fencing, dozens of KEEP OUT signs attached in multiple languages. If you were just a visitor passing through, all of this reeked of urban decay. To me, Arleta was like a grandmother whose skin was wrinkled and whose bones were fragile, but whose smile could never be outdone by any younger and more beautiful supermodel.

Aside from the old cars and the cheap shops, one thing that Arleta had a lot of was churches. I passed at least five before I finally saw the tall, pointed steeple of my target ahead. ST. LITA'S CHURCH, read the sign in the grass out front. I brought my bike to a stop in front of it, catching my breath.

The main part of the church was built in a traditional style with giant wooden doors behind steps leading from the sidewalk, all surrounded by neatly clipped trees. There was a parking lot to its left with people hurrying to make it inside before the service began. Most of them were Hispanic, all dressed up far better than I was, and at once I felt out of place.

I hid my bike behind the bushes and dusted my clothes off with my fingers, ridding my shirt of the grass and bugs that had flown there. I strolled up to the doors with as much faked belonging as I could—covering my burning hand in my pocket—and stepped inside.

I was immediately greeted by a host of scents that were foreign to me: candles melting with gently smoking flames atop their glowing white pillars, and perfumes and colognes from the churchgoers around me. The chill of an overworked and buzzing air conditioner carried the smell of incense from the front of the church: a smoky and exotic sensation that entered my nose like crushed flowers and spices.

The stained glass windows glowed from the evening sunlight outside. Likely accustomed to visitors, the families around me didn't even notice that an outsider was in their midst. I quickly stepped out of the entryway, finding an abandoned spot at the end of a pew in the back. When I sat down, something beside me caught my eye: the blue wall with the golden angels. There was no mistake; it was the same from the photo.

Where to begin my search? I wondered. I knew that Spud was right: there wasn't much hope in finding one person out of this group. The children stuck close to their parents, families and groups of old ladies scattered about—none of them looked like conspirators. The church was merely one long room with two columns of pews, split through the middle by a walkway leading to the cloth-covered altar. A woman sat behind the keys of an organ, and began to play.

Everyone stood so I mimicked their actions, picking up a hymnal and mouthing the words along with them. A bespectacled priest appeared with two altar boys in a line, one bearing a tall crucifix and the other a gigantic bible. They all wore robes: the boys in white, the priest in green, steps so practiced that none of them even came close to tripping over the ends of their clothes. Behind them strolled a single monk dressed in brown with a completely bald head. When the priest reached the front, the music stopped, and he started to speak.

I didn't really understand much of what he was talking about because I never went to church, but I followed along with the people nearby. They would stand for some things and sit for others. I found the uneven harmonies of the old people mixed with the children to be soothing—so powerful, it even calmed my own tension.

It went on for about half an hour. My eyes continued to scan the faces around me. I couldn't see a true Glimpse, but even without that I felt I was in the wrong place.

None of these people even appeared slightly out of the ordinary. Not a single face there could have held the secrets of a plot to murder me. Even as the priest finished the reading and began his sermon, the only disturbance in the room was the snore of an old woman who'd fallen asleep.

I turned my head to study the people who lurked in the back pews with me. One of the men from the opposite corner stared at the priest, almost too intently. Another woman two rows ahead of him didn't seem happy to be there. *Dissatisfaction*, I recognized. But murder? I couldn't see that in either of their eyes.

I sighed, slouching a bit against the hard back of the pew. *Maybe this was a waste of time.* I might have had better luck hunting for a penguin in a desert.

"*For the time is come*," the priest's monotonous voice suddenly rose to a boom through the speakers, breaking me out of my reverie, "*that judgment must begin at the house of God: and if it first begin at us, what shall the end be of them that obey not the gospel of God?*"

My concentration was drawn to him again, his eyes reading from the book. I hadn't been paying attention until now, but the fervent insistence in his voice was too much to turn away from. The priest was patriarchal and almost ancient, a short gray beard and wrinkly skin on his face, hands holding the side of the pulpit to steady himself. His eyes were bright blue, a color I could see even from across the church.

"Brothers and sisters," he said after a pause. "Listen to those words of Peter the Apostle. Listen, for soon the judgment foretold shall be upon us—'*And if the righteous scarcely be saved, where shall the ungodly and the sinner appear?*'"

The language was so treacherously dark that it felt out of place with these people, yet all of them listened closely. The priest's eyes scanned their faces, pausing and considering his next words.

"Who knows when this end shall come?" he proclaimed. "Ten years from now? A month? A week? Where will you be on Monday if it happens then? Will your soul be ready?"

He nodded at all of us, his croak of a voice seeming to command the very air we all breathed.

"And what of the unrighteous—those who lead our souls astray?" he went on. "For if we are the sheep, we must follow a shepherd. But what if we find that we have been deceived, and are living in the herd of a shepherd only leading us to slaughter?"

An unusual gravity had taken over the entire room. He bowed his head for a moment, tilting the microphone away a half-inch to ease the power of his voice.

"Listen for the voices that warn of the coming. Listen for the voices that cry out for the purification of your soul before the farmer comes to harvest," he said. "*Because only those who listen can hear what is true.*"

Like they had been spoken in a deep chamber, the priest's final words reverberated in my head, my hands freezing as they clutched at the wooden armrest.

The priest was done. He turned and walked back to the altar. The Expositor had been in front of me all along.

It's strange how many motions a body makes all on its own. Even standing up is a symphony of legs pushing and arms supporting, an endless and yet unconscious attention that no one really notices before they're on their feet. All of a thousand things happen in the span of a second, like a set of instructions your brain has so you don't need to remember the steps.

However the moment I'd identified the Expositor, I became conscious of every motion I made. Suddenly it was as if everyone else in the church had disappeared, and if the priest were only to look up he'd pick me out at once. My breath was too loud so I tried to slow it. My arms were crossed so I uncrossed them. Breathing slower started to make me dizzy, which only made me feel more evident. I simply couldn't get the autopilot turned back on.

So I sat with my back pressed into the corner of the pew, trying as hard as I could to keep my eyes from the priest as he went through his long-practiced motions of finishing the service. *It was him.* I knew I was right.

Soon the organ's sounds filled the halls with a final song, as the priest and his assistants filed out and around the opposite side of the church, disappearing into a small room. As the song finished, everyone around me started to buzz with low greetings to their neighbors, some leaving hurriedly and others grouping into friendly pockets of conversation.

I managed to stand. But what next? I'd watched the priest go into a side room in the front of the church, and I could see his shadow and the shadows of others as they performed their cleanup duties.

I wasn't about to let him dart out a door and disappear before I could find some answers. But it wasn't like there was any good way to start this conversation either. *Have you heard any good conspiracy theories lately, Father?*

Frosty air blew at me from vents against the wall, an usher switching off some of the lights that were over the altar just as I got to the pulpit. He nodded at me as I walked up the steps. I could hear the monk talking merrily with another usher, something about the old woman who'd been snoring, and they all laughed at once as I turned the corner.

The room was barely the size of my bedroom, mostly one wall with a long counter and many rows of cabinets. A table was beside the door, holding up sconces and a tall chalice that sat upside-down on a towel to dry. There was a tiny open closet with just enough room for about a dozen colored robes that hung inside, and at that moment the priest was hanging his robe up, now dressed in an all-black suit and white collar of clergy. He turned just as I walked in.

"Can I help you?" he said. His voice was cavernous and mellow, the warmth of a person who lived off speaking. I stopped in the doorway.

"Um…yes." Any words I'd prepared departed at once. The priest looked at me, his ocean eyes even more piercing now, set in the circles of age on his face. Certainly not a man who knew dark secrets—certainly not a man who knew why I'd almost been killed?

"I have a question. About…what you said earlier," I said. He closed the door of the closet.

"Yes?" he prompted.

"Did you write it yourself?" I blurted. The lines in his face showed confusion.

"Of course," he replied. "Well, I didn't *write* it. I merely spoke from the heart. The Spirit works best when we let it guide us."

The priest picked up the chalice and placed it in the cabinet. I glanced at the monk and usher who were still in the room. They were bantering loudly but I wasn't sure if taking chances would be in my favor.

"I'd like to talk to you," I said. "Alone."

The priest raised an eyebrow. "What about?"

"I...I can't say."

His face twisted up. "Can't you talk about it with me here?"

"I don't think it's safe here," I said. The priest did not look convinced.

"Well I don't know what you want to say that you can't tell me here with Brother James," he said. "I've got tomorrow's mass to prepare for. If it's not a time sensitive matter, maybe you can drop by the office tomorrow evening at—"

"I've seen the blog," I whispered, hoarsely because it had slipped out without warning. Immediately his hands stopped, hovered in the motion of picking up the sconces, face frozen like a stone cutting. In the shock I'd given him, I saw one of the clearest and most unhindered Glimpses I'd ever witnessed. *Raw terror,* like the fleeting thought of a person one second before a car was about to crush them. It was paired with a feeling of entrapment and a second where he wondered just how short a time he might have left to live.

His lips parted to say something but in mid-thought he must have realized that he'd already given himself away, and there was no use in denying it.

"I won't talk about this," he said under his breath, moving to place the sconces into the cabinet and closing the doors.

"Please, just—"

He pushed me aside, moving to escape through the doorway I'd been standing in. In my desperation I grabbed him by the arm of his shirt, causing him to spin around, arms coming up to defend himself.

"Stay away from—!" he shouted, but his voice cut off like the breaking of a tree branch. His eyes had locked with the hand I'd lifted to stop him, straight to my black birthmark now throbbing and red.

"*Daniel...*" he whispered in shock. Then realizing that the room had gone silent, he blinked and looked up to the monk and usher who'd turned around to see what the trouble was. His face went paler.

"I—I'm sorry," he said. "I will...I'll hear your confession now, if you'd like," he said to me hastily. "No sinner should be forced to wait for forgiveness, yes?"

Without another word, he turned and started away, so I followed. He headed straight for the back of the church, hands nervously grazing the tops of the pews as he went, head darting to each side as he checked the room. All of the parish members were already gone.

On the wall near the entrance was a set of wooden boxes that looked almost like closets, a pair of doors going in with a light over one. The priest said nothing, darting through one of the doors and closing it behind himself. On it was a plaque that read: FATHER LONNIE PETERS.

I swallowed hard as I reached for the metal handle of the other door. There was no time to think about it, not with the frantic curiosity that had taken over me. What would be said inside that room would change everything I knew.

My fingers grazed the handle and in that instant my hesitation vanished, and I slipped inside.

7

CONFESSIONS

A wall with a square metal grill in its center separated me from the priest's side, our faces masked from each other. There was little more than that and a padded kneeler. Through the mesh of the anonymity window, I could see the faint outline of Father Lonnie leaning near the divider.

"Close the door," he muttered under his breath. I couldn't tell if his tone was annoyance or fear, but I obeyed. Light from outside disappeared, replaced by a glow that came from a box in the ceiling and washed over the fake wood paneling and the brown leather of the kneeler. Something about the light was upsetting: a yellowish, artificial hue that was just bright enough for me to see by, but dim enough that I always felt I was struggling to make out where I could stand without hitting my toes. This, paired with the narrow room and the soundproof seal of the door, made it feel like I'd been buried alive.

"I don't know how you found me," the priest started. "I don't know why you came here or what the hell you want, but for the sake of us all our lives you should *never* speak of the blog aloud."

His voice was so muffled that I kneeled in front of the window just to hear him better. He shifted, the outline of his hands and face appearing only as silhouettes.

"I just…I can't believe I lived to see you," he said. "Anon wrote of you, but I never thought *I* would…"

His voice trailed off. He was speaking so quickly that he sounded manic.

"How did you find me?" he asked. "I'm not even safe anymore. Damn it, I'm not safe."

"I found the blog," I told him. "But I only found you and your church through…random chance." My hands squeezed the wooden top of the kneeler, mind still whirling from the fact that I was actually speaking to a man who, just a day before, I'd been certain I'd never find. Even his existence hadn't sunk in yet.

Father Lonnie huffed. "There's no such thing as an accident," he muttered. "Coincidence is merely the puppeteers' curtain, hiding the hands that pull the world's strings. But you—"

I heard him scratch the wood of his chair nervously. "I…I don't understand. Why aren't you dead?" He realized his abruptness and drew back.

"I almost was," I murmured. "I think I killed my killer instead."

Father Lonnie shook his head. I knew he and I both regarded each other's existence with equal suspicion.

"So," he said, "this isn't their doing at all. You've managed to…oh good God."

His forehead hit against the wood panel in weakness, his breath now so close that I could hear it going in and out of him. I couldn't tell if he was simply lost in fright or if he was silently weeping, eyes closed and fingers over the front of his face.

"You're supposed to be dead," he told me bluntly.

"Tell me something I don't know," I replied.

"*No*," he insisted. "You're *supposed* to be dead. You being alive…it changes everything. Everything for me. For us. For the whole world."

His voice stayed at its steady, quiet volume, but I could hear the terror in his tone, the thoughts and calculations that were going through his head even as he spoke. Behind the old man, crazy from fear of conspiracies and plots, was a machine of a mind that sped sharper than ever—one that my appearance had sent reeling from miscalculation.

"Look, I don't know you," I told him. "I came to you to get answers. Why would anyone want me dead?"

I could think of a few examples, actually. I'd exposed a lot of cheaters and liars before. But none of them would have been criminal enough to pull off what Mr. Sharpe had done—or so I thought.

"Do they know you're alive?" Father Lonnie asked, ignoring my question.

"Whoever tried to kill me is dead now, if that helps," I said.

"It'll throw them off for a day or two, at most," he replied. "You're only alive now because of their overconfidence. It was so easy for them the last few times..."

Father Lonnie was blathering to himself more than he was to me. He mumbled things I couldn't even discern, muffled curses as he pressed his head harder against the wood paneling and winced as the thoughts continued to bubble inside of him. I wondered if he even heard me when I spoke.

"This is good though," he said. "This is a change, a hope. You've still got a chance. But I—what do I do?"

He looked up, but I couldn't see his eyes through the panel, only the frightened outline of his hands and face as they tried intently to sort through a thousand thoughts at once.

"Your birthday," he said. "How long until you turn seventeen?"

There it was: the same question about my age that Mr. Sharpe had asked, minutes before he'd attempted his murderous dissection.

"Three days." I replied.

"Good God," he said. "They're looking for you again by now, for sure. And your Chosens are nowhere to be found? You don't have a chance. It might be best to let you die and try again in another seventeen..."

"What are you talking about?" I burst shakily. "There's someone else who wants to kill me? If you know something then I need to go to the police."

"Going to the police is the quickest way for you to get killed," Father Lonnie said, his voice turning sharp. "You don't think they have the police? It's not much use going to anyone. You're unguarded now. You've got three days and you don't stand a chance of making it."

"Why are you so certain I'm going to die?" I protested.

"If they knew you were here, you'd be gone the second you stepped out of this church," Father Lonnie said, with such strong resolution, any doubt I had was erased at once. The protest that I had already prepared to counter him vanished.

"If that's true then why am I not dead now?" I asked. "Who are *they?*"

Had I somehow been confused with someone else? Someone who owed a debt, or had killed someone, or knew some great secret that couldn't get out? There was no reason for anyone to kill me. I was sixteen, I went to school, and sometimes I read eyes for clients. But never anything worth being killed over. Never anything worth the giant plot that Father Lonnie was too fearful to speak of.

The wood of his chair creaked as he shifted. How could this be so difficult, especially for a man who from the pulpit had appeared so fiery and so mentally disciplined?

"I—I don't know what to call them," he said, still resisting.

"Don't give me crap answers," I spat, tired of the games. The confessional fell silent again, the very walls seeming to wait upon his answer.

"Some people call them *Reptilians,*" he finally whispered. "Or *Lizard People.* But that's not what they call themselves. They're…*the Guardians*…at least, that's what Anon has told me."

"Why did they send someone to kill me?" I pressed. But that hardly contained every question I wanted to ask at once. *The silver claws? The flying? All the things I'd read on the blog?*

"Nothing is what you think it is," Father Lonnie said, hitting the wall between us in frustration. "You have no idea what is happening around you—what *has* happened around you your entire life, for decades…"

He hit the wall between us again, his energy already waning. "I don't have the strength to be an instrument of this capacity. I can't hide you. I can't protect you. I am just a blogger…a messenger. There's not even a reason to be speaking to you now if your Chosens aren't here. You could be dead tonight or even by the end of the hour—"

"Then if I'm going to die, there's no reason for you *not* to help me," I cut him off. "No one will ever know."

"You don't understand," he said. "They'll kill me regardless. I've spoken to you. I've seen you. I've got to die now, too."

Unexpectedly, he broke into a light sob so earnest that my anger was immediately broken. I could hear the terror in the priest's weeping, a fear he tried to disguise from me but could not.

"You don't even know who you are," he said. "You're the *bringer of the dawn*, right here in front of me, right now. I'm ecstatic. You don't know how much this world will change if you live to see the next two days."

He gasped in and out painfully like a trapped animal. He was so intent on my importance that I was startled. I thought he might be insane, but that didn't feel right.

"And I *want* you to live," he said, "but I don't know if it's possible. I don't know if you *can*. I don't even know how you've lasted this long alone."

"I don't understand," I said. My voice broke midsentence.

"You're a threat," he said. "To yourself, to the ones you love, to me...to the entire world. I'm going to die. They're going to die. Everyone you love is going to die if you stay alive now. The Guardians will make sure of it, just so you're gone again. And even in the end—if you *do* live, and everyone else dies—it will still all be worth it. But only if you live."

I had no reply. Even swallowing was painful. I could hear the depth of truth in the priest's voice, such terror to overtake a man who knew so much, who'd seen so many days and decades, and yet appeared to hold our meeting as the pinnacle of his lifetime.

"I would help if I could," Father Lonnie said. "But not now. Not when you're alone. Not when I and others will die just for you to fail in the end."

"You're so sure I'm going to fail," I said as my eyes narrowed. I'd never known anyone to have such little confidence in me. "I could go into hiding if I need to."

He shook his head.

"Every inch of this world is controlled by them," he replied. "The police, the media, the government. You think that your mayors and governors run your tiny piece of a country? They are sheep. Humans are like bugs on the sheep. And even the sheep have shepherds who herd them into circles, separating one for slaughter and another to be sheared at their whim."

He laced his fingers together, almost as if he was praying for strength to continue. "But if the sheep have shepherds, who then are the masters of the shepherds? *Those* are Guardians. Everything you do, everything you say, everything you write and transmit and read—every piece of your minuscule life is followed like germs under a microscope. Since the day you are born you are placed into

89

the maze, with shifting walls and doors in place so you continue to run but never find the exit: never see the hands or faces of those who master your life and death."

Father Lonnie had taken a nosedive into things I couldn't bring myself to fathom or believe.

"But you know?" I whispered. "If something is so secret, how did you find out?"

"I have a source," he said. "Someone outside the maze."

"Anon?"

The priest nodded slowly. Even after all he'd said, Father Lonnie still struggled to identify this person.

"He tells me everything," the priest went on. "It was so long ago I can hardly remember how it started, but for a decade I've heard from Anon. Always letters, never a phone call or a visit. Always typed and signed, always with the direction to scan and post them onto my website…to observe the Guardians and make records of everything."

"And you believe him?"

"Not at first," Father Lonnie said. "I…I theorized on these things before, but never to the depth that he wrote of. Never with the information he has, and the names and charts and pictures. Never with the proof: predictions of elections, businesses going bankrupt, so-called natural disasters. He's spoken of them to me in letters months before they even happen!"

"But where do I fit in?" I said, trying at least to sort through my burning questions. I could almost hear him trembling, so many things that he wanted to say to me but unable to choose which to start with. I couldn't read his eyes through the screen but I knew he wanted to go on, even though he felt it was a waste. He was certain I was going to die anyway.

"Because you're a threat," the priest said again.

Suddenly, there was a distant knock from his side of the box. Both of us jumped.

"Father," came the low voice of the monk. "Not to intrude the confession, but they're locking up the church."

"We'll be done shortly," Father Lonnie replied. The monk lingered.

"The lights are all out too, Father," he insisted. "Just so you know."

"I'll be out in a minute, Brother," the priest said. I panicked.

"You can't leave now," I said quickly, pushing closer. "I need more answers than this."

"Keep your voice down," Father Lonnie commanded, this time through clenched teeth. "Do you not think I know the urgency at hand? But already we've brought too much attention to ourselves."

He leaned closer. "I'd hide you here if I could, but that wouldn't help either of us. It's too suspicious, too unusual—someone would whisper about it and Guardians would know you were here in a heartbeat."

"I have to go home," I told him. "My mom will call the police if I don't."

"And that's the worst thing to happen now," he said. He drummed his fingers on the wood nervously.

"I can only risk a little now," he resolved. "I don't even know how close they are to you. You might not live past tonight. But you've gotten this far and there may still be hope yet. And there's so much to tell you…"

He sighed. "But I must. I'll tell you everything I can—everything Anon has sent me, and all the research I've done in my lifetime. But we can't draw attention to ourselves by meeting tonight. I—I'm only alive now because I've kept my identity a secret."

I drew in a breath and let it out. I couldn't simply go home after all that he'd told me—I'd never sleep. But there was no other option.

"Tomorrow, after the first mass," he said. After lingering a few moments, he stood up and pushed his confessional door open.

I hurried to follow him, but the old wooden door had become jammed. I fought against it frantically, only to find that I'd been pulling on a door that swung out.

I found myself alone in the back of the church, the monk folding a cloth near the pulpit, which was obviously only a thinly veiled ruse to stay in the room. Cool air rushed to greet me, the stuffiness of the box gone. The monk looked up at me so I turned for the door.

I don't have to believe him, I told myself. As I stepped out of the church, the incense filled air dissipated and my thoughts became clearer. Nothing was scary in the blinding sunset that washed over the surrounding houses and parishioners who still chatted in groups.

Even so, I couldn't shake the horrible feeling in the back of my head: the senses that made my eyes dart from one side of the church lawn to the other. *Could* I trust the priest? Could I at least give him an ounce of belief, that maybe some parts of his words were true? I didn't want to, but then again, I hadn't wanted a man with silver claws to attempt my assassination.

Evening brought me no comfort. As I slowly faded into an exhausted sleep, every shadow in the room was a hunter coming to finish the job that Mr. Sharpe had started.

*   *   *

The shattered pieces of a window hit a tile floor...

I snapped up like a bent spring bounding back into shape—asleep in my room one moment, on an unfamiliar leather couch the next.

I heard sounds of scuffling and rushed movements as someone frantically ran down a hallway. The room was dark but I could see well enough to know that I was somewhere I'd never been before. From the couches that lay in a U shape to the pictures and paintings going all around, I could tell that I was in the living room of a house, but not mine, not a friend's. The walls had cheap paneling and the floors were covered in carpet, gentle light from the boxy television illuminating the room with static-filled white and blue flashes. These flashes reflected off the silver ring now returned to my right hand.

I heard another crash, this time closer than before, and suddenly the silhouette of a person appeared from around a corner. It was none other than the girl who'd died in my last dream—Callista, whose face I'd already memorized.

In reaction, I tried to say something to her. But like the dreams before, I was merely a spectator in this movie-like sequence, my body moving on its own accord, jumping to its feet.

"Who are you?" I asked, the voice not even sounding like my own. Just then, the boy with the long black hair slid out from behind her. They were startled to see me already awake, their faces showing exertion from running. That didn't stop them from springing into action though, as they dashed forward and grabbed me, one at each of my arms.

"We've got to run!" Callista said urgently. My body protested against them but they were far stronger than I was, pulling me around and toward a stairway. I fought them but the girl pressed her face close to mine.

"I can't explain now," she said, "but you better not fight us now or he'll get here."

There came another smash, louder and more viscous than theirs had been, like an ice pick being driven against a screen door and ripping its mesh apart. I heard the door's remains kicked across tiles in rage, and somehow that horribly determined sound convinced me that these two were not anywhere near as bad as what was coming. I ran with them, up the stairs and around a corner, someone else's shoes striking the bottom step just as we turned the bend.

The boy went ahead of us, throwing open doors in the narrow hallway and checking inside, only to find a bathroom behind one and a closet behind another. The hall was lined with family portraits and its carpet fought in vain to mask our footsteps. Finally, at the end, the boy found a room and the three of us rushed inside.

"Block the door!" he said, his black hair now running with sweat from his forehead. They already knew what they were doing, the girl lifting one of the chairs and the boy—muscles flexing—heaving the long dresser from the wall, sliding its weight against the door. Then they moved the bed against the dresser, faces filled with such a terror of whatever was behind us that even in the dream, I couldn't help but feel my own fears increase.

"Take him out the window!" the girl commanded, but there came a sudden blast against the door that shook the entire house, rocking us off our feet. The boy grabbed my arm again, pulling me toward the window.

Wait! I tried to say, but my mouth still wouldn't move. I wanted to stop running for just a few seconds, only long enough for me to ask a question, to find something that I could use when I woke up. I knew I would awaken at any second—I already knew that whatever was chasing us would cause this dream to end just as horribly as the previous.

Then, as if the dream itself was eavesdropping on my fears, the door split apart through the center. Its pieces exploded away with a force like a cannon, and behind it appeared our pursuers.

The dark-haired woman stepped through first, olive skin set against her black clothing and gray eyes picking us out of the dark without a moment's uncertainty. Her hands were stretched out in front of her, fingers spread, shaking once like she was flinging water from them. Except instead of water, bits of wood and metal were stuck in ten long, silver claws that came from the ends of her fingertips.

The silver claws had split through the wood like they were axes, though they were each no wider than her fingernails—long and curved like a lizard's. With inhuman strength, her palms knocked the dresser and then the bed frame aside, parting the blockade like the waters of a sea.

A step behind her was a man I'd already seen before in a different dream: the man with the white eyebrows, with claws like hers. The woman's eyebrows matched his. So did the red ring on her right hand. Just as before, he carried a pistol.

They disregarded the other two in the room and looked straight at me, the man lifting his gun. Suddenly, there was a flurry of motion, and the boy leapt up from the floor, jumping between us: now bearing silver claws of his own. He held his hands out like bladed shields but the woman was prepared, her right claws striking out at once and catching his hand by the side. There was a sharp clang of metal like swords striking each other as she shoved him away. He lost his footing and fell, and I was exposed again.

"Are you happy, mother?" the man said, trying to align his gun as my defender fell.

"After you pull that trigger, Wyck. Then I will be," she replied coldly.

The girl slid from behind me with a shout, claws of her own now out and ready to fight. But it was already too late. For one second, the path between the man and me had been cleared.

There was a shot. It only lasted a millisecond before the world that surrounded us was bludgeoned to death.

My eyes flew open immediately, sitting up in bead, sweaty and breathing heavily. I was still in my bedroom.

I checked the face of my alarm clock: *3:14 AM.*

So this is how it's going to be.

It was too early to turn my light on. I reached up to wipe my eyes and felt something wet touch the side of my face. Thinking I'd drooled in my sleep, I went to my desk and searched the mess for a rag or shirt or tissue or… anything? My hand didn't come across a single cloth. So I reached to switch on my computer screen for light.

I froze.

I shoved my hand closer to the glow of the screen.

Like a scene in horror movie, my entire hand was covered in blood, now staining my shirt and neck. I felt its warmth against my face from where I'd unknowingly pressed my hands to it.

In horror I turned to grab something to stop the blood, only to find that beside me were the open sheets of my bed. Long streaks of red now stained the white like the grisly aftermath of a murder.

I dashed to the bathroom on the balls of my feet so that I wouldn't wake anyone up. I closed the door and punched the lock, diving to the sink. The bandage I'd put on the night before was still stuck to my right finger, sliding and unable to stop the gentle blood that had been coming from underneath it. I pulled it off sharply.

A stab of fiery pain shot through my finger. I had to grind my teeth together to hold my voice in. *The sting!* Tears burst into my eyes as the sharp feeling coursed throughout me. To my horror, I saw that with the bandage, the adhesive had also pulled off a thin layer of my own skin.

My breath came in sharp gasps, barely getting air out before I was drawing it back in again. With the fingers on my left hand splashing the flow of water from the faucet, I struggled to wash the gash. This only made me bite back another yell.

"Stop, stop!" The blood washed away and I saw the blackened skin of my birthmark again, now looking like it was singed and dead, like plastic wrap over a bone. The water continued to burn against the raw skin so I pulled my hand back out, fire shooting through every nerve.

My birthmark was raised even higher than the day before, looking like it was about to pop, fresh blood emerging from the skin that had peeled from around it. Edges of more skin were lifted up beside it and itching, bits of the bandage's adhesive still stuck.

I carefully reached to pull it free. The layer of skin peeled further. Blood was coming from the open wound. I knew if I stopped now it might only close up again, so I pulled more, closing my eyes and gritting my teeth.

Pain throbbed from the gash as air hit. To my horror, I saw that I had peeled away my own skin. Now between my two shaking fingers, I held a thick strip of black. It hung loose like a dead flower petal.

But what terrified me most—and what burned throughout my mind even more intensely than the pain—was what had emerged from hiding beneath my now-absent birthmark.

It was a silver ring on my finger.

8

SILVER AND RED

More blood, more gnashing of my teeth to contain the torture. The water from the faucet fell clear from the spout but hit the sink red.

Something kicked in and my finger soon became numb, until the awful burning actually started to recede. It didn't feel right for the pain to go away so quickly, but it wasn't like I was going to complain about that. The blood began to slow as well, and within seconds all that was left was the clean, silver ring that had, by all appearances, come from nowhere.

The metal was very smooth and polished to a shine as the water washed over it. It was strangely pure: thin with rounded edges, a gleam to its surface, three simple lines cut into its top. I never wore jewelry. But it looked expensive and I might have liked it, if it hadn't come out from under my own skin.

When I tried to pull it off though, the ring would not budge the slightest of an inch. Even though it didn't feel tight or painful anymore, the ring felt like it was attached to bone.

I wasn't about to spiral down into questions, asking how any of this could have happened, because I was too far past asking things I knew had no answer. Seeing the ring made me remember Father Lonnie's reaction when he'd noticed my birthmark: had he known?

Of course he'd known. He'd been looking for the ring all along, even when it was still hidden.

The bleeding had stopped entirely and the redness had receded. No need to wrap my finger in gauze anymore. So I scrambled back to my room in a daze, locking the door, pulling the bloodied sheets off of my bed and balling them up on the floor. Such a tedious thing to busy myself with in an attempt to forget the ring, though its weight on my finger refused to be ignored.

I hid the sheets in my closet behind some old laundry. But now I had nothing to sleep on.

I laughed. Sleep? Did I expect to ever sleep again?

Is that enough concrete proof for you? I thought. Something supernatural? I could handle that now. A conspiracy? I might even believe that. They wanted me dead? I could deal with that too. As long as I got answers. I *needed* the truth.

I was out of bed again as soon as the sun poked up, pulling the same church clothes from my closet, struggling to get them on. By then, my finger appeared entirely healed. Even bending it felt natural, though the band of the unusual metal felt like a weight. I shoved my hands into my pockets as I walked downstairs, my family still asleep.

I got onto my bike and started toward the church. Even the way the ring pressed against the handlebar was jarring.

I pedaled quickly even though being late for mass wouldn't have hurt, since I was only interested in grabbing the priest after he finished. I guess some part of me hoped that if I went fast and down streets that no one frequented, I could avoid the attention of any of those people the priest had said were watching for me— *Guardians.*

Anytime I heard a car door open or brakes squealing, I had to glance over just to make sure no one was taking aim at me as I rode. Would there even be enough time for all my questions before the next mass? I had so many now. My anticipation only grew as I turned the corner for the church's street.

From afar, I could see a crowd gathered outside the church, people again dressed up in their best shirts and dresses. Was church already finished? I couldn't possibly be that late. But everyone was outside, walking away from the church instead of toward it, covering their mouths, pulling their children by the arm frantically.

Finally I was close enough to see panic-filled faces and tears dripping from their eyes and hear confused weeping as they stumbled away from the church. I glanced over the flashing lights that were further down the street, and saw police cars and ambulances, yellow tape around the front of the church blocking the parishioners from going inside. Traffic on the street was lined up as an officer tried to manage the chaos of people standing around, looking toward the sky, and pointing in disbelief. I skidded my bike to a stop and looked up, all the way up past the church door and the circular stained glass window, to the pointed steeple above the bell tower.

I squinted because the sun was behind it, nearly blinding me. But in the outline, far at the top, I could see something that should not have been there. All in an instant, I realized what they were looking at.

Father Lonnie.

The morning sun streamed around his silhouette, his body bent backwards with arms extended, legs the opposite way, mouth and eyes open as if in a scream. The spire poked out of his chest, his corpse spiked through the middle like a nail through paper. He looked at us upside down, his body facing the sky but his eyes facing us with their lids open: skin white, a line of blood already dried from running down the steeple and onto the roof of his church.

My bike dropped from under me and crashed to the sidewalk. Every ounce of energy inside me felt like it was sucked away by a vacuum, I couldn't even stand, falling onto my knees in the grass as I stared up, unable to tear my eyes from the horrible sight. I could hear the sounds: the crying of the people, the frenzied questions, the police officers ordering everyone to leave. A fire truck with a long ladder had finally arrived and they were extending the arm out, doing their best to reach Father Lonnie and at least take the ghastly site down as more people began to gather. I could only go on kneeling, staring up at the man I'd spoken to not many hours before: the man who'd told me he'd die if I lived.

The bloodstained roof of the church was a message to me.

"*Please go home,*" I could hear the police say over a megaphone. "*Please let us do our jobs. Take your children and go home.*"

I managed to get to my feet, forcing myself to walk closer. Even when I looked away I was unable to get the horrible image out of my head, seeing the outline of the priest in the corner of my eye, feeling like I would vomit if my own body had enough strength. The crying got louder as I came closer, the grass trampled flat from high-heels and dress shoes, car horns honking as they tried to avoid pedestrians hurrying back to their vehicles.

"It's horrible…" I heard an old woman say.

"God have mercy," another whispered.

"This was by the gangs. He tried to help them but God knows they'd kill a man this way."

Others hugged in circles, supporting each other just enough so they could walk away. The police and paramedics weren't rushing though. They knew they were far too late now.

I'd never felt so truly lost. What was I supposed to do now? Where was I supposed to go? I fumbled to take my cell phone out of my pocket, thinking that I'd call Spud and ask him to come get me, but realized I had forgotten my phone back on my dresser.

I didn't know if I needed to hide. Whoever had done this was likely still in the crowd, watching and waiting for me to pop up. I was almost certain that they'd found the priest by following me. Or was it the other way? Had they come to him demanding to know where I was, and he had refused to tell?

I drowned in the unanswered questions. In my daze, I ran right into a police officer. He shoved me away and back into my senses.

"Look, kid, you need to go home," he ordered me, pointing away. "I'm not gonna tell you again."

I almost protested that I'd just seen Father Lonnie the night before, and that I knew who'd killed him. But all at once I remembered what the priest had told me: I couldn't even trust the police.

I couldn't trust anyone at all.

I mumbled an apology, turning to leave as quickly as I could. The loud engines of the fire truck rumbled, the ladder clicking as it extended high into the air toward the corpse. I reached the concrete and started back for my bike.

"Michael!" I heard someone whisper, making me jump. Over my shoulder, I saw someone else was now walking beside me. It was the monk, Brother James.

"Don't look at me, look straight ahead," he whispered, so I obeyed. Gray, unshaven stubble covered his chin and his eyes were bloodshot and terrified. His hands were folded in front of him, the long sleeves of his brown robe swishing against his shoes.

"Walk with me," he said. "Around the side and to the back. Don't look at anyone, all right? Just look ahead. Stay close to me."

Maybe it was my fright that caused me to do what he said without question, or the urgency in his voice. I stayed at the same pace as him, stepping into the damp grass and crossing the lawn beside the church.

We passed through the shadow of the steeple and were out of view of most of the bystanders. The church had a side door with steps leading up to it and at first I thought that was where Brother James was leading me. But he passed it, going around the church. Behind the large building were some storage sheds and beyond that was a waist-high white fence surrounding a small, one-story house—the rectory, where the priest had lived.

He pushed the gate open. The walkway was made of large and carefully placed stones lined by yellow and white flowers. In the tiny yard there was a corner garden and a giant, ancient satellite dish the size of a car, now rusted and filled with rainwater like a dish. Bees darted in and out of the flowers and grass, unaware of the nightmare that'd happened nearby.

"Lonnie told me this would happen," Brother James said under his breath, closing the gate behind me. "I knew when you showed up that there'd be trouble. And I tried to warn him but..."

"You saw who did it?" I asked.

"No," he replied. "But I know who. I don't have a single doubt it was Guardians." He sighed, rubbing his arms. "How'd you get a man all the way up to the steeple, eh? How'd you spear a man atop his own church? You'd got to fly him there."

He pushed ahead of me toward the house. So he knew. I followed him quicker than before.

He pulled the screen open so I could pass through and then locked both doors behind us. The inside of the house was yet another piece of Arleta trying to prove we'd never left the 1980s: old orange carpeting, wood panel walls, pictures in old frames and wooden clocks covering almost every inch. It stank of air fresheners and cologne, rocking chairs and small tables and old upholstered couches stuffing the living room from the far wall to the linoleum-covered kitchen on the end.

The monk moved to the windows, glancing outside before he let the metal blinds fall. He darkened the room one window at a time.

"Am I safe?" I asked. It was odd for me to wonder it, when all other times I'd never been fearful of such things.

"Not anymore," the monk said shakily. "But I don't think anyone noticed you outside. Not anyone who'd be able to describe you, not with all the shock they're in. Go close the blinds in the kitchen."

In seconds there was nothing left but dim light peeking through the slits.

"This way," he said, voice still low. He passed the kitchen, down the narrow hall and around the corner into a bedroom.

I knew immediately that this was where the attacker had found Father Lonnie. The furniture was a knocked-over mess, wooden dresser with drawers and clothes spilling out, a smashed chair in the center of the room as the only remainder from a short-lived struggle. The bed frame itself was sliced up and down like the claws of some attacking beast… or the knife-like edges of claws I'd seen before.

But no blood. No sign of the dead man here besides the fight. That must have happened outside.

"It's just…I knew this would happen. But I can't believe it," Brother James said painfully. "I just can't. I thought Lonnie would never get caught, but then he was."

He was coming close to sobbing but his hands continued to move, pulling open the closet door and shoving the clothes to the side. Beyond the clothes was a hidden, undersized door with two locks. He sniffled as he pulled keys from his pockets, undoing both locks and pushing inside. I had to bend over to step through the low doorway.

The room was musty, smelling of wood and dust like an old shed. It was long and thin, no windows or any other doors, a single air vent poking through the wall. Scattered around were desks, two giant safes in the corner, lamps and magnifying glasses and computers all around. There was a couch in the center with many of its buttons ripped out and some rugs covering the ugly concrete, the wooden support frames of the walls exposed with wires running in and out. A rickety, metal furnace sat in the corner with an exhaust pipe poking up to the ceiling; a fire going inside it though the room was much too warm already.

"What's all this in here?" I asked. I heard Brother James lock both deadbolts behind us and the keys rattle back into his pocket.

"This is the home of the blog," he told me. "Or at least it was. There won't be any more of it now, I guess."

Curiosity got the best of me, so I approached one of the desks. The computer was running a procedure, a green progress bar at 79% completion and files being listed below as they were erased one-by-one. All of the computers were doing the same thing. The desk was covered in papers and printouts, though I could see by following a trail of dropped notes that most of them had already been thrown into the furnace. Three empty document boxes sat beside the fire.

"I can't believe I'm burning all of this," Brother James said beside me. "This was Lonnie's life. This was all he did: this and the Church. But it's too dangerous to keep them now."

"What is all of it?" I asked.

"Everything you could imagine," he said. "Government emails. Memos between businesses. CIA, FBI, royal families, foreign officials. Leaks to online databases full of this stuff that no one's even dreamed of being true."

He breathed out despondently. "It's all from Anon. Lots of truth no one gets to see."

He sounded close to sobbing again. He obviously wasn't going to stop me, so I grabbed some of the papers from the mess. The topmost one was written in what appeared to be Russian, but there were notes scribbled in the sides: a sharp handwriting that said to "POST THIS" with an arrow to a circled paragraph, and "REDACT" next to a part that was scratched out with black marker. There were pages of that report stapled together, with diagrams of an airplane and arrows denoting specific seats.

I pushed it off and found more beneath that. There were memos bound by paper clips, messages exchanged in a circle of email addresses that were jumbled letters and numbers. The message chain was long but the newest post was circled by a highlighter pen, which only read:

TO: 100-964
FROM: 1094-57

Confirmation of activity in Japan, now moved to March 16, earthquake. Keep away from the area for two days leading up and following the date.

Relocate all invested assets from Dreycorp a week preceding.

It was odd, until I recognized what they had been talking about. That was the earthquake that'd hit Japan days ago—the same that my teacher had shown us in class.

At the top of the page, a date marked when the email had been sent...four months ago.

I remembered suddenly what I'd read in the eyes of Dreycorp's own CEO, that dramatic change that had overcome Harold Wolf some time before his death. Now it clicked into place: the fear of something that he was certain was coming to get him. He'd known all along, too. Maybe he'd been running from them, hiding in another country to escape the inevitable. It became painfully obvious to me that the earthquake—all that massive destruction, and all the lives that it had taken—had somehow been artificially created to kill this one man.

"How does Anon get this information?" I asked, looking up. "This is...this is almost unbelievable."

And a treasure trove for me—a strange feeding of my addiction to truth. I didn't give the monk a possibility of answering, digging further into the papers. There was a chart attached below the email, showing two graphs side-by-side. The one on the left showed a large circle with DREYCORP typed in the center, dated this year. There were uncountable smaller circles inside its bounds with even smaller names: food companies whose brands I saw all the time when we went grocery shopping.

The graph on the right also had DREYCORP, but it and its circles were now far smaller and beside two others, all three enveloped by another that simply said EXCELSOR. This chart was dated ten years into the future. A predicted merger, I guessed. Or rather, an inevitable one.

It was like crawling down into a hole only to find that just around the corner was another world, right under my feet the entire time. An email spoke of a nationwide banking chain that was going to fail, the deadline still two months away. It was brief and to the point: *Pull your assets. Place them as investments in this other company.* They were like instructions with no signature, no way of telling the author or the receiver. There were other attached pages detailing numbers and figures I didn't understand, lines of text in some finance language. The email circle appeared to be a group of moguls and investment operators, sometimes posting emails that were forwarded to them by others. There were never any names: only the codes as identification.

Everything was a photocopy. Who was Anon to have access to all these things?

"That's just some of the finance stuff," Brother James said from beside me. "These are nothing. They're far down the chain of power. We've only identified a few based on their anonymous handles. Have you ever read an email to a president before?"

"I didn't even know the President had email," I said in a quick breath, taking a paper that the monk slid in front of me. It was one page, dated for 2012 and addressed from 916-88 to 55-614, which only said:

Stay out of NY this October.

"You think you know what the world is?" Brother James said. "A lot of people think they do. But people are sheep. Humans are easily led when they don't know they are following."

"And Father Lonnie..." I said. "They killed him because he knows."

"Because he *knew*," Brother James corrected. Past tense now; Father Lonnie was already gone.

"But he had proof," I said. "He could have gone out and told someone. He could have used all of this to expose who they are!"

"You don't understand," the monk said. "It sounds so easy: take these documents and expose them. But to whom? The police? The FBI? Late night radio shows who'd broadcast us in the same segment they talk about alien space saucers?"

He scratched his arms. "They control *everything*, Michael. They command *everything*. Do you know how large the world is? Can you imagine how much power it would take to run the *entire* world, when few can even run an entire country?"

His voice had started to rise as he became more frantic. He yanked the papers out of my hands, tossing them across the desk into the pile.

"Some people believe in families that run the world," he said. "Rich, powerful families who have been around since kings, still commanding countries in secret, causing wars on a whim to build their wealth and releasing plagues as a part of procedure. But the families still report to these... to the Guardians."

He shrugged. "But you probably think I'm crazy, still. You're like everyone else. But the Guardians made it that way. They control the media and thus control the way people think: make anyone who believes in this to be a 'conspiracy theorist' or a 'crazy old man talking about Illuminati'. But we're not making it up. We're *right*."

I was becoming more and more alarmed as the monk's voice sped up, his hands shaking as he grabbed papers from the desk and stacked them up, then shuffled them, only to reorganize them again.

"Look at Lonnie," he said. "You don't think this happens all the time? They want someone dead, so they *make* him dead. And not just his body: dead to anyone who'd loved him before. Tomorrow they'll find meds in Lonnie's room. Some prostitute will say his name in the news. They'll spread all these lies so that people will *want* to forget him, think his death was his own fault—a suicide by a drug-abusing, tithe-stealing, whoremonger of a priest. 'Not Lonnie!' they'll say. But even his friends will believe it just because they're told to."

The monk hit the desk, making it rattle. "Anon didn't do anything to save him. He just let him die. Where was Anon when Lonnie needed protection? Did he just let him die because it was for some greater good? To keep *you* safe?"

The monk pulled open one of the drawers and shuffled things around in it furiously. I glanced at the locked door. My heart had started to beat faster, afraid that the monk would soon faint from shock. Which pocket had he put the keys in? Would I be able to drag him out to get the paramedics, who likely were still outside?

"I wish I was Lonnie," he went on. "I wish I could be as brave as he was. But I'm not. This isn't my war. And I've got a family: I've got brothers and sisters and both my parents."

"Calm down, you'll be all right," I told him, holding my hands out.

"No it won't be alright!" he exploded into a scream, and suddenly his hand whipped out from the drawer. In it was a pistol, aimed at me.

"Nothing will ever be alright now!" he shouted at me, his voice bouncing off the bricks and the metal furnace. I was frozen, hands extended, heart nearly stopping. The gun was a 9-millimeter: long and slender chassis, black and metal. It was so close I could see its front sight.

"What the hell are you doing?" I demanded. But the gun didn't waver, even as the sweat that glistened in his palms threatened to make it slip.

"I can't be Lonnie!" he said through clenched teeth. "I can't die that way."

"I'll leave then!" I told him, lifting my hands. "No one will ever know you had me here."

"It's too late for that," the monk said. "I can't let you go. Not if I want them to let me live. You've got to stay here until he comes back."

Everything hit me at once, and I realized just how stupid and blind I had been. In my fright at seeing the corpse atop the church, I hadn't taken a moment to dig for a Glimpse from Brother James, to even wonder if I should trust him at all. Now, across the room and deep in the eyes of this crazed man, I could see answers to all the questions that had appeared. *Threatened. Cornered.*

Someone had gotten to Brother James before I arrived.

"Are they here?" I asked, knowing full well what was happening, why I'd been led back here. My mind raced for an escape.

"Soon," he replied. "I—I told him you'd be back this morning after mass. I'm sorry, Michael. I just couldn't do anything else when he…"

Then I saw why he'd kept his arms crossed all this time. His left hand was bent painfully forward and still didn't move, scaling and red with the worst burns I'd seen. Parts of his skin were blackened even past his wrist, dried blood around the white gauze he'd tried to wrap around it. When he saw I was looking, he hid his hand away again, still trembling.

"You don't have to do this," I said. "I'll disappear. They'll think you killed me."

"They want you alive," he whined. "They want to make sure. If I don't keep you here, he'll know. He'll get me, just like Lonnie. You don't think they can, and kill my whole family too?"

"But we're on the same side," I said, though I already knew the attempt was in vain. His mind was made up, strengthened like a barrier of fear he'd been building ever since the night before. I could imagine the horror he'd witnessed: the killing of his friend, the threat from a Guardian... who even now was likely on his way back here to collect me, and finish what Mr. Sharpe could not.

Never had such terror washed over me as I remembered the chase from nights before, and realized that I had fallen right into a trap. They wouldn't make the same mistake twice. I had to get out of there.

Brother James' gun hand had started to shake. I moved to the side, trying to get out of its way, but he stepped between the door and me again.

"I'm sorry," he said, and even then I could tell that he meant it.

So I tried to run, knowing his conscience would make him hesitate to shoot. But he was fast, diving to the side, slamming into me and throwing me hard against the wall. I yelled, pushing him off of me, running again only to be knocked hard against my back, falling over and gasping for breath.

He was kneeling on top of me in a second. I grabbed the end of a fire poker that was next to the furnace, swinging it at him. I knocked his arm and he screamed, but he managed to grab it and wrestle it from me. I heard the reverberating metal fly to the other end of the room, smashing through a computer screen. All the while I continued to shout for help, my words bouncing uselessly off the walls.

I tried to roll over but he held me down, pushing my back with his knee, pressing a cloth against my face and blocking my mouth and nose. I gasped and got a whole lung-full of whatever chemical he was trying to get inside of me.

It hit suddenly, such a strong smell, like alcohol and a doctor's office. It only made me gasp more, dizziness racing through my head as I struggled to fight against it.

"Quiet down!" he commanded me. Something was banging above our heads, each sound like it was in an echo chamber. There was a crash. A pounding against the locked door.

Was it someone coming for me? Had they heard me?

But I wasn't screaming anymore: *why wasn't I screaming?!* I drifted on a magic carpet that hovered from the floor, room spinning, muscles still trying to lift me though nothing ever brought me up more than a few inches.

I could feel things happening inside me: strange sensations that felt like a dam threatening to explode, making me want to vomit. My finger throbbed where the silver ring was. It felt like it was tightening slowly, like the device that nurses put around an arm to check blood pressure. All of my skin felt like it was constricting, floating, plummeting...

I could still hear the sounds though. I heard a creaking of hinges, a crashing of wood being shredded. I heard two voices yelling, just before the pressure holding me down disappeared.

There was a shot.

Gentle arms lifted me.

Warm sunshine fell on my arms and legs.

Then I was going up...up...up into the air, until all I could hear was the wind and gentle echoes.

Sirens.

Birds.

Silence.

9

CESSATION

I dreamt of flying.

One moment I was frozen in a chemical blackness, and the other I was surrounded by blue and white, soaring and free of the wooden, dirty smell that had enveloped the secret room. Warmth ran against my back and down my legs and arms as the wind flew in my face. The smell of salt water rushing up from below awakened me.

My eyes were already open but it took some time for anything I was looking at to sink in. I was soaring high above the coastline, the people below me little more than specks and the cars and houses like faraway models. Like a toy town. It was so peaceful, so silent besides the muted buzz of air as it pressed around my head like bees. My eyes were not bothered by the rushing: it was as if a glass cone was over my head like a helmet, keeping me safe, sealing me from the air and the sky. Gravity couldn't keep its fingers on me. I floated free of the Earth. I was invincible, and I was silver.

It startled me only slightly. I had looked down and seen my hands firmly pressed to my sides and noticed something was different. Silver covered the outside of my hands from my knuckles to my wrist in overlapping, reflective scales like the skin of a snake. They moved when I clenched my fist. The scales mirrored the sun into my face.

In the dream, this didn't feel strange at all: the glow of the silver on my hands seemed no more unusual than that of the ring still on my finger. And the flying too. I simply willed myself to go higher and suddenly I was heading upward on my own accord, legs and arms pressed together like I was a long silver bullet. I was actually *flying.*

I wasn't alone either. The girl from my dream suddenly appeared from over my shoulder, hands with scales just like mine pressed to her sides. The magnificent silver was even more vibrant in the sunlight. I grinned then leapt higher, as if trying to tempt her into racing against me. I heard her laugh from over my shoulder, a sound I'd never heard from this girl in any dream before. It was enough of a distraction for her to dart ahead.

On a plane, a jet engine and babbling passengers would have drowned the quiet of the sky out. But here, where we were alone, the silence was omnipresent: a beautiful emptiness of yellow sun and perfect clouds that made all the vast cities and shining coasts and bustling cars below seem insignificant.

She stopped to float as I tried to catch up. Her feet dangled lightly in the air, arms crossed now. I could see every line between the scales on her hands, like miniature black creases dividing tiny mirrors.

I took a labored breath of air and let it out in contentment.

10

REBIRTH

I awoke to a gentle rain drizzling down the sides of my face: the misty spray of a storm coming to its close. It smelled of rot and acid and all the hideous chemicals that permeated the city air, and tasted even worse when it dripped through the corners of my lips and down my dehydrated throat. I rolled over, groaning in pain. My torn clothes were already soaked through to my skin. They squished miserably against the wet rock beneath my body.

I was disoriented but managed to force my eyelids open. My forehead rested on my arms, elbows covered in gray rock chips. So I wasn't going to die in my dream this time? How lucky I was.

Even then, the final dream was blemished by memories of something else...a priest on a steeple. A gun pointed at my face. Chemicals that had forced me to sleep. Arms picking me up, and carrying me into the sky. I couldn't put them all together at first. Had my entire morning been a part of a dream all along?

I barely registered that I was outdoors. The rain poured harmlessly on me, cool at first, then warming like sweat when it ran down my back and through rips in my white undershirt. Had I fallen asleep in the yard? I lifted my head.

I wasn't in my yard at all. I was at the top of a canyon somewhere, tall rock was all around me and my body lying in the middle of a thin, open path. I sat up quickly, water falling from folds in my shirt. Everything was dark under the heavy clouds but even then I could tell I was far from home.

Something itched on my right hand. The ring was still there.

I was on my feet in an instant, the lethargic feeling dashed from my bones. I remembered! Brother James had handed me over to the Guardians. And now I was outside? Had something gone wrong, or had I escaped them somehow but couldn't remember it? I'd already had enough experience with these Guardians to know I should get away while I could. I stumbled ahead in a stupor.

The opening in the rocks was not a path at all, but a sudden cliff drop-off that had been hidden in the mist. I came upon it too quickly to catch my balance and slipped as my shoes hit the wet rocks.

I fell over the edge.

For a moment I tumbled into nothing, unable to hold my balance, arms rushing in front of me to catch my fall. But then I wasn't falling any longer. I found myself floating in midair, feet dangling inches away from the edge and an unfathomable distance from the rock-covered valley below. My hands were still frozen in front of me: hands now covered in silver scales.

The scales brushed against each other, feeling strangely natural. My hands trembled, some unfamiliar sensation coursing out of them that caused me to remain afloat. The energy came from the tops of my hands and burst invisibly through my skin and bones and out the other side of my palms. I was carried backwards to my feet again and dropped heavily to solid ground.

The moment I was safe again, the silver scales sudden drew back, hiding themselves beneath my skin as if they'd never been there at all. In seconds, I had once again returned to normal, except for my heart pounding louder than the rain.

I shook. Was I still dreaming? I couldn't be. I'd already awoken, and that sensation—that real, unmistakable feeling of *something* within me, fresh and powerful like the beating of a new heart.

"Try *not* to die so quickly," I heard a male voice behind me. I spun around and my hands reacted again, the silver scales bursting forth in the same way they had seconds before. This time, however, ten long, curled silver claws slid from my fingers, bursting from the cuticle and covering my nails like armor with razor-sharp ends.

I don't know what scared me more: the claws, or the person I saw across from me.

"You!" I gasped. I could hardly believe my own eyes—the boy who'd appeared in my nightmares was now sitting in front of me, deep in the shadow of the high stonewall beneath a tree that left him in a dry circle. His clothes were far more modern than before: a black tank top that left his muscled arms exposed, and faded blue jeans above navy-blue Converse scuffed by dirt stains. His hair was still long and black, tied behind his shoulders. There was a silver ring on his finger, exactly like mine. Not to mention the most unusual thing about him, which frankly was beginning to lose its novelty: silver scales on his hands and long claws on his fingers.

The moment I saw the silver, I panicked and stepped back. He looked at me and I at him, neither of us able to speak at first. Then, as if judging me to be no threat, he leaned back again, and the claws and scales withdrew back into his skin.

"I'm Thad," he said calmly. "Stop that before you hurt yourself."

"Did they send you to kill me?" I demanded, and at this accusation my fingers twitched. I wanted them to stop but I wasn't controlling them, their movements involuntary.

"I sure hope not," he said. "You've been laying there for hours and I haven't sliced you to bits. I'd be *the worst* assassin the world has ever seen."

He regarded me with a slightly amused, crooked smile. I didn't know how to respond to that, except to feel stupid. My claws retreated again, as if they could sense there wasn't any danger. I tore my eyes from him slowly, looking down as the scales vanished too.

Impossible…

But too real for me to deny.

I studied Thad but was unable to voice any of the questions that I had—questions that only continued to multiply.

Thad pushed himself up from his slouch and dusted his hands on the knees of his jeans.

"Maybe I should have left you back there," he said in reflection. "I'd get a whole lot more appreciation from those Guardians."

"I…I'm sorry," I said, swallowing hard. "I just don't know what's going on. I don't know who you are." I stopped, correcting myself. "Actually I do. You're the guy from my dreams."

"That's the first time I've heard *that* from another guy," he murmured.

I wasn't amused, even though Thad was fighting valiantly to end the heavy air between us. I was so confused that I didn't know which reaction to go with.

He gestured to a dry spot next to him.

"You want to get out of the rain at least?" he suggested. As he spoke, he reached into his pocket for something, but finding that it wasn't there, he glanced to his wristwatch swiftly.

"I'd give it about ten more minutes," he said. "Then we've got to run. Just enough time to figure out how we both got into this mess."

He tapped the dry spot again. "Come on, just a few minutes. I've been running all over the place trying to save you in time."

I relented, but more because I felt that my knees would soon give out if I didn't sit. I still wasn't sure if I could trust him, but he had made a good point: I'd have been dead if he wanted me that way. I sat an arm's length from him and shivered.

"What do you mean you saved me?" I finally mustered up the courage to ask.

"I mean if I'd been a few minutes late, both of us would be dead now," he replied. "You think that monk was keeping you in that room waiting for your mother to arrive?"

I twisted my lips up wryly. I could recall most of it clearly and Thad was right. Why *wasn't* I with the Guardians, locked up wherever they would have taken me after Brother James had handed me over? The sounds flooded back too: the loud scuffle and the gunshots. I began to realize that all that fighting hadn't been between Brother James and a Guardian after all. Thad had appeared instead.

"I must've given that monk quite a fright, tearing down the door with these," he said, flexing his claws. "He shot himself in the head when he saw me."

Obviously, Brother James had thought Thad was a Guardian come to kill him and collect me. I didn't know whether to feel sympathy for him or to think that it'd served him right. It was too late now, though. Whoever was returning to the church to pick me up would be greeted by yet another corpse—the latest in a long line.

"I—I don't even know where to start," I stammered. "How do you even know who I am? And how'd you know I was in there?"

"Psh," Thad said with disgust. "Those are all the same questions I have and I was hoping *you* could answer."

I didn't have any.

"Look," he said. "Give up now on getting the answers you want. They're not going to appear. I've already tried."

He scratched the knees of his jeans, looking blankly toward the cliff edge. "That was the first thing I learned, when the dreams started..."

So, he'd had them as well. I shifted a bit.

"You sure act like you know me, though," I noted.

"Yeah?" he said. "I guess you're right. I kinda feel like I do. Enough to risk my life to save yours, at least."

He checked his watch again. As he did, I couldn't help but notice that even the skin around his ring was still bearing the light red inflammation, like he'd gone through the same transformation as I.

"Did it all happen the same for you?" I asked, now letting my curiosity take over. I looked down to where my scales had been but now the skin was smooth and unbroken, as if it had simply healed itself back into a human disguise.

"I'd think so," he said. "If you mean the dreams and the ring that just came out of nowhere. The claws happened a day before my seventeenth birthday."

"My birthday is tomorrow," I said.

"Of course it is," he replied matter-of-factly. "That's why they're so desperate to make you a dead Michael."

Did growing claws make a person impervious to empathy? I'd known this Thad person for ten whole minutes and I already wanted to shake his hand in thanks and punch him at the same time.

"Just think like one of them," he said. "You know what Guardians are. Do you think they'd let anyone who can fight them stay around?"

"It'd help if I knew what any of that meant," I said.

"It's because *you're* a threat," he said insistently, as if I was missing some obvious point. "You haven't realized it yet? You're one of them. *You* are a Guardian."

He looked at me like I should have expected his answer, as if somehow I should have known that this was coming. But nothing so far had prepared me for it, and suddenly I was unsure if anything surrounding me was real or if Brother James' chemicals were still at work.

"Me?" I said, the fright causing my voice to rise in pitch. An unwanted feeling began to creep its fingers up the back of my neck. I wanted to say he was lying but I couldn't form the words.

"You have claws and scales," he said, gesturing in my direction. The proof was attached to me, after all. My insides didn't feel any different. I still felt like a human, and my mind still functioned in the same way it always had. In fact, the very mind that should have been helping me understand what he was saying was busy fighting against what appeared to be the inevitable truth.

"What do you think Guardians are?" Thad asked. "You're not human, that's for sure. At least not entirely."

I wanted to curl up into a ball and block out his words, that flippant, uncaring tone like this was all so natural when absolutely nothing about it was. I realized why he bothered me so much. I'd just lost control over everything. Or rather, I'd found out that I'd never had any control to begin with, but had been a pawn in some greater game. And Thad, irritatingly calm, appeared to have already come to terms with all this.

"How did you find me?" I asked. The more answers I could get, the more I'd feel like I was actually sitting on solid ground.

Thad gave an unexpected grin.

"Ah," he stated. "The start of all of this mess for me. If only I *didn't* know."

Again, his fingers twisted at the ring, almost like he wished he could remove it but it simply wouldn't budge. "Don't even ask me how. It started right after the dreams and I still didn't know who you were. Then all of a sudden, I woke up—on my seventeenth birthday—and I had this bizarre feeling. Like I had to find you."

It felt like he was leading up to some big joke, but he never reached the punch line.

He shrugged. "It was weird. I just knew where you were. I mean, I'm looking at you now so I know you're right there. But at the same time I *know* you're there."

He gestured at me. "I could go a mile the other way and still now you're *right there*. I could stand and point to you from where I was back in that white room they had me in. That's why the Guardians took us."

He looked up, gaze stronger now. "They wanted us to take them to you. Luckily, that gave them a reason to keep us alive."

I blinked. His positivity had only suffered a tiny crack as he spoke of his own possible demise. But I'd caught something unexpected in his words.

"Us?" I echoed. "There are others?"

He nodded. "Yes. Don't you remember? Wasn't Callista in your dreams too?"

"She's alive?" I burst with dismay. Keeping my outbursts in check had become an impossible task.

"I read in the newspaper that she'd died in a fire," I blurted. Thad gave me a quizzical look.

"Obviously you've been doing some research," he said, a little impressed. "But no. That was a cover-up. Guardians have had her for weeks, I think."

"So she's alive?" I said again, unwilling to believe until I was certain.

"I hope so." His face fell slightly. "Last time I saw her she was..."

His voice trailed off, and I couldn't help but notice that his shoulders sagged lower, and the nonchalant gaze changed to something more of concern. That wasn't exactly the answer that I'd wanted, but for some reason I felt my insides soar because it was far more than I'd had earlier. She was actually alive somewhere? All this time? Of everyone I'd tracked down so far, this girl had always seemed the most important. Finding out that she hadn't died was like erasing a history book chapter and starting over—a mental rewriting of what I'd thought was concrete truth.

Nervously, Thad glanced at his wristwatch again. Then he stood abruptly, the rain already having slowed from before, and started toward the cliff edge so that he could see over. He studied the horizon, checking his watch yet another time.

"You know the Guardians will go back to the church and find I'm not there," I said. "That's if they haven't already."

I didn't know what to do next. I'd reached the end of my plans long ago when I'd found the priest, and everything after had only been venturing further into the dark. Intuition told me I could trust Thad, as strange as that seemed. He looked up from his watch.

"Don't worry yet," he replied. "Callista made a plan."

"And what's that?"

He opened his mouth to answer, but instead something else chose to respond. It came in the form of a dramatic, faraway explosion, with a burst of orange light flashing from the coastline. It made me jump, then a second later I heard an echoing roar like a bomb going off. Seeing a tall curl of black smoke heading for the sky, Thad smiled.

"That," he said, "would be Callista's plan."

He leapt off the cliff edge. In that same second, the scales appeared on his hands once again, and he rose into the air a few feet as if there were gentle rockets at the bottom of his shoes. The motion caused water to sling from his clothes and into my eyes. His motion seemed as natural as walking.

"Come on then," he said, hovering with his feet now at the level of my eyes.

"You still have a lot to explain!" I protested. It was a wonder I managed to speak at all.

"Well," he replied, lowering himself a bit, "I could stick around and tell you everything, or we could go down and see what horrible thing Callista's done."

He shot up and away. I was left alone on the cliff, and watching him rise into the sky, I came to the rim and stopped. What did he really expect...he couldn't actually mean for me to...?

I'd done it before but that'd only been by instinct. It had felt effortless. But I didn't even know *what* I'd done or if I could do it again. The rocks below seemed so far away. I licked my lips, stifling a sudden urge to jump, as if even my body and mind were telling me to just do it, to just step over that edge, to let the air carry me...

I felt like a tiny child about to skydive out of a plane, a sinking feeling inside that maybe this wasn't such a good idea. But Thad beckoned me, and I looked up and saw his head blocking the sunlight that had just begun to clear the storm clouds. He looked impatient. So I jumped.

It was a stupid thing to do. I wasn't close enough to the edge to clear it, so my heels ended up slipping on the end, my arms waving frantically. I was entirely unprepared for having nothing beneath my feet, falling like a stone toward jagged rocks and trees. I choked out a squeak because I couldn't gather enough air for a full shout, feeling the scales emerge on my hands again...

I was caught by the air.

With a whoosh, my plunging dive turned in the opposite direction, my body soaring up like I'd leapt out of a swing. Fear had pressed my arms to my sides, but though I trembled, I continued to rush up with such grace that I knew I was not consciously controlling my motion. One second I was falling, the next I was floating.

Air ruffled my hair as I rose, arms still pressed tightly against my sides because I was too fearful to move them, afraid that any motion would upset whatever force held me aloft. And yet it all seemed so *normal*. So natural. I simply wanted to go closer to Thad and with less than an active thought, my body started toward him like an arrow.

The motion was smooth and I closed in on him in seconds. Thad regarded me with approval.

"I can't promise I won't make fun of you for that sound you made," he said. When stopped, our bodies righted themselves, so that our feet dangled below us. Thad's hands were out as if even he was still getting used to balancing in the air. I struggled to get a feel for what I was doing. When I willed myself to climb an inch, I did, and when I turned my head to look back at the cliff that I'd been on moments before, my body turned midair to follow.

"You'll get the hang of it," Thad said. "Let's go see Callista."

We headed toward the blue as the distant black smoke continued to crawl its lazy way into the sky.

11

PYROMANIA

If I'd had any lingering fears that I was still dreaming, they were beaten in a moment. I could not have invented such a feeling even in my imagination, as we broke through low tufts of cloud that fought like vapor while we fell toward the miniature ground below.

I finally dared to look down at the houses and buildings, spots darkened from the rain. The smell hit me in a rush—a mixture of dust and smoke and smog. Gravity seemed to have less power over me. *Everything* seemed to have less power over me.

How can no one see us? I wondered. Was that another part of the supernatural powers: something in the semi-invisible shell that allowed me to breathe and kept my eyes clear? We were either invisible or camouflaged. Or maybe we were merely faraway birds darting between the clouds to everyone below.

I saw another explosion in the distance, a belch of black smoke erupting from a fire on the beach, followed by a boom. We were nearing the Pacific coastline, the long stretch of sand bordering the blue water like some type of cream-colored road. The rain had left the beach abandoned but I could already see the flashing lights and hear the sirens of police cars and fire trucks rushing toward the flames. I looked closer and saw that the fire had consumed the wreckage of a small executive jet.

Thad began to dive so I followed him toward the ground. The plane had been absolutely obliterated, a mangled clutter of wreckage with pieces of it floating in the water, a wing poking from the sand and another tossed a few hundred feet away. Even as I descended, it was hard to take my eyes off the destruction.

Until, of course, I spotted a figure sitting in the shade of a tree, staring out in my direction. It only took one fleeting second to recognize Callista.

I wasn't watching where I was going, so the ground came upon me quicker than I could react. My shoes scraped a pile of sand, making me fall forward and roll, dirt and sticks clinging to my already-tattered shirt. I fell onto my back, eyes flying open. No more clouds or sky. I was surrounded by palm trees.

Sand flew at my face as Thad leaned over me with his head blocking the sunlight. He shook his head.

"Watching where you're going is supposed to be the easy part," he said. He offered me his hand, and with some flailing I managed to catch it and pull myself up. Both of our scales had disappeared.

We were in a shaded area on a hill, the breeze blowing in from the coast and the sounds of the waves hitting the beach like endless radio static.

"What happened over there?" I asked, smelling the smoke even from where we stood. Thad didn't answer me, hopping across the slippery rocks in the direction of Callista. I hurried to follow him, hearing the sounds of police shouting to residents to stay away from the beach. I'd probably heard more police megaphones this week than in my entire life.

Callista sat with her back to us, knees pulled up to her chest with arms hugging them for warmth. She wore a simple gray shirt with the back torn in uneven slits. Her hair was a mess from the wind that whipped at it, as dark as I'd seen in the dreams.

"I could have blown the plane up sixty seconds earlier," she said, with some measure of discontent, never looking up at us. "That extra minute of jet fuel would have tossed the tail a bit further out into the water."

"I still think you made a fine explosion," Thad replied, sitting down beside her.

I awkwardly sat on her other side, trying not to stare or blurting something out that I knew would sound stupid. But who could blame me? There was the girl who'd haunted me all week, talking about the mechanics of blowing up planes.

The fire trucks were having a hard time getting out to the beach thanks to the wet sand, and there was another loud pop that sent tiny bits of metal flying like bursting popcorn. The destruction looked pretty complete to me. I watched with alarmed attention as the fire licked through the air, feeding on fuel and whatever had been in the plane before it'd hit. Its middle was split, windows blown out and spewing more smoke.

Callista still didn't look satisfied.

"I just wish they'd packed more bullets and guns on board," she said dryly. "You know, all that stuff they were gonna use to kill us. I really wanted to see some fireworks, Thad."

"I'll make a note of that for next time you need to take down a plane," he replied dutifully. Behind her back, he gave me a feigned look of terror, before hiding it when she turned to look at me.

It was the first time our eyes had met, in real life at least. They shouldn't have surprised me, but they did—seeing them so close, so vibrant that I blinked, thoughts scattering like fish before a shark. Their blue didn't even seem to fit in any normal spectrum.

I was never a person to be intimidated, so I kept her gaze strongly.

"Fine, I'm a pyromaniac," she burst, opening her hands defensively. "What can I do?"

Still, she refused to break my gaze. I didn't know what that meant.

"You could... *not* crash planes?" I suggested.

To my surprise, she didn't frown, but instead exploded into a fit of laughter. She laughed so hard that she fell backwards, hair going around her head like a dark halo, face staring up at the sky that was now entirely clear of clouds and rain.

"Yeah, that'd be a good start," she agreed, closing her eyes, leaving me even more confused than before. I looked up at Thad, now unblocked by Callista. He glanced from me to her, then back to me again, but refused to comment. Callista breathed deep, unimpeded even by the burnt smell that drifted our way, and the sound was filled with a strange relief.

"Um..." I started. I cleared my throat. "Can I ask why there's a plane crashed on the beach?" I said, trying to force as much command into my voice as I could, but failing.

"Because if it'd landed, the eleven men on board would have killed you," Callista said, without even opening her eyes.

"And Thad, and me too," she added. "They were armed like the military. Tell him our plan, Thad."

She poked him with her knee and he straightened up to attention.

"Right, the plan," he said to me. "You already know Callista and I were caught before they found you. When they got the lead that you were out here, they sent this guy named Mr. Sharpe. But he must not have killed you, because he never came back. And because she and I never died. See…" He opened his hands. "That's what I heard from them. If *you* die, then for some reason Callista and I are supposed to die immediately as well."

"Right on the spot," Callista said, with some disdain. "Because you're a Guardian, and we're just Chosens—that's what they called us. We're connected to you. Whatever that means."

"Yeah," Thad said. "So when we didn't die, and Mr. Sharpe didn't come back…well, Callista and I knew you were fighting. So it was our turn to put in some effort."

He nodded excitedly. "Since you'd gotten the first guy, his boss went out to do things right: Wyck is what they called him. But when he left, all that was guarding us was his team of cheap expendable gunmen."

He gestured at himself. "Easily outwitted by me. The plan was for me to escape, which I eventually did, to go save your sorry life. Callista would stay behind and keep the henchmen at bay."

"Basically, throw things into chaos," Callista broke in, still laying down, eyelids shut.

"Because with Thad out," she continued, "it wasn't going to be so easy to kill you. There was someone lurking around who could challenge Wyck. So he got scared and had his henchmen get on that jet to move me out here, where he could make certain I didn't get away either. But it's like one of those two-ended rabbit holes."

She held one hand up. "On this end, you have Thad running to save you. And on this end," she held her other hand up, far from the other, "you have little old me, suddenly breaking locks and blocking bullets and cutting my way through the walls of a plane and slicing its wing off midair."

To accent her words, claws flew out from the hand she'd marked as herself. They slid forth like hidden blades, making me blink, which by the look in her face was exactly the reaction she'd wanted.

"The little fox just gets trapped running from one end to the other," she said. "And down go the henchmen, away goes the Callista, and safe goes the Michael."

She hit my arm with the back of her hand, claws gone. I didn't know what to say in response to their plan. It was either the stupidest thing I'd ever heard, or the most brilliant.

"So now they're really going to panic," I said with a hint of dread.

Callista nodded. "Like a bunch of bees when you hit the nest," she said. She turned to look at me.

"Please don't say I shouldn't have," she warned. "I don't want to think about what I just did for you. Even if it was eleven trained killers without a single moral fiber in their bodies."

"I think that we can agree on the fact that they started it," I said with a long release of nervous breath. It was worrisome though, how that statement seemed to be the extent of emotion she had after killing eleven people. I remembered the newspaper article about her family's fiery death…maybe her emotional fuses had been burned out with them?

Callista leaned away from me to look at Thad.

"I remembered," she told him, pulling something out of her short pocket and placing it in his hand. It was a flawless bronze pocket watch, the type that gentlemen might wear on chains in old England. Except this one was unusual in its design: formed with two disks that met as a lid, but the top bearing two small, metal skeleton hands that reached for the lock. Thad took it without smiling, though he looked relieved.

I didn't understand what'd just happened. I also didn't like the way that Callista was simply laying there, as if we weren't in any danger at all.

"So what now?" I asked nervously, as the fire truck hoses burst with solution that crackled over the flames.

"The moment Wyck hears about this, he'll be coming this way," Callista said. "So we've got to be out of here by then."

"But as soon as he finds out…" My voice fell to a whisper simply from the weakness that suddenly overtook me. All at once, I realized what this meant. Somewhere, perhaps lurking in the sky or just now arriving at the church to find that I wasn't a prisoner there, was a person who hunted me. Someone even more terrifying than Mr. Sharpe had been.

All at once, I realized the first place he would think to look for me next. *My house.*

"I—I've got to go now," I told the others, scrambling to my feet, slipping but catching my balance as I stood. The others looked up at me in surprise.

"What? Where?" Callista asked, bending her head up. "We're gonna leave in two minutes."

"No, I've to go now," I burst. "My mom and sister can't stay in that house. He'll come for them next!"

I spun around and tripped off the rock, not even pausing as I heard the others scratching up from the stone, making sounds in protest. I was already rising into the air. I didn't care what they were going to do, all I could think about was my mom and Alli sitting in the house waiting to be attacked. Would the Guardians go so far as retaliation? I didn't put it past them. I needed to get—

Hands grabbed me around my middle, tackling me midair and throwing me down onto the sand. I would have shouted if the hard beach hadn't pushed the air out of me.

"What the hell are you thinking?!" Callista was on top of my back, holding me down with the help of Thad, her voice hissing into my ear.

"Stop fighting!" she told me.

Without command, my claws and scales appeared again. I swung my arms wildly, the back of my hand catching Callista and throwing her off me like springs tossing her onto the beach. I pushed up from the ground and reached for the air but her hand caught my foot, slamming me onto the ground again. I hit my back hard, and Callista and Thad were suddenly on top of me again.

"Put the claws away!" Callista commanded me, her face pressed close to mine, red with rage. Her claws were out too, burying into the sand like bars in front of my face. I swung again to be free of her, instinctively slashing to punch Thad, though again forgetting my claws. With lightning-fast motions, he caught the blades with the back of his hand, the scales clashing against them like metal on metal. The rattling force jolted me back to my senses.

So I obeyed, and my claws slid across the sand as they went back inside, leaving long marks. Callista and Thad lifted from me slightly, breathing heavy with exertion.

"The hell you're going back home," Callista said between breaths. "Do you have any idea how much we've both sacrificed for you to even think about going *home*?!"

Thad had already gotten off of me, but she remained pressed on my other side.

"My family's still there!" I protested, wincing. She ground her teeth together.

"Well I'm sorry to hear that," she said. "But for now, if you try to run off, I'm bringing you right back down again."

She gave me a hard push when she got to her feet, rolling me over. I stood without hesitation, eye to eye with her.

"That's my family!" I said. "I can't just leave them there!"

"And if you go back, they'll follow you there, kill them anyway, and us too," she told me, but this time she didn't yell. It was more of a fact that she was merely broadcasting.

I let my breath out, looking from her to Thad for support. His eyes turned away from mine, and I knew that if I couldn't get him on my side, then there was no use in fighting. Inside, I knew Callista was right. If I went back home, who knew what would follow me there.

I spun my back on them with discontent, walking away toward the beach. Neither of them chased me this time.

I didn't speak to them, even when the beach became darker and the lights from the police cars and the receding fire became the only colors we could see nearby. I found a spot and sat there, staring at the water that came closer to my feet with every wave. My arms remained crossed, as if by keeping my hands out of view I wouldn't think of the silver that hid beneath my skin. I couldn't make the feeling of the ring disappear, though. It was impossible to escape the reminders of what I'd become.

When we heard a helicopter flying our way, Callista and Thad came to get me, and we flew into the sky without saying anything. This time, flying was no joy. Already it had devolved into a simple method of transportation, a way for us to leave the beach and head for the mountains, a way that drove me further from Arleta. They tried to hide it, but I could tell that Callista and Thad were taking turns flanking me to make sure I didn't run off.

When we landed, we were back on the cliff where Thad had taken me. The first thing Thad did was break the watch off his wrist and fling it over the edge; it didn't even make a sound as it fell.

"Don't be down," he told me, where Callista couldn't hear. "Tomorrow is your birthday, and we'll figure things out then. Nothing's worse than being dead, and you're not that, right?"

He'd meant it to console me but I was far past words. I walked away from him and stopped when I got to the end of the cliff. The sun cast a tall, inhuman shadow onto the rocks beside me, appearing almost as if a monster was creeping up behind me.

I looked out over the Valley. I could see far—maybe further if not for the sun reflecting on the fog. My mom was probably already out pestering the police to find me, and they were likely sighing and insisting to her that this was simply another one of my misadventures. Officers would take a report but toss it into a pile on someone's desk. *That's the kid who drove his car over the cliff,* they'd say to each other with knowing grins. My friends would think I'd just disappeared on a job. Nobody would even worry for days.

I heard Thad and Callista whispering to each other but I didn't care enough to hear what they were saying. I sat with my feet hanging over the edge of the cliff and tried to find Arleta in the horizon. The ever-darkening clouds made that impossible.

*   *   *

Another dreamless night, another morning for me to wake up in a place that wasn't home. This time it wasn't nightmares that broke me from sleep, or that awful rain I could still taste in the back of my throat. The sun was up, warm rays gently rousing me, light spread over the precipice.

Drowsy and exhausted as I was, I could smell trees and rocks and damp ground, reminding me of the few times I'd gone camping with my family in parks near Arleta. I soaked in the silence, all the echoes of the cars and people hardly reaching this high. I didn't want to get up. I felt sore, like the morning after a lot of swimming.

But at least I wasn't running from assassins for five whole minutes.

When I tried to lift my arm, I realized that I was in a black sleeping bag, zipped up to my shoulders. I pulled at it and managed to get my arms free. I didn't remember getting into a sleeping bag... maybe I'd been too tired to notice much after the sun had set. I rolled over.

There were two other new sleeping bags arranged on the flat rock, and plastic bags in the corner of our camp. Someone must have left and bought them after I'd fallen asleep. With what money, I wondered? Again, I couldn't complain. I'd probably be in a lot more miserable position if I'd slept only on rocks all night.

One of the sleeping bags was empty but Callista was in the one closest to me. She was lying on her back, staring awake at the sky above us. It was hard to tell if she was ignoring me or if she hadn't realized I was awake too. I followed her gaze up and saw that the rainclouds from the day before had now been replaced with puffy white shapes drifting across the blue.

"I've decided I don't have to hate you," she said without warning. I cleared my throat.

"Is that...an improvement?" I asked.

"Yes," she said bluntly. "Until ten minutes ago, I hated you. Now I don't."

She sighed and rolled over onto her stomach, flinging her hair back behind her neck. I tried to keep from studying her, but every time I took my eyes away I only found them glancing back at her again.

"Did I do something ten minutes ago that changed things?" I pressed, hoping to keep this conversation going but also fearful that my insistence might convince her I was worthy of being hated again. She still didn't meet my gaze.

"It's more of what you *didn't* do," she replied. "You didn't run off last night. I was certain you were going to disappear and run screaming to the police, and sit there waiting for a Guardian to show up to shoot you in the head."

"You think I'm that stupid?" I was almost insulted. Few people had ever spoken to me that way.

She shrugged. "You haven't done much to convince me otherwise."

This was not going nicely at all. Had I lost all of my powers of persuasion that had helped me with my clients? Or maybe this girl was simply invincible to my attempts at lightening the air.

"I've stayed alive this long," I tried.

"I know, it's shocking," she said. "You're arrogant. Selfish. Overconfident. You have no respect for how much danger you put other people in. You think of yourself more than anyone."

"Because I'm in *shock*," I defended. "I've just had the most terrifying week of my life. I grew *claws* and…and a ring from nowhere. I think I'm allowed to worry about myself."

"There you go again," she countered without a second of hesitation. "You don't think Thad and I haven't been through the same thing? Rings, claws…all of it? But on top of that, *we've* been stuck in a cell. *We've* had needles shoved into our arms, we've been beaten and yelled at. We've been waiting to just turn into dust any second when you got yourself killed."

Her voice had started to rise with anger, but she managed to force composure at the end. I was left in shambles again. Why was I letting this girl have the power to tear me to shreds?

"And this is you *not* hating me?" I said. "I'd be terrified to see you when you love someone."

She rolled over on to her side, facing me but closing her eyes as if she was going back to sleep. *Damn it, Michael.* I needed to learn when to keep my mouth shut. But I wasn't used to someone else being right.

Quiet fell again, leaving us to the sounds of birds and the wind in the untamed grass. Part of me wanted to just give up on Callista. I didn't deserve this treatment from her—I'd just been nearly murdered twice in the past week. It wasn't my fault that she'd become a part of it.

There you go again… again, her voice echoed in my head. My thoughts had immediately turned back to myself, and my problems, and how much my life had been in danger. I'd completely forgotten the very newspaper article that I'd first seen Callista in: the one about the deaths of her family.

Was I completely blind? Her family had been killed so the Guardians could catch her. And she'd been caught so the Guardians could find me. I was the reason that she was now alone.

Of course she had every reason to hate me. Here I'd been running free, while the only thing she had left—her own life—was hanging around me like a fragile glass necklace, just waiting for me to stumble and crush it. If I were her, I'd have hated me too.

And yet she lay with such a mask of calm control. I could never have held it together as well as she did.

"I—I never said thank you," I broke the silence. "I don't know any other girls who'd take down a plane to save me."

Finally, *something* worked, because I saw one end of her mouth fighting against a smirk that threatened to reveal itself.

"I don't do it because I care," she told me. "I do it because I have to."

A tiny victory for me, at least? As if reading my mind, she narrowed her eyes.

"Look," she told me, "if I didn't need to keep you safe, I wouldn't be here. I'd be out there chasing each and every one of these Guardians myself and blowing their brains out."

I swallowed. The harsh words were like poison.

"But I'm stuck," she said. "The Guardians seemed certain I'd die if you did, and after everything I've seen, I'm leaning to believe them."

"Have you even stopped to ask why?" I said.

"Does it really matter?" she muttered in reply. "We're here now. We better start getting to know each other because I think we'll be stuck this way for a while."

I wanted badly to read her eyes. I still hadn't had a chance to. With her back to me now, she'd erected the wall between us even higher. All I got was the emptiness and hopelessness in her voice, and a future devoid of anything other than survival. Her only reason to live was to stay alive.

I almost asked more, wanting to know why we were so supernaturally connected. But I was done trying to break through her shell. So I rolled over too, and we lay on the rocks with our backs to each other, letting the whistling wind fill the void instead.

*   *   *

Not much time passed until Thad returned, carrying two plastic grocery bags in his arms. He regarded me and Callista in our opposing positions with some worry but didn't ask, because he was a smart person and knew when to keep his mouth shut, unlike another male on that cliff. I sat up as he dropped one of the bags, filled with bottles of water. He held the other out toward me.

"Happy birthday," he proclaimed, sweeping the plastic away to reveal a boxed-up birthday cake hiding inside. It was one of the cheap, undecorated cakes that grocery stores sell in their bakery. At the sight of it, I felt a thrill. I was seventeen now. I'd forgotten but Thad hadn't.

I nodded my thanks at Thad. He looked quite happy that he'd been able to brighten things up, and he waved an arm for Callista to come with us.

"Forks?" Callista asked. Thad stopped.

"Plates?" she tried. His face fell slightly.

"I—I just thought of the cake…" he said defensively.

"We can use our hands," I said, sitting down and putting the cake in front of me. Thad and Callista sat down and we made a small circle with the cake at the center, and dug pieces of it out with our fingers. Icing got stuck all over our palms but in the end none of us really cared. The cake tasted glorious, and served as a much needed distraction.

When I was done, I licked my fingers clean and stood to roll my sleeping bag up. The others went on gobbling bits of cake, and I figured it was because they hadn't had much real food in a while.

Absently, I leaned forward to pull the edge of my sleeping bag up. To my surprise, I found that under my bag—down where my feet had been—was a piece of paper. It'd been there the entire time without me noticing.

"What's this?" I asked them, gesturing. I bent down to grab it.

Suddenly, before my fingers could touch the paper, I was lifted up from the ground from behind, two arms looped around my shoulders. I gasped as I was whisked through the air.

"Don't touch it!" I heard Thad say from behind me. In a second, he and Callista and I were against the stone wall.

"Where did that come from?" Callista demanded—claws out. The cake had been overturned in their outburst, splattered onto the rocks. I fought against Thad and he finally dropped me to my feet.

"What was that?" I shouted. "What's wrong with both of you?"

"Did you put it there?" Thad asked Callista, ignoring me. She shook her head.

"I didn't even see it until now." She looked at me. "Did you bring it? Was it in your pocket or something?"

"No!" I told them. I didn't know why they were reacting this way. Callista saw my confusion and swiftly grabbed me by the shoulder, spinning me back to look at the envelope.

"See?" she said, pointing.

Now I knew why they'd gotten such a fright. On the front of the envelope, written in large letters, were three words: *TO: MICHAEL ASHER.*

12

ANONYMITY

The lonely white envelope sat amidst a sea of gray stone, its edge lifting slightly in the wind though never overturning. The paper was crisp and new, and its center bulged out from something held inside.

"This isn't good," Callista said, looking up at the sky and then around the edges of the walls that hid us. "Someone had to have come here last night and left it. That means they know where we are."

"Just to drop off a letter?" Thad said. "Does that make sense?"

"What have they done that's ever made sense?" Callista countered, waving her hand toward the envelope. "Thad, you've seen some of the crazy stuff they have."

"He's right, though," I said. The others looked at me. I swallowed quickly.

"I mean, we aren't dead," I told them. "We could be getting all worked up for nothing. And we won't know unless we open it."

The morning air and some food in my stomach had revived me a little. So without allowing for any more arguing, I stepped across the rocks and grabbed the envelope.

"See, no explosions," I said, watching as both of them relaxed, if only slightly. I turned the envelope over a couple times in my hands, studying the edges and finding that the paper was dry, some dirt stuck in the edges but sealed tightly in the flaps. Whatever was inside wasn't stiff, so I figured it was safe enough. I glanced up at the others, staring across enraptured. All attention was on me now.

To make it more dramatic, I flicked my finger, and a single silver claw appeared. I liked the surprise on their faces: it made me feel like I was in control again. I drew my blade across the top of the envelope.

Callista appeared by my side as I pulled the halves apart. Inside was a single, folded piece of paper, thick like the expensive letter stock my mom sometimes used when trying to impress her clients. I could feel the anticipation as Callista and Thad pressed in closer. I unfolded the top third of the letter with fingers holding it gingerly by the edges, trying to put on a strong face so they wouldn't know I was just as nervous as they were.

When you open a letter, usually you start reading at the top. But in my case, when I bent both of the folds down, the first thing I saw was at the bottom of the page simply because a word on it leapt out at me.

"Anon!" I couldn't help myself as the name slipped out. The others looked up at me.

"You know who this is from?" Callista asked. I wasn't sure whether I should shake my head or nod.

"I don't *know* him," I said. "But I know who he is. He's…someone on the inside."

Nothing I could have said would have alleviated the questions I saw on their faces. My eagerness was too great to finish an explanation, so I looked back to the letter and read:

To Mr. Asher,

You have finally survived. Your lack of decease shows promise.

At the moment, you are safer than you will ever be for most of your existence. The group sent to end you is under the belief that you perished while attempting to save your Chosen in their plane crash. I am partially responsible for this deception. With your death, your family is now temporarily out of harm's way. I believe your pursuers will not realize otherwise for a few days, after which you will be in danger again.

Already, I am sure you are feeling lost. You do not know your place in the Grand Design. But I wish to assure you that you do have a place, your place serves a purpose, and all will soon be revealed, if you choose.

Your two companions have a place in this Design as well. The duty of your Chosens is to protect you, their Guardian. This is their obligation. Their failure means their demise.

At the bottom of this page is the address of a house. The owner is of no relevance. The window beside the chimney is open for you already. At this house, you will find the answer to who you are, why you are here, how you got where you are, and what you are to do. I cannot promise that these answers will make you happy.

The house will remain untouched for three days, after which time it will find itself burned to ashes in an unfortunate electrical malfunction. Any evidence of your presence will disappear with it.

If you desire to know the truth, you will follow my instructions. If you desire to disappear and pretend that you are not who you are, then you will never hear from me again.

Choose wisely. Don't trust anyone.

ANON

While the address at the bottom was circled in pen, there was no written signature. By the time I had reached the ending, the paper was shaking between my hands.

No one said anything at first. An unfathomable silence fell upon us.

My family is safe. It brought a racing feeling of relief, even if just a little. Maybe if the Guardians thought I was gone, then they'd simply let my death vanish into the cases of unsolved mysteries. But how long would it last?

"So what's that about?" Thad finally said. I met his eyes but looked away quickly, back to the paper, reading it a second time. *The mysterious Anon strikes again.* I remembered how secretive Father Lonnie had been even with this man's reference, frightened at the mere thought of saying it aloud. How had Anon gotten the letter to me? Had he crept up sometime in the night and slipped it under me without being seen? Sent an associate? I doubted he'd risk telling someone else where we were. But I also doubted he'd risk his own safety. If it'd been anyone else, I'd have felt stupid and defeated. But all the secrecy that surrounded Anon had built him up as someone who could remain concealed no matter how much effort we'd put into hiding ourselves.

"I really don't know," I replied exhaustedly. That was the best I could do. I waved the paper. "It's probably stupid but I feel like I believe him."

"I don't," Callista said, breaking her silence abruptly. I hadn't expected her to agree with me, but I was open to listening.

"If he's on our side, and he's been watching all this, why didn't he show up to help when the plane was going down, and you were nearly being killed?" she said. "What is he talking about, this *obligation*?"

"I think he means the part where we *die* if Michael does," Thad said under his breath.

Callista slid a step away from both of us, hands out defensively.

"Listen, I don't even know you," she said. Then, as if everything began to sink in to her at once, she blinked quickly and a frightened look overcame her. "I blew up a plane for you, and I just met you." Her voice collapsed mid-sentence. "I blew up *a plane*. I'm a *normal* person. I don't *do* things like this. I'm supposed to be at school right now. I'm supposed to be home. I don't know how I got here!"

If she'd had been anyone but Callista, she might have broken into tears then. But she only clenched her fists and composed herself.

"I think I've already done my fair share," she said. "I'm not a part of whatever this Anon person is talking about. I just want to disappear and try to go back to normal."

"And what do you think normal means now?" Thad broke in. I picked up on some already-begun conversation they had been having; something they'd already argued about before I'd even arrived. Callista's fists tightened even more.

"What do we have to go back to?" Thad continued. "Normal? They've already taken normal from us. You know that."

"I could go home," she whispered through her teeth.

"To what?" Thad argued. "They'll find you there and kill you."

"But I don't want to be *here*!" she shouted.

"*None of us* want to be here!" I burst, the fury that I'd been withholding finally popping like a balloon.

It shut her up instantly, her mouth snapping closed as she stared at me with pain on her face. It shocked her so much that it forced a Glimpse: *terror, sadness, ferociously bitter fury mixed with vengeance.* It was like a cocktail of mental agony, so strong it felt like a nail punched into my chest, and I immediately regretted my words.

But I was right. We'd all been thrust into this against our will. That fact was only strengthened further when I looked around our tiny circle at the faces that stood across from me. Callista, the girl who I'd once thought was dead. Thad, the boy who I knew so little of, I had never even heard his last name. I doubted the three of us would have ever met had it not been for this chain of horrible events. It was like fate had unceremoniously shoved us together, but hadn't been polite enough to provide an introduction.

"I know you wish you were back home," I pressed on, my voice calmer now. "I do too. But we're here now. And there's a whole lot of people out there who seem to not want us around, and sooner or later they're going to realize we're still alive."

The sides of Callista's jaw bulged, her teeth ground together as tightly as she could force them. Her gaze wasn't pointed at me though, looking downward, fighting to remain in control over herself. She knew I was right; she just didn't want to admit it—not because it'd mean I won, but because it'd be admitting that going home wasn't an option anymore. I found no victory in being right this time.

"And I don't trust him either," I said, lifting the letter. "But he's right, we don't have any other choice. You said it yourself yesterday: if we go home, they'll follow us. And I'd rather spend the few days we have of not being chased down and shot at actually finding out *why*."

I shifted my gaze to Thad. Out of both of them, I knew that he'd be the most likely one to support me. Already—and as much as it was against our wishes—we'd become a group, and when Thad nodded, it was a majority vote.

*   *   *

We rolled our sleeping bags but in the end figured that it wasn't worth carrying them along. So we bunched them up into the corner of the cliff along with the bags of now-unneeded water bottles, hopeful that a wandering homeless person might find it and feel lucky. At least something positive might come out of our situation.

Taking flight was far easier this time than the others had been. The strange familiarity helped to calm my soul of its troubles. Part of me feared that I would soon take it for granted, that it was already weaving itself in as part of my being. If I just continued to believe that all of this would be over soon, then I'd be alright. It'll all go back to normal, I tried to convince myself. But what if this was my new normal? The thought terrified me.

I had a good sense of where Anon's written address was leading us: somewhere in Beverly Hills, no less, otherwise known to me as "that place where all the rich people live". I'd been there a number of times, spying on targets while trying to disguise my long-range camera so I wouldn't get thrown out. Sometimes I'd even gone down there on my own to get pictures for my walls. It was almost sad how tourists would stand outside and take picture by the neighborhood's entrance sign. It was as if that was the most they ever aspired to be: a person left standing outside a gate, the lesser-known subject in a picture of them and a wooden sign.

We cut over hills and communities until we crossed out of the San Fernando Valley. The buildings were stacked together in clusters like shining gift boxes sorted into piles. A steady stream of heat hit me from both the sun above and the roads below, but the wind in my face managed to cool the sweat away. I could see different collections of buildings far off, cars darting in and out and massive jets passing unhindered above us.

I led them now: it was strangest because it felt right. As we flew, the landscape below changed again, becoming more suburban with sprawling houses dotting the ground between heavy trees and clipped yards. When the attached garages got to be larger than my entire home, I knew I was nearing the right place. We descended slowly upon a street until finally the tops of the houses were so close I could have scraped them if I'd reached. There were expensive cars shining in the long driveways, vast rows of extinguished lights leading up to grand entrances. I doubted my life savings could have even bought their doorknobs.

I kept checking the street signs. I realized how close we were to the ground. I still didn't know the depth of my powers—how did the strange invisibility work when we flew, while I could still see the others near me? Was it true invisibility, even? Or just some type of chameleon-like effect? Either way, I was thankful because I could already see people walking and driving not far below us. We threw shadows, but the people were too distracted to notice.

Finally, I spotted the house's number, painted against the curb for emergency crews to find at night. I swooped down and landed on the top of the mansion, my palms instantly burning against the red Spanish-style roof. I winced and stood up straight as the others fell to a stop beside me.

From where we stood, I could see a vast horizon of rooftops and chimneys—not nearly the view that had been in the sky, but at least a more telling one. Trees and fences blocked a lot of the houses. It felt too quiet for midday so close to Los Angeles, little more than the snipping of garden scissors and water hoses running. I guess you can get serenity if you pay for it.

"Is this it?" Thad said, stumbling on one of the looser tiles.

"You sound so unimpressed," I replied. "You might be able to play basketball off this roof."

"If it wasn't so bumpy, I'd try." He grunted. Callista, whose severity had lightened up during the flight, ventured away from us. She found the brick chimney and waved for us to come over.

"If we're gonna do this, let's get inside," she said. "I haven't figured out how no one can see us when we fly. But it's not a good time to start testing it out now."

"That's exactly what I was thinking," I said. So I went to the edge and jumped over, hovering around in a circle as I descended. I saw the window right below the chimney and pushed myself toward it. There was a screen to keep bugs out so I extended a claw and sliced through it. The glass was unlocked, just as Anon had said it was. I grabbed both sides of the frame and pulled myself through.

The floor was further from the window than I thought. My face slammed into the carpet. A painful snort erupted from my nose.

Unfortunately, the other two had been right behind me so they'd seen the entire episode. I heard Thad and Callista trying to hold in laughter, even as they landed beside me. Neither of them volunteered to help me up this time.

"Come on, guys," I told them, rubbing my now-sore nose.

"Shut up, Thad," Callista commanded him, though she was having a harder time being quiet than he was. Inside, I was relieved that something had dispersed a little of the tension.

I brushed the dust from the roof off my hands as Callista shut the window and pulled the curtains closed behind us. Our surroundings went dark as the window's glow disappeared. We had entered a room of white and gray, a giant bed with folded sheets and an abundance of pillows against one wall, and opposite that a couch and flat-screen television nearly as tall as me. The floor was carpet, the softness of which my nose was still grateful for.

Everything from the intricately threaded rug to the glass cabinets filled with pottery exuded wealth and perfection. Even the way the blanket rested languidly on the couch looked like a photo from an advertisement.

"This feels weird," I observed.

"But we *were* invited, weren't we?" Thad said.

None of us really dared to venture from the window at first, looking for any signs that we might have come to the wrong place—or worse, fallen into a trap. But Anon had been right so far, and the silence that embraced us and flowed freely throughout the vacant house only strengthened the truth in his directions.

"Who do you think lives here?" I asked them.

"*Does* someone live here?" Thad said. He gestured at the bed.

"That doesn't look like it's been used in a while," he pointed out.

"Could be someone's second home," Callista suggested. Both Thad and I looked at her in disbelief.

"Come on," she insisted. "You're in Beverly Hills. People here have a few homes. Maybe they're only here in the winter."

"And Anon gets to send people here all the other seasons?" I pondered aloud. I felt a strange thrill at the idea of traipsing through this giant house—maybe finding pictures of its owner on the walls or family portraits scattered throughout. It could be a treasure trove for my Great Work.

The others followed me to the door and I could feel their anticipation as we crept out—everyone taking quiet steps even though we didn't have to, whispering even though we quickly realized there was nobody around to hear us. The hallway was just as magnificent as the bedroom, walls lined with rich paintings illuminated by sunshine that streamed through skylights. The carpet was so thick it was like a layer of white moss beneath my shoes.

There were several doors on each side of the hall, all open and inviting us in. As I passed, I glanced inside them: a blue bedroom, a green bedroom, a tiled bathroom with two sinks and sparkling-clean mirrors. Everything was neat and made up like a model home, the only sounds coming from the gentle hum of the air conditioner. Oh such lavish extravagance: a house with air actually circulating. Should've invited my mom.

"This place smells like a department store," Callista observed in a low voice. "It's like the scary furniture section."

"That place scares you too?" I said, grinning. "I thought I was the only one."

"It's a bunch of rooms with no walls," she insisted. "It just doesn't feel right. Ever since I was a kid I've hated that place."

"Imagine it at night," I said. She shivered.

"I don't know what you two are talking about," Thad said under his breath. "There's nothing scary about a bunch of empty furniture and bedrooms."

"But there's *no one* here," I said, waving my hand in front of us as we crept ahead. "That isn't a little creepy to you?"

"I think it'd be much creepier if we ran into somebody," Thad said. "And it'd be a bit hard to explain how we got in through the second story."

"'Sorry, a random letter we found on a cliff told us to break in,'" Callista said in dry retort.

We reached the end of the hall. It opened up to a balcony area with shelves of books against the walls, light streaming from a giant circular window that was high above the twin front doors, a chandelier hanging by a chain from the ceiling. A stairway with white railing curved down to the ground floor.

Everything was decorated beautifully. But no photographs, I noticed. Not a single portrait of a person, not even a painting of a face. All the artwork was of bland, nondescript things: flowers, animals, and shapes. No clues to the owner. No eyes for me to read.

We were all pressed together, having gone silent unintentionally. When we reached the top of the stairs, though, I finally spotted something that was out of place: three propped-up paper bags sitting by the front door. They were from Trader Joe's, the grocery store. Beside them was a thick white package.

"And there's the note," I told the others, already hurrying down the stairs. Hearing them so close behind sent a wave of *déjà vu*: hadn't I dreamed of running up stairs with them? I pushed the feeling away in time for me to reach the bottom and pick up the envelope.

Just like the first letter, this one also had my name printed on the front. But the envelope was heavier: something far bigger than a letter inside. Anon must have had a lot of confidence in the fact that I would follow his instructions, or at least a lot of hope. I glanced around at the other's faces, already full of so much expectation that I ripped the envelope apart.

Two things tumbled out. I managed to catch one but the other slipped out of my hand. I'd grabbed a rectangular and bulky object, wrapped in plain red gift paper. An old VHS tape had fallen to the floor, with a white note taped to its front. Callista swept it up.

"Be careful!" she told me. "You almost broke this thing."

I reached to snatch the letter from the tape, but she was already opening it herself. Thad and I leaned over her shoulders:

To Mr. Asher,

I am grateful you are reading this. My hope in your survival has increased. You are already proving many people wrong.

By now, you are likely wondering who I am. Unfortunately, I cannot remedy that. Though we will correspond, you will never see my face, and you will never meet me. To risk myself being discovered will obliterate any chance we have of succeeding, now or forever. This is a more important part of the Grand Design than who you are in this life.

You may also be wondering why you are here. I have promised to answer this. But to tell you all the things about who you are in this page would be of no avail. You would not believe me, and I would be unable to answer all your questions.

However, I have been keeping some things for you for many years. One of those things is this videotape. The other is in the safety deposit box listed at the bottom of this page. Now that you have proven yourself in this further step, you should have them.

I have also included a gift for your birthday. Do not unwrap it until you have watched the tape.

Have courage. Don't trust anyone.

ANON

13

DANIEL ROTHFELD

The moment we read the final words, the three of us spun around, immediately searching for a television. We didn't need direction: I shot off one way, Callista the other, Thad up the stairs, our feet pounding against carpet and tiles and hardwood floors from different parts of the house.

Finding a TV was not hard at all in that well-furnished place, but finding a TV *with a VCR* proved to be far more difficult. I dove in to an office with eerily empty bookshelves and a desk with fake flowers in pots, and checked the TV on the wall to find that it only played DVDs. I bumped into Callista as she came out of another room.

"There's a whole entertainment room but no stupid VCR," she told me. Who even used VHS tapes anymore? Finding a cart and buggy might have been easier.

In the end, Thad called out from upstairs, and Callista and I stepped on each other's feet in our haste to get to him. He'd gone into the green bedroom and found that the small television had both DVD and VHS players embedded in its front. Callista pushed the tape in without hesitation, flipping the TV on and finding the correct channel. Thad and I sat on the bed and she squeezed between us while holding the remote.

The tape started. We had fallen into such a hush of anticipation that I could pick Thad and Callista's anxious breathing apart from each other.

There was a little rolling static in the beginning of the recording, but that ended in seconds. Then it showed a blank screen, and finally a face.

It was a man filmed shoulders up, sitting in front of a nondescript white wall. He wore a black button-up shirt but no tie, his skin white but not pale enough for me to think that he was unhealthy, slight circles under his eyes from lack of sleep. He had a carefully shaven face, leaving a slight stubble that looked too intentional to be unplanned, hair swept to the side leaving his forehead exposed. His eyes were hazel staring straight into the camera, making certain it was filming before settling back a few inches in his leather chair.

He hesitated, just looking at us. It was almost like he was studying us, or rather debating what he was about to say. He cleared his throat.

"I am Daniel Rothfeld," he began. "When you see this tape, I will have already been murdered many years ago, because tonight I will die."

Hadn't Father Lonnie said something about a Daniel before? The man on the screen didn't show any feelings of fear or even sadness. His eyes didn't quiver as if he was reading a script behind the camera, though he appeared to have practiced his speech.

"There are some things you should understand about me," he said. "First, is that I didn't want it to happen this way. If I could rip the conscience out of my chest then I would, even if it meant ripping my own heart out with it. But I cannot, just as I cannot go on ignoring what I know needs to be done."

He took a deep breath. "Secondly, this world is not what you think it is. If you are watching this tape, then I'm sure you already know that much. You likely know of the Guardians, have seen an inkling of their hold on this planet. By the time you watch this, their grip will have worsened. I know, because I am partially to blame; I am a Guardian with them."

I heard Callista swallow hard beside me, her hand tightening against her knee.

"But despite what they may tell you, their plans are not a part of the Grand Design," the man continued. "All is not right—in fact, few things are. The powers of the Guardians were never meant to establish them as a superior race on this planet. They have done well to hide the truth of our history—of how we really came to be in power."

He stopped for a moment, as if considering delving more into the past, but deciding against it.

"I discovered a plan of theirs," he said. "I only had to look back—history repeats itself. The world is growing too quickly for the Guardians to keep their hold. Their power is slipping as human numbers grow. Then like a reaper, they will cleanse the world of all they deem unnecessary. It is genocide against humanity."

He shook his head. "When you have seen the great evils that Guardians have caused, when you have seen the manner in which they have enslaved the earth, you will understand why they can no longer remain in power. You will understand why I have come to this decision."

He finally glanced away from the camera. "I must end the Guardians. The darkness of their power must end to bring the world into a new dawn."

A flare of static caused the tape to shift, but it restored itself a moment later.

"To do this," he said, "means to betray who I am, to betray those who I've wrongfully trusted. But I have no choice. Because I am the only one who can stand against them, I am the only one who can complete this. This was the true Grand Design."

He spread his hands. "You should also understand this: Guardians do not die natural deaths, and are therefore impenetrable to natural law and order. We will never die of age. If we are killed, there is no corpse: we turn to dust. Our essence is then reincarnated into another body, hosting off a human to continue our line. In this way, we never end, and continue to return forever."

Mr. Sharpe, I realized. His body had disappeared! After all this time, suddenly I had an explanation for how he'd left no trace behind.

The tape went on:

"So even if I was to alert the world, as unlikely as they would be to believe me, and even if I was to form another army against the Guardians, it would be no use. Killing a Guardian would only make them return again. I found myself in a dilemma."

Then, leaning back, his face opened with a slight, triumphant smile.

"But I made a discovery," he said. "I do not have the time to tell you how. But I found a hope."

Here, he reached to his side and off the camera. When he pulled his hand back in front of us, he was holding a knife.

The opaque black of the dagger's handle looked like it was made out of charcoal, wrapped in complicated swirls around a yellow guard for the bearer's hand. The weapon was no longer than his forearm from hilt to tip, and the way he held it so lightly made it appear almost weightless. The long edge itself grabbed my attention at once because it didn't appear to be a knife. In fact, the entire length of the razor looked exactly like a giant feather.

"This is the Blade," he said, voice dropping to a strong tone filled with intensity. "This is what they fear."

He was holding the Blade a safe distance from himself, but still his other arm and shoulder were drawn back. He looked nervous just holding it.

"This dagger has a power opposite to theirs," he said. "One cut from this weapon strips a Guardian of their power: making them just as human as those they despise."

The three of us sat dumbfounded, and I closed my mouth when I discovered that it was hanging open. My eyes crept to the side, trying to gauge their response, trying to see if their breath had also increased its pace with every sentence the man on the screen had spoken.

Thad's eyes were still locked on the television. Callista's hands were now clenched. Daniel Rothfeld paused, letting the weight of his words sink in before going on.

"So this was my plan," he said. "I was to remove their powers, to make them human. To force them to be equals. But I have already failed in my mission. I've been found out. I know I will be killed tonight."

He said this flippantly, like it was merely a small roadblock. *But of course,* I realized. He was a Guardian. If they killed him, he knew he'd just come back in another life, right? That piece was so vitally important that I was shocked I hadn't figured it out on my own.

"I could try to run, but it is too late for me, and the risk is too high—they would catch up, and then have the Blade," he continued. "They are on to me, and I have been told by a confidant that they will end me tonight."

Finally, there was some inkling of emotion, just a prick of sadness in the man's blankly staring eyes.

"When a Guardian is killed, his two Chosens vanish immediately as well," the man continued. "But that is their duty. My Chosens will die with me. It is the only way. But we will see each other again."

Even such a small reaction to the thought of his Chosens dying felt considerable, because for it to seep out meant that he was feeling great inner pain. He managed to push it back inside.

"So I am hiding the dagger," he said. "They will never find it, and even if they do, only I can obtain it. And that is why I am making this tape."

He nodded at us as if he could see through the glass of the TV. "At this very moment, I walk among you. At this very moment, I am with you. I have left everything that I need to continue my mission as if it had never been stopped. You only need to find me…wherever I am. Find me, and aide me. I will do what is right."

There was a click from the tape. The screen went black.

That couldn't possibly be the end!

A burst of empty static shot through the speakers in answer, making all of us jump and Thad swear. Callista leapt to her feet to eject the tape and switched the awful noise off. The screen fizzled as it disappeared.

She spun to Thad and I, but stared at me. The room was hotter, my hands uneasy as I tried to digest what we'd just watched. I wished that I could have read a Glimpse through videotape, but alas I could not.

"W—what do we do now?" I asked. They were both looking at me. Their eyes made me uncomfortable, as if they thought I should have the answer to my own question.

"I don't even know what to say," Callista replied. She crossed her arms, still not seeming to believe what we'd heard. There was so much that had just been dumped on us at once.

"Well if they—we—reincarnate," Thad suggested, "do you think that Anon was Daniel Rothfeld?"

I didn't know whether to nod or shake my head. Why would Anon give us the tape if he already knew who he was? Was this his way of enlisting our support, to make us part of some army of his?

The most perplexing part was *why*: we'd gotten so many questions answered, but now had an equal amount new ones.

I was still holding the red gift-wrapped present from Anon, the final thing from his letter. Callista and Thad looked down at it the same time I did.

"That's too small for another tape," Callista observed as she slid closer, Thad inching across the bed to be next to me. I turned it over to find the edge, ripping the paper across and tossing it onto the comforter.

Underneath, I found a stack of three metal rectangles, with hinges on their sides that connected them together. I guess I'd been expecting a cassette or a tiny box with something important in it. I lifted it by the edge and found that the three pieces folded out into a line.

Now there were three rectangles next to each other attached by the hinges. They were small picture frames, silver and new. At first glance I thought it was odd, until I saw that there were already photos in them, some that I recognized.

The bottom picture was of me, smiling in a gray sweater and white t-shirt against a marbled blue background. It was my latest high school photo, the same that my mom kept sticking to the side of the refrigerator even though I'd tried to hide it dozens of times.

Stranger were the other two pictures. The center photo was of a boy who was also my age, but who had black hair combed back and deeply emerald eyes. He was far tanner than me too, relaxed and smiling without showing his teeth, a leisurely grin telling the world that he didn't have many monetary cares. The paper on which it was printed was old and bent at the corners, carefully placed behind the glass so it would stay together.

Then there was the third picture, at the top. It was a photograph of Daniel Rothfeld, looking much like he had in the film but not nearly as tired or afraid. It intrigued me how I hadn't picked up much strain from the man when he'd been on the tape, but now that I saw him in this picture and could compare the two, I realized just how different he was. It was almost like that picture had been taken before he'd gained his conscience.

We continued to study the faces, trying to unravel this code. I couldn't ignore a strange feeling emanating from the pictures. Something kept biting at me every time I looked from one to the other.

I tried reading their Glimpses. That was easy. Daniel Rothfeld—finally, in a photo—was molded out of confidence, so filled with power and prestige that it practically shone from him. I knew it came from his power as a Guardian.

Strangely enough, though, when I looked at the center picture I began to detect a similar feeling. It wasn't as strong, just power and command deep in his eyes. Something…similar between the two.

I finally looked at the bottom picture, and read my own Glimpse.

And then it clicked.

The three eyes—though all different colors, and all with different shades of feeling—were exactly the same. Even when I hopped from the center, then to Daniel Rothfeld, and finally to my own, I knew that what I'd just discovered had been lying in front of me all along, and I—the Eye Guy—had just been too blind to see it.

"I'm Daniel Rothfeld," I realized.

14

NIGHTLIGHTS

If there was a way to describe the feeling that overcame me, it was like my entire body was being pulled down the drain of a tub, water fighting to drown me as my bones were mashed together. No matter how much I struggled or how badly the force mangled me, I could not fight hard enough to escape.

I looked up from the pictures, letting them fall into my lap, staring at Callista and Thad with fright and inwardly hoping that one of them would protest.

They were looking at me with wide eyes, probably a mirror of my own face. But they didn't say anything. Why weren't they arguing, why weren't they at least trying to prove me wrong? Didn't Callista always try that—why wasn't she now?

Thad bent forward, resting his head on his knee and running his fingers into his hair, leaving them there, letting the realization flow through him.

"The dreams were real," I said, pieces still coming together like keys into locks. "We've lived before. Everything I saw…those were my lives. I've already failed twice."

I pointed to the pictures. "This is what Anon wanted me to know. That's why I saw both of you in my nightmares. We were running from the Guardians in the first, and you tried to save me in the second life, but it was too late. And now we're back."

"This is insane…" Callista breathed out, her voice dropping to a nearly indiscernible level. It was affecting her just as much as me. All along, we'd been far more important than we'd thought. Suddenly, we all knew why the Guardians wanted us dead so badly. *How could this have happened?*

Nothing we could have spoken would have been of any comfort. What we'd thought was larger than us was now even a hundred times bigger. But who was I supposed to hate? Myself, for dying and pushing it onto me? That was the worst part, because if what I'd found was true, I was the only person to blame for it.

"We need a plan," Callista said.

"I don't have one," I replied, unintentionally whimpering.

"*We need a damn plan!*" she exploded at me, screaming so loudly that it bounced off the walls and the furniture, ringing on the glass of the TV.

"*I don't have one!*" I barked, my head snapping up as the roar left my throat, so harsh that it was painful. She didn't back down.

"Do you understand that they are going to kill us?" she shouted straight into my face. Her hands were in fists so tense that her knuckles were white.

"Do you understand how big this is?!" she said. "We will *die.* They will *make sure.*"

"You think I don't know that?" I was just as loud as her, refusing to back down. "They're after *me.* I'm the target. I'm the one who has to die."

"And if you die then we do too," she said. "So if you let yourself die because you don't even have any of this thought out, then you're our murderer."

My hands slid down to my sides on the bed, ready to push myself up and face her, fury pumping through my veins. I moved but only made it to standing halfway before Thad lashed an arm out, slamming it across my chest, forcing me to sit.

"Sit the hell down!" he yelled at me. I fought, but the muscles on his arm were almost twice the size of mine.

"You too!" he ordered Callista, just as harshly. "Sit down, now!"

Callista didn't take orders. But I'd never seen Thad so furious, arm still latched across me like an iron brace, fire in his eyes as he glared at Callista—lions in a war of territory. She bit her lower lip, but in the end, she sat halfway on the edge of the dresser, turning her head away with hot, angry tears in the corners of her eyes.

"That's enough from *both* of you," Thad snapped. "We're not going to get anywhere if we're fighting with each other. That's not what we need right now."

"What we need is a plan—" Callista started. He lifted his other hand.

"Do you see I have another arm right here?" he growled threateningly. "I could pin you to a chair, and Michael here to another chair, until both of you *shut up.*"

She shut up.

"Don't you dare yell at Callista again," he told me. "We've given up a lot for you already, and we don't owe you a single thing anymore."

I pressed my lips together tightly, teeth together too. I *knew* they'd given up a lot for me, and just having them there with me at that moment was something I should have been extremely grateful for. There was just no room for feelings of appreciation amidst everything else in my head at that moment.

When I said nothing, Thad turned to Callista again.

"And you," he said. "We're all upset right now. But you need to keep in control. None of us want to be here, but we're here now. And we have to move ahead from that."

He took a large breath and let it out quickly in exasperation. "You two are gonna drive me crazy if you keep this up."

Finally, his arm slid away from me, and I sank back to let some of the tension ease.

"Am I allowed to ask what the next step is?" Callista said. Thad cleared his throat.

"Michael," he said. They were looking at me again.

"Um..." I started. "Well there's the bank cash box at the bottom of the letter."

I produced the paper. The number was typed a space below an address in downtown LA.

"We can go down there and take a look," I said. "That's the next obvious thing to do."

"Are we actually going to go after this Blade?" Callista said. Thad didn't move but I could sense that the same question was on his mind too. Because that was really what all of this had pointed to, wasn't it? I'd been led down a winding path to find the truth, and now that I knew, it was time for me to pick up where I'd left off, decades before.

I knew I was a Guardian. And with all I'd found out, I couldn't just stop there.

But I couldn't expect myself to go deeper, a part of me cried. I was just a teenager. My goal was to go home somehow, right?

"I don't know," I replied, just like I'd replied to so many other questions.

"And that's going to settle it for now," Thad said, standing up quickly, clicking his pocket watch open. "It's two-forty-three PM. We're not going to argue. We're going to stay here tonight, eat something, and tomorrow we will go to the bank, and take this one step at a time."

That sounded very anti-plan and I knew Callista wasn't happy about that. She managed to keep her dissatisfaction to herself by promptly leaving the room, but the heat of her anger emanated down the hall.

"You really get on her nerves," Thad told me, shaking his head. I sighed.

"Don't worry," he said. "She'll be alright."

"I didn't mean to yell at her," I said.

"Look, this is a lot," he told me. "We're gonna deal with it in different ways."

I turned to him. "How come you seem so calm about this?"

Out of all of us, he'd reacted the least, and actually seemed to have already adjusted to our new discoveries. I could sense his coolness under pressure, the calculated way in which he absorbed everything. I envied his ability to let go of inhibitions because I was so much the opposite.

With questions still in the air, we left the room and headed in search of something to eat. Why did things have to be tenser now, even when we weren't running from people trying to kill us? I felt stupid. I'd had to go and fight with Callista when that was the last thing I wanted us to be doing.

I thought about apologizing, but I never ran into Callista as Thad and I got to the stairs. When we reached the bottom, we saw the paper grocery bags at our feet.

"This was thoughtful," I said, reaching in to the first and pulling out a sack of almonds. All of the bags were full of food: green apples, more almonds, a handful of fresh avocados, cans of white tuna, boxes of cheap crackers shaped like animals, and jars with some type of dough and fruit. The bags were full of them, assorted throughout like someone had picked them up from the store in a hurry and dropped them there.

"Glad he gave us something to snack on," Thad said, taking one of the apples and biting into it. I was far hungrier than I had realized, so I grabbed one of the tuna cans and ventured off in search of a can opener.

Around the corner, the area opened up into a gigantic kitchen with the same gray tiled floors as the entryway. The counter was made of smooth blue granite and seemed to go on forever around half the parameter of the room, not a spot or smudge on it. In the center of the floor was an island, covered by another slab of granite at least twice the size of my bed. The walls were full of cherry-colored cabinetry and drawers, except across the room where tall windows were covered by blinds. A small table sat beneath the windows.

The kitchen was stocked with plates and cups and utensils hiding in the cabinets. But the pantry was entirely empty and the fridge's shelves were so clean it appeared it'd never been used.

It was difficult to let my surroundings sink in. Any other time, I'd have leapt at the opportunity to stay in a house like this. Spud would want to hear all about this giant home, only to be bored by the things I'd actually used it for: hiding upstairs at night and watching out the windows with my camera, attempting to see the neighbors as they got home. Most times, wealth didn't impress me. Being star struck was a waste of time. I wasn't the person who stood outside the gates of the Beverly Hills taking pictures; I was the person who grew scales and flew over.

I grinned at the thought of Spud seeing me now. That was if I ever saw anyone I knew again. The possibility of never being able to go back sank in. It was nearly unfathomable. Never? Of course I'd be going back. Maybe if I waited a week, or even two weeks, all of this would blow over? Maybe I could fix all this, then sneak home and take my family far away, where we could get new identities and hide so deep that the Guardians would never find me again.

A week or two weeks? another part of me thought. *Are you serious, Michael?*

The Guardians had tracked down a billionaire hiding in Japan. If they could find him in a crowd of millions and orchestrate an earthquake just to get him, surely they could find me anywhere I went.

I sighed. I didn't want to think about this, so I dug the last bite of tuna out of the can and chewed it slowly.

*   *   *

As darkness settled over the mansion, we found ourselves growing restless. As large as the house was, it still felt like being trapped in a trench. I tried to step outside, just for a few minutes onto the back porch, but Thad wouldn't let me. We had to stay indoors for now. If we were going to follow Anon's instructions, we couldn't take any chances of the neighbors alerting the police about trespassers.

In the interest of not calling attention to ourselves, we knew that turning on lights would be a bad idea. Thad found flashlights in the kitchen though, unscrewing their caps so that the bulb was like a candle. We sat in a circle in the first bedroom we'd entered and had a light dinner of mashed avocados and more tuna fish together. I pulled out the bag of crackers.

"Animal crackers and tuna fish," Thad observed, grabbing some. "A fine and fitting meal for this beautiful mansion."

"I don't think I'm using the proper tuna fork right now," I added.

"I can just feel the walls trembling with disdain," Callista said, taking a handful herself and dropping them into one of the crystal cups I'd found in the cabinet. The room was still very cold because even though we'd searched, none of us could find the thermostat controls.

I was thankful that we were able to talk like that, because earlier I'd been wondering if Callista would ever speak to me again. Her anger quelled itself over time: I was slowly learning that about her. I chewed my food slowly as we passed the box of crackers around.

No one spoke of what we'd discovered earlier. Callista picked the lions out of the animal crackers and then started stealing Thad's lions too. We even laughed together quietly.

When we were full, we laid around continuing to snack. I leaned against the side of the bed while Callista lay on her stomach nearby. Thad kept trying to balance his plate on his knee by placing crackers on each side like weights. It kept falling over. So in the end, he dropped it to the floor, and reached into his pocket, clicking his watch open.

"Oh, hello there," he piped up. "It's 11:11 right now. Make a wish everyone."

I threw a cracker at him.

"Why are you so obsessed with that stupid watch?" I said, laughing.

The cracker hit him straight in the face: unflinching, his hand not moving to catch it as it fell to the floor. The room dropped into a hush.

What did I say this time? I thought, food still in my mouth, hesitant to chew. I looked to Thad, but he'd already caught himself. His face had gone stony.

"It's just a watch," he said in a hurry. *Not true.* He was covering something up.

"I'm sorry," I said. "I didn't mean—"

"Let's watch TV," Callista suggested, standing up abruptly and grabbing the remote from the stand. She switched it on before Thad or I could say anything else. The static burst swept throughout the room but I could feel that I'd touched a nerve.

"It's alright, man," Thad told me, cutting his hand in the air dismissively. I chewed slowly, watching Thad stuff the watch back into his pocket. He didn't appear angry... but there was hurt on his face. If he'd shown a Glimpse, I'd already missed it. His teeth were clenched slightly, though he pried them apart as he turned around to face the TV.

I just can't keep my mouth shut, I scolded myself. This was why I didn't have many friends in real life. I just couldn't deal with all of this, people and their problems. *Their feelings.*

So we watched TV. Callista had turned it to an old black-and-white sitcom, so hyper with its canned laughter and sound effects that it became the room's anesthesia.

"We should talk about before," Thad said suddenly.

"No," Callista replied without hesitation.

In this, none of us had turned to each other, staring ahead as the screen fizzled lights onto our faces. It was something we'd been avoiding.

But it *had* to be brought up. We were here together in some strange house not knowing what would happen the next day, the next week...the rest of our lives. It was the three of us against everyone else; a trio who, by fate or chance, had been shoved together against our will.

"I think we do," I said in agreement. Callista's head bowed forward slightly—there we went again, two against one. Thad cleared his throat.

"I don't know my parents," he began. "Not even since I was a kid. They're either dead or too high right now to realize I'm alive. I live—I *lived*—with my uncle in Washington. He won't go looking for me, so I'm not worried about going back."

He uncrossed his legs, tilting them in front of himself and draping his arms over his knees. "So if we get shot at again and I can't make it, and I die, not many people are going to really care all that much. Just so you know."

It was such a despondent thing to say. It was almost like Thad was outing himself as expendable, telling us to not worry about police being sent to search for him. He didn't say it in a self-deprecating way: just a fact.

No one volunteered to continue. I swallowed nervously.

"I live in the Valley," I said. "It's this town called Arleta. I have my mom and my sister...that's mostly it. If I can keep them safe long enough to figure this out and take them someplace else, I'll be happy."

And if not? I didn't want to think about it. There wasn't another option. I *would* go home, and I *would* get my life back in order. I could fix this. I could make all of this better and make it all go away. I'd never faced a problem I couldn't solve, so I could solve this, right?

There was only one person left to talk. At first she didn't, and so much silence went on after me that I assumed she wasn't going to speak at all.

"My family is dead," Callista's voice cracked.

It took great effort for her to get the words out. She wiped her eyes swiftly.

"That's all," she said. "They're gone. I watched them being killed. It was nighttime. I watched that Guardian with the white eyebrows—*Wyck*—he shot them all. He shot my mom first, then my dad, then both my brothers. They were just crying."

A quick breath tumbled out of her.

"They weren't doing anything but crying," she insisted. "And he just shot them in the back of their heads. And then they put the bag over me, and Wyck took me away, and when I woke up I was in the white room."

Callista curled into a sitting ball. *The white room.* The way she said it made me feel cold inside, bumps rolling across my skin at the desperation and terror that had infused her thoughts of that place. It hit me how long she'd been kept a prisoner, not even allowed a few moments to recover from the death of her family before she was thrust into whatever living nightmare I could see scrolling through her eyes.

"So even when this is over, I don't have anywhere to go," she finished.

She stood up suddenly. Neither Thad nor I acknowledged her as she left, staring at the floor, the weight in the room pushing against our chests. The door opened and closed behind her, and then it was only Thad and I. Again.

The TV babbled on.

*   *   *

When I regained power over myself, I stood, picked up my plate and the cans of food, and left Thad. I crossed the hall, toes sinking in to the gentle carpet. Callista had taken the blue bedroom, the door now closed, so I went into the green one. The door clicked solidly behind me.

I shone the flashlight into the dark corners, checking the closet just because I knew I'd feel safer if I made sure nothing was in there. The shelves and racks were empty, no clothes or even a single coat hanger.

The bed's mattress was so thick that it nearly went up to my hips, and the sheets were so tightly pressed that I had some difficulty getting them pulled back. I pushed most of the pillows off onto the floor and chose the flattest of them, which was still overstuffed. I flicked the flashlight off.

In the sudden darkness, I could have easily been disoriented into thinking I was in my room, until my eyes adjusted and my surroundings proved otherwise. As I lay facing the ceiling—which had no fan on it, and made me miss my room even more—I realized that I'd already been away from home for far longer than I'd ever disappeared before. Surely my mom was already at the police station, calling my friends, calling the school. She wouldn't find any information on my clients because I kept those locked away. But she'd worry. That was the worst part. There was nothing I could do about it either.

It felt like ages ago when I'd first found the website with Spud, first heard the word *Guardian* from Father Lonnie, first seen his body dangling from the church. I'd only uncovered a scratch of what the Guardians did, and already I'd seen earthquakes that killed hundreds, people stuck through steeples, cars and planes blown up. What else might they be responsible for?

Sleep drifted over me slowly, but as I was exhausted I couldn't resist its pull. I floated away into the black, and soon I was gone.

It seemed as if no time had even passed between the closing of my eyes and their opening again. I was still in the dark, thinking a second that I was home and then finding to my disappointment that I wasn't. Would I ever wake up again and not think that everything previously had been a bad dream? I sighed, rolling over.

There was a dim light shining under my door, unnaturally turquoise.

It didn't move like someone walking by with a flashlight. I didn't know if I should be worried—it hadn't been there when I'd gone to sleep. And now I wasn't going to fall back asleep because I'd already spent too much time concentrating on it. So reluctantly, but with some curiosity, I slid my feet to the floor and walked to the door. I peered around the corner of the doorframe.

Callista was sitting on the carpet at the end with her back against the wall. Her face was illuminated by a multitude of softly glowing nightlights, one in each plug going across the floor—six in all on both sides. She was absently flicking a cigarette lighter in her hand, letting the flame pop for a second before killing it and starting over. She didn't appear startled, turning her head up at me.

"It's past your bedtime," she said in a low voice. No malice though.

"You're the one who's sitting out in the hall," I replied. When she didn't seem suspicious, I stepped outside. She leaned her head into the corner. *Flick. Flick.* The tiny flame kept flashing and disappearing.

"Where's Thad?" I asked.

"Sleeping," she replied. *Flick.*

"You're not tired?"

Callista shrugged passively. "I don't sleep easily."

159

I glanced across the curious line of nightlights, their bulbs casting little glowing circles on the floor and tall ovals on the walls. I had no idea where she'd gotten them from, unless she'd somehow collected them from the bathrooms. I didn't feel right just leaving her there, so I walked across and slid to sit a few feet from her against the opposite wall.

"You can't sleep?" I questioned, rubbing my eyes. "It's got to be super late by now."

"I don't like nighttime that much," she said. "Insomnia."

"You can take something for that," I offered, trying to be as considerate as I could, to make up for earlier. "We can get you some sleep aid tomorrow." *Or Valerian Root*, as my mom would have corrected.

"That won't help," Callista replied. At first I thought she'd stop there, then she shrugged.

"Actually," she said, "I'm tired, but...well, it's hard to sleep in the dark now."

Immediately, her face told me that she regretted saying that, though it'd tumbled out in her exhaustion before she could catch it. I figured out the scene at once. From her position pressed in the corner of the room, to the lights that protected her in a soft circle, it hit me all at once that Callista was *afraid of the dark*.

That came as a shock. Callista was the most brutal of us all— she'd taken down a plane! But the anxiety on her face was real.

In the low lights, though, I watched her relax slightly, now that I didn't look to be leaving anytime soon. Her finger stopped and she set the lighter next to her. Thoughts of our fight were still swirling in the air.

"I'm sorry for earlier," I said. It was hard to say the words but I managed to wrestle them out.

She didn't reply. So we both sat in the empty quiet, listening to the sound of the air conditioner. I let my head rest behind me.

"Wyck came at night," Callista broke the silence. I opened my eyes. She was staring straight ahead.

"If I'm in the dark, I start to see their faces," she continued. "My mind makes shapes with the dark and they just slip out. Sometimes it's my family, sometimes it's him. That's why I don't like the dark."

I said nothing. Inside, I felt arrows going through my chest.

"He didn't have to kill them," Callista said. "But he did it anyway, to make a point to me. He wanted to break me down so I wouldn't fight them later."

Her gaze remained distant. When I dared to venture a look at her eyes, it was almost like I could see a movie of the horrible night she'd gone through playing behind her pupils.

Guilt crept upon me. *I still had my family.* How could I have dared to think that I'd given up anything when I still had something to go back to?

I wasn't sure if it was a good idea, but I couldn't just leave her sitting there like that so I turned around, switching to the other side of the hall to sit closer to her, a safe five inches between us. At first she looked at me as if wondering what I was doing, but when I settled down she relaxed again. She didn't push me away at least; that was good.

But again, more quiet. More wordless novels created between us by our breathing. The silence composed a sonata of loss.

I absently studied her resting hands, the skin uninterrupted by lines or cuts that should have marked where the scales would emerge. Just an eternity of skin that continued up her arm and to her neck and disappeared where her hair began.

She looked uncomfortably tense. Suddenly I had an urge to reach across the four or five inches between us, to touch her shoulders and try to ease the anxiety out of her with my thumbs. Seeing her bent over made me ache. And it just looked like she needed that.

But I wasn't brave enough, and I figured she'd recoil and ask why I was being ridiculous if I tried. Thad maybe could have, if he was there. They'd been stuck together for days before I'd even arrived, and in our situation that was almost like years. He felt like her brother, and I still felt like an outsider.

I let the inches remain, and crossed my hands so they wouldn't wander away against my will. I just wanted her to feel better.

"Do you want to know a secret?" I said abruptly. Callista gave a half grin, her head still resting and eyes closed. It was almost a whole grin, but she suppressed it; I didn't mind because her attempts were telling.

"Alright," she said, playing along.

161

"So, when all this started," I said, scooting down on the wall so that my head was level with hers, "I was with one of my friends, and we found a newspaper article about you...dying."

Of all things, to bring that article up. So I deflected quickly.

"It had your picture," I said. "And when I pulled it out, the first thing from my friend's mouth was something like, "That's a shame, she was hot.""

Callista couldn't hold in her hiss of laughter. It came out as a snort through her nose, and that ridiculous sound made me chuckle too.

"I mean," I went on, "he'd just found out you were dead, and he was sad because he thought you were hot. That was the worst thing in the world to him."

She couldn't wipe the grin off her face, because even when she pulled one corner down it went up when she pictured the scene again. I felt a thrill just watching her struggle. *Success...*

She shook her head at me in a scolding way, finally opening her eyes to glare at me. "You're ridiculous."

"You thought it was funny," I told her, and she didn't argue. The way she rolled her eyes away grabbed my attention. I'd never actually been that close to them since she'd come out of my dream, so I found myself almost enthralled by their blue infinity. She caught me staring.

"There was something else too," I said, trying to act nonchalant as I looked away.

"More about how hot I am?" she said, giving a slow and unimpressed blink.

"Do you not want to hear the story?" I asked with a faked sharpness. She snapped her mouth shut, lifting her eyebrows innocently.

"That's better," I said, pulling my knees up. "So, after I got the newspaper article, I actually sneaked it back home with me. Because I have a wall, see..."

How was I going to explain my Great Work? It was impossible to boil it down into a few words.

"Well, I take pictures," I tried. "See, I can read emotions through people's eyes."

She looked at me strangely. I guess I'd forgotten to explain that part. I stumbled on my words again.

"It's a long story," I said. "But keep up with me. I can read people's emotions and mental reactions through their eyes, especially in photographs: I call it the Glimpse. So I just take pictures of people all the time, and then I put their faces on my wall. And... and..."

You're going downhill, Michael. You're boring her. Pull up before you crash...

"Anyway," I said, "so I had your picture. And on my wall there are different places for different emotions I've found Glimpses of, like love and anger and sadness and stuff. But I couldn't figure out where you were supposed to go on my wall."

"Did I not look happy enough for happy?" she said. I shook my head.

"It didn't fit there, there was something stronger," I said. "I had to pick the strongest one out of a million, and I couldn't figure you out. But I think I just did."

I held up a finger. "You belonged on the Love wall, up on the ceiling. I got confused because you weren't exactly in love with a person; you were just in love with your *life*."

I heard a long and deep breath go in and out of her, difficult but not painful... just lamenting. *Remembering.* I'd stepped onto dangerous ground, bringing up her old life. It could have been the right thing to say but I found it tough to gauge her thoughts. Maybe I'd dug too deep.

"That's really sweet of you," she said. Then her head bent over and fell onto my shoulder.

I froze into ice. The top of her head was now pressed into the side of my neck, the dark strands of her hair against my ear and flattened around my cheek. She had leaned over the four-or-five-inch ravine, her warm shoulder against the side of my arm.

Had she done it on purpose? Was she just using me as a prop? What was she doing? Why did she just do that?

She was bent against me, her arms still around her knees. I'd never gotten that close to her before. I'd never smelled her before.

Could she tell that I had turned into a statue? She had to hear my heartbeat because I could feel it pumping through my neck so close to where her ear was.

What's wrong with you? What's going on? Michael? Are you functioning? My brain was resetting its internal computer, trying in vain to compensate. I wanted everything to stop because I was too confused to figure out what was happening, but I *didn't* want it to stop—*no, don't stop. Don't move.* I had to keep my shoulder as still as I possibly could so she wouldn't leave.

She jumped, as if realizing what she'd done. Her head jerked back up as she sat straight.

"I—I'm sorry," I said, even though I hadn't done anything. Then I saw what was probably what I wanted to see the least at that moment: tears, falling out of Callista's eyes. She wiped them away quickly but was unable to hide them in time.

"We can't do this, Michael," she said. Her voice was hoarse, eyes filled with guilt.

"I understand, you're just…tired," I said, trying to brush it off. I still didn't know what'd happened.

"No," she said, shaking her head, wiping her eyes with her sleeve in a vain attempt to dry them. She looked wrecked. I shouldn't have let that happen. I'd done something, and I didn't know what… maybe I shouldn't have even stepped out of my room at all.

Callista shook her head again as if she could flick out whatever painful thought was in it.

"I lied to you," she said.

"When?" I asked.

"Earlier," she replied, sniffing again, face full of even deeper remorse "I didn't…I didn't actually lie. But I didn't say something when I should have. A long time ago."

She cleared her throat. "I knew that we'd lived before and had other lives. I just didn't say anything."

All along? Had I missed so many clues that she'd put it together long before me? Confusion hit and a barrel of questions broke open in front of me.

"How?" I asked. She scratched the back of her head, ruffling her hair nervously before pulling it back behind her shoulders.

"I—I had different dreams than you," she admitted.

"Why didn't you tell me that before?" I felt lost. I couldn't think of any reason why she'd have withheld that. It wasn't like I'd have been angry with her. It just might have helped me to figure things out much faster.

She shook her head. "It's not what you think, Michael. It was about us. You and me."

I wasn't sure what that meant and her voice refused to give me any indication. She gathered her courage and pressed on.

"I think I had more dreams than you," she said. "Maybe Thad did as well; I haven't asked. I didn't just dream of finding you and then getting killed. I dreamed of other things."

She nodded. "You and I and Thad, in some other life. In my dreams, I called you Daniel but I didn't see him, I saw you, just like you are now."

She waved her hand at me. I remembered how my dreams had also shown her and Thad as they were, not who they'd been in the other lives. I guessed it'd been a part of our connection—something that'd linked us in this real life.

"We were outside, in a garden," she continued. "It was giant, like a courtyard, with all red flowers hanging from the trees and the ground just…littered with them. Like that *was* the ground, these bloody-looking red flowers all over the place. And I just stood there with Thad next to me, there was nobody else but us and you."

She lifted her right hand. "Thad was whispering something to me and showed me his silver ring. It only had one mark on it then. He said that every Guardian has two rings for picking their Chosens: two humans that a Guardian trusts more than anyone else, and wants to keep for eternity. It was almost like he was reciting something from a ceremony."

"Then you started talking," Callista went on. "You told me I could still leave if I wanted. If I wasn't absolutely sure of what I was doing, that I shouldn't go ahead, and you wouldn't hate me."

She shook her head. "But I wasn't going to hear any of that. I didn't have any control over myself, but I *knew* that I wanted it, back then. And when you finally got your hand up and put the ring on my finger, everything just went black, and I woke up."

Here she reached over her shoulder, massaging the back of her own neck just like I'd wished I could have done minutes before. I held my hands as she eased her own pain out.

"Then all the other dreams kept going. Can you imagine what that did to me?" she said. "This real-life ring started growing from my finger and I was still dreaming about you night after night. My parents already had me going to a psychiatrist for the nightmares. I think that's how the Guardians found me—all my wild stories in my medical records about claws and Chosens and someone named Daniel Rothfeld…it had to have sent up a flag to them somehow."

165

She was fighting back tears. "Then they found me, and…you know. But the dreams kept going until the scales appeared while I was lying in their cell. I kept seeing you at night, watching you die in your lives, watching Thad die…watching *me* die."

She sighed, the sound almost agonizing to me.

"I couldn't help it," she said. "I couldn't stop watching you get killed. Every dream just made me *remember*. Like those other lives are still buried somewhere in the back of my head: just old torn-out chapters to my life now. And I *begged* for the memories to stop: how many dreams do I need to endure? How many times do I have to die before I can live with you again?"

The words rang like a funeral bell, so permeated by lost hope that they were excruciating just to hear.

"I missed something and I didn't even know why," she said. "I missed you. It was like an echoing feeling that stuck around from the other life. And I fought it, and that worked for a while, but now…"

Her hand stopped rubbing the corner of her eyes to wave once with dissatisfaction at me, sitting so close to her, unaware that my presence had unearthed something she'd tried hard to bury.

"So you have to understand," she said, grabbing my hand between both of hers, squeezing them like she'd fall if she didn't hold on to me.

"I *don't* hate you," her voice broke, weakly forced. "I just *can't* get close to you. Everyone I've known in every life I've had is dead. And I know you're trying, but I can't risk it. You've already died too many times to me, and I can't go through that again. I can't get close to anyone, especially you."

Our eyes were locked with each other's, the corners of hers red and leaking tears that ran down her cheeks in zigzagging lines. She was begging me, pleading that I not let happen what had already sealed her fate. In some other life, when she'd been such a close person to me—however impossible that seemed— she'd given herself up to become my immortal Chosen so that we would never be separated. But in that forever, somehow it had become her downfall, and that was why she was there, thrust into a war that wasn't hers, crushing my hands, regretting a decision she hadn't even made as herself.

I swallowed hard. Her gaze didn't break, studying my face like it was the first time she'd ever really seen me. Her hands shook; or maybe they were my hands that moved?

"I want to promise it," she whispered. "It's for both of us. If we're going to be stuck here, we can't let it happen again. We can only work together; we can't be what we once were."

I'd never consciously thought of it. The idea of having the slightest attachment to Callista hadn't even presented itself to me, so unfathomable that I'd glossed over it. Or had I? From far away, I could sense the thoughts nipping at me, as I stared at Callista and her anxiously waiting eyes, ready for me to commit to the promise. This should have been easier. I didn't even know her—the promise she asked for was like me promising to never be a trillionaire. It wasn't like I was ever getting close to her anyway, so what did it hurt to promise what would never be?

"Alright, I promise," I finally conceded. It was much harder than I'd expected. Callista's chin trembled. But she understood me, in the fewest and strongest words I could muster. So she gave my hands one final squeeze, our silver rings touching each other as she did.

"Thank you," she said, letting out a breath. I couldn't tell for sure if it was relief or not. Then she let go of me and settled back into the corner, and closed her eyes.

Why did I feel a pain inside my chest? It made me sick. I wanted to sleep again. I could have gone to bed, but I chose to stay with her, four or five inches away again.

15

THE VAULT

No one was around when the scents of food cooking woke me up, my arms touched by noon sunlight that streamed through the tall windows. I stumbled down the stairs in the direction of the rattling pots and pans.

Thad was in front of the giant metal stovetop, warming slices of apples on one side and pancakes in the other. Beside him on the counter was the jar filled with the strange doughy mix.

"Like apricots?" he asked me in a rush. I nodded.

"Good," he said. He pointed to the jar of mix. "These are pancakes. He didn't forget that breakfast is the most important meal of the day."

He flipped one of the pancakes over onto a plate and slid it across the island counter to Callista. She was perched on one of the stools, holding a glossy guitar that she'd found somewhere, attempting to tune it. She glanced at me and gave a cynical half-smile.

"Obviously," she said with disgust, "whoever owns this house is a habitual instrument abuser. This thing is vastly out of tune."

"Maybe it's just for looks?" I suggested.

"Leave it to the uber wealthy to keep such a wonderful device just for *looks*," Callista murmured. I was relieved that she appeared to have forgotten—or at least was trying to ignore—our late-night meeting.

Callista strummed the guitar, smiling when she was satisfied. She started with chords again and Thad picked up on it, singing a hoarse rendition of "Every Rose Has Its Thorn" from Poison. I knew that band well because my mom still had an old record of theirs, and sometimes on weekends she'd break it out. I had been born with no vocal talent whatsoever, but the feeling of the three of us together—just like I did back home with Mom and Alli —was far too inviting to resist.

After we'd eaten our fill, Thad dumped the remainder onto our newly ordained trash plate.

"So in the words of our dear friend Callista," he said, "what's the plan, Michael?"

We all knew why this decision fell on me—I'd naturally been pushed forward as the leader ever since the truth had come out about whom I'd been. I drank my water down until the glass was empty and left me with no remaining excuse to keep from talking.

"We go to the bank," I said. "That's the next obvious step."

I still had the paper in my pocket, so I pulled it out and spread it onto the island countertop. We all slid closer to look, my finger underscoring the address.

"I was thinking about this last night," Thad said. "I know it's a long shot, but if we get you to the Blade," he tapped my shoulder, "and you actually have it, won't the Guardians be afraid enough to back off from us?"

"Maybe," I said, trying to be hopeful. "Then again, the last time I had it was the first time they killed me. So we might have some fighting to do after all."

We all knew that we'd be no match for what the Guardians could throw at us. I wasn't even sure how much more time Anon could buy for us. But it wasn't like there was another way.

"How are we gonna get there?" Callista asked.

"Same way we get everywhere," I replied.

"Think that's a good idea?" she said. "Isn't that downtown? Where will we land? It'd seem a bit suspicious in the middle of the day."

"You're right…" I admitted. That would certainly be a problem, as mundane as it seemed. I scratched the side of my face as I tried to think of a solution, surprised to feel stubble growing since I hadn't shaved for half a week.

While Callista and I were debating our options, Thad had been searching for a garbage can to dump our trash plate into. I heard a sound of surprise from Thad when he opened a door.

"I've found a way to get there!" he called to us, standing right outside the kitchen. Callista and I jumped to our feet, scurrying to him. Since we'd gotten to the house I'd thought that door led to a closet, so I hadn't opened it. But behind it was a garage.

To call it a garage would have made anyone I knew back home fall over in disbelief. There were no bins of junk, no ripped cardboard boxes on wooden shelves, no bicycles hanging by hooks from the ceiling. When Thad reached around the corner and flipped a switch, suddenly the polished concrete floor glimmered as the place became illuminated by intense ceiling lights. These same lights shone upon five polished cars sitting in a row.

My heart nearly stopped beating when I saw the fourth.

The magnificence of this mansion, every piece of expensive furniture it housed, I would have eagerly thrown away for the device before me now. I'd glanced over the black Bentley Coupe, the silver Maserati Gran Turismo, and even the white Audi R8—locking on the single piece of flaming red glory behind them.

A Shelby GT500. The most glorious car the world had ever been graced with; the car no road deserved to feel trample its gravel. My BMW would have melted in jealousy at the sight. Its wheels were the blackest of black, windows tinted, the sweeping red angles of the hood and side and door like a carefully crafted ship. The silver cobra on its front whispered seductively to my heart. If I'd had my camera, I could have photographed its two front lights, and likely would have been able to read nothing but eternal bliss behind their pupils.

Did it matter that I couldn't remember what its V8 engine could do, or what its lack of a white racing stripe meant, or that the other cars were far more expensive? Did it matter that I'd seen more than my fair share of nice vehicles when working with wealthy clients? I was still captivated by this piece of machinery.

Callista punched me in the shoulder, finally breaking in to my thoughts.

"I take it you're going to marry the red one?" she snapped. I heard Thad laughing at me from the corner.

"You're just better at hiding your admiration for this god-machine," I told him. I approached the car with caution, hands out until I'd touched its warm metal. Callista tilted her head at me in surrender as I ran my fingers over its hull.

"Well good," Thad called. "Maybe your admiration will make you a safer driver."

The shadow of something came flying across the room from Thad, and I yelped and grabbed it out of the air before it could dent the Shelby. I was about to hurl obscenities at him, before I realized that I was holding a ring of keys.

I looked from them to Thad in alarm but no words would come out, because I saw that he was standing next to a row of key hooks on the wall. He was already heading for the Audi with another key in his hand. I turned my head and saw that Callista had climbed into the passenger seat of my new car.

"Let's go!" she demanded.

I could have won marathons at the speed I got to the door. I tore it open and dove into the chair before I had fully realized I was even moving. The black leather formed into my back, a button on the side adjusting the seat to be just right, the slam of the door snapping like a battle tank's hatch. I turned the ignition and the engine sound sent a thrill to my heart.

The garage door opened behind me, letting sunlight stream in. It felt like the first time I'd seen the outside world in ages. With shaking knees I pushed on the gas to ease us out, and suddenly I was going down a driveway, passing trees and a yard, then out an open gate, then facing the runway of a road before me. I pressed the brake a bit too quickly, not accustomed to its taunt control.

Thad was at the end of the street already, waiting impatiently for us to follow. We sat in the center of a beautiful lane, trees overhanging the street blissfully.

Not for long. I switched gears and pressed the pedal, and we shot off.

Riding in the Shelby was like traveling by road submarine. The world outside was entirely blocked out by the tinted windows and the thick metal as we dashed across the Beverly Hills, following the car ahead. Had Thad punched the address into his GPS? I certainly didn't know where we were going, so I hoped he had. I just knew that I was driving a Shelby GT500. When a person is driving a

Shelby GT500, it doesn't really matter where they are headed, because anywhere they end up becomes a landmark.

"I think I'll name her Ophelia," I said over the hum of the engine.

"Who?" Callista whirled to me in alarm.

"This car," I said, rubbing its dash. "This wonderful car. This piece of dreams."

I'd never felt more thrilled to irritate a person before. Callista grabbed the radio dial and spun it up so high that it suffocated my voice. But I was too far on top of the world now for anything to dampen my spirits. So I flicked the volume up even more than she had put it, feeling the bass beat against the inside walls and the chairs and my foot as it pressed the pedal.

I glanced at Callista, whose lips were pressed tightly together, and when she looked at me she pushed them even tighter, though I could tell her disgust was mostly faked. She was biting her tongue to keep from making fun of me.

Soon I was forced to slow the car down as Thad took an exit in front of us, and we began to venture down the streets into the heart of Los Angeles. There never really was a "good time" for traffic in LA: the only times it really let up was between 2 and 4 AM, and then only if there wasn't late-night construction. It was midday so the lunch hour traffic was out, and I had to dodge my unfamiliar car around blocks and up busy streets as Thad weaved in and out of the lanes insubordinately. People would stare at my car when we stopped at a light but luckily none of them could see me inside. I was horrible at being covert. In fact, flying might have brought *less* attention. We hadn't thought this one out well.

Finally, I saw the massive bank building: a towering behemoth of crystal black windows that reflected the city, straight and tall without so much as a single curve to interrupt its sharpness. The only things that broke the black were two clear, revolving doors at the bottom, people going in and out in a constant stream. And at the top of the building was a red sign that said, in blocky letters: **VERSTONE BANK**.

Thad swept his car around the corner and onto a side street. I parked behind him, forcing myself to turn the key but hesitant to get out. I came around the front where Callista was waiting with a raised eyebrow.

"She'll still be here when we get back," Callista growled.

"Are you jealous of a car getting my attention?" I asked. She refused to acknowledge me.

Thad gestured between us at the building, which now rose so high in the air that I had to bend backwards just to see its top. I'd probably passed by this building hundreds of times while driving downtown—it was just one of those bank skyscrapers so common in the city that nobody'd look twice.

"I think Callista and I should stay out here," Thad suggested. "It might be suspicious for a bunch of teenagers to walk in and ask for a bank box. We don't know what's in it yet. And besides..."

He spread his hands over both our cars. "We don't have quarters to pay the parking meter."

"Well *that* decides it," Callista said, hopping onto the hood of my Shelby. "I can face ruthless murderers who control the world, but please not a parking cop."

I rubbed my hands together nervously, trying to think of any flaws in Thad's logic but finding none. So I turned and left them for the sidewalk, pushing my hands into my pockets to try to calm some of the nervous tension that had begun to creep up again.

I'd been through this before, those minutes preceding some event that would reveal terrible secrets or answer some of the million questions that faced me. I still couldn't calm myself though, as I turned the corner amidst lines of cars that rolled down the hectic streets, pedestrians babbling to one another, crossing signals whistling to let the blind know it was safe to go. I looked back to Callista and Thad but they were already out of sight, so I pressed on through the revolving doors of the bank.

The squeak of my shoes made me feel more conspicuous. The inside of the bank sprawled on with counters below windows of inch-thick Plexiglas plates, people standing in lines to make deposits or withdrawals or open accounts. They babbled incessantly as the ceiling speakers struggled to fight back with cheap saxophone music.

My back was hit by the revolving door.

"Excuse me!" a brawny woman barked, her two children in tow. I came to my senses and pulled my hand out of my pocket, taking the letter and looking at the access code that Anon had given me. There were two numbers, actually: one, a 16-character, and the other a 4-digit PIN code. I approached the back of the line and waited.

I was easily distracted so the line seemed to move quickly. All the people around me were simply going about their own business, few even glancing my way. I saw rows of pictures going around the upper wall, showing the long line of Verstone CEOs and board members. In my boredom, I picked out which ones had been stealing from the company, two that were having affairs and one who might have been a murderer. I hopped from one Glimpse to the next—it was like a game.

The teller coughed loudly at me and I realized it was my turn. I stepped up.

"I—I have a deposit box here," I said.

"We use electronic access codes here," she told me through the speaker. "Do you have yours?"

I nodded and punched the long password string into the box. She checked it with her computer then told me to go wait at a side door. I stood there for a few minutes until I heard it click, and she ushered me in.

"You'll need your PIN to open it," she informed me, all business. The hallway was tiled, fancy marble on the walls covered by more richly framed portraits. As we walked, we started to pass wooden booths with thick red cloths hanging from poles covering their entrances. There were numbers over the booths, and when we came to the one marked "43", the woman stopped.

"When you're done, press the call button and the guard will retrieve your box," she said. She held the red cloth open for me insistently, so I slipped under.

I heard her high heels clicking against the floor as she left. I was now in a boxy room, identical to the others I'd seen on my way up. Harsh lights glared from the ceiling and scrubbed the place clean of any sense of uniqueness. A simple leather stool sat in front of a counter. I heard the teller open a door far away, a few seconds of outside noise, then silence when it clicked shut.

In the center of the counter was a small safe deposit box, lonely and out of place in the grandeur of the room. It was black and metal, the lid sealed by a digital keypad on its top. I stepped closer, glancing over my shoulder to make sure the cloth had fallen into place. It didn't seem secure enough, not as my expectancy rose, hands gripping the box. It took great effort for me to lift it even an inch.

There was no reason for me to waste time, so I set the paper next to me on the counter and carefully typed in the PIN. The box took a few seconds to register and I thought for a moment I'd punched it in wrong, until there came a single beep marking my success. Something inside clicked. I lifted the lid.

Yet another white envelope with my name was resting on top, so I took it out first. I didn't have a chance to open it though, because there were more things beneath it that distracted me. I fished around in the box, pulling out two blocks of paper, stiff like tall notepads. It wasn't until I had them all in the light that I realized they were bound stacks of cash.

I nearly gasped. They were all hundred dollar notes bound together in their center by a strip of yellow paper, each stack marked as "$10000". There were two of them. I'd never seen so much money all at once, even at my hourly rate. This type of money would have changed our lives back home...free air-conditioning in abundance...a new car.

I cautiously reached into the box again with my right hand. I didn't find anything else but a bumpy base, until I realized that it didn't feel right and I had to peer inside again. At the bottom of the safe deposit was another box.

I unwillingly let go of the money to grab this new contraption, grunting at its weight and struggling to set it on the counter without making too much noise. Even the tiny click of its edge touching the countertop echoed in the booth, though luckily the heavy cloth wouldn't let the noise escape.

It was one of the most unusual devices I'd ever seen. It was no thicker than two inches but long and rectangular, like the case that my mom kept her old china silverware in. There was no place for a lock, though the lid was stuck tight, every part appearing to be made of something like brass.

The most unusual part, though, was the top of the lid. It was embellished in a strange metalworking, the design swirling up and down intricately with lines and curves that whirled into shapes at the corners. In the center of the box's lid was a raised piece, with two circles side-by-side, embedded in the metal and bulging out unusually.

I licked my lips. This was something different. I'd learned, however, that Anon tended to do things in an order, so I reached for the abandoned envelope and tore it, pulling the paper out.

175

To Mr. Asher,

This will be my final correspondence for some time. I must be brief.

This money is to aid you in survival. The bills are untraceable and will provide for your food and basic needs. Do not feel inclined to repay this to me: this is a portion of funds that you left in my care before your passing.

You also asked me to keep one other thing for you. It is the box. Only you can open it.

Do well. Don't trust anyone.
ANON

It was very brief in comparison to all his previous letters—almost a letdown when I got to the end. I'd wished for a few more answers...but then again this was Anon.

So I set the paper and the money aside and reached for the box. Shouldn't Anon have at least given me some instructions on how to get it open? I searched all around it but couldn't find a hole for a key. In fact there didn't even seem to be any edge where the lid would part: the entire thing all one piece of uninterrupted metal.

I ran my fingers around its sides, trying to find a button. Instead, as my fingertips crawled the top's design, I accidentally hit an edge of one of the corners. At first I was frightened that it'd broken off, then I saw that I'd actual hit a hidden lever, which had turned down like a switch.

Nothing happened. So with haste, I searched the other corners, finding that the matching pieces there also moved, shifting all three remaining levers until they faced the center.

I heard the mechanical clicking of tiny gears being forced into motion and felt a gentle vibration from inside the box's metal shell. Then, like twin doors, the protruding circular pieces started to split apart at their centers, opening like eyelids until they exposed what was beneath.

It was a pair of glass orbs filled with clear liquid, still unsteady from when I'd moved the box. Floating inside them was what appeared to be two human eyeballs.

There was one in each orb, both staring straight ahead with no socket or muscle around them: blank, expressionless gazes missing their frame of a face. It was almost grotesque, until I convinced myself they weren't actually human eyes…or were they? I couldn't tell for sure. If they weren't authentic, they were at least realistic.

I stretched over the countertop so I could see the eyes more clearly. Their irises were both green with wide-open pupils, almost like a cat's in the dark, staying straight even when I tilted the box forward at me so their gaze met mine. Was that all I was supposed to see? Maybe the box didn't open after all.

I found myself falling into my usual habit, and without even thinking I'd gone beyond the gaze of the eyes and spotted a Glimpse. Immediately, I withdrew with fright.

That was odd, these eyes shouldn't have shown anything at all. But it'd certainly been there, inviting me in.

So I did it again. I leaned the box forward, studying the gaze, trying to read what was behind it just because that was the only success I'd found so far. I saw a Glimpse that was certain. But there was *nothing* there. It was like the eyes were open and surprised and caught in their exposing second, yet didn't have any emotion or secret to tell.

Suddenly, the pupils narrowed.

I jumped, dropping the box at their unexpected movement. The pupils had squeezed inwards into thin slits like a lizard's eyes. The box slammed back onto the counter with a crash. In my surprise, it'd felt like the fake eyes had leapt straight from their metal sockets, entering my mind and then slithering back all in the same second.

It was violating, like hands crawling up and down my skin, squeezing and touching me and giving me shivers. It was like I'd had something pulled straight through my gaze, and I realized that the eyes I'd been trying to read had sucked in my Glimpse instead.

As if in confirmation of this, the box gave another click, an invisible seal glowing light orange around the parameter before cooling back into its regular gray. Some type of Guardian lock that worked through reading eyes? An alignment in the box that only allowed it to open at my Glimpse?

I shook the feeling away from me in shivers, hesitant hands reaching forward to remove the lid. It slipped off like the top of a gift box, revealing a tiny space lined with rich, black velvet inside. In the center was a single piece of thin paper.

I lifted the forlorn page out gingerly; it looked so fragile that I was afraid even a gentle blow from the ceiling A/C would make it tear. It wasn't folded, the writing revealed on the opposite side as I flipped it over and set it flat on the counter.

It was mostly blank. The only part with marking was in the center, black hand-written ink. At the top was a set of numbers and decimals with two letters: *coordinates*. Below these was a simple note, written in scratchy cursive so harshly that the pen had cut into the page at parts:

IT IS HIDDEN IN THE CHURCH.

Their simplicity only made the words all the more severe. What I held in my hands was a treasure map already solved, directions that I had left for myself in some other life. It sank in that the last person to touch this page had been me, decades before, when I'd first been certain that I was going to die.

Was it going to be that simple? I couldn't shake the feelings of uneasiness, some foreboding now that I had these instructions. Did I even understand what it would mean for me to find the Blade, how much of a chain reaction that would set off?

I placed the lid back and it sealed itself immediately. I turned to the cash. All this time I'd been trying to avoid looking at it. I peeled a stack of the bills from the block, stuffing them into my pockets: I could always come back if I needed more. Then I locked everything up and pushed the buzzer for the guard.

Even the heat of the day felt colder and more tinged with anticipation as I walked through the bank's doors again. I rolled the paper up nervously as I turned the corner, seeing Callista and Thad still sitting on the cars. They both slid down to their feet.

"Anything?" Callista asked. I didn't reply, nodding toward the Shelby. They understood, climbing in with Thad in the back seat and Callista beside me, no one speaking until the doors were sealed.

I handed Thad the paper and let him unroll it.

"The Blade is there?" he said after reading it.

"I'd think so," I replied. "I can't think of anything else that I'd have kept exact coordinates of."

While I was saying this, Callista reached forward to turn on the GPS system. Thad and I figured out what she was doing at the same time and fell into a hush. She clicked through options until she found an input for coordinates—it was likely a feature used only on unusual occasions, but it served us perfectly. The GPS mulled for a few seconds, then the screen changed to show a path.

"Ten minutes away," Callista said. "Twenty in traffic."

"That close?" Thad said with uncertainty. "Why would you hide it out in the open somewhere?"

"Maybe because nobody'd think to look in the open?" I replied, pulling the car keys out of my pocket and slipping them in to the ignition. Thad slid out and walked over to his car, leaving Callista and I again as the engine growled to a start.

It just didn't feel right to make light conversation anymore, as I made a U-turn and got back onto the main street. Our tension had risen to an almost unbearable level, leaving both our eyes locked ahead but mine still distracted enough to nearly miss turns and red lights. We were actually about to find what all of this had been leading to, what had started this entire fiasco decades before we were even born.

The GPS announced that we'd reached our destination far before I'd expected it to, and its voice caused me to whirl around in my seat.

"Do you see a church?" I asked, but Callista was already searching for it herself. There wasn't a church in sight: we were in the thickest part of downtown, surrounded by cars parked against the street and pedestrians wandering through the restaurants and shops.

I hit the brakes at an abrupt red light, still searching for anything that might resemble an old church. Nothing. No steeple, no bell tower, and no giant doors—everything here was modern.

I turned the corner with Thad's car still tagging close behind, going around the block again and stopping carefully where the GPS directed. I pulled onto the side of the road and parked.

"I still don't see a church," I said nervously. Callista grabbed the GPS again, confirming that it had been programmed correctly. She looked out her window.

"It should be there," she pointed.

I strained my eyes looking, but it was no use. No church was on that street.

16

RESTLESSNESS

Callista and I waited stoically in a corner booth of the restaurant that sat where the church should have been. Businesspeople held loud conversations in the tables near us. Scents of oregano and basil wafted through the air from the bustling and noisy kitchen, my spaghetti and Callista's small pizza still steaming but untouched, ordered mostly so we could get a table. My fingers drummed as I stared at Thad's empty seat.

Finally, Thad came walking through the restaurant doors, sliding to sit beside Callista.

"Good and bad news," he said, picking up his fork and stirring his food around.

"Bad news first," Callista said. He cleared his throat.

"We're in the right place," he explained with an unfortunate tone, twirling his fettuccini noodles onto his fork and taking a bite. "I looked up what I could online at the place next door. Saint Winslow's Church used to sit on this exact spot, before it was burned to the ground thirty-four or something years ago. They built Fabolli's on its foundation. You know what that means?"

Both Callista and I stared at him blankly. He swallowed a bite down first.

"Thirty-four is seventeen times two," he said. "Two lifetimes ago, the church that was here just happened to be burned down."

"The Guardians knew I'd hidden it here," I said, nodding my head forward into my hands. Thad lifted a finger.

"But there's the good news," he said. "They must not have found the Blade, or else they'd have used it on you by now, right? I mean, isn't that the whole point?"

He pointed his fork at me. "Think like them. They have to keep killing you every seventeen years. If they had the Blade, and that'd make you die once and for all, they'd have gotten rid of you with it last time."

"Good point," I admitted. Maybe the Guardians had given up on their search, thinking that I'd hidden it somewhere else.

"So where is it now?" Callista pressed. Thad swallowed his mouthful down.

"I read a little more," he continued. "After the church was burned down, all of the relics and anything important were retrieved and moved."

Callista's fork scraped against her plate.

"So the Blade is just hidden with all the old stuff," she said when it hit her.

Thad nodded deeply, smiling too much for him to be hiding bad news.

"They took it all north," he said with excitement. "Everything is being stored at the Cathedral Of Saint Helen in a little town called Lodi."

"And nobody ever thought otherwise," I said, a thrill of relief driving through my heart. For once, fate appeared to be working in our favor. I shoveled a bite of my food into my mouth as some type of victory stab.

"Let's get there fast," I told them through my full mouth. "We can make it tonight."

"Flying might not be the best idea," Callista broke in. "It's too much of a risk. All it takes is one Guardian or Chosen still hanging around this area to spot us, and it's all over."

It could have been the usual, paranoid Callista-speak that Thad and I were learning to ignore. However, we contemplated her words for a bit, and she was probably right. It wouldn't be smart to take any unneeded risks now, not when we were so close and were still undiscovered.

"Dangit." I grumbled loudly. "This is one of those rare occasions when Callista is right."

The way she glared at me, I knew if I'd been sitting in range I'd have gotten punched.

"So let's stay as much under the radar as we can," I went on. "We'll sleep tonight and drive it early tomorrow."

None of us were interested in finishing our meals, not now that we'd found a lead and were too eager to concentrate on something so mundane. But we gobbled down our food because we were all getting tired of little but albacore tuna and crackers back at the house. I paid with one of the $100 bills, Callista and Thad sending me curious glances when I produced the money. We climbed into our cars and drove back to the house with few words passing between us. Anytime one of us tried to start a conversation, it would end abruptly. Pretty soon we gave up on trying, and separated throughout the house.

*   *   *

We went to our rooms early, knowing that we'd need rest to face whatever was coming the next day. However, I turned in my bed repeatedly for hours as I tried to sort through my thoughts.

Restlessness held me like the grip of a noose, choking any sense of peace out of me that might have led me to sleep. The house had become unsettlingly quiet, the missing hum of my bedroom ceiling fan causing the room to feel even more vacant. It was just too big of a bed; the walls were too far away. There were none of my familiar photos on the walls either, those faces that most people might be frightened by in the middle of the night but I found strangely comforting. Maybe reading their eyes had made me feel like I wasn't so alone in my room. Or maybe they'd just reassured me that I was home.

I occupied myself by flexing my hands, claws slipping in and out like familiar allies—how quickly they'd become commonplace. The scale-like armor appeared over my hands with them. I scratched the outside of my left hand with my right claws but the metal shield refused to budge. I didn't feel the razors even when they touched the scales. Stupidly I tried the claw against my lower arm, wincing when they sliced through. I grabbed my hand tightly as a thin sliver of blood appeared, claws retracting immediately. *Bright idea, Michael...*

What had I turned into? Did my power to read eyes play any part—had it been a forewarning of what I would transform into? Mr. Sharpe hadn't had that ability. Why was I different?

I kept falling into that endless rut of questioning. Usually on nights like this, I would wander out and take pictures of people as they walked through the parks or up and down the sidewalks. I thought about how simple life had once been. There hadn't been deaths and chases and plane crashes. There'd been work and school and sneaking out. My mom yelling was the worst I'd ever gotten. I missed Arleta, but I missed my family even more.

What would it hurt? I began to wonder. Arleta was so close to where I was, so much that I ached just thinking about it. And besides, we were driving a long way in the morning. Who knew? Tonight might be my last night in Los Angeles for a while.

As soon as my mind was made up, I planned my escape. Callista and Thad couldn't know: never in a million years would they let me go. But I was confident that if I crossed the city under cover of night, I would be safe enough, and they wouldn't even notice.

I locked my bedroom door as a safeguard, checking to make sure there was no turquoise glow underneath—Callista wasn't in the hall. I parted the curtains and blinds as quietly as I could. With careful fingers, I unlocked the window, wrestled the screen inside, and stepped onto the sill.

A cool breeze hit my face as I stood unsteadily, letting the air awaken me and clear my senses. Was this really a good idea?

I refused to let indecision get the best of me. So I jumped.

I fell a few inches, many more than I had intended. The rush of air sent a similar rush through me. I yanked at whatever invisible muscle controlled my powers, catching the air just before I would have hit the yard. Bushes and trees muddled the shadow I cast on the ground.

Time was nothing to me as I wandered through the sky. The sight of the glittering city was familiar to me now, but still no less dazzling as I soared over Los Angeles and its cars and buildings, most of them powered down like battery-drained robots. I kept below the clouds so that I could watch my path, struggling at first but soon falling into autopilot.

Arleta did not shine nearly as brightly as Los Angeles did. I had to fly lower if I wanted to touch those old rooftops, the smell of lawn mower gasoline and road tar and car exhaust invading my nose. But that odor was such a holy sting. It reeked of plainness. I knew those broken streetlights in uneven lines, the old cars on the curbs and on concrete blocks in driveways, the grass not mowed, the badly-painted houses, the dirty pools, the wild dogs barking at the newly risen moon.

And the blue bug zappers! I could not physically hear them from as high as I was but my mind could still place their unmistakable buzz as I flew over, hearing voices from people sitting on a porch. Nothing here was fake. Insincerity died before it could crawl to Arleta.

I flew just over the tops of the cars, everything unchanged but appearing different from above. Branford Park was empty except for some stragglers smoking on a bench. I kept turning corners until I got to Hogan Lane and saw my house.

Gone were the thoughts of the glorious mansion I'd just left, the dream car that I had driven, and the bricks of cash. Nothing compared to the plain wooden sides, the regular door handle, and the red chimney with its broken bricks. I didn't care that we had cheap plastic blinds on our windows—I flew to my house like it was a treasure, landing on the roof with excitement.

The sound of the shingles cracking under my shoes brought joy to my ears. Every 4th of July, my family would pull out the long ladder and climb onto the roof to watch fireworks unopposed by the outlines of trees and neighboring houses. We would sit with our backs to the chimney and watch as the colors exploded into our faces. Alli would point into the sky trying to guess where the next ones would go off, so it would look like she was doing some sort of wicked magic in the air.

But July 4th was a long time away. I was by myself on the roof. I took a deep breath of the air and let it out slowly. If only I could put that Arleta air into bags and carry it with me, all of the danger I ever faced might be weakened.

I walked to the edge of the roof but there was no ladder. So I hopped off and let my powers lower me gently, wanting to peek in to my sister's window. But the moon reflected on the glass and her blinds were closed. I touched the window to see if I could catch just a small peek, and I was surprised to find that it moved. Alli had left it unlocked.

A thousand thoughts went through my head at once. Did she actually think that I had sneaked out and would need to get back in secretly? I knew her too well to think otherwise: of course Alli would hope for that. Even after all the days that I'd been gone, and after they'd surely become convinced that I was either kidnapped or dead, she would still leave her window unlocked, hoping for me to return. She watched out for me even when I had abandoned her.

With my free hand, I slowly lifted the windowpane as silently as I could, pushing the blinds apart with my foot and stepping in. I could feel the air conditioning as I crawled through: I felt guilty for that. My mom must have had more important things to think about than the electricity now.

By crossing through the window, I immediately stepped back into my old world, covered by blackness but my eyes still recognizing every detail. Alli had a cheap desk that was exactly like mine—a two for one deal at a garage sale. She had tiny shelves crammed with pink book covers from her aunts, zombie comics hidden in the back. Her bed was in the corner of the square room.

Alli was under the sheets but had her thick blanket pushed against the wall, lying on her side so that she was facing me—fast asleep. I hadn't realized how much I missed her until I actually saw her. A heavy lump formed in my throat that I just couldn't get down. She slept so peacefully. I knew she had been worried for me though, because her bed was littered with books and a flashlight, and she had likely been restless until a short time before I'd arrived.

I knelt beside her bed, careful not to jar the mattress. With claws and scales gone, I now looked just as human as I'd always been, and suddenly felt like it too. I lay my head as gently as I could across from hers, listening to her breath and watching her still and silent face.

How can she rest safely when there were things like me around? This torturous question plagued my mind. How could people like her and my mom just go on living, millions like them too, never having any idea that they were slaves at the whim of creatures I didn't venture to think were fully human. Was it better that way? Could it be a good thing for Alli to go on living blind and having no idea what was out there?

I remembered something Alli had told me before: *monsters are never as scary if they eat you before you see them.*

She took a deep breath and let it out in her sleep. I hoped that she was dreaming of something sweet – of riding in fancy cars and living in mansions and flying above the city. She deserved those dreams more than I did.

Part of me wanted to slap myself as I slipped into the sad and sentimental. But I argued straight back at whatever caused those voices, demanding to know why I wasn't allowed to miss my family, why I wasn't allowed to wish that I could just be normal again. There wasn't anything wrong with normal.

"*There isn't anything wrong with normal?*" it screamed. What's happened to you? Where's the Michael who loathed the very basis of the word *normal,* who hated the abyss of ordinary that sucked almost everyone around you in?

Normal? it spat. *All along, you've never even been human.*

I couldn't take its vicious onslaught so I left the room. Unlike the mansion, the walls of our balcony were plastered by framed family photographs and mementoes, no shortage of smiling faces and captured moments of excitement as I walked. Most of our family pictures had been taken by my mom until I'd gotten older and picked up my own camera. Then, I took most of them. It was easy to tell the difference: my photography was clean, all my mom's were crooked and some had heads cropped off.

Since I was already in the house, I didn't think it would hurt to stick around for a little while longer. I checked in through my mom's open door. She was in bed too. Her hand clutched the cordless phone, tired bags beneath her eyes, random papers in a clutter around her on the sheets. I guessed she was waiting on a phone call, hoping the police would find me.

Part of me wanted to leave a short note that might comfort her. But I knew that might only open a lifetime full of questions for her. And worse, she'd never understand why she couldn't go to the police.

I ventured back down the hall, prepared to leave but seeing my own bedroom door at the end. It stood welcoming me like an old friend I'd almost forgotten to visit while I was in town.

My door was closed and as it had a squeaky hinge, I felt only safe enough to open it a few inches and push myself through.

Everything was exactly as I'd left it. The piles of papers all over the desk, socks littered around the chair, camera lenses and tripods and lights...no one had moved a thing. Even my bed, which I had left unmade on that fateful Sunday morning, still had its sheets pulled back.

186

And my photographs—not a single one was missing from my Great Work. I sat on my bed and its springs creaked. A gentle whirr continued from the ceiling fan above my head. Even it said hello.

It was like I had traveled back in time. The world seemed to say that if I only crawled back in to my own bed and fell asleep, I'd wake up in the morning to the sound of my mom knocking on the door, yelling for me to hurry up and get to school. I'd go out to my car and it'd be parked there, just like always. I'd see Spud at school and we'd argue about why we never got dates. I'd drive home, edit some photos. I'd sneak out to see a client. My mom would act like she didn't know. I'd sleep again. Repeat forever.

As if to shatter this possibility though, my hand—which had been absently running across my desk—uncovered the newspaper article with Callista's face on it.

I couldn't look at it. I covered it again, and left.

I headed back for my sister's window, but when I reached her bed I stopped and knelt again, just wanting one more minute. I would have stayed all night if I didn't feel like a prodigal serpent attracting danger to this holy place.

I sighed. A lock of hair was in Alli's eyes so I reached to brush it away.

Suddenly, her hand slammed down, and before I could react, she'd grabbed hold of my wrist in an unbreakable grip. Her eyes flew open, and I was caught.

Alli swung up from the pillow and slapped me across the face with her other hand. The sound of the strike clicked off the walls like a tiny firecracker.

"You jerk!" she said through her teeth. "How could you do this, Michael!?"

Her voice was a type of screaming whisper, as low as she could manage in her fury. The darkness did little to cover her reddened face and eyes brimming with tears.

"I didn't—!" but she wouldn't let me get more than that out before she slapped me again.

"I've cried for you for days!" she said. "Mom and I thought you were dead."

I finally freed myself from her grip, grabbing both of her wrists before she could hit me again, holding them down as she fought me. She was a mess of tears and fury, struggling to breath and to keep quiet at the same time but failing miserably at both.

"Shh!" I commanded. "Don't wake Mom up!"

She wrenched herself free, feet getting tangled in the bed sheets as she tried to sit up. I got one more strike, this time from the other direction.

"Where have you been?" she demanded. "Have you been out on some job all this time? Because if you have then I'm going to tell Mom."

It was the strongest menace she could muster. Her hair was in chaos over her shoulders, strands of it sticking to the tears on her cheeks. I was still in shock—everything had happened so fast, and now that I'd heard her voice for what felt like the first time in forever, I didn't know how to react.

There was really no easy answer to her question, either. I sighed and sat deeper on the bed, pushing my legs up from the floor: she wanted to know I wasn't going to bolt.

"You didn't even call," she said accusingly. "You didn't send me one text."

"I didn't have my phone," I said weakly. That only made her angrier.

"What sort of a lame excuse is that?" she replied with shoulders lifted in disbelief. "They still have pay phones. I don't care if you're in trouble or you've killed somebody or if you can't talk to mom. But you call *me*."

She broke down after that. She didn't weep or sob, but her head fell forward weakly, like there was no more energy left to fuel her anger. She pulled her knees up close to her chest like they might protect her, laying her forehead on them and creating a wall between her and I.

"I'm sorry," was all I could muster. No words would equal the apology I wished I could have said. What confession could I offer that would make up for the pain that she was in? I had abandoned her. I'd disappeared and let them come to their own conclusions. Even if I was running away—even if I'd planned to kill myself—I'd have left a note. Somehow I'd plucked myself from one world and moved to another, and forgotten the fissure my absence would create.

Her back pressed against the wall, eyes staring at me over the tops of her arms. She wanted more of an explanation. There was no way I was going to give her one—I didn't care how much she begged, how much she cried or hit me, I was not dragging her in to the peril I'd found myself in.

So I said nothing. Eventually she picked up on my silence and tried to break me down with her gaze, but I still refused.

"How did you get in my window without a ladder?" she asked instead, voice muffled into her knee. She was trying to keep her eyebrows narrowed at me, though her relief at seeing me again was beginning to wear down her wrath.

"I climbed," I said, reaching to brush away the hair that was stuck to her face.

"You're not part spider now, are you?" she asked, only with half sarcasm. I sniffed.

"I think that's more ninja than anything," I replied. She let out a slow breath, looking away from me and then back again.

"Don't try to make me laugh," she said. "I'm still mad at you. Why'd you go?"

"I can't tell you," I said.

"Then what *should* we talk about?" she asked with an irritated shrug. "You just disappear and make us think you've been kidnapped. The police think you've just run off because of the car crash and won't do much to help us. Mom's been trying to hack into your computer for days now to find your clients."

"Any luck?" I asked.

"What do you think?" Alli said. "Mom can barely type."

I sniffed in amusement. It was true: she hated most computers.

"Then she wanted your cell phone to dig in that," Alli went on. "She told me if she could find it, she knew the password because she'd seen it over your shoulder: 3140."

What was up with my mom always being a step ahead of me? All at once the pages of data and contact lists and snapshots I'd collected on my phone rolled through my head. And worse, I hadn't cleared my web history from reading Father Lonnie's blog.

Alli stared at me strangely. "You look nervous."

"Did she get it open?" I insisted. "Don't look at me that way, what happened?"

Alli pressed her lips together, suddenly enjoying this control, or rather the fact that she was finally wreaking her vengeance. When my face didn't soften, she relented.

"No," Alli admitted. "She never found your phone, because when she told me that, I went in your room and hid it."

Alli reached across the blanket and past me to her tiny bedside table, sliding the drawer open. Inside and beneath some papers was a small rectangular object that I knew very well. I dove to take it but she snatched it out before I could.

"What was she gonna find if she did?" Alli said, putting the phone behind her back.

"Just give it to me!"

"Why can't you tell me?" Alli pressed.

"I just can't."

"You know I can keep secrets," she told me.

"This is bigger than a secret," I said. That wasn't the answer she wanted to hear, but it was all I had.

Silence fell over us both again, Alli full of questions and me holding answers that I wished I could tell her. *I shouldn't have even come back*. Now Alli was a partner in crime, now she'd have to keep a secret as my mom went on searching, begging for someone to help find me, wondering if I might be dead. Alli would have to watch all that. And I knew she'd go on keeping the secret anyway, no matter how much it tore her up inside.

"Alright," she gave up, voice breaking. She dumped the cell phone into my lap.

"Now I promise I won't tell," she said hoarsely. "But you can't disappear. I won't ask questions or try to find out what's going on, but you *can't disappear*."

I gripped the cell phone tightly, pulling Alli close to me in an embrace—we never did that, but it just felt right. I didn't want to let her go. But I knew that I couldn't stay. Every moment that I lingered only brought more danger into that house.

She let me pull away from her. I could see in her eyes that it was far too soon. She looked panicked when my feet touched the floor again.

We didn't bid each other farewell because to say the words would have held too much finality. When I got to the window, I turned the cell phone on and held it up, waving the colored light over her face like it was a tiny flashlight, then shining it on the floor as I mimicked sweeping my tracks away. She finally grinned back at me. I climbed out the window, and heard the blinds clatter back into place behind me.

I swung myself to the side and out of her window's view before I allowed my powers to lift me higher, whirling to the rooftop. I waited there, hands clutching the edge until I heard the sound of her window sliding shut. I knew she'd be watching there, hoping to see which direction my shadow would run. She wouldn't think to look to the sky.

When I was certain she'd finally given up and left the window, I sat up. Part of me hoped that by the next morning, it'd be like I'd never been there. She'd wake up and doubt herself, thinking that my return had all been a dream. Even if my mom or the police squeezed it out of her, they'd say it was delusions too. I figured I was safe enough.

"Having trouble sleeping?" came a sudden voice from behind me.

I spun around, hands out at once with claws and scales following in the same second, hovering at the ready.

Sitting in the shadow of the chimney was a man with white eyebrows, the same man I'd twice seen in my nightmares: *Wyck*.

17

WHITE

The claws on Wyck's hands were spread apart like the teeth of a shark, his gray eyes trained on me with fierce intent, lips parted in a smile. His breathing was so even that I knew he'd been waiting while I'd been inside the house, preparing for the moment I would emerge. His face hadn't aged a day from the man I knew in my nightmares.

I'd been in that position so many times in my dreams that I knew there was a pistol in his right hand. But when I looked and saw no weapon besides his claws, the shock broke me out of my deer-in-the-headlights petrification.

Seized by internal programming I didn't fully control, I launched into the air, claws extended fully for Wyck's throat.

Wyck was faster. In a flash, he cut through the air, the scaled back of his left hand catching my jaw like the strike of a steel hammer. The thud and crack were deafening, throwing me off my feet and into a black void.

My back slammed into the grass, muted colors spinning above me. My jaw felt like it had been dislocated below my ear. The ringing in my head was unbearable as I tried to lift myself, waving my arms to find which way was up.

"Of course you weren't *dead*. I knew better than to fall for that," Wyck's leering voice came from behind me as he landed on the grass. He spoke like all of this was merely play to him, a slow singsong quality in the way he accented his words. He laughed in victory, a tiny sound coming from deep in his throat.

"You're much too *smart* for that," he went on. "But I'm smarter than you are, it seems. Smarter than Mr. Sharpe, too—the idiot bastard."

There was twisted glee in his voice, a maniacal cadence that caused him to accent certain words oddly and wheeze as he tried to breath in and out. I choked for air that'd been knocked from me in the fall. He watched as I struggled, tilting his head down over me.

"You're bleeding," he told me. Wyck studied the blood as it ran down the side of my face with an odd interest. I could feel the liquid dripping from somewhere on my lip where his red ring had grazed. I gagged on it, spitting and choking.

"It's just a *little* blood," he said. "No need to thrash. I'll get it."

He bent closer to me and I tried to move, so he slammed a knee onto my shoulder in response. I groaned out a cry that refused to escape as I felt my bone ground into the grass, his head nearing mine from the other side. He extended a single silver claw, hand wavering as it came closer to my face, ignoring my squirms of pain under him. For one terrible moment I thought he meant to slice my throat, but instead he only wiped the blunted flat side of his claw across my lip, staining their silver with my blood.

He looked at the blood and finally released me. *I've just got to stand up.* If I could stand then I could get my hands from under me, I could slash him across with my claws...

I found a sliver of strength and dove to grab his legs, but he stopped me with a swift knee to my stomach that sent me curling up again. I managed to get onto my side but my arm had too little strength to keep me up, so I fell over onto my front. I struggled to put my hands out but only managed to tilt my head and see the sides of Wyck's black leather shoes as he knelt beside me. He continued to study the red on his claws before finally retracting them, the blood sliding to stain his fingers.

"I'm just so happy that we *finally* get to meet this time," he said. "I've met you *so* many times before that it's almost like I *know* you already. Maybe we should introduce ourselves again?"

If someone standing nearby had heard his tone, they never would have thought that he was kneeling over my beaten body. He was so calm that it was frightening, a control that told me that he'd already accounted for any possible means by which I might escape.

He reached out and grabbed me by my chin, squeezing it so tightly that the inside of my cheek felt like it was being cut against my own teeth. He pulled me to look at him, his grip around the side of my neck and upper throat.

"I'm Wyck Alyson," he said. "I'm Morgan Alyson's Chosen, and her son too. I've killed you a lot. And now you're mine. *Mine!*"

He tapped me with his thumb. He tilted his head again. "Now it's your turn. Tell me who you are, Michael."

I gritted my teeth together, refusing to play a part in whatever sadistic game was going on in his head. But he became impatient and tightened his grip.

"*I'm Michael Asher,*" he said in a high voice, squeezing my lips to move. "*I will rip your skin into tiny pieces, Wyck—if you'll just help me up off the ground, please.*"

Another tiny laugh, like a child playing with dolls, but maniacal when coming from such a man. I wanted to run, to fly, to draw him away from that place, so close to my sister who probably was in her bed again, thinking I was far away.

I just couldn't. I didn't have the energy. I didn't even have the breath.

Wyck grew tired of waiting. He pushed his shoe under my chin, lifting my face up with its hard rim. I couldn't cry out, even as the pain in my back burned from the impact I'd made. I ground my teeth together until I was up and staring straight at him, his head bent over to see mine. He looked confused.

"And you're supposed to be humanity's hero?" he said. "It's times like this I wonder if I've tracked down the *wrong* person."

He dropped his foot and let my head hit the dirt again. *Fight, Michael! Get up!* No matter how hard I tried, I just couldn't. He stepped over me, shoes on either side of my face, and methodically pulled a black bag over my head, tightening the string around my neck. I could see nothing.

"Feel free to sleep for the rest of our trip," he told me. I felt a gentle prick like a mosquito bite on the inside of my elbow. Something cold ran into my arm. Then I was gone.

*　　　　　*　　　　　*

A tinny cry slashed through the silence, a long pronunciation of an insistent, mechanical beep that refused to be abated. It was like the painful burn of an alarm clock buzzer, broken so that it continued as a single tone, screaming for attention, never giving any indication that it might fade.

Someone shut that off, I thought. *Can't anyone hear that abysmal noise?*

I couldn't tell from which side of me it was coming from, or if it was actually behind my head—or above me, even? It came from all directions, confusing me, continuing with the same force as it had when I'd awoken. So I opened my eyes to investigate further.

White.

All that surrounded me was so bright that nothing could be distinguished from the glow, blinding me the moment my eyelids parted. My vision blurred like I was peering through an out-of-focus lens—then again, when all there is to see is white, it's impossible to focus on anything.

As my vision cleared and adjusted to the light, the nothing faded into a something. The source of the light was a giant, circular arm of bulbs that hung over me like a medical examiner's lamp, so powerful that I could feel heat radiating from them. As I blinked, I began to pick things out in the brightness: corners and ends high above me that were slightly grayer because of shadows. I heard someone breathing sharply in and out, only to realize that the reverberating sound was coming from my own mouth.

The beep continued. I still could not find its source.

I attempted to roll over only to find that the motion was impossible. I looked down, unable to even lift myself more than a slight tilt of my head, and saw to my horror that my arms and legs were held down by black straps.

Being unable to move sent a jolt through me. All at once it hit that I was lying on a gurney, arms and legs and neck strapped down to the table like I was an experiment. My head jerked from one side to the other. Everything in the room was white, from the thin sheets under me, to the metal bars that held up the bed, to the tiny tables with vials and needles and sharply edged tools shining in the glare.

I heard the click of a door behind me, hidden in my blind spot. I instinctively tried to look but was unable to do more than twist my neck up, vision blocked by the edge of the pillow under my head. In the strained corner of my eye, I saw the white-jacketed outline of someone moving around the room behind me, reaching to my other side and clicking a button. The droning alarm ceased.

I turned to look but wasn't fast enough to see the person before their form disappeared behind me again.

"Hel-lll-lo?" I said. Even forming the single word was a struggle. It didn't sound right, it was all slurred and messy. I didn't even say the full thing, like I'd groaned it halfway and then let it trail off.

"Hello?" I tried again, saying it slower, enunciating it out this time. But the person behind me did not respond, moving to type something into a keyboard with a steady stream of clicks.

I slid down painfully, noticing more of my surroundings with every second. My arm hurt and when I looked down, I saw there was a needle poking from the inside of my left elbow, attached to a long tube that went up to a nearly-empty bag of liquid. On the wall to my left were small diagnostic screens with meters and buttons, something else was monitoring my pulse. There were no windows, no skylights or any clue to where I was. The room itself was anonymous.

I moved my other hand to pull the needle out, but of course my arm was still stuck and didn't move more than a half-inch. My efforts only made me dizzier.

"What's going on?" I said, all of my words clear now. I could still see the person in the white coat hovering just out of my eyesight, still engrossed in the computer. I saw long, blonde hair—not Wyck.

"Please, tell me something," I said, breathing heavily. "What are you doing to me?"

Still, no response. I wanted to scream, hoping that a doctor outside the door behind me might hear the noise and check in, someone who'd at least say a word to me. I couldn't plead with someone who didn't listen.

But my senses had been slow in their return. All at once, before I could open my mouth to cry out, I realized where I was. *The white room*. The same room that Callista had told me about, the room where she'd been kept a prisoner.

No…!

I was fighting against the straps again, kicking and flopping and bending trying to break free. I knew screaming was of no use because no one would hear me, but I shouted as loud as I could anyway. The bed shook and its screws creaked as I moved, the sheets coming off from under me as I tried to roll over. The pillow fell to the side and off the bed, the tube in my arm shaking like a whip, but I could not move to free myself, and when I finally fell exhausted again, the only result was a raw redness left on my wrists and ankles.

"Let me out!" I shouted at the person. Finally I heard her stand. I relaxed unwillingly, my eyes following her as she came around my right side. But she wasn't moving to attend to me. She pushed a rolling table around the edge of the room, its wheels creaking against the hard tiles.

Her face looked almost like that of a cat, puffy cheeks and giant lips below a straight nose that looked like it'd been traced on by pencil. Her skin was frighteningly lineless, like old movie stars' after plastic surgery disasters, even down to the skin on her hands that showed the frailty of age disguised behind medical stretching. Her hair was bleached and straightened and went past her shoulders, a sickly-thin frame obvious even beneath the jacket. She didn't look at me as she passed.

"Please?" I begged. "Where am I?"

Still no answer. It was almost as if she wasn't even in the room with me at all, looking ahead and not reacting in the slightest to my voice. She rested the table against the wall across from my feet. On it were two television screens.

The woman turned around, but didn't look into my eyes, just over to my arm where the needle was, face not showing any reaction.

"Are you a doctor?" I asked her. "You have to tell me what's going on!"

She walked up to me and readjusted the pillow behind my head. She started to disappear so I resumed my shouting and thrashing, demanding that she turn back and respond. My pillow fell again so she returned, but only to pick it up from the floor—humming disjointedly to herself—and push it back under my head.

She reached behind me and adjusted a dial on the drip going in to my arm. I felt something cold going through the tube.

"Please…" I begged, voice falling even though I'd tried to continue in a shout. The liquid made me lightheaded. I felt my muscles relaxing against my will. *No!*

In seconds, I was a shell again, breathing in and out madly, unable to lift my limbs or fight anymore. The woman continued

197

humming to herself as I became silent, the rumble of an air vent clicking on to make the room even more refrigerated.

I couldn't move. I couldn't speak. They'd taken away all of my control.

As the panic set in, I heard a new, gentle buzz behind me, like a cell phone on vibrate. The woman arose from her stool, crossing the room again to go back to the table she'd pushed across from me. She clicked buttons and the screens fizzled on, then she turned to me and adjusted my bed so that I was angled higher.

One of the televisions gave a high-pitched sound and I tilted my head to look. The screen on the left had come to life. At first, the camera was unmoving and focused on a pile of torn papers and broken glass spread in a mess on a floor. It was day there, dim because the window blinds were drawn, but I saw someone's fingers as they lifted the camera up, turning it around to face them. I heard a scrape across the microphone, which popped static through the TV.

It was Wyck. His back was to a blank wall. He sounded out of breath.

"Hello?" he called, that awful voice stinging my ears. He appeared grainy in the bad lighting of where he was. He tapped the lens on the camera.

"I can see *you* but can you see me?" he said, playfully again. I didn't reply, but he caught my eyes flicking around nervously from his voice, and he smiled.

"There you are," he said, face brightening but eyes nearly dripping with his tainted enjoyment. "You're very lucky today, because today you're getting television *straight* to your bed. And you don't even have to *worry* about changing the channel if it gets boring."

He was looking straight at me. I noticed a tiny camera poking from between the two televisions. Sweat rolled down my forehead as his words crackled through the screen. The most movement I could muster was to tremble and to lick my lips that had split dry in the chill of the room.

"You look unhappy," Wyck observed, not seeming to like this, or at least acting so. He couldn't keep the camera still in his unsteady hands, making the screen bob and shift as he swayed. The wall behind him remained blank, continuing to hide his location from me.

"I mean, you shouldn't be," he said. "You're about to see the *greatest* show on earth, I think. A *stupendous* show. Impossible to forget afterwards—or your money back!"

Everything about him was so premeditated—so unconcerned that it scared me. What was he doing? It was almost as if he was leading me along, letting the awful anticipation become a part of the torture I knew was coming. When would he order the nurse to reach for the tools, when would she begin slicing away parts of my skin and digging it into my side, hoping that I would tell them where the Blade was.

I was already steeling myself. I had a low threshold for pain, as evidenced by my earlier birthmark experience. I even became squeamish around too much blood. But how much could they know? I was a professional at seeing truth, so I knew how to tell a better lie. I could easily bluff them, lie and scream that I didn't know where the Blade was. They'd try hard, but they'd never kill me. They'd never hurt me so much that I couldn't find the Blade for them.

Eventually, Callista and Thad would notice I was gone and they would come running. Their connection to me would lead them straight to this room. I only had to last until then.

As I thought these things, Wyck seemed to not like whatever passed over my face.

"Oh Michael," he said, voice so low that it now almost resembled a growl. "Michael, Michael. Oh *Michael*," he'd distracted himself, blinking. "That's such an...*interesting* name. Do you know what it means?"

His eyebrow perked up hopefully, gaze shifting to look at some screen through which he was able to see me. I didn't respond.

"It *means* 'who is like God?'," he revealed, showing his perfectly straight, entirely white row of teeth. "It's a Hebrew name, with a question inside. I bet you didn't know that though."

Another scratch of his shoes, another dizzying turn and twist of the camera. He was amusing himself again, like he was already thinking of the punch line of a joke as he told it.

"Are you like a *god*, Michael?" he asked, lifting his free hand as if in deep question. I still couldn't reply. He stared through the camera for a few seconds, waiting on me. Then, as if realizing why I wasn't responding, he straightened up.

"Leilah?" he said. "Please adjust Michael. It slipped my mind that he should be *awake* for this."

The woman arose from her seat again and went to my left side, turning the dial. Then she went to one of the metal tables, taking a needle and syringe already filled with liquid. She turned my other arm over, pricking me with sharp end. I didn't feel the needle sliding in, but whatever was inside the syringe revived me quickly enough to make me feel it going back out.

All of my muscles constricted at once, then suddenly relaxed, and I fell back onto the bed shaking uncontrollably.

"That's better," Wyck said through the sound of my painful wince. "I'll repeat: are you like a god, Michael?"

I didn't reply. I wasn't going to talk to him, not even utter a single word. I knew that he was playing some sort of mind game, and once I allowed myself to talk he'd use that to keep me going. It was a trick that I'd used on my harsher clients: small talk would lead to deeper things. Tiny victories would win the war. I refused to entertain Wyck.

He detected what I was doing immediately. His eyelids fell halfway and I heard the plastic of the camcorder being squeezed between his hands.

"*Are you like a god?*" he roared suddenly, voice going so deep that it was like the scream of a death metal singer, making me jump in terror as his teeth nearly slammed with the camera. The speakers threatened to burst under the onslaught of his yell.

"No!" I shouted, immediately cursing that I'd allowed myself to be cracked so easily. Wyck was left out of breath, bloodshot eyes wide with the rage that he'd let loose. Then, realizing he'd lost his cool, he forced his breathing down, spluttering until it was cleared, straightening his hair back into position.

"But you kind of are," he said, clearing his throat, voice returning to his regular sneer. "Can't you come *back* to life when people *kill* you? You can, right? How interesting."

As he said this, he started to sway from side to side, turning around so that I could see the rest of the blank wall. Then when his movement exposed just a few more inches, I knew exactly where he was. The wall was from my kitchen back home.

I wish I were wrong. But I saw the dishes we'd used now broken in pieces across the counter, my mom's herbs dangling in the window, the metal faucet on our sink cracked off from some

200

violent scuffle and dribbling water everywhere. Wyck secured the camera in his hand, wobbling unsteadily as he wiped his forehead free of perspiration.

"But what about other people, Michael?" he went on, continuing to rock back and forth as if unaware of my horror. "Can you bring other people back to life after *they're* dead, too?"

No. You can't be there. You can't! I was petrified by the insanity in Wyck's eyes.

"I don't think you can do that," he said. "In fact, I *know* you can't."

Then he tripped over something and threw his hands in front of himself to catch his balance. I heard a shout of pain through the screen, a terrifyingly familiar sound that made my eyes go wider. The camera's view dipped when Wyck caught himself, and for a flash of a second I saw my mom.

She was curled up on the floor, her face under her arms and her back pressed into the corner of the room next to the wreckage of what had been our dining room table. I screamed as loudly as I could, suddenly a furious beast tearing at the straps again.

"Don't hurt her!" I shouted at the top of my lungs, my own voice paining my ears and scratching like sandpaper against my throat. Wyck realigned the camera so that I couldn't see my mom anymore.

"Please!" I screamed. "Don't hurt her!"

"Now you suddenly seem so eager to speak to me," Wyck said in observation. "How nice of you. For a minute I thought this conversation would be completely one-sided."

He looked through the camera and beyond me, tapping the glass of his camcorder lens. "Leilah? I think you can turn on the other screen now. Mother will want to see."

The nurse walked out from behind me as I gritted my teeth and pulled at my wrists. Inside and out, my body and mind cried. It was like being stuck in a nightmare after taking sleeping pills, begging to be awoken but physically unable to escape. I fell back on to the bed, voice gone. I didn't want to think of what Wyck was doing, what he'd already done.

Leilah flicked the switch on the other screen and it came to life at once.

On screen were now a woman and a child. I recognized the older instantly: she was the same olive-skinned, black haired woman

201

who'd appeared in my second nightmare with Wyck, the one who'd ordered him to kill me. *His mother, Morgan.* Just like Wyck, her eyebrows were solid white, and the gaze of green that she stared with showed as little emotion as I'd seen in my dream.

She was sitting in an ornate wooden chair whose back was so tall I couldn't see its full height. Most of the room behind her was too dark to perceive. In her lap was a child who couldn't have been older than eleven or twelve, a boy with hair in black curls on his head and eyes that matched hers. His eyebrows were white, and also like her, he had a red ring on his right hand. He looked at me intently.

"Ah, mother," Wyck said, breathing out quickly, looking excited that she was watching. "I've—"

"That's him?" the younger boy broke in, with a hint of an English accent that his brother lacked. Wyck spluttered to a stop, blinking at the interruption.

"Yes," Morgan replied. "That's Daniel Rothfeld."

"Why is he in bed?" he asked. "Make him stand up for me."

"We can't, Teddy," she replied gently. "He'll run away."

"Can you still hear me?" Wyck said, unable to disguise his irritation at being interrupted. The eyes of the other two moved away from me and to his screen in their room. Wyck hesitated under his mother's gaze, still panting for air through his mouth.

"We can hear you," she said with coldness. "Go on, Wyck."

"Yes, yes," he stammered, trying to bring himself back on track but put off by their disruption. He turned again, looking around for something that he'd left leaning against the corner of the counter: a broomstick. He seized its handle.

"Well, we've been through this so *many* times, I figured a repeated episode would get mighty boring," he said, swallowing. "You see, we keep *chasing* you, Michael. We keep *running*. I don't like to run! I'm *tired* of it. I'm ready to end this whole thing."

He furrowed his brow. He gestured to me.

"It's like…you're a *disease*," he said, coughs punctuating his words. "We've just been treating the symptoms of you for decades. But now it's time to vaccinate the *source*."

My brain had started to clear itself again. I knew that Wyck was talking about the Blade—he probably already knew that I'd gone after it as soon as I had escaped them.

"I don't have…the Blade," I told him. I didn't feel the denial was giving him too much.

"No no no no no," he broke in, waving his hand furiously. "You don't have to lie *yet*. I'm not even *asking* you yet. We'll *get* to that."

He turned the broom over, exposing its bristles on the other end. Then, with a wild swing, he slammed the end of it down onto the counter. I heard the crack echo in my old kitchen, the long pole breaking off into a splintered spike.

"Just while you're watching," Wyck said, spinning the broken handle back over, "be sure to come up with a good lie. And hold onto it. I'm gonna want to hear it after class."

"My family doesn't have anything to do with this!" I burst. Even when he sniffed at my objection there was a lack of care…an inkling of entertainment lapping up my pain like it was nourishment to him. But he paused nonetheless.

"Well," Wyck said after thinking a moment, "I guess they're *about* to have something to do with it."

He shrugged. "And besides: the color red looks good on a human."

He looked to the floor.

The camera jerked, a whoosh as the broom handle swung down in Wyck's fist. I heard the painful scream of my mother amidst the crack of something striking her. It was almost like one of my own bones had broken, so harshly that I couldn't make a sound.

She yelled for him to stop and he did, turning to look up at the end of the stick. He studied its jagged edge as I watched in wide-eyed, wordless horror.

"Nope, still no blood," he said with dissatisfaction. So he struck again and I screamed so loud that I couldn't hear the sound my mother made, struggling to pull myself from the bed even if it meant tearing my own arms out in the process. But my claws refused to emerge.

"Stop! Stop!" I shouted, but Wyck refused to. I shook, feeling my ankles hitting against the straps. I heard the whistle of the stick again, the sickening snap, the weak sob.

Morgan sat back comfortably into her chair. How could she simply ignore the sounds, to let it go on? Wasn't she even going to ask for something, to at least attempt to get the location of the

Blade from me? She just watched my reaction. And Teddy slid to sit on one of her legs as she wrapped her arms to hold him up.

"I'll tell you!" I yelled. "I know where the Blade is!"

My mom's screams had left all of my defenses broken, so that absolutely nothing else mattered to me at that moment. I heard another shout, and another...

Don't tell them, Michael!

You can't tell them!

You can't ruin everything now, not when you're so close!

"See, right now," Wyck said, pausing to catch his breath and wipe his sweaty forehead with the back of his hand, "my goal isn't to *kill* you."

He took a deep breath, readying the broomstick again, lifting it back behind him, gritting his teeth together.

"It's just to—" He swung the staff forward. "—make... you... *feel*... dead."

Every word: another strike, another scream, another crack that drove itself through me. I cried horribly, unable to see, unable to shut out the sounds.

"It's in Saint Helen's Cathedral!" I broke out in a moan, unable to fight any longer. The words spilled from my lips, eyes sagging, and arms weak now in the bonds that held me down. Wyck, hearing me, looked up at the camera. He seemed surprised that I'd broken, as if all along he'd been expecting me to resist to the end.

"What city?" he asked. He didn't even give me a second to get enough breath to reply before he'd kicked my mother on the floor, a crash as she hit the bottom of the dining room table.

"In Lodi!" I shouted. Wyck's eyes shifted to look beyond me.

"Is he telling the truth, mother?" he asked. I realized that Morgan had been staring at me intently, and when Wyck had startled me, she'd been reading a Glimpse in my eyes.

It was too late for me to look away. *So my power was Guardian after all.*

"He is," she confirmed.

Teddy clapped with glee, his eyes jumping from one side to the other as he watched Wyck and I with rapture. Seeming satisfied, Wyck finally stopped his beating; sweat now rolling down the sides of his pale face. I couldn't even hear my mother's weeping anymore.

"That was...tiring," he said, unaffected. He lifted the end of the broom handle, and smiled when he saw that it was stained with a splattering of red.

He tossed the broom across the floor and I heard it clattering away. I felt limp, worthless, discarded. I wished I could have passed out; anything to block the echoes of my mom's screams.

Wyck, though, started to pull something off our counter, mixing jars of liquid together while the camera swayed in his uneven grip. He grabbed something out of his pocket: a cigarette lighter. He flicked it and suddenly a tendril of flame flared up from the side of the camera.

"Wait..." I said, lips barely able to move. Wyck didn't listen.

"I...told you the truth..." I said, blood pounding through my neck. *No, Wyck. What are you doing? Don't...* I stared at the screen with tear-filled eyes. He shrugged again.

"This place could use a little brightening up," he said, and then turning from the camera, he threw the lighter and the jar. The contents sprayed across my kitchen, immediately feeding the tiny flame and flaring up into a burning trail. When the rest of the can hit the ground, there was a massive explosion like a bomb going off, and the lights burst into Wyck's face.

He readjusted the camera, and in this motion I saw my mother lying unconscious on the floor, in a mess of blood now lit by the growing fire. Unmoving. Trapped.

18

SNOWFLAKES AND FIRE

The moment that the fire licked its way across the floor and hit my mother's medicine cabinet, suddenly everything on screen went aglow. Her alcohol-based remedies and mixtures began to pop and feed the flames as Wyck walked slowly through the kitchen door, and I began my screams again.

The absolute silence of Wyck was now even more terrifying than his incessant babbling had been. I yelled to him but he didn't stop. He'd gotten what he wanted.

"See, Teddy?" Morgan went on. "This is what makes us different from the worthless eaters. It's called death. It's most curious. It's like an end—to everything—for a human."

She gestured at the screen. "He lived with that human for a very long time. He might even think he is a human like her. I don't understand it."

Teddy grinned. He wasn't watching me anymore, he was watching Wyck's screen, reveling in the fire as it slid across the carpet in the place I'd once lived in. Morgan, seeing that her son's interest in me had waned, reached forward and pressed a button, and her screen died.

I was left with only the cracking sounds of the fire, the breathing of Wyck as he moved toward my house's back door. The smoke began to gather and mask the walls and the pictures that hung there. Surely the fire department would come! Surely they would save my mom and Alli—where was my sister? Had Wyck already shot her and left her dead upstairs?

The fire was too powerful. The police would never arrive in time.

My gaze spotted something off the screen's reflection. Beside my bed, on one of the tables, was my cell phone. I could grab it...I could call the police! I stretched my hand out. My phone was only inches away. I pushed harder, letting the strap pull higher against my arm, cutting off the blood pressure so much that my hand went scarlet. My bonds slid up, tightening on my arm, the chemicals on my other side again starting to take over.

The end of my finger scraped the volume button on my phone. *One more inch...*

The woman in the white coat turned around from her desk and spotted me. Gently, she reached out and touched my phone, sliding it across the table, too far away from me. I collapsed. She shook her head in scolding.

"You're a very difficult person to sedate," she said, voice like the croak of a frog. She took my outstretched hand and slid to place it back beside me on the bed.

But that was close enough. I seized her by her wrist, pulling her toward me with all the rage that I'd pent up behind my tears. My motion took her by surprise and she fell over across me. Her flailing arm hit the I/V from my other elbow, ripping the needle out.

The moment the chemicals stopped, my mind emerged from the muddy water. The woman fell over, but in the second between her falling from my bed and when she would have struck the floor, I exploded in all directions.

There came the sound of four giants tears as the straps and mattress burst into frayed string and material, a crash as the table beside me went flying when the scales on my hand hit it. I erupted from the bed so wildly that my razors cut the plaster of the room's walls, the back of my other fist landing squarely into the woman's chest, sending her flying into the television screens.

All in the space of a second, I was free.

The room rang with crashes as the tables went flying, the instruments clattered against the floor, my claws tore at the tiles and the computers until they were sliced into bits of metal and glass on the floor, pounded like dough into each other. My shout was a roar of fury, sparks flying from the television screens as I spun and turned the room into wreckage.

The lights disappeared over my head, likely as a result of my claws tearing them straight from their sockets. I was immediately engulfed in darkness but I didn't stop, taking to the air, pounding the backs of my hands into the ceiling. Every strike was painless, the scales like armor protecting me as the ceiling buckled. I was so filled with rage that I was nearly blinded until I'd carved a hole in the roof: tiny at first, then growing with each punch, until daylight streamed through, and all the processed air was replaced by the scent of outside.

I gave the ceiling one final slam, the floor rocking beneath my feet and the room swaying on unstable supports. Grabbing my cell phone from the floor, I launched into the air, sliding through the hole that I'd created, blinking as I found myself escaping into another world.

I had erupted from a trailer that was hitched to the back of a large truck. It came as a shock—the fresh air, the sunlight, and the clouds in the sky. The room of horrors had been a small square box that nobody would ever pay attention to, parked behind a grocery store. I could see people driving around the corner, pulling in to parking spaces, picking up food for their families, while I had just emerged from a prison they didn't even know existed.

There was no time for me to let the alarm wear off. I rose higher against the heat of the sun. The ground disappeared, the trees and the battered trailer left behind. The moment I could see the city I knew exactly where I was—not even a few miles from Arleta.

At first I thought that I could call the fire department from my phone but I was in too much of a panic to get my fingers to press the right numbers. I was focused on a single, desperate thought: reaching the house in time. I would fight Wyck off with my own hands if I had to.

Don't die! was all I could think, a painful internal sob like a black hole threatening to consume me from the inside out. I couldn't cry now. I couldn't waste what precious breath I had.

I saw smoke in the distance: thick, black and repugnant, like the morbid breath of a volcano. My eyes and throat burned as I found myself in the way of the smoke. I coughed but didn't pause, diving from the sky and ignoring the flashing lights of the fire trucks as they raced down the highway far below.

The ground came upon me in seconds. I hit my backyard and rolled in a flurry of grass and dust. I got to my feet instantly, shaking my hair out of my eyes, looking up in horror for a moment just because I couldn't stop myself. The entire house from floor to rooftop was already burning, shingles and wooden supports breaking off, red and orange fire flaring out of the broken windows. The back porch had collapsed onto my mom's swing and my sister's now-melted drawing easel. I could see through the kitchen window that fire and ash continued to rain inside. A firefighter's water would do nothing to stop this in time. Even the roof that I'd sat upon not many hours before had already caved in with crater-like holes.

I heard a pop like a gunshot and the back door of my house exploded, shaking me as a rain of shrapnel and splinters flew in all directions. I dashed towards the house anyway, the heat rising with every step as I ran up the porch and shot through the door.

It was an inferno. Fire had crawled up the walls in erratic patterns, the ceiling ablaze and dropping ash where giant, jagged pieces of wood had already fallen. Furniture was alighted like giant torches, the noise deafening as everything crackled and flames leapt from one end of the room to the other. And the smoke! It burned my nostrils and lungs and eyes, like airborne toxins entering me, so that I stumbled back toward the door again just to breathe.

"Alli! Mom!" I yelled, but the fire masked my voice. I got to the kitchen but my mom wasn't there anymore. I called for my family, spinning in a circle and hoping that maybe my mom had awakened and crawled to safety. All of my skin felt sunburned at once.

There was a crash as something fell through the ceiling from the second story. Orange and black and red rained like hot sequins around me as I dove for cover in the doorframe. I still couldn't see my mom, and I was running out of time. Could Wyck have dragged her somewhere?

I found one safe step then another, trying to reach the stairs as the broken boards wobbled under my shoes. My mom's medicine cabinet was wrecked. The couch was destroyed. Everything I'd once known was melting away before my eyes.

At the bottom of the stairs, I saw the most horrific sight of all.

A body lay crumpled like a discarded doll, only the head visible beneath giant beams of fallen wood that had crushed her body. Her eyes were open but stared blankly, emptily—wide in shock, but showing no Glimpse.

I was too late. My mom was dead.

Everything stopped.

The hallowed face of my mother was a single fragment of peace in the hellfire. Her face, though bruised and beaten, showed no fear of death—no concern for herself, dying in the same way that she had lived. I stumbled forward, falling to my knees in front of her, trying not to look at her blood soaked shirt. I touched her open fingers but they did not move to curl around mine, her empty eyes continuing to stare, her lips parted like she had tried to utter her last words but had been cut off by the unrelenting fire.

A falling beam smashed our coffee table behind me. The chairs scattered when the ceiling panel above them crumbled. It was as if a tragedy film was playing out around me and I was stuck in its script. Kneeling before the broken body of my mother, I was merely an actor in a screenplay. A puppet in a show.

This isn't how it was supposed to happen...

I was broken from my tears when part of the second-story balcony collapsed behind me, striking me in the back and hurling me forward. My hands flew up into a mask that deflected the debris from my face, but I was now perched against the wall across the room, coughing for air. I inhaled smoke. My mom's face was already gone, now covered by what had been our ceiling. I'd seen her for the last time.

I couldn't mourn for her any longer, not as the house was collapsing and there was still one hope left. I soared into flight over the stairs, shouting my sister's name. I hit the floor above but had to catch myself as the wood crumbled beneath me. Alli's room was already taken over by the flames. But I knew if she had run to hide anywhere, it would have been my room next door.

The burning had not neglected my bedroom. My dresser was toppled with my clothes spilling out in piles—likely the work of Wyck as he'd ravaged my house in his quest to defile it. All the camera lenses were knocked to the ground and shattered, thousands of dollars of my life's savings spilled across the room.

But worse: *my Great Work.* As I spun, I saw that every photograph was on fire; the ones on the ceiling breaking off and fluttering like flaming snowflakes to the floor. All of the faces were blackened with holes through them, their eyes fading against the smoke. It pierced my heart to see all of them dying like the slow-burning carcasses of old friends.

I panicked and almost ran to save them. But my sister was still somewhere in the house. My Great Work was nothing.

I threw my closet door open. She wasn't there. I stepped back and the floor shifted from under me again. Where was she? I spun to get out but found that the floor outside my room had already collapsed.

I wasn't ready to give up. So I slammed shut what remained of my door and went to the wall I shared with my sister's adjacent room. Even then I hesitated, though only for a second, before my fingers went flying to rip my work down, tearing the photos to pieces and letting the shreds hit the floor without so much as a glance. The wall beneath it was already hot, my fingers stained black. But I went on, slamming with my fists and digging with my claws into the already weakened panels, hoping that I could break through.

My eyes burned as ash and wood stuck to my sweaty face. An opening finally broke. It was like I had opened a furnace. I could not step inside, fire leaping through the wall at me and my scaly hands flashing once again to my protection. Still, I forced myself ahead, trying to look inside, to see if I could drag my sister out.

I saw her shoes across the room, shrouded in smoke.

"Alli!" I shouted again. But there were just too many flames to see, and the smoke only served as a precursor to the explosion that threw me off my feet.

I was standing one second, vigorously fighting to press forward, and the next I was in the air, powers struggling to catch me, my back slamming into the opposite wall. I tried to get up, but couldn't as the smoke slowly began to seep through my lungs.

Hands grabbed a hold of me. I was pulled through the window, hit with fresh air that expelled the smoke.

Someone held me up. *Wyck?* No. Someone else.

I struggled to keep my eyes open, and through slits I saw that I was hanging over Callista's shoulder. We were high in the air, the wind whirling in gusts against my face.

"I couldn't save them," I said. I collapsed into her arms and didn't even try to hold back my tears anymore.

19

SOPHIA

With her arms wrapped around my middle and mine around her shoulders, Callista carried me across the city until I couldn't smell the smoke or hear the sirens anymore. Thad appeared beside us, guarding the air as we went, his claws out and ready to defend.

Even after we'd landed she still wouldn't let me go—or maybe it was me who wouldn't? I was in a daze. I wavered between being awake and falling into sleep-like shock, where I would just stare silently, my body trembling, my hands clutching each other to keep them still.

Thad and Callista never left our sacred circle on the mountain, the same edge of the cliff where I'd first woken up with scales and claws. Neither of them spoke. Their mere presence brought me some tiny comfort.

I wasn't a crier, and yet I'd already cried more that day than I had in my entire life. I'd always thought that weeping over dead people merely stretched the period of pain out longer when it should have ended when they did. It wasn't like tears would bring anything back.

Still, I wept. I just couldn't stop myself.

A time came when I could not cry anymore. When the tears dried, I told Thad and Callista everything that had happened. When quiet finally set, so did the sun, and we pressed close as the chilly night swept over the hills. Thad gathered enough courage to leave and get food and flashlights, Callista remained standing over me like a guard. Even when he returned, we continued to sit in the silence and listen as the voice of the city as they rose up over the cliff.

"Why are we out here instead of at the house?" I asked. The bed would have been far better than the rocks.

"It isn't safe anymore," Callista replied. I dusted off my hands.

"Nowhere is safe anymore," I spat. She walked away from me to ignore the sourness in my voice. Thad came between us.

"Callista is right," he told me. "We need to move. We can't stay in Los Angeles."

His voice dropped. He didn't want to say what was coming next, but he knew he had to.

"Right now, I guarantee you they're headed to Lodi," he said, avoiding my eyes. "The least we can do is use that as a head start…to get away."

"Once they have it, we can't be here," Callista said with insistence. "We have to leave. And we need a plan, Michael. A real one."

I drew in a quick breath, feeling my muscles tense. I knew what they were thinking: *Michael had run off and nearly got himself killed again. Ruining everything, as usual.* I straightened my shoulders.

"Here's a plan for you," I said, picking at rocks on the ground. "Let's go right in the middle of the city, and stand on top of one of the buildings, and shout the truth to everyone. Let's make the Guardians send someone to shoot us down, and kill that person."

I piled the pebbles into my hand in angry motions. "Then they'll send another, and we'll kill him too. Then we'll track each and every Guardian down. And we'll keep killing until every one of them is dead, or we are."

Callista shook her head disdainfully.

"What is wrong with you?" she said with dismay. "Do you have any idea what you did earlier? Do you have any idea that every time you put yourself in danger, you put Thad and I in the same spot? We didn't even have a choice."

"Being out there is better than sitting here waiting for them," I said.

"And if you go out, they *will* hunt you down!" Thad shouted suddenly from the other side, in an irate tone that I'd never heard him use before. I pushed myself up to my feet, throwing the rocks to the ground in fury.

"Then why the hell did he let me go?" I yelled back. "He had me and he could have killed me in a second."

"Because he wants to come back and kill you with the Blade instead!" Thad's voice roared into the trees above us. "He knows you're giving up. You've gone *weak*."

My jaw tightened, hands now fists to hold the claws in.

"Now you have nothing left," he said. "That's what they've wanted all along. To break you, just like they broke us. They want you reckless so they can calculate everything you do, until you're theirs. Callista's right—we need a new plan."

"I don't *have* a plan," I said.

"Well you need to come up with one!" Thad waved an angry hand at me.

"Why?" I returned sharply.

Thad let a quick breath out but I refused to relent. He turned away, walking off as if he wasn't going to stoop so low as to reply to me.

"Because you're the one who got us into this mess," he muttered over his shoulder.

He could have shot my knee with a bullet and it might have hurt less. All of a sudden, hot tears of rage brimmed in the corners of my eyes, and before I could stop myself, I was dashing toward Thad with my fists out.

He reacted faster, hearing me and spinning around. I hadn't realized that my claws were out too, and our silver edges clashed together like swords. But he was far better than me, far more prepared, and in one swift motion his blades wrenched in a circle, catching against my scales and flipping me over onto my back.

"Stop!" Callista shouted, though the short-lived battle was already over. Thad breathed heavily, standing away from me at the ready. I coughed and rolled over, the impact having shaken my urge to attack, but not my rage.

Callista held out her hand, but I hit it away, getting to my feet on my own. I turned from both of them and started to run for the edge, and before anyone could stop me, I was in the air again. I heard Callista calling after me but I ignored her voice, and flew all the faster.

Being solitary was almost painful. As soon as there were no voices, the sounds in my head bubbled up with memories of my mother's screams, Wyck's ghastly voice, and the laughs coming through the screen.

Had I really meant what I'd told Callista and Thad? I was such a mess that I couldn't trust my thoughts anymore. I had never believed in capital punishment before. Who is a judge to say that someone doesn't deserve to live? Life isn't something that is given on loan by a government, a privilege they can recall if someone doesn't follow their rules.

Sometimes, though, I would watch the news about death row prisoners and study the Glimpses in their eyes. Most would have a dazed, empty space inside, like they'd already died and were simply waiting for the formalities to wrap it up. But the serial killers and the psychopaths were different. Their faces might be calm but inside their eyes was still a terrifying, uncontrollable urge to kill, like kleptomaniacs addicted to stealing lives.

When I put the pieces together, I saw the Guardians as genocidal psychopaths. How many disasters had been by their hand? How many more would they kill, if someone didn't kill them first? Was that to be my grim responsibility—to kill the killers?

Who wept when Hitler died? Murder is good sometimes.

I wrestled with these heavy thoughts as I flew, until exhaustion sank in and I was forced to the ground with the ache of thirst. I walked the sidewalks of an unfamiliar part of the city. No one nearby even glanced my way. I was like a ghost.

That association fit me far too well. I felt as empty as a ghost inside. Without my mother and sister, I had nothing to go back to. I had no hope, no reason to fight. There would never be a normal again. Everything I'd once known was now turned to ashes.

I wandered in this aimless state as the night darkened further and the sidewalks began to empty. My surroundings became lonely and decrepit, slovenly-kept shacks and buildings growing like fungus against the sides of the road. When I spotted an open door radiating light ahead, I turned to go in.

It was a messy bar that I was too young to enter, neon beer advertisements glowing on the walls and animal heads studying me with blank gazes. Even at that hour, the bar was nearly deserted, only two men talking in a corner booth with their voices masked by low rock music and the television. The bartender behind the counter turned to me.

"Can't come in here, kid," he said, eyeing me as he cleaned the inside of a glass with a towel. He had long dreadlocks and a black tattoo on the right side of his face like a half-skull. The inside smelled of old sweat and cheap alcohol.

"Do you have water?" I asked in a soft voice, because it was all I could muster. He glared at me.

"You're too young to be here, man," he said. "There's an *In-N-Out* down the road."

"I just watched my family die," I replied. "Can I just have some water?"

The bartender didn't have an answer. In my life's study of eyes, I'd discovered that sometimes, even people who didn't have my power could read the gaze of another person. This was simply part of being human—the ability to see fear in enemies, or pain in a friend, or affection in a lover. The bartender must have read such intense pain in my own eyes that he was forced to concede, and he filled the cup for me without any more objections.

I swallowed all he gave me, coughing up smoke. He poured more then went to the other side of the building to clean a table.

The television was on, so I watched as it played rerun shots of a football game. The fat reporter spit his "S's" and "P's" so much that I expected the camera lens to become covered in saliva. Why did I hold so tightly to these tiny details now?

Unexpectedly, the report changed, and before my startled eyes, my own face appeared on the screen. I nearly choked.

The anchor turned to the camera with my photo hovering at his side: my school portrait, zoomed in so closely that it was pixilated and made me look far more sinister. The subtext beneath my photo read: *TEENAGE TERRORIST MICHAEL ASHER MURDERS OWN FAMILY, DISAPPEARS.*

My mouth hung open in shock but I immediately had the sense to shut it, to turn around in the stool so my back was to the booth of men and the bartender. There was another television across the room playing the same thing: TVs all around, so that any of the patrons could just look up and match my face to the one on the screen. My heart beat faster, but I didn't move, fearful that anything would bring attention to myself.

It was hard to hear the anchor without straining, so I leaned in as best I could.

"...Asher displayed sociopathic tendencies as early as six years old..." the reporter said, emphasizing all the right words with a professional—but obviously uncaring—tone.

"...but like all psychopaths, he managed to stay carefully under the radar so that all the signs went ignored," she continued. "Brushes with police. Car crashes. Even cyberspace hacker friends. And a hobby that Michael called his "Wall of Death"."

Here, my picture finally disappeared, only to be replaced by an even larger photograph of my old bedroom. Taken at a horribly crooked angle, the photo provided by the police department displayed my wall of eyes, all of the pictures now ruined by dust and ash and crinkled edges that gave them a degenerated look.

Of course they'd skip over the Joy and Love walls. Of *course* they'd go straight to the Sadness and Anger, panning across the terrified eyes of the anonymous people like I'd trapped them in cages and tortured them to get my pictures. Nobody would explain how I got the photos. Nobody would tell them to turn around and look at the glowing faces on the other side of the room. That wouldn't have made for a good Wall of Death, now would it?

Go ahead, squeeze as much out of this story as you can. I clenched my fists.

But the reporter hadn't even gotten to the best part yet—the part that'd gotten me labeled a terrorist. Next, they shifted to shaky video footage of a crashed jet on the beach, smoke dominating the sky as the flames roared through the remaining fuel. My photo hovered on screen beside the plane that Callista had crashed: I was accused of hiding bombs on board and destroying the jet via remote control.

I couldn't believe what I was watching. It was so obvious...*so fabricated.* The anchors just continued on with their reports as if there wasn't even an inch of doubt, throwing in the casual *accused* and *alleged* to stay barely in the bounds of honest journalism.

And Arleta—they loved their sinister and gory tales. They would eat all of this up. Everyone would watch the updates every day, talk about it at school and their jobs until my reputation reached local-celebrity levels. They'd all say they knew it all along, that they were right to have never trusted me, that they were lucky to have not been my friend.

I wanted to curse at the news that they were getting it all wrong, that all of this was a lie about me. But suddenly I knew what was happening.

They control every inch of the world... I remembered Father Lonnie so clearly, his whisper tinged with fear. This was the Guardians' doing! They were feeding these stories to the media to ruin me even more, to give me nowhere to run.

My chin sank into my palm weakly as the report continued, showing interviews with kids I'd bumped into once or twice— suddenly, former best friends or ex-girlfriends. That part almost made me burst with laughter. Then it switched to the reporter walking down a sidewalk with my school in the background.

"Parents have to wonder that if a boy of seventeen can murder his own family and burn their house down—how close was he to your own children? Are they safe while he runs free?"

"I have a message for Mr. Asher." It showed footage of a short and rotund man in a police uniform, standing behind a stack of microphones. He looked nervous, lacking the public speaking skills to even look up from his pre-written statement on the podium. "No matter what it takes, we will find you. We will draw you out from where you are hiding, and bring justice to your family."

I'd seen better-written threats in chalk at my sister's schoolyard. There was a shuffle of stock music, ushering in an animated bumper that sent them into another segment. My face disappeared.

I sank back into the chair, looking across the counter at nothing. In one sweep, the Guardians had taken from me anyone in my old town who might have come to my support.

My throat had gone dry again. I heard footsteps in the doorway behind me but was too distracted to turn until someone slid into the chair next to me. I turned my head sharply. It was Thad.

"Did you follow me?" I said quickly. I would have jumped from him if I wasn't sure it'd cause a scene. He was by himself.

"You can't be alone," Thad replied simply. "You know that."

I let my breath out. Having a bodyguard stalking me was not something that I found appealing. Likely it was because they'd already seen that if they took their eyes off me then I'd go off and nearly get myself killed. I cursed under my breath.

The bartender clinked a glass of water down in front of Thad and left again. He began to sip slowly, eyes staring blankly ahead at the television.

We sat like that for a while, neither speaking. Thad put his glass down.

"What are you thinking about doing?" he said, almost painfully. I wished I could have dodged his question but he was looking straight at me.

"Thad," I replied, "my family is dead. My house is burned down. Everything is gone. Do you understand what that means?"

"That you're blinded with anger," he suggested. "That you'll do anything to get your hands on Wyck for what he did. Even if it's suicide for you and us."

The words slipped out and he immediately knew how cruel it sounded. I cringed and turned away, drinking more to hide my face.

"I'm sorry," he relented. "I shouldn't have said that."

Talking about it was not making me feel any better, and every time I let my mind wander back it was overcome by images of the burning house. I couldn't escape it, like a brand seared in to the back of my subconscious, always popping up no matter how hard I tried to block it out.

Thad picked the glass up, drank the rest down, and then stood.

"Come on," he beckoned. "I want to show you something."

"No," I said. "Just go."

"Please," he said. It took me unawares. He nodded toward the door.

I gave in. It wasn't like I had somewhere else to go. I put some cash on the counter and Thad lead me outside. He went down the neighboring lane and into the shadows, where we jumped into flight and headed away from the Valley.

At first I was afraid that he was bringing me back to Callista, and I just didn't have the heart to hear another scolding from her. But to my relief he turned away from the hills and in the direction of a different part of town. His motions told me that he knew exactly where he wanted to go, so I followed.

We passed Beverly Hills, our short-term home. Surprisingly, only a small distance from the beautiful neighborhood, the buildings below us changed into messy structures again. You could easily tell where the rich people had stopped building their rich people homes, because that's exactly where the roads began to fall into disrepair, and the trash began to be piled higher in the alleys, and the dogs appeared to run free from one lot to the next. Everything stank of rot.

Thad found the rooftop he was looking for—long and flat above an auto garage. This building was not much taller than the bar we'd left, surrounded by others in similar concrete construction. Wind rustled black tarps and broken crates that polluted the roof. I could hear multiple pounding subwoofers below, warring each other to dominate the beat.

Thad hopped onto the wall with his back against the bricks of the corner pillar and his shoes on the concrete edge in front of him. I wasn't surprised by the lack of concern on his face for the edge, even as the sounds of the cars in the nighttime traffic rumbled below us.

I walked to the edge and peered over, using it as a distraction for my aimless gaze, trying not to look at Thad. Multicolored lights laced the street below us like an array of cheap carnival games. Buildings blocked most of the view but the little I could see was magnificent enough. Los Angeles signs sparkled like purple and green gems, reflecting into the faces of the people and the cars going about their frivolous and self-indulgent tasks. On the surface, everything glittered in LA. Even when I stole a glance at Thad, I could see the city continuing on the other way—ever sparkling, ever alive.

There were high towers in the distance, pinnacles of construction with so many offices and businesses housed within that the radiance of the windows were like tiny cubes of light. But those were far from us. In contrast, the buildings on the streets below were littered with pawn shops made of wind-worn bricks, nightclubs with flashing lights and provocative window signs. Patrons wandered in and out, getting into cars and swerving onto the road, three drunken girls leaving in a limousine. Their clothes sparkled vibrantly and their fake laughs rose to the sky. They were counterfeit diamonds: beautiful outside, repulsive within.

"I bet this would make for a lot of good pictures," Thad said.

Pictures. I hadn't snapped a picture in what felt like decades. All of my stuff was destroyed now. But that couldn't stifle the urge that managed to crawl from under the ashes in my heart. *Taking pictures always makes you feel better, Michael.*

It just wouldn't feel the same now, though. My Great Work was gone. A part of me had died with it.

"I already have loads," I replied emptily.

"You could take more," Thad said.

"Where would I put them?"

"Well I don't know," he said, eyebrows furrowing. "Look, I'm trying to make you feel better but you're really trashing it all."

I almost reared up in anger again but chose to glare over the edge instead. After all, I was the one who'd just lost everything. Who was he to tell me that I shouldn't feel this bad?

A girl in a black dress caught my attention, stumbling between her friends drunkenly and shouting indecipherable nonsense into the night. She and her posse were migrating from one nightclub to another next door, obviously not satisfied by their levels of intoxication yet. *Ugh.* That type of shallow pointlessness was exactly what I loathed in the normal people who surrounded me at school. Another reason I never fit in with them.

"It's weird how those people have no idea," Thad said.

He'd followed my gaze down. Confusion was etched on his face. He studied the people further, almost in the grief of jealousy—the way a lepidopterist might study a butterfly and yearn to be as beautiful.

"I mean," he went on, "how can we be up here flying around and they're just down on the ground living their lives? Why were we picked? Why are we sacrificing all this when they don't even seem to care?"

I didn't respond. What had been such a fine canvas was now a melancholy portrait of the city below. He was right. Why was this our duty? We were only seventeen.

Thad shook his head, gaze following the people as they disappeared. He looked more worn than before, the façade to keep Callista and I in some semblance of order now removed. He wasn't even studying the people anymore—he just stared down into nothing.

"I loved people too, before this," he said abruptly. "So I know how it feels to lose everything, Michael."

He didn't look at me as he said it. My hands froze against the flat top of the wall. He cleared his throat.

"I don't know if she's alive or dead," he continued. "They just took her."

He shielded his face from me by looking at the street, probably not wanting me to read the anguish in his eyes. At first he hesitated, then his fingers slid away and pulled out the shiny skeleton pocket watch. He clicked the watch open out of habit and glanced at the time, before he snapped it closed again and hid it in the fold of his hands.

"Her?" I pressed. He nodded slowly.

"Yeah," was all I could get out of him at first. There were volumes of stories behind that single word just itching to be free. Thad was doing his best to keep the covers closed. In the end though, he sighed.

"It's a funny story how we met actually," he said. "See, my uncle is kind of a bum. He lives in this old singlewide trailer in Washington and drinks most of the day, so I'm the one who has to run out and get jobs if I want food to eat that's not like…microwave macaroni. Or sardines. I got to be a waiter, so I'd take all the money I made and put some of it to pay for my truck, and some of it for gas, and the rest I'd either save or buy food at the Walmart."

He couldn't manage a grin, but his lips turned slightly upward at the memory. "I liked the frozen stuff because it could sit in the freezer all month and I wouldn't need to waste time going to the store every week. So I'd pile things into my basket and go check out. That's where I met Sophia."

Thad said her name sweetly, like the way a composer might speak of his most enthralling composition. He shifted one of his legs on the ledge.

"She was the checkout girl," he went on. "I was piling all my frozen pizzas and frozen noodles and frozen lasagna on the belt. She looked at me weirdly and said something like, 'Should I be worried that you're feeding an Italian army at your house?' I laughed like a crazy person."

He finally smiled at that part, though he had to lift a hand to wipe away a tear.

"So that was our thing," he said. "Every month I'd go in to the store, buy a bunch of frozen food, and she'd make fun of it. If I bought frozen enchiladas or burritos, I was hiding the Mexican army. If I got rice she said the Asians were coming. I started doing it on purpose, and then I started going back more than once a week because it started to get funny."

Thad shrugged. "But then they started to cut some of the checkout jobs. Sophia lost hers. So the last time I was there, she told me that she had to start working at another grocery store way down the road. She didn't think she'd see me anymore."

He crossed his arms. "I didn't think so either. And I felt silly to be sad about it. But the next week, when I went to go get food, you know what I did? I drove all the way across the whole town to go shop at her new store and check out in her line again. It was like a habit. I couldn't help myself."

"I told her it'd be much less of a drive if we met somewhere in the middle. So the next day we did, and that was our first date."

His voice had gone warm with the recollection. With some hesitation, he lifted the skeleton watch between us.

"Neither of us wanted to go home," he said. "So to get out of the rain we went in to this old shop. Sophia had this grand idea for us to pick cheap things out for each other and then use them as surprises at the end of the day. I was nervous so I got her something boring, some pin-thing for her hair. But I think she already knew me well. She got me this watch. It was crazy and I loved it, because you know me—always checking the time, and this just made it more fun."

He brushed his fingers through the sides of his hair tensely.

"That was six months ago," he said. "We've seen each other every day after that except three…"

His voice trailed away. "Well, now that count's off, since they took her."

He didn't want to go in to this part of the story; his desperation to stay afloat had turned into an anxious flailing. But he had to go on.

"It was 4:56 PM on March 15th," he said. "We were walking in one of the parks near the trailer. I'd just checked my watch and told her how all the numbers were consecutive. Then all of a sudden, there was this—" he stopped, then shook his head. "I don't need to go into it. But I was knocked out, and when I woke up, I was in the white room."

Each word was a heavy block of stone he had to heave out of himself.

"Maybe it was a different white room from yours," he said. "Maybe there are a dozen white rooms all over the place. I don't know. But they had Sophia there too, and I just barely remember seeing them drag her out the door screaming for me before I was dozing off again with a needle in my arm."

His jaw clenched. "I haven't seen her since."

He never wept. Somehow, in all the time that he'd been a prisoner, Thad had managed to build such a mental fortress that not even recalling the girl he loved was enough to break through. It could have been his resolve to find her, the uneasy platform on which he stood to keep telling himself that she was alive, when both of us knew she probably wasn't. The Guardians didn't have any reason to keep her.

It left us in a heavy gloom. I breathed slowly, trying not to let the torment carry me away.

He finally lifted himself up so that his gaze could meet my eyes—his were bloodshot and filled with haunting memories. The city reflecting in them looked like a desolate wasteland.

"I lost Sophia for you," he said bluntly. "No...not for you. *Because* of you. So did Callista with her family. You are important enough for all this, and *I* know that, but I don't think you can see how many things people have sacrificed to give you a chance at finishing what you started when you were Daniel. You're that significant, Michael."

He nodded at me. "Who you are now is always more important than who you were before. And if you can't bring yourself to do it because it's right, then do it for the ones who care about you."

In so few words, Thad had summed up the invisible foe that I had been fighting: *myself*. Because now, I wasn't *just* myself. I wasn't just Michael Asher who could go on taking clients and driving nice cars and sneaking out and back in at night. Father Lonnie had been speared on a church. Callista's family had been murdered. Anon still risked himself just to help me. How many others did I not even know about who were, at that very moment, praying secretly that I would somehow survive? Everyone that Callista, Thad, and I loved had already placed his or her lives as collateral for my victory. The debt was now mine to bear.

All along, I'd known what I needed to do, and yet I'd tried to deny it. If I let the Guardians continue, I knew how this would end—I'd already predicted it in another life. I *had* to take the Guardians' power.

Thad held my gaze for a few seconds and then looked back to the street. The nameless people had vanished, music still pumping through the walls but the streets momentarily emptied. I replayed the dreams like movies in the back of my head, retracing every step from end to beginning. Thad and Callista had run to save me in the second life, even jumping in front of me to block the bullet. And in the first, they had hurried with me up the winding stairs, knowing full well that there was no escape, that the moment we dashed out into the night we would be caught and killed. They'd done it for me.

"Underground," I gasped suddenly.

Thad looked up at me. "What?"

All at once, something from the dream that had been pushed to the back of my subconscious leapt into the forefront. It was so obvious that it was nearly blinding.

How could I have missed that?

"What did you say?" Thad demanded, rising up as he looked at my stricken face.

"M-my dream," I managed to force out. "The first one, from my first life when I hid the Blade. There were stairs. You and Callista and me were running up *stairs* from a basement."

Thad comprehended what this meant at the same time I did.

"The Blade is *under* the restaurant!" he realized.

20

DÉJÀ VU

I whipped my phone out of my pocket immediately. Not even a genius would claim wide enough knowledge of random trivia to match the Internet. It only took a few searches to find the answer we were looking for.

"The restaurant is built on the church's foundation," Thad told Callista, after a whirlwind of a flight back to the cliff. She stood with arms crossed, dubiously looking from his face to mine.

"There's a basement under it," Thad insisted, like she hadn't heard him. "Somewhere in that basement is a door that nobody knows about."

She still didn't look convinced. I held my phone out so she could see what was on the screen: a history of the restaurant on its website, detailing how the original owner Gustav Fabolli had bought the worthless spot from the Catholic Church and turned it into a family business.

"It's from the dream," I said. "In the first one, we were running up stairs behind a hidden door. So if nobody knew it was there, then nobody's moved it, and the Blade is still inside."

"So there's some secret door under the Italian restaurant?" Callista repeated. I caught the skepticism in her voice instantly. I'd thought that Callista would feel the same rush that Thad and I had, and her disinterest was throwing a damper on our discovery.

She twisted her face up and looked to Thad. "I thought we decided to hide for a while."

Thad was taken aback too. He blinked a few times, unable to gather his words.

"Yes..." he said slowly. "But things have changed."

"You know what this means, right?" I insisted to her. "Wyck *thinks* the Blade is somewhere up north. But it's not. So while he's traveling all the way up there, we have a chance to get it. Then they won't touch us. What's the one thing they're afraid of more than anything?"

Being human: I knew that for certain. I'd already seen that on their faces, their utter disgust for the creatures they deemed so inferior. Fear of death drove them to insane lengths.

She was right, though. The Blade was why I'd been killed in the first place. But what was I supposed to do? Run off and hide even though I was so certain the Blade was there? I might have done that a while ago. It was different now.

Callista appeared to be thinking the same, debating it inside though still not looking convinced. She'd changed too. Maybe it was because of my recklessness. She didn't want to fight now. She wanted to retreat and regroup in a safe place.

"Let's try," I insisted. "Just one more time. And if it's not there, we'll go east and disappear. I just can't leave without taking this one chance."

That decided it for her. Maybe the renewed determination showed in my gaze. Her shoulders fell as she uncrossed her arms. Thad and I turned, and with running bounds, we flew off the cliff like a small formation of birds, heading in the direction of Los Angeles.

*   *   *

The moon was masked behind heavy clouds, throwing the city into an even darker gloom than usual. Scattered cars and people continued on their duties, unperturbed by the time. It was as if Los Angeles simply refused to bind its life to the hours of day, lights in the tall skyscrapers still burning for late-night workers and the windows of cheap fast food restaurants still alit.

Luckily, though, the darkness managed to conceal us when we landed in a deserted alleyway. And just in time too, as a group of rowdy pedestrians walked by the opening. We startled them and they scraped to a stop—a group of rough teenage boys in baggy clothes—but when Thad stood up to his full height, they continued on in a hurry.

"You're good at scaring people," I murmured to Thad. "I could use you, if…you know, I ever go back to taking clients."

"How so?" Thad asked, as we started to walk toward the end of the alley, wind whistling around the corner.

"I think I caught four Glimpses when you stood up and puffed yourself out like that," I told him. "Those guys thought about robbing us for a second, then you changed their minds."

Thad gave a tiny chuckle. Callista shook her head though she was obviously entertained. Our banter lightened the air and made my steps stronger.

We turned the corner and continued along our quiet path on the sidewalk. Tall lamps lined the street and continued so far that they only disappeared when the hill blocked them from view. Only one car drove far off in the distance, and even though I studied the windows of the buildings around us, each step only confirmed to me that nobody was watching. I saw Fabolli's from a block away.

Callista fell beside me as we walked, stony and determined. I knew she didn't like this idea, especially now that we were out in the open for these few minutes. She kept studying the windows and dark spaces, hands swinging tensely and always ready to produce her claws the moment she might need them.

"We're alright," I assured her. She nodded.

"If it's there, then we're safe," I said. "We'll have an upper hand. It'll throw them off."

"One bullet and you're dead," she reminded me. "You don't think they'll sniper you out? Having that Blade just makes you more of a target than before."

"And it makes them far more scared than ever," I replied. She pressed her lips together, choosing not to continue. We crossed the street, our steps the only sound besides the whistle of the crossing sign and the fizzle of a neon light. The green shutters on the restaurant's windows were now nearly invisible in the shadow of its porch overhang.

I led them around to the back. Breaking in to buildings was not my specialty, but I'd been forced to do it once or twice when clients had conveniently "forgotten the keys". Picking a lock brought my heaviest surcharge because it carried such a high risk of prosecution. Also, when chasing down cheating lovers, sometimes picking a locked door revealed sights I never wanted to see—I kept the charge high in case I'd need therapy one day.

As I expected, there was a door tucked away in an alley behind the restaurant. I didn't have my picklock set. It didn't really matter though. A quickly lifted hand and the slashing of five blades all at once took care of both the lock and the handle. The noise sounded like swords grinding against each other—or on this side of town, more likely a drunk scraping the side of his car against a wall he'd swerved too close to. When the employees arrived the next day, they'd likely think an animal had mauled their door.

I grinned and shoved what remained of the door open with my shoulder. There was no alarm. That was one of many mistakes the owners of this shop had made. I should have offered security consultations too.

The thrill of my easy entrance pushed me faster, even allowing some excitement to seep through. With cautious steps, we entered in to the kitchen: long countertops sitting above cheap floors, spatulas and utensils and knives hanging in rows against the wall. I couldn't see much more than a flicker from a pilot light inside an oven, the lights from a refrigerator door, the red glow of a digital clock on the wall. Everything was heavily noiseless.

I held my hands out to avoid bumping the edge of something. I heard Thad fiddling with his flashlight and he finally got it on, but the beam was so weak that it would only shine a few feet around our shoes.

"Sorry guys," he apologized. He took the lead though, sweeping the ground in front of us with the flashlight. The light gleamed against the bottoms of hanging pots like they were misted mirrors, onto the metal of the industrial freezers and sinks, across the knives and cleavers washed and ready for the next day's business. If we were lucky, we wouldn't even need to leave this room. If there was a basement, surely the door would have been designed to sit in here.

Unfortunately, though Thad swept the walls with light on all sides, there were no doorways other than the one we'd passed through and the exit to the dining area. So Thad continued ahead and pushed the flapping doors apart with his side.

When we stepped through and into the nearly pitch-black hallway, suddenly my outstretched hand was caught by another. I jumped, but recognized the soft fingers instantly: Callista's. She clutched mine, riveted in terror and trembling. Her fear had been disguised by the inky darkness that she was so afraid of.

It distracted me immediately. My mind traitorously started to debate what her hand in mine meant. Was she actually trying to hate me less? We walked like this behind Thad, searching the walls for a door.

The blinds on the front of the restaurant were closed so the windows provided only minimal light. Cleaned booths and tables were lined up in neat rows; Thad's light skimmed over them, careful to avoid the windows and door. He let the beam go up the wall, across the old jukebox, around the cashier's computer.

We all spotted it at the same time: a wide-open frame with no door beside the counter, obviously leading down because of the sloped roof beyond. We darted toward it until we'd all gathered in front of the entrance.

"There's our basement," Thad said. His light revealed a set of wooden stairs. He didn't wait for us to reply before heading down.

The steps creaked unsteadily beneath our feet. At the bottom lay a giant room with green carpet, and wooden paneling on the walls littered by outdated neon signs and old license plates. Four pool tables sat in a neat row in the center, with chairs hijacked from the upstairs tables in disorder around the games. A row of pool sticks hung on the wall beside a change machine. The ceiling was so low that it was only a few inches above Thad's head. *A game room.*

I was about to say something snarky, but was cut short when Thad's flashlight shone onto the corner of the room. All of a sudden, I was hit with a strange feeling of déjà vu so strong that it caused me to turn and look back up the stairs, trying to shake off the momentary dizziness.

"This is definitely the right place," I spluttered. Thad shone the flashlight at me.

"I *remember* this," I went on. "It wasn't this place, but looking up that stairway, the flat roof. It's weird. Claustrophobic."

"Familiar?" Thad pressed. I nodded.

"Definitely," I replied. He was relieved.

"Then we're in the right spot," he said. "But unless the Blade is a pool stick, we're still looking for another door, right?"

I nodded, drawing away from them but finding that Callista wouldn't release my hand. So I pulled her along with me, hoping that my palms wouldn't sweat into hers as I nervously studied the walls, trying to recall my dream. Obviously, this basement was part of the heavy foundation from the original church. It hadn't changed at all since my first life, except for the new walls and the tables. If I was only to line this up with what I remembered from my dream...

It clicked like a peg sliding into a slot. When I stood in the far corner of the room, suddenly it was like I was back in my dream again. The familiar urge returned: the push to run away, to hurry up the steps and outside, even though I could see that there was now a restaurant beyond the opening.

"Over here!" I whispered, running my free hand along the wall. Finally Callista let me go so that she could press her palms against the walls too. The wood paneling fought to throw me off so I had to imagine it wasn't there.

"That spot?" Callista checked. I nodded, then dove out of the way as her fists suddenly came forward. With sharp, commanding jabs, her silver hands pounded the wood like eggshells in two strokes. Thad and I jumped forward to peel the wrecked panels off, revealing that behind it was a wall of solid white stone.

Instantly, the newly revealed walls fell into place in my memories. In another life, I'd pressed against this wall and sealed a doorway behind it. I ran my fingers across the flat panel instinctively, feeling the cold rock, discovering the thinnest of seams too small for even a fingernail. As the memories of the dream came back, a lump formed in my throat. I knew that if I tore all those hideous panels off the walls and threw the games upstairs, then this room would be the exact same as I had left it minutes before I'd died the first time.

We were so close to finding the Blade that when I whirled around to look at the others, I saw that their faces had matching expressions of anticipation.

"There's no hinge or anything," Thad observed.

"If I remember correctly," I said, "the whole thing kinda just sealed into the wall. I don't think we're going to get it open in a normal way again."

Thad shrugged. "Not like that's ever stopped us before."

Callista nodded with a knowing grin. Seeing her face brighten gave me the confidence I needed. So with renewed power inside, I spun back to the wall, claws out. I wasn't sure how much strength those blades could take before they'd crack off. They'd been rather strong against everything they'd faced before. No time for hesitation.

I jabbed my fist forward. Their bladed tips slammed into the wall so heavily that I was pushed backwards, shoes sliding. They'd broken deep chips off, though, so that was encouraging. I shook my head. This was going to take some extra work.

I started again, this time with legs spread to support myself. I'd slam with the scale-covered back of my hands and then dig at the cracks with my blades, sending slivers of rock and whirling streams of dust flying through the air. I had to close my eyes as the stones darted at me, my blades hitting like picks then slashing like saws, grating the stones down with such a horrible noise I feared someone outside would surely hear.

But no one came, so I continued to attack. It was working. I beat it again and again, and before I realized it, I was hitting the wall with angry, vengeful growls, striking it as if the stone was Wyck standing before me. It was a thousand screams of pent up anger let out soundlessly, my voice replaced by the cries of the wall as I tore it to bits.

The smooth outer surface was soon wrecked and slowly began to thin out and turn gray. Suddenly, at the very center I saw one of my blades break a tiny hole through. I felt a spray of cold air hit my face.

I battered the wall with even more passion. In seconds, the center of it crumbled, and all at once there was an opening covered in falling dust and debris. I beat it again and again, and the wall crumbled even further.

I felt a hand on my shoulder reaching to stop me and all of a sudden I was back from my frenzy. I coughed when I breathed in too quickly. Thad motioned for me to lift the edge of my shirt to my mouth.

The dust was thick and refused to settle easily, and even Thad's flashlight wouldn't cut through it. But sure enough, I saw that there was now a hole in the wall, and beyond it on the ground, a wide metal plate. It was a single stair, and as the dust fell to the ground, I was able to see that others curved down behind it.

The circular stairway.

When I saw it, I drew in air too quickly again and fell into another fit of coughs. Thad patted me on the back as I doubled over.

"Should I run and get you water?" he offered. I shook my head and waved a hand at him. I wasn't going to let that stop me now. I knelt toward the opening I'd made so I could see through the hole better. I took the flashlight from Thad and shone the light down.

I couldn't see far around the corner. But when I turned the beam of the light downward, I saw through the large slits in the steps that they wound far out of my eyesight. I kicked the lower part of the wall, widening the hole and placing a foot through.

The others didn't seem as eager to step inside, so for a few moments I was entirely in the dark of the tunnel by myself. One of my hands rested on the cold stone, the other waving for them to follow me. Callista went first with widened eyes as she crawled through the jagged hole, and Thad went last.

"We're so close," I whispered to them, voice echoing like we were standing in a metal can. At first, none of us walked ahead, studying our new surroundings. The tunnel was no wider than a car, like a tall chimney vent from some underground base the military had forgotten about. When I shone the light up, the ceiling was just inches above our heads, and when I turned it down the middle, it wasn't bright enough to see the end.

I took up the lead. The steps were hollow and metallic, supported by heavy beams. The stairs were so tightly packed that their bottoms nearly touched our heads as we walked below them.

It was difficult to feel any eagerness when I was surrounded by tons of rock. Who knew how sturdily this place was constructed? After all these decades, maybe the walls had worn down, and if we only touched it in the wrong way, it would collapse and bury us alive. We were so far underground that nobody would hear us screaming. The tunnel would become one tall, triple-occupied coffin.

Step. Step. Step. The metal reverberated. *Step. Step.* I quickened my pace, feeling that the ground was coming up soon.

A few seconds later, I left the last step abruptly. The solid ground took me by surprise and I had to catch my balance. The flashlight spilled all over the room.

Where the stairs ended, a gray carpet began. The walls were so narrow that I couldn't have stretched my elbows out. They were lined with bookshelves going as high as the ceiling. Glass panels in front of the shelves guarded what appeared to be an assortment of old tattered books and bound up stacks of paper, mostly eaten by age and appearing too weak to touch without turning to dust. The hall ran at least ten steps like this until the next opening. I shone the light into the shelves curiously, wondering if the Blade was anywhere in them. What was I even looking for, exactly? How would I have hid it in my first life?

I didn't think it was there, and by that time I was content with trusting my instincts. So we continued to the end, where the room opened up one final time.

The crypt was circular with a roof that domed over our heads. It was about as large as my living room, the walls made of rough, undecorated stone that was chipped and cracked in many places, lines running through it like the marks of marble. The space was incredibly empty. The only thing inside was a rectangular pillar in the center that looked like it had once held a coffin.

Something was on the pillar, but it wasn't a casket. It was a rectangular box with a design on its top so intricate I couldn't help but recognize it right away. In the midst of the swirling artwork and the sweeps of expertly molded metal were two orb-like stalks protruding from the center of the box. Just like the box in the bank.

No less than a perfect place to secure the Blade.

We all laid eyes on the box at once, and suddenly the room became a rush to see who would reach it first. Thad managed to grab it, heaving its bulk up into his arms and trying to open it with his bare hands. I stopped him quickly.

"Let an expert do it," I told him with a grin. He dropped it into my hands and I sat on the low stone pillar, turning the box so its eyes would face me when they opened. Thad pointed the light straight down as I moved my fingers along the sides of the box, clicking down the levers just as I'd done before.

I'd moved two of them, when suddenly there was a noise.

All three of our heads shot up to look toward the source. It'd been so soft that if they hadn't reacted at the same time, I'd have thought it was only my imagination. I'd heard a tiny, hollow clang, like a pencil being dropped on a metal desk. But in the silence that was the crypt, even that sound felt decibels louder.

"What time does the place open?" I whispered to Thad. He'd darted the beam of his flashlight down instinctively, covering it with his palm. I felt Callista's fingers tighten on my shoulder.

"Not until ten," Thad replied. "I checked. They do lunch and dinner."

We sat in a hush, no one moving, all of us hardly daring to breath. The only light in the room now came from Thad's red, glowing hand that hid the flashlight. We listened. My fingers still hovered over the third lever.

Nothing.

"The wall," I thought aloud. "One of the chips fell off onto the stairs."

They let out the air they'd been holding. Thad uncovered the light again, Callista shaking her head and grinning at how ridiculously skittish we were. They leaned over me as I worked the lid like a master, finding and clicking the next lever.

As I did, the tiny gears started to whirr, the two pieces over the eyes parting. Callista stood beside me enraptured, her hand on my shoulder to support herself as she leaned over for a better look.

The gears continued to turn on their own unhurried course, winding until the metal eyelids stopped. Eerily, there were now four pairs of eyes in the room. The ones set into the box hovered in the same clear liquid as I'd seen before. Except these eyes were bright and brown, almost the color of white oak wood. Their pupils were wide as if already detecting that it was dark in the room, or maybe because somehow after all these years they recognized me.

A scrape.

I jumped, all three of our heads going up again. Had that been another sound?

Thad extinguished his light yet again. What was making that noise? It was like we were in a cave, all senses heightened by the silence. If a mouse had ventured down that far and bit into a kernel of corn, the noise might have made us jump.

"I heard it," Callista confirmed shakily.

"Was it another rock?" Thad whispered. I clutched the box close in my arms. Was that faraway sound the creak of a shoe or just my imagination playing with the emptiness?

"Silent alarm?" I said. I wanted to see if Thad was shaking his head but I couldn't see him at all. We sat like statues, waiting, letting it sink in just how cornered we were if...

Psss.

It came from the doorway: a tiny hiss like a snake.

Then a flash of light burst so powerful that all of us lifted our arms to cover our faces. The room that had been black was immediately white for half of a second, like a camera bulb going off across the room.

It disappeared as quickly as it had exploded.

A fizzle of smoke.

Another pop.

Another flash.

This time, I saw everything. In the doorway were the figures of three people, two of them wearing police armor with long lenses on their goggles—*night vision*. The man in the center was Wyck. In his hand was a long tube that continued to explode with light like a rock concert, popping like guns and spraying smoke all over the room. He threw it at us, and like a stop-motion movie, I saw the flare cutting through the distance.

They'd found us!

The flare went on and I found myself running, seeing Thad and Callista dive across the room to escape the two men that came after them. Then the room went black and I shouted for them, voice echoing as I struggled to find where the door was, where it was safe to stand, where the arms that clamped over me were coming from.

The room went white again.

Black again.

I kicked and yelled and fought, getting free only to be thrown into the wall with a heavy body leaning against me. The case fell from my hands as the light flashed again.

No, no, no. Not now! How did they find us?

The room went black. I heard Wyck shout an order, a scrape as the Blade's case was picked up off the ground.

White. Callista screamed for Thad and I screamed for Callista, a flying punch from Thad knocking one of the men to the floor as others stormed in, ordering us to the ground. The sounds of their megaphones burned my ears in the cramped space.

Black. My fist threw the heavy man off me and I heard his back hit the opposite wall.

White. The lights shone off claws that now filled the room. Wyck still had his claws hidden but now he was holding the Blade case in his arms, grinning as he stared across the room from me.

The officers slammed in to Callista and Thad, who were trying to get around the masked night-vision men who'd cornered them. *Get out. Run, both of you!*

Black. There were shouts and grunts of pain. My claws sliced ahead by instinct and I heard them slash across something sickeningly, the front of my clothes sprayed with a warm liquid.

White. I saw the door. Wyck had his back to me, already leaving. Callista and Thad beat the men away.

Black. I made a run for it.

The rapidly pulsating light and the smoke clouded my vision. The noise deafened me. But I was able to run, to chase after Wyck. I heard the guards shouting after me, reaching to grab me by the leg, so I pushed them aside as I stumbled into the hall.

"Go!" I heard Thad shout, pushing me ahead. I needed the Blade! Where was Wyck?

Thad pushed me harder so I obeyed, with him and Callista right behind me. I heard one of the officers shouting for others in the hall to grab us but I leapt over their heads, throwing myself into the air and crashing against the glass of the bookshelves. I heard things clattering, my feet catching faces as I went over them, then I was on the stairs and running, running, *running.*

"Hurry!" I shouted to Callista and Thad, not able to waste a second to look back. I heard the men behind us, the same who'd been so stealthy now caring nothing for how much noise their boots made on each step. I was going so fast that I knew any second I would trip, my foot would catch the end of one of the stairs and then they'd have me. But somehow I managed to keep going, always staying three steps ahead of our pursuers.

I could see the top! The gray glow of morning spread down through the basement and through our hole, so dim that if I hadn't been underground I wouldn't have been able to notice it. The clanging behind me continued, the yelling, the pops and flashes…

I dove through the rocky opening in the wall, rolling across the stones and scraping my arms and cheek. I couldn't stop, scrambling up the steps, around the counter and back into the kitchen now lit by the morning. *The door was still open…*

I skidded through and suddenly I was in the air. The slam of clear, smokeless sky was the greatest relief, clearing my senses, giving me the strength to fly even faster. The ground was already disappearing and the dark clouds were within reach.

Suddenly, I was hit with a terrifying awareness. *Where was Callista? And Thad?*

Like a freight train driving over me, I realized that they weren't with me anymore. I nearly stopped, but my flight continued on its own, pulling me higher into the sky. Where were they? Hadn't they been right behind me seconds ago?

Maybe they'd escaped through the other door? Or they'd gone another way? I searched the sky to see if they'd scrambled off to hide. I was already so far from the restaurant that I couldn't even see it. Everything had become a mess of buildings and shadows from the sliver of dawn that'd appeared. Cars were out in droves now, drowsy people walking with coffees in their hands and breakfast drive-thru's filling up.

I hovered in place, feet dangling beneath me, eyes searching wildly for any sign of the others. It was hard to see with the fog. No! I couldn't have left them behind!

Suddenly, I was slammed into from the side.

Like a missile coming out of nowhere, someone had flown out of the cloud and rammed into me, sending me into a spiral. I struggled to regain my balance, twisting only for me to be struck by my attacker again from the other side. I couldn't find which way was up and went plummeting toward the earth.

21

DESOLATION

I fell like the shattered pieces of a clay target. The treetops neared, spinning in circles as I whirled uncontrollably. I tried in vain to catch the air, to bring myself up as the gray concrete rushed to meet my face.

Arms grabbed me around my middle, slamming with me into the ground and rolling in a bout of grass. The momentum carried us until we rammed into the side of a tree and stopped abruptly.

I sprawled beside it to catch my breath, dizzily trying to roll over. I shook my head, clearing my vision of the haze, looking up to find that I was in the middle of a large park. Trees that surrounded the concrete path blocked me from view of the cars I could hear already racing nearby to go about their business, drivers oblivious to my latest almost demise. Sensing danger was near, I scrambling to my feet—only to have the back of my shirt grabbed and my body slung against the tree.

"Don't run!" came a sudden, mechanical hiss. I spun, ready to fight, but a hand hit my side, grabbing for something in my pocket, taking it before I could react.

I leapt away as my attacker threw whatever he'd grabbed onto the concrete beside us. With his back to me, he began stabbing at the device with his foot. Before I knew what was happening, his boot had already cracked the screen of my cell phone. The next stab split it into crumbled fragments.

"Hey!" I shouted. He struck it again, glass and plastic going everywhere. My mouth hung open for a moment but then I realized he wasn't even watching me anymore. Let him keep the stupid phone.

"You...are...an...*idiot*!" the mechanical voice continued before I could run, the boot stabbing my phone with each word. Finally, satisfied by the dusty pile that remained, the man spun back to me.

He wasn't any of the people I'd expected, the claws that I'd lifted to slice him hesitated. He was dressed in a sweeping black coat much too heavy for the sun of California, the cloth gathered around his legs and the collar turned up over his neck. He wore gloves on his hands. His face was like a block of stone, middle-aged and entirely hairless.

But that was only for a second. Before my eyes, the face of the bald man suddenly changed. Like they'd turned to putty, his cheeks sank in, the bones shifted out, his eyes became thinner, and the irises faded from brown to gray. Black hair grew from his head like grass, a covering of stubble on his chin.

I wanted to run.

"Don't you dare, Mr. Asher," the voice warned from the mouth of the new man. The sound was the same as before: deep and processed, like a computer was speaking the words with incorrect pitches and accents.

"You're a master of idiocy," the voice proclaimed. "It's a wonder you live an entire day without supervision."

He waved his hand at my destroyed phone. "Did you even think *once* that maybe you should get rid of your phone? That maybe they'd had time to tinker with it while you were strapped down and immobile in the interrogation room?"

I was at a loss for words. The man was furious and yet wasn't making any move to attack. I drew back a small step.

"How do you think they've been following you, Mr. Asher?" he continued his tirade. "How'd they know you went to that tunnel? Because of your damned phone. Because you're a damned idiot."

He kicked the shards and sent pieces skittering down the concrete walk. It hit me all at once: somehow, Wyck had followed me by using my phone as a tracking device.

240

"W——who are you…?" I demanded with an unintentional stammer, still ready to fight if I needed. I could feel the blood going cold in the ends of my fingers as I realized that I'd led Wyck right to us without even knowing—and according to who?

The man spun back to face me. He had a new face again. Now, his skin was wrinkled, his eyes and hair a matching gray. He looked like one of the gentle old men I'd sometimes see wandering in the park and feeding the ducks, if not for the fiery rage in his eyes.

"Who do you think I am?" he spat. "Who else would risk everything to save you once again when you've just gone and blundered it all up?"

He scoffed distastefully at me. "Your brazen disregard for all the sacrifices made for you only proves you are not prepared for a part in restoring the Grand Design."

When he said that, I knew exactly who he was.

"Anon!" I gasped, but he sliced a hand through the air to silence me. I was left with my mouth open, fingers that had been fists loosening, feeling my face go pale.

As if to prove just how anonymous he still remained, his face had continued to change as we spoke. He was old then he was young again, then in the seconds of dumbfounded silence, I watched his skin sink into bags and hang off flabby cheeks. No matter how many new people he became or how many times the irises changed colors, his eyes continued to glare at me with distaste. I noticed that around his neck, nearly hidden by the collar of his jacket, was a black circle, almost like a thin, mechanical scarf—some device of Guardian technology, no doubt.

"I'm sorry," I said, feeling wretched inside. Even the ever-changing disguises could not mask the urgency and importance I felt radiating from this man.

He showed me no sympathy. He shook his head sharply, changing form again, growing hair that was parted over his forehead.

"Do you have any idea how much you've ruined?" he went on. "Searching the Internet on a phone they already knew was yours? Carrying it with you everywhere you went, so they could trace your exact location any second of the day or night?"

"I—I thought I'd led Wyck to go north…"

Anon would hear none of it.

241

"Because of you, they now have the Blade," he said. "They'll do anything to get you to open the case. They'll pry bits of your skin away piece by piece until you can't tell your screams from the sounds of their tools. They'll get you to *open that case*."

He threw both of his hands apart in exasperation. "But I've been the stupid one. I'm to blame for helping you, when I should have let you die long ago when you first started doing things wrong."

All of his horrible words were bullets. It was all sinking in at once what had just transpired. How could I have been so stupid?! I hadn't even taken a second to think of all these things that now looked so obvious, and with every word Anon's rasping voice said, I only felt all the more dejected, all the more a failure.

And Callista and Thad…were they still left behind? Were they even still alive?

"I…tried," I said, voice cracking. I was not going to tear up. I was not going to let Anon see me even weaker than he already thought I was. Because I *had* tried. I *had* put everything I could into getting the Blade, to finishing what I hadn't managed to do two lives ago. I'd lost everything for this stupid plan, and yet Anon, in all his forms, only looked at me like I was the worst disappointment of a person he'd ever met.

"When has trying ever been good enough for you, Mr. Asher?" he said. "You are not a try-er. You make things happen. You live when you should die and you fight when you should give up. So don't tell me that you '*tried*'."

He shook his head again. "I should blame myself. Perhaps I haven't instilled in you how important you are. Perhaps you still have no idea that the entire world rests on your shoulders."

His voice was getting lower, shoulders falling in resignation. I didn't want to see him giving up like that because it meant that he was giving up on me. But what could I say in my defense? He had a reply for everything.

"What do I do?" I asked him.

"Nothing," he said. "You do nothing."

"But what about Callista and Thad?" I said. "And the Blade?"

"The Guardians have it now," he replied. "There's nothing you can do."

He shoved his gloved hands into his pockets. "It's over, Mr. Asher. It's time for you to let this go."

"But *where* do I go?" I couldn't get my voice much higher than a whisper. What little I'd built up from the ashes of my lost life was now crashing around me again, like it'd been made of sand all along. I didn't have anywhere to run even if I wanted to.

"It doesn't matter," Anon said, now with pale, bald skin again. "I can't risk helping you anymore."

He gave the already-destroyed phone a final crunch under his boot. "They won't find you for a while. Stay away from phones and don't check your email. Use the cash."

As he said this, he was already starting to turn away from me. But his departure was all too soon. I still had no answers, no direction.

"I—I can't do anything?" I said, desperate to hear *something* from him. If he was giving up on me, I knew I didn't have any hope. I was like a ship approaching a harbor without a lighthouse, a pilot with no ground control.

He shrugged with a reluctant surrender.

"You can die," he said, empty of any malice but still edged with ice. It was spoken just as simply as he might have told me the time.

"Come back in seventeen years," he told me. "You'll have a better chance then. I'll be waiting."

And with that, Anon pushed from the ground with the tips of his shoes and was carried over the trees.

He disappeared from view. I was left in the hush of the park. Empty. *Alone.*

*   *   *

I found a park bench, and sat.

Early morning walkers strolled by, but didn't acknowledge me.

Pigeons fluttered down to the grass around my feet as if I wasn't even there.

I was a statue bent over with my head resting in my palm, as the sun rose like a golden coin and threw my ever-shrinking shadow across the dewy grass.

A fountain trickled nearby, water splashing in a static noise.

A driver slammed on the brakes, tires squealing against pavement.

I lifted my hand to stare at it. *What have I become?* I thought.

With no one around—not that I truly cared anymore—I allowed my scales to slide out from under my skin, each poking forth slowly before overlapping with those beneath. They were like tiny panels, mirroring slightly so that I could see the misty reflection of my face, as if my hand was a shattered mirror. Would seeing those scales enmeshed with my own skin ever become natural? Would they ever allow me to go back to just being Michael Asher again?

My eyes shifted and I saw the only answer I needed in the irremovable silver ring around my finger. Even the birthmark I'd had all my life had been blotted away by a new one.

Such a fitting metaphor for who I was now. The old Michael had transformed. The snake had shed its skin for a new one.

But not entirely, I countered. Most of my real skin still remained just as most of my identity did. But I couldn't deny it: enough of me had changed. My old life had withered away and fallen off just as my birthmark had. I was bound like a slave to this ring: a slave to the silver. This was my reality now.

*   *   *

As time wore on and the brightness of day began to shine against my face, I managed to lift myself from the bench and take to the air again. I could have turned in any direction and it would have been just as good as any other, because there was no real destination anymore. I didn't have a family to rush and save. I didn't have a Blade to go hunting for, or a letter from Anon to track down, or anything left at all for that matter.

But habits had a strange way of working in me, so I chose to fly toward the cliff where our trio had taken refuge so many times. To my surprise, as I neared it, my eyes caught the form of someone who'd already gotten there before me. I saw her hair flying from the heavy wind. *Callista!* I swooped down and landed hard on my feet.

"You made it!" I gasped, dashing over to her in disbelief. She dropped the sleeping bag and ran for me too, standing on the ends of her toes so I could wrap my arms around her. I crushed her to me so tightly that she was lifted from her feet, and I didn't even try to hold back my tears of relief as they dried against the shoulder of her shirt.

"I thought for sure you were caught," I said, still not letting her free. It wasn't like I'd be able to, anyway—her arms were wrapped around my neck just as tightly.

"I knew you were alive or else I wouldn't be here," she said, voice muffled. But she was gasping small sounds of relief with tears at the same time. We both trembled, the terror of the ambush still racing through us. Her arms were scraped from the scuffle in the crypt, both of us covered with gashes that showed through lines of dried blood. But at least having her there made things a tiny bit better.

Something was missing, though. I let her slide down to her feet, holding her by the sides of her arms, glancing around the precipice in case I was mistaken.

"Thad?" I said, not wanting to hear the answer. I felt Callista's arms loosen.

"I—I saw him…taken away." She had to force herself to say it. I wanted to disbelieve her but a single look at her face told me how certain she was. Her eyes were bloodshot, cheeks red and lower lip shaking.

My hands dropped from her sides. *Not Thad.*

She looked like she wanted to say something else but instead she turned and went back to the work she'd been doing. Two of the black sleeping bags were sitting near the end of the cliff, and she seized one of them and ripped it apart, shaking the stuffing out over the edge before tossing the material away. She continued with this on the other, as I sank to lean against the rocky wall. Not Thad. We *needed* Thad. He should have been there trying to regroup us, trying to convince Callista and I that things weren't nearly as bad as they looked. How could he have been left behind? He was the strongest of all of us!

I guess I knew the answer to that. After all, he was Thad. He probably tried to take on our attackers at once so we could get away. It was just the type selfless thing Thad would do without hesitating.

Callista tossed the last sleeping bag over the edge, a strong wind sending the stuffing whirling like snow, the last of any evidence we'd been there. The air hit us in gusts, like a storm was approaching, sending waves through my hair as I sat in the corner. Callista walked over to join me and we pressed close beside each other.

When the quiet became too heavy, she slid her hand across the distance to touch mine. I grasped hers like it could keep me from being swept away. We became each other's anchor.

"What will they do to him?" I asked her.

"They'll want the box opened," she told me. "They'll do things to him until he tells them where you are."

I looked down, feeling my heart sink.

"If he dies before I do," I asked, "what happens?"

Silence. Her breathing was sporadic, heavy, labored.

"He'll be gone," she said. "If one of your Chosens dies before you, they don't come back the next time. Wyck made sure we knew...one of us was always dispensable."

Her hand quivered in mine. I couldn't lift my eyes from the expanse of rock around my feet, the grass that brushed up and down my leg, like fingers.

"You know he won't give us up," I said, choking. "He'd die before."

And at that, Callista's tears began to fall. She leaned over and laid her head against my shoulder, and I held her up as best I could, a tiny cry escaping before she forced it back down. I couldn't bring myself to wrap my other arm around her because I was just as heartbroken as she was.

"I'm sorry," she said into my shoulder. "I did all this."

She sounded so guilty—more than she should have. I wanted to counter her remorse, to say that she'd had no choice at all. That really, this was on my conscience, that I was to blame for all our lives being lost. But there was something different than that behind her voice, something that went much deeper than her hurt. She sniffed and tried to regain control of herself but only ended up pushing away from me, wiping her eyes with her wrist.

"There's stuff you don't know," she said. "I didn't tell you and Thad because I knew you'd hate me. But all of this is my fault."

"Why would we hate you?" I said in disbelief. My first meeting with Callista had been after she'd taken down a plane to keep me safe. Of all of us, she'd been the safest, done the most planning, held Thad and I back when we were going to do something stupid. What could she possibly be talking about—*hating her?* That was impossible.

She shook her head.

"I—I was caught by the Guardians before you or Thad," she blurted. "I didn't know what was going on. They just…they just killed my whole family."

Her shoulders slumped even further. "And I couldn't take it. So I just told them where you and Thad were. That's how they found you in the first place. *I* told them."

The guilt she'd been feeling and hiding all this time was finally out in the open, but it burned like a splinter being drawn from a deep wound. What was I supposed to say? I wanted to comfort her, to tell her that it was alright, that she'd just made a mistake, that it wasn't that bad after all. But to say those things would have been an insult to everything we'd lost. That it was alright that Thad had lost Sophia, that I had lost my family, that we had lost the Blade, and now that we'd lost our friend.

So I said nothing. She said nothing. The silence meshed with our grief, with Callista's guilt, with my failure. We were empty, hollow, and futureless.

"Kiss me," Callista said suddenly. She hadn't turned, hadn't looked at me, just continued to stare ahead at the edge far away through her glassy eyes. I didn't move.

"Please," she said, voice cracking. "Make me feel happy again."

So I turned and kissed her.

All at once, every other thought and fear and melancholy misery that had been around me vanished. She moved closer, leaning in so that the back of my head was pushed against the heavy stone, my hands sliding to keep myself supported, hers running through my hair. She moved my lips for me, and my conscious mind—whatever part of it still existed—was swept away.

Everything around us—the net of trees, the tornado of wind, and the people who wanted us dead—disappeared. I could feel her warmth radiating against my skin. This was what I'd wanted without knowing. This was the dream I'd wished I could have had all those nights ago, when instead I'd been fed nightmares about Callista instead.

It crushed the pain out of me like there was no room for the both of them. Callista or the sadness. Callista or the horrors. I chose Callista.

She breathed sharply, her hair a canopy over my face as she leaned over me on an incline, blocking everything out save for her now-opened eyes. It was a rare second when both of our gazes met, when I was able to stare into hers without feeling like we should have been running, or planning, or saving someone else. For a moment, it was just us. I couldn't have said my own name if someone had asked.

Callista pulled away.

Tears had come up in the edges of her eyes again, running down her face. She looked at me, and then her face fell with regret, with shame, with absolute remorse.

"I'm sorry," she said, pushing away from me, curling back into her ball.

"No," I whispered without meaning to say it out loud, my tone hoarse from having not spoken in so long. She shook her head.

"I'm sorry," she said again. "I shouldn't have done that. It was selfish. I broke our promise."

How could she think that I even cared about the stupid promise anymore? I shook my head. I wanted to tell her all the things that I'd wanted to say. With her, I had someone else. With her, I had something left to live for that before, I hadn't even realized was worth it.

I just couldn't say any of the things I wanted to. Her kiss had taken all my words.

She wiped her eyes. "I didn't mean that. I just did it to make me feel better."

Her tears had stopped. She was hardening again. So I sat on one side of her wall and she sat building and mortaring it on the other, until we were safely separated again. Merely allies. I pushed my legs in front of me and took a deep breath.

"You know I have to go back for Thad," I said.

She drew a breath sharply: the reaction I'd expected but hoped to not hear.

"That's suicide," she said callously.

"I know," I replied. "But Thad already did the same for me. Twice."

It didn't seem to make a difference to her. She pushed her teeth together, squeezing herself even tighter. My mind was already made up though. To leave Thad behind would mean that I was unfaithful, a coward, a failure—to be everything that Anon believed of me.

The end wasn't a fear of mine anymore. I could live with dying.

Even though I hoped she would, Callista never relented. So with no other choice, I stood.

She lashed out, scaled hands catching me like a net and slinging me back into the corner. The rocks bruised the skin against my spine painfully but I sprang back. In the next second I was standing across from Callista, claws out, facing her as she growled at me viciously.

"You're not leaving!" she shouted, ready to knock me again if I tried. I tested her with a mad dash in the other direction, only to have her claws slice through the air in front of me, slamming so hard into the stones that they tore deep chips away. My hand flew up to push hers out of my way. My fist was met with the back of her hand, scales colliding so powerfully that I was thrown off my feet.

"I have to go!" I yelled just as loudly. "You want me to leave Thad to them? You know what they'll do!"

"If you go, everything he's done will be worth nothing," she told me, sliding to corner me again, spreading her fingers and claws menacingly.

"So you want me to leave him there?" I said. "You're just giving up on him?"

"He wouldn't *want* you to save him!" she said in a near scream. I jumped into the air, trying to rise over the rocky wall only to find that she was faster, raising to bat me back down again. I crashed to the ground, instinctively swinging to catch my claws against hers. They clashed and I tried to push her over, but she managed to shove back against me with a matching strength. I was caught off guard and fell again, her blades slipping down and slicing the unprotected inside of my hand before she could stop herself.

She tumbled to the side but was back up instantly, gritting her teeth.

"You can't die," she said, sobbing again through her fury. "I was weak before, but I can't be now. I can't let you die."

I bent over, out of breath. I was bleeding from my hand. I looked up to her and saw that her face was covered in alarm at the blood she'd drawn, her claws pulling back quickly.

"You'd rather let him die instead?" I said through my teeth. I wiped my hands down my jeans, trying to clear them of the red, to wipe away the sting.

"You're the only hope left," she begged me. "You can't. You have to let him go."

"I won't," I said with resolve. "You can't keep me here. I won't let him die alone."

Finally, she broke down. She spun, throwing her hands down so that the end of the cliff was open in front of me.

"Fine!" she shouted. "Go, if you want. But I'm not going to die fighting again. I'll just die here when you do."

She backed away, gesturing toward the open edge in bitter insistence. The whole of the San Fernando Valley spread beyond her, painted over by the sun's rays, calling me to go out. My urge to fight her vanished the moment she gave up. I could see behind her insistence was a longing to hold me back—a duty, even, because she knew exactly what would happen to me when I left.

I knew what I would face. It took all of my strength to tear myself from against the rocky wall, to walk past Callista who still remained hopeful that I would change my mind. I got to the edge and stopped.

Callista stayed behind me, refusing to follow.

"Will you look for me in our next life again?" I asked her. I should have wished she wouldn't, that somehow she could be disconnected from me so in our next life so she could live as a human and never face any of this again. But I didn't want to leave her. Deep inside, I hoped that if I died, she would be there again in seventeen years, and somehow we would rediscover everything again, and pick up where we left off.

She didn't say anything back. Maybe she had finally hardened her heart enough to be strong, to keep our promise. So without another word, I pushed myself from the cliff and left to save my friend.

22

DANGER TO SOCIETY

When you are a seventeen-year-old suspected terrorist, there is no shortage of ways to get yourself caught. If I'd wanted fanfare, I could have walked in to a TV news studio and announced my presence, to allow the cameras enough time to grab their startled close-ups before the police arrived. If I wanted to perpetuate the dangerous image they'd already created for me, then I could have walked through the park in the daylight, acting suspicious until someone finally recognized me and a special team was dispatched with helicopters lest I escape. They were all very good options, and I thought hard over my choices as I flew over the city.

In the end, though, I went with the simplest and most boring. I walked in to the first police station I spotted and told the uniformed woman at the counter that I was Michael Asher. At first, she didn't seem to believe me, telephone resting an inch from her ear, the person on the other side still babbling away. One quick glance of her eyes matched my face to the one on the wanted poster already pasted to the wall beside her.

What followed was a flurry of boots, of shouts for me to kneel and place my hands on the back of my head, to lay flat as a startled set of officers rushed to check me for explosives. I lay still as they patted me down, handcuffed me, checked my pockets and under my shirt and around my legs, certain they were overlooking weapons of some sort. When they ran a metal detector wand over me, I expected it to beep when it passed over my hands, but it didn't.

I was hoisted to stand, pulled by a hastily formed battalion of officers through the back door and toward a cruiser already waiting for me. Somehow the press had gotten wind of my capture. The second the door popped open, a flurry of camera flashes and yelling rushed from gathered reporters. The officers formed a wall around me, struggling to keep the cameras away as I was dragged through the crowd. I tried to push innocence onto my face; I knew this scene would appear on the evening news. When they showed my picture across all the screens in Arleta, I wanted to look as little like a murderer as I could.

But what was the point, anyway? They'd made their judgments long ago. When I met the fleeting gazes of the reporters, I could see they all feared me, frightened that such a normal-looking teen could have committed such horrible crimes. I knew they'd go back to the office, shaking their heads, saying to themselves, "Of course, all the worst criminals look just like us."

The officers shoved me into the car and I was driven away with my hands still bound and the bars on the windows blocking out some of the cameras as their lenses scraped my window for a shot. I wondered what my Glimpse was showing at that moment. If I died that day, would I find all these articles about me seventeen years in the future, and get the chance to look back and read myself?

I pushed the thought aside. I had to focus, to plan, to find a way to fix all of this. I would. I always did, in the end.

The line of police cars rocketed off, leaving the shouting flood of reporters behind. I tried to settle down into the uncomfortable seat, to calm my nerves with slow and deep breaths. Nothing helped.

At the next station, I was locked in a holding cell by myself. I sat on the hard metal bench against the wall, surrounded on all sides by thick metal bars that offered no privacy from the security camera in the ceiling. My presence had thrown the entire department into disarray, no one knowing for sure who should call who, if the FBI or the CIA were coming, if they should question me or wait. My mother's death made things worse because I was still a minor and so there was no parent to call. Anytime an officer passed, their eyes

252

would stray to me then dart away again. It was like they kept waiting for me to say something, to make a threat or confession. I just sat wordlessly.

The Guardians already knew I was there. Now, it was a waiting game.

As the hours passed, I lay down on the coarse bench and stared at the fluorescent ceiling panels. The floor of my cage and of the large room outside was made of a dull concrete that echoed sounds through the door and the hall beyond it. The voices of the panicked officers outside were masked by the sounds of the television that hung high in the corner of the room, its old speakers buzzing anytime a commercial got too loud. Its picture was yellowed and had a static line going through the middle.

Surely the Guardians would send someone soon? There was no way everyone in town didn't know by now.

As if on cue, the commercial that had been blathering away on the television ended and the evening news started. I turned my head to the side to see better. As expected, my face was the first to appear.

"Local terrorist Michael Asher has been captured by Beverly Hills police officers in what has been one of the most dramatic and horrifying cases to sweep Southern California this decade," the female anchor said, an absolute void of empathy behind her tone. *Local terrorist?* I pressed my lips together wryly. Now there's something to add to my résumé.

She listed my suspected crimes, which had grown from mere family murdering and house-burning to an inventory of previously unsolved murders and bomb threats. Again, they pulled up all the necessary sources: kids from school thrilled to talk about that weird Michael Asher kid who read their minds, but was obviously just a clever fraud. Our former next-door neighbor, who said she'd seen me sneak out late at night to practice witchcraft. And finally, Mrs. Milo, wide eyed with her hair all a mess, proclaiming that she couldn't find her husband anywhere now and that I had surely kidnapped him.

I wasn't amused by the idiotic report for long. I knew that almost everyone in town was tuning in, believing every lie that was said about me. I couldn't blame them. If I'd been in their position, I probably would have believed the television too. The news never lied. The news was never biased, or tainted, or controlled by

253

anyone. And certainly not some ridiculous, supernatural secret society. That would have been silly.

I heard a clang from down the hall and pushed myself up to sit. Heavy footsteps pounded against the concrete, the handle on the holding room's door bobbing. I gripped the edge of the bed, expecting Wyck.

Instead, I was greeted with someone entirely the opposite.

"Spud!" I gasped. He appeared around the corner of the door, turning to the sound of my voice, eyes widening when he saw me behind the bars. His arms hung loosely beside his wide middle, hair still a wild black mess on the top of his head, moustache even more pronounced than the last time I'd seen him. He looked exhausted, but when he saw me his face went cheery.

"Man, how'd you get stuck behind bars before I did?" he burst, spreading his hands out with disbelief. I couldn't help grinning, jumping from the bed to stand.

Another person appeared behind Spud: a female officer I could never have forgotten. *Officer Delaney.* I stopped in my tracks. She crossed her arms, keeping the door open with her foot, narrowing her eyes at me. Weaker people might've melted beneath the fury of her glare.

"Yeah, I figured I'd see you here soon," she said grouchily. She glanced at Spud then back to me again.

"I'm staying with you," she said. "You're not supposed to be here. I'll give you five—"

"What am I gonna do?" Spud exploded, whirling to face her. "Give him a file to saw his way out? And then what, run? Ha. Me. *Run.*" He beat his own belly as proof. "I'll come get you in a minute."

She didn't look pleased with this proposal but Spud must have had some influence. With a huff, she turned and left, closing the door behind her. I breathed a sigh of relief.

"I think I just got my Christmas present downgraded," Spud complained, throwing me a fake glare. I wanted to run up and pound him on the back heartily but the closest I could get was to stand near the bars. He looked to where they met the ceiling and the floor, then over to the cameras and the locks.

"I could hack this place's lock system," he said with a shrug. *Oh boy.*

"Don't start that," I told him, shaking my head in surrender.

"You wouldn't welcome my presence back there?" he said, still studying the room for weaknesses. I huffed.

"I probably would," I said. "But I don't think that bed would fit the both of us."

"I call dibs," he said, grabbing the bars between his hands to test their strength. And like that, Spud—without any effort at all—had taken me back in time. Despite the bars that now stood between us, it was like we were out on another crazy escapade, kicking rocks out of our way on the road, complaining about all the seemingly important woes in our life. He completely ignored the news behind us that continued on about my various misdeeds, showing interviews of more and more so-called "friends" eager for five seconds of airtime to bash me.

The reporters clearly needed to do better research. My only school friend was with me.

When he was finally certain that the bars wouldn't fall off, he met my eyes.

"So," he said. "Did you do it?"

Leave it to Spud to never dance around a question. I shook my head.

"Of course not," I said, voice lowering to a whisper.

"Then why are you in there?" he asked, matching my tone but trying not to lean in too close, already wary of the ceiling camera. I hesitated. There wasn't much that I was willing to tell him but I knew he'd see right through me if I avoided the truth.

"Is this because of that guy with the car?" he said. "The guy who tried to kill you?"

"Yes," I confirmed. He shrugged.

"Figures," he said. "Someone tries to kill you, *you* end up in jail. Judicial system logic."

"It's not their fault," I told him. "There's just…bigger stuff going on."

He lifted an eyebrow, now wary of the way I was talking and the bits that I was leaving out. Secrets never flew with him; I'd always told him all of mine. I sighed.

"It's just… stuff," I told him. "They're pinning a lot of things on me that I didn't do, but I can't tell them that. I need to be here. There's…bigger stuff going on."

"Bigger stuff?" he echoed. "You mean… like a *conspiracy?*"

The last word was spoken with an air of fake mystery, twirling his fingers like a cheap magician. He said this while trying to hold himself back from laughing, so I took a swing at him with my hand through the bars.

"You've become one of them!" he chuckled. "You're a conspiracy theorist now!"

I would have hit his shoulder if the bars hadn't held me back. He leaned just out of reach to make this fact all the more obvious, taunting me playfully.

"Come on," he told me. "I've known you're clear since I saw the first news thing on you. So why're you letting this happen? It's ridiculous. We gotta get you a lawyer and get you out."

He looked at me hopefully, suddenly going serious. It caught me off guard.

"I can't, not yet," I told him.

"Why?"

"I just can't."

He crinkled his brow with frustration, but he knew when to shut up, so he finally—and unwillingly—dropped the subject. He leaned against the bars.

"Do you at least want anything?" he said. "I could try to get you some candy in here. Or air freshener."

He sniffed. "Wait, that's you. Maybe you just need a bath."

I rolled my eyes and leaned against the barred wall beside us. "Yeah, a bath would be nice."

His offer had made me think of something, though. I considered it a few seconds, wondering if it was worth asking. I glanced to the TV and saw that the report had finally changed, and realized how much time we'd already spent together. At any moment, his aunt would return.

"Actually, there is something," I said. He straightened up.

"Yes, master," he said in his greatest evil henchman impression. I glanced up to the camera on the ceiling, trying to lean closer to him without seeming overly conspicuous.

"Remember the blog?" I whispered close to him. He nodded.

"Do me a favor and download it," I said. "If you can find a way, hack it and save all the files. But at least get everything you can from the pages."

His gaze met mine, looking confused. He already knew he wasn't going to get an explanation, though he still looked hopeful for one.

I heard a door open far down the hall, and footsteps approaching us. Was that all the time we were going to get? It seems like it'd passed so quickly.

"Keep it somewhere," I told him, speaking quicker now. "Just keep all that stuff, and whatever happens to me, don't get rid of it. Don't tell anyone you have it."

"What are you talking about?" he said in alarm, having caught my disturbing choice of words. *Whatever happens to me.* I knew my situation. If things went wrong, I might need that website again in seventeen years.

He suddenly realized just how serious all this was, and in reaction he pushed himself from the cage and blinked at me. But it was too late for him to ask any more questions because at that moment the door creaked open and his aunt stepped through again.

"You gotta go," she told him. "They're coming for Michael and if you're in here, I'm gonna lose my job."

Spud, who normally would have protested with something sharp, was frightened. He just stared at me with a paled face until his aunt came over and took him by the arm.

Spud threw her hand off, jolting back to life.

"Get off me," he told her, turning around and walking ahead of her to the door. Officer Delaney looked at me suspiciously, though appeared relieved that Spud seemed upset and had turned his back to me. She followed him to the door.

At the last second, while she wasn't watching, Spud turned. He gave me a small thumbs-up with a nod. For all the support I felt coming from him, it might have been a legion of flags with my face on it.

The door clanged shut behind them and I heard their footsteps disappearing down the hall. I heard another set of shoes, like a small army coming back in my direction. The squeal of boot soles against cement sounded through the room as two guards entered, dressed in black with what appeared to be riot armor. They had rifles held between their hands, rough faces that refused to show me any regard as they approached my cage. Behind them were two others in similarly overdone garb, and finally the most wretched

257

man I'd ever had the misfortune to meet: Wyck, dressed in a business suit, eyes on me immediately.

My fingers became fists the moment I saw him, feeling the pent-up rage breaking the dam inside me. I struggled to keep myself under control, though I'd begun to seethe involuntarily. All I could see was the reflection of my mother's face in his eyes as he'd slowly let her die at his feet, and my sister's body as she'd burned alive by his hand.

He regarded me with a depraved, amused expression.

"I didn't believe it when they *told* me," he said, astonished. "And yet here you are. Unless you use very convincing decoys now?"

The first guard had begun to rattle a set of keys against the door, clicking the locks. Wyck studied me up and down with a flick of his eyes as the door swung open.

"Nope, it's you," he confirmed with a sniff. "There's no way to fake that smell of smoke that's still on your clothes."

Suddenly, the metal gate had parted and there was a second of a clear path between us. Without even taking time to think, I dove forward, slamming my hand down into his face with all the strength my vengeful rage could muster. I caught his cheek with a massive, echoing slap, amidst wild shouts from the officers who fought to pin me down.

They wrestled me to the ground. I could barely breathe under the weight of all the officers piled on top of me. It took the entire group, one for each of my limbs, just to keep me down as I struggled, until they'd knocked me hard enough that I wasn't screaming and fighting anymore. It took all of my remaining strength to keep my claws hidden. *Not yet.*

They lifted me from the ground at once, holding my arms at my sides and roughly turning me back around. Wyck was there, wiping his mouth that dribbled a satisfying stream of blood. He spat it out onto the ground, twisting his mouth up to realign his jaw.

"My God," he told me. "You are *quick*, Mr. Asher."

Then, in front of all the officers, he drew his fist back like a backwards-swinging battering ram, and crashed it forward into the side of my face.

WHITE.
BLACK.
WHITE.

No one really sees stars when they're hit. They see flashes and pops and explosions of color, hear the crack of their own bone in their ears and feel the pounding of their heart as it speeds to compensate. His ring struck my skin. It was like my head was encased in a drum, and he beat that drum with a mallet.

I felt blood running from my nose but I couldn't wipe it, my hands bound and held down by the guards. My eyes were fixed in a wide stare and I felt dizzy, sick, focusing on the wall for a second only for it to go blurry. I would have fallen to the side if they hadn't held me so tightly.

"How terrible!" I heard Wyck saying with mock sympathy. "Please, officers, keep this *disturbed* boy from beating himself against the walls."

We started down the hall. I heard gasps from the police, hushed telephone conversations as I was dragged down steps, across another hall, and out the door. I tasted the blood as it ran onto my lips, like salt water.

My vision still swam in front of me so I was not prepared for an entirely new set of lights and flashes and noises. The media was waiting for me outside again, a loud gasp from the gathered crowd at first but even more flash bulbs following. Wyck casually moved so that everyone could get a shot of me: Michael Asher. Bleeding. Dizzy. Blinded. The boy they said killed his own family, unable to walk on his own two feet.

I was lifted through the back door of a waiting vehicle, hearing it clang shut like the sealing of a safe behind me. When the harsh sunlight was covered again, I was finally able to open my eyes weakly. We were inside an armored truck much like the type that carried funds back and forth from banks. Instead of shelves, there were long benches on each wall, the metal so thick that even the calls of the crowd were drowned out.

Wyck sat across from me with a guard on each of his sides. He straightened his suit.

"Let's go," he told the driver, tapping the window impatiently. "They got their pictures."

I heard the heavy engine roar to a start, and we were off.

I was too weak to sit up so I bounced between the unmoving shoulders of the two guards beside me. No one looked at me when I forced myself to glance around, their eyes fixed straight ahead dutifully. Where had Wyck found officers so jaded that they were willing to follow his orders as he beat a teenager? Or maybe they'd been warned about my crafty ways, that even one misstep might give me a chance to escape and then kill their families too.

It made everything worse when I thought about it. The Guardians didn't need henchmen. When everyone followed orders from someone higher, and those people followed orders from someone higher than them, eventually the pyramid came to a peak of command. When Guardians stood at the top, the police might as well be their personal army.

Every bump in the road made me bounce and feel sicker. The drive continued longer than I'd expected, and partway through Wyck whispered something in a radio to the driver. We took a sharp turn and started down another way. We could have been anywhere for all I knew, heading deeper in to a maze from which I knew there would be little chance of escape.

The longer we rode, the more edgy the four guards became. Each was nearly twice my mass. It didn't make sense for them to be so afraid and yet I didn't need a Glimpse to see the anxiety lurking in their eyes.

Soon, the truck slowed and I heard a massive grating outside. Then we pulled ahead a few more feet, the windows darkening as we entered a building. The guards glanced at each other but still said nothing.

The back door opened. The guards beside me seized my arms again, pulling me down the steps and onto the ground. Lights from our single police car escort flashed against the walls.

We had parked inside what appeared to be a giant airplane hangar. I wasn't sure at first until I looked over my shoulder and saw far off in the corner was a small, Gulfstream G650 executive plane. That was how large the space was: a small jet could sit tucked away in one corner and go unnoticed for a few seconds. The roof towered above my head and the walls were made of long metal sheets, everything lit by skylights. There were five silver sedans parked neatly against the wall, all bearing the Maserati trident on their fronts. Two other people were standing behind racks, shuffling around with cables and a row of screens, paying no attention to us. Other things were scattered about under tarps and behind tables but I was pushed ahead before I could see them.

Wyck got out of the van last, approaching the guards and me after a quick check of his wristwatch. He took me by the arm.

"Stand over here," he ordered, as the men let go of me uncertainly. I could see they were confused about what was going on. I was shoved from Wyck's hold into the grasp of the driver, as Wyck tossed his coat into the man's other arm.

"Good work, men," he said, spinning around. Claws slithered out from the ends of his fingers. The men didn't even have a chance to gasp.

In a single twirl of motion, Wyck slashed around on either side of him, slicing the men across their middles. Their bulletproof armor did nothing to stop the silver blades, blood splashing in a watery line across the floor as they cried out. But their noises were short—he swung the claws back down, stabbing two through the center then drawing the blades back again.

The men gurgled, trying to choke in air, but they were dead before they could get a single breath more.

Wyck turned around—his face was blank. No vengeance, no enjoyment, not even a second of killer's glee. Just frigid, unaffected calm, like he'd squashed mosquitoes between his fingers. His claws disappeared, the blood wiping against his skin and staining his fingers as it did. He retrieved his jacket and swept it back on.

"We won't be late for the meeting," he told the two remaining officers with a satisfied nod. They turned me around, forcing me to walk again, and I realized that these two officers were on Wyck's side. Humans actually helping the Guardians? I thought of the nurse in the white room and the other technicians still plugging the televisions together in front of me. Why would any human ever help a Guardian?

We came to a square of tables and I was pushed down onto the cold metal chair at their center. The other two people were bustling around the area, keeping their heads down and their faces turned from mine. I managed to see bits of their faces: a man and a woman, both middle aged. It was hard to tell exactly how old they were though, because like the nurse from the white room, their faces had received vast surgical work. Their chin and cheeks were puffed up over plate-like bones, all their skin stretched tightly. It looked like they'd only made minute changes but with all of the alterations added up, they appeared disfigured.

I wanted to look in their eyes, hoping somehow I'd capture a Glimpse—to find out why they continued to move at the command of these Guardians who despised their entire race so much. Was it fear? Had they been brainwashed against their own kind? Every time one of them accidentally glanced in the direction of Wyck, they lowered their heads even further, almost as if through some spiritual devotion. They were like cult members.

The metal rack they were setting up held a row of television screens, a large video camera poking from the center and aimed at me. Far off, I saw another row of vehicles: massive trailers like the one with the white room. There were no windows for me to see through any of them. I felt a shudder go up my back when I thought about what might be inside. Was Thad already in one of them, suffering at the hands of another brutal nurse?

One of the tables screeched as it was slid in front of me, the edge bumping my chest. The men placed my hands in top of the table and undid my handcuffs.

I was still shaking lightly, unable to control it. The bleeding on my face had stopped but my head continued to pound, and I had to keep blinking so that my vision would stay clear. I wanted to sleep, to give in to the black that seeped in around my vision.

Wyck slammed both of his hands down on the metal tabletop.

"Awake?" he checked, tilting his head. I licked my lips and tasted the salt of blood. He reached to the side and picked something up with both arms, dropping it on the table with a crash. It startled me and I blinked again, vision clearing as the sound reverberated back and forth in the hangar. It was the metal box, the eyes of it still open and waiting for me, just as it'd been when Wyck had plucked it from my hands in the crypt.

"Where's Thad?" I spoke my first words in what felt like hours. It wasn't even a question, really. It was my demand, one that I knew Wyck was smart enough to have figured out hours ago. He knew why I'd turned myself in. One glance up at his face told me that much.

He conceded immediately. Lifting a hand, he gestured for one of the two workers to carry out the command, and I heard her steps leaving and a door cracking open. My eyes remained locked with Wyck's, refusing to look away.

I heard the creak of wheels behind me and stiffened. It was a slow, unhurried sound, like that of a grocery cart being wheeled down an aisle. My teeth tightened together. Wyck was too close to me. My hands were free—I could have slapped him again, ripped the skin right off his cheek before the meager guards could have stopped me. But I held myself back, squeezing my hands together to keep them from moving on their own as I heard the wheels continue around me and come to a stop.

I didn't want to turn. Wyck nodded to the side. So finally, I forced myself to look.

Thad was lying on a stretcher with white sheets, arms exposed and flat against his sides with wrists facing up. His long hair was ruffled around his scalp, matted by sweat that ran down his forehead in long beads and lines. He was strapped down just as I had been but didn't try to shift when I saw him—or rather, he couldn't. I saw why: a tall metal pole on wheels sat beside his bed, and running from it was a tube with a needle poking his left arm.

Only his eyes moved. Their lids were stuck open, bloodshot, and unable to bat the dust away. But with great effort, his irises turned down, stretching so that they could see me out of the corners.

He drew a breath in quickly.

I let one out.

"You don't need to do that to him," I said, casting away all the façade that I'd been hoping to keep. I lifted my hand to wipe my eyes and both of the guards jumped, grabbing my arm, smashing it back onto the table. I spun to look at Wyck.

"I've been good so far," I told him. "You can get that out of his arm."

"Ha!" Wyck gave a laugh like he found my request hilarious. "And what then? Let him go *flying* around the room to save you? Be thankful he's still alive."

"I won't open that box until he's free," I spat.

"And I won't set him loose until that box is open," Wyck returned instantly. "Do you see me as a fool?"

"Then we're at a stalemate," I said. "You can kill me."

Wyck suddenly rang out with another laugh, terrible and frightening all at once. He clapped his hands together, turning from me and stepping over to the row of five television screens. There was a keyboard beside them. He started typing as his forced chuckles shrank.

"We've been through this. We don't need you *dead*," Wyck told me, as he flipped switches on the screens to turn them on.

"We just need you *gone*," he insisted. "That's all there is to it. We just need the Blade to do that. One tiny *prick*. Then we don't care about you anymore."

He spread his hands to accentuate his promise, as if his desires were so obvious that I should have guessed it myself. On the outside, he looked so innocent behind his request, like I'd be a fool to turn down such an easy offer.

Yet I still had the upper hand. He might not have showed it, but all of us knew that if he shot me right then and there, he wouldn't get what he wanted. The Blade would still be locked away and I'd just come back in another form. Eventually, in time—even if it took millennia of reincarnations—I'd find some way to get it back and end them.

The screens came on one by one. They caught my attention as the static faded and was replaced by a row of faces. Four men in a row, and the fifth a woman I'd already seen: the Guardian named Morgan, now without her young son. The first four all had different faces, but as I looked, those faces changed. Just like what had happened with Anon, all of the men were wearing the identity-concealing devices, so that even in the space it took Wyck to turn to me again, they'd all changed twice each.

But their eyes, those stayed the same. In their eyes, even without needing a Glimpse, I knew who these people were, why they were all gathered to watch from safe places far away. Power. Authority. Anticipation. *Guardians.*

It was impossible to identify any of them in that state, besides Wyck's mother Morgan. She seemed unconcerned for her identity, relaxed into her high-backed chair and blinking at us.

So there are five of them: five Guardians. Did each of them have two Chosens? That meant at most, there were fifteen in total. That seemed like such a tiny number when placed against how vast the world was, how much of a reach they'd need in order to control so many things at once. It was startling, but also encouraging. I only had fifteen to take down.

Fifteen minus one, I corrected myself. Mr. Sharpe was already gone. I wondered whose Chosen he had been. I scanned their eyes, wondering if I would see any of them with extra hate to identify Mr. Sharpe's Guardian by, but they only stared through the screens at me unfeelingly.

"As you can see," Wyck said to the screens, angling himself toward Morgan, "I have brought Mr. Asher in as promised, and he will give us the Blade."

"What is that over there on the side?" Morgan said, ignoring Wyck. She leaned over in an attempt to see something that the camera did not reveal entirely. Wyck, blinking, looked to his side, then pulled the edge of Thad's bed toward him.

"This is Mr. Asher's Chosen," he said to her, now looking a little flustered.

"Why isn't he dead yet?" she asked. "Haven't we made this little mistake before, Wyck?"

Before my eyes, I watched the unshakable man crumble. The absolute assurance that Wyck had displayed so far was betrayed by a single, thin line of sweat that ran down the back of his neck, so insignificant that I almost didn't notice it.

I sat up straight. Something was going on between Wyck and his mother. It looked like she'd struck him through the screen.

Wyck coughed, ignoring me. "The dilemma with killing Mr. Asher's Chosen is that... Mr. Asher will not be as inclined to open the box if—"

"Can we just carry on with Mr. Asher?" one of the men said, the second screen from the left. He had just changed from a middle-aged, bearded gentleman into a sallow-faced elderly woman with discolored wrinkles across her skin.

"Hush, Arthur," Morgan commanded with an impatient wave of her hand. "Just kill the Chosen and take the ring and be done with it."

Wyck, seeming incited by her sharp words, turned to the guard next to him and seized the gun from his hands. In a flash, he cocked it and—

"Wait!" I burst in a scream, standing up with the chair dropping behind me. It fell with a crash that brought Wyck's head around.

"I'll open the box!" I shouted at him and the screens. "I'll open it now. But if you shoot him I swear I won't."

I shook with intent, trying not to show my fear but unable to mask it from my widened eyes. The gun hovered over Thad's chest, his eyes rolling away from where they'd locked on the barrel. Now he looked at me.

265

"If he dies, I'll scrape my own eyes out," I said through my heavy breathing. "Then you can torture me all you want, it won't get the box open."

The gun didn't move. Morgan looked upset.

"Well?" she said, leaning back and drumming her fingers on the chair's arm. "One or the other. Let's hurry."

Seeing my hesitation, Wyck lifted the gun to his shoulder again. So I threw my hands out, seizing the box and spinning it around to face me. I leaned over the table so that my eyes were aligned with those in the box, looking up to make sure that the others saw me.

Thad's bed had begun to shake, such tiny movements that they'd have been imperceptible if not for the way the wheels creaked on the floor. Tears ran down his face, eyes his only way of speaking. They begged me to stop, to run, to leave the Blade, to do anything but allow it to fall into their hands and forfeit everything that we'd already done, everything that we'd already given up.

I couldn't look at him. I couldn't see his tortured face and push myself to continue. So I swallowed hard, turning away from Thad, and looked down to the box.

Its designs appeared all the more intricate in the glow from the skylights, as if every detail was heightened and I could pick out even the tiniest, most miniscule stroke from the expert's knife. I hadn't been able to see it in the dark of the crypt, but now I could tell just how different this was from previous case. It was longer and the designs were darker with more points. Its eyes were dilated: waiting for me, calling for me to read them.

So with the seconds passing, with me wondering if I was making the worst mistake of my thrice-lived life, and the stillness of anticipation enveloping the room...

I looked.

A simple, fixed stare was all it took, locking my eyes with the pair below mine. I waited for the eyes to change, for the lock to shift, for a gear to spin, for the box to open so that finally, all of this would be over.

The eyes in the stalks rolled forward to meet mine. In a flash, they narrowed into black slits.

The box gave an immediate shift. The lid beneath my thumbs moved a millimeter upward, releasing itself from the rest of the box. I heard a sharp intake of breath from across the table, Wyck lowering his gun, as if even he hadn't believed that I would do it.

And that was all I needed.

The moment that the box was open and the lid had brushed the ends of my waiting fingers, something inside of me came back to life. Maybe it was because the lingering pain in my head had finally faded. Maybe it was because the guards' fingers on my arms had loosed slightly at the box's sound. But more likely, it was because when the box opened, somewhere deep in the recesses of my mind, I remembered the last time that I'd heard that sound: two lives before, when I'd locked it away.

Like an explosion going off with me at its center, suddenly things went flying.

A backwards swing of my scaled fists sent both guards through the air. I seized the box's cover so quickly that my now-extended claws threw sparks against its surface, the lid torn from the case. I grabbed the handle of the Blade and pulled it from the sheath before I even had a chance to look at it.

I darted in front of Thad like a shield, shadowing him as Wyck's gun went off. Instincts now out of my control, my left hand moved on its own in a blur of motion. I felt something strike the outside of my hand but the impact was as gentle as a pebble, and it wasn't until I heard something clatter across the room that I realized I'd blocked Wyck's bullet.

Without a second to dwell on my newfound defense, suddenly my legs pushed me from the ground, launching me forward into flight. My shoulder caught Wyck's side and sent him crashing into the rack of screens.

All of this had happened in mere seconds. I was suddenly on the other side of the table, eyes filled with fire, hands covered by scales, and a short, silver Blade clutched in my right hand.

My teeth ground together, all the pent up fury coursing through my body and feeding me strength. Wyck stumbled against the rack, knocking the screens over, scrambling as his claws ripped through the cables he attempted to use to help him to his feet.

"One tiny prick!" I said, lunging for him as he pushed himself backward, arms and legs diving away from the Blade. Now that I saw the weapon, I recognized how identical it was to the one from the video, entirely unchanged by age. The black metal handle was tight in my grip, with indented bumps to secure it against my fingers and a golden hand guard. The knife's edge—as I'd seen before—was like a large feather, narrowing to a point at the end.

I couldn't marvel at it though, holding it out as Wyck lifted his claws in defense. The largest knife I'd ever held was a meat cleaver and thus at first the Blade felt wobbly in my grasp. It was nearly weightless. I heard the men trying to crawl up behind me so I pushed Thad's bed backward, brandishing the knife between them and I.

"Just one prick," I told him again. Wyck circled us, forcing me to turn the bed again so that it remained protected behind me. I jabbed the Blade in his direction, startling him, and in that flash of a second, I caught a Glimpse.

Fear and terror. A panic that consumed him from the inside out.

Never before had I seen such in this man's eyes.

And yet the calm, composed, ever-present emptiness on his face displayed none of this on the outside. I wanted to run across the space between us and bury the end of the Blade into his heart, knowing that it would be hardly an increment of the pain that he'd already caused me.

"You don't want to do this." Wyck's voice was laced with warning. He held a hand out like he was calming a misbehaving child.

"I think I know what's better for me than you do," I said. Wyck just shook his head.

"But I *counted* on this happening," he said. "That's why I prepared myself to raise the stakes if needed."

His eyes weren't on me anymore. They were looking over my shoulder, head tilted up to see what was behind me. My first instinct told me that it was a distraction; that he wanted me to turn so that he could take me by surprise. I refused to, ready to run forward with the Blade.

But I heard footsteps, gentle and scratchy on the floor behind me. The sounds made me freeze. The feet stopped at the same time.

I grasped the bed with my free hand, rolling it back again so that I could see both Wyck and whoever had approached me. Wyck insisted that I look. Warily, I turned my head.

The two workers were standing there now. The woman had one of her arms up and around the shoulders of someone beside her in a neck lock, while the man held a pistol.

White gauze was taped over the girl's eyes, arms down as the woman led her to stop a few feet away from me. The girl's blonde hair was clustered on her forehead from the sweat of panic. She breathed in shallow, scared gasps, too afraid to lift her arms from her sides.

No, I thought.

No. No.

No.

Then the woman reached forward, and taking the two pieces of gauze by their edges, ripped them off the girl's face abruptly. But I didn't need to see her eyes or to hear her shout of pain to know who she was.

"Alli..." I whispered. She looked up at me, and all my plans of escape vanished.

23

TO BE HUMAN

Alli blinked at me as if she couldn't believe what she was seeing.

"Michael!" she choked, but when she tried to run to me, the woman held her back with a steel-like grip, the man pressing the pistol even deeper into the top of her head. The woman showed no reaction as Alli kicked and screamed and beat her with fists. I slid a step in her direction only to see Wyck move out of the corner of my eye in response.

I jumped back again, slinging the Blade out to him in warning.

"Don't move!" I roared, and he stopped in mid-step. Alli ceased her fighting, breathing heavily from her struggle and looking to me with wild eyes.

"They told me you were dead!" she screamed, her neck locked in the woman's elbow. And all of a sudden, I realized why I'd never found Alli in the burning house.

I exploded with a mixture of so many emotions at once: a feeling that all was not lost after all, followed by a sinking terror when I saw the unaffected expression on the woman's face, looking to Wyck for her next orders. I twisted to look at Wyck again, and in that motion, betrayed myself. His eyes filled with an eager vengeance—a merciless delight. He stood up straighter, brushing his bruised hands against the front of his now-ruined suit coat.

"So you're defeated!" he burst with glee. He didn't laugh any more than a small huff of enjoyment, reaching over to pull the heavy rack of screens upright again. Two of the screens had fallen off and their wires were ripped but the other three remained attached, with the faces of the Guardians behind them still struggling to see. It fell back into place with a crash, the camera wobbling forward to look at the room again.

"You're one of us but you could *easily* be one of them," he told me, as if finally enlightened to some truth that he'd been missing. The speakers that the people on the screens had used to communicate with us had been destroyed, so we could not hear their voices as their mouths moved. Morgan was yelling at Wyck but he didn't see her. His claws twitched eagerly.

"You won't leave this room," he said. He was far too correct. If I moved for Wyck, the workers would kill Alli. If I moved for Alli, Wyck would slice Thad through the middle with a flick of his finger. *Thad!* I thought. If only I could get him awake, if I could somehow get the I/V from his arm... but Wyck was too close.

Wake up, Thad, I can't do this alone...! I thought, but it was in vain. Thad's eyes had slumped forward halfway, his body having given in to weakness.

"Just give me the Bl—" Wyck started.

CRASH.

The room was so large that when the noise interrupted no one could tell from which direction it had come. Almost immediately, there came tiny, tinkling noises as glass rained down to the concrete and broke into bits.

All of us looked up at once. And there, diving down through the very skylight she had just smashed through, was Callista.

Beams of sunlight shone across the glimmers of falling glass like they were airborne diamonds. The silver of her claws spread majestically, frighteningly, like the attack of a bird as it swooped toward the ground.

She'd found me.

The two workers who held Alli turned their heads up. In the second it took for them to see Callista's claws, their faces paled in a startled awe, looking like they were seeing a goddess soaring from the clouds. Their knees bent slightly, as if unsure whether they should fall to kneel, the pistol falling from Alli's head and to the man's side.

271

Callista hit the ground with a smash, two inches from them. Their heads followed her down, petrified as Callista threw both of her hands forward between them. With one sweeping part, she threw both of them aside, the pistol firing a string of pops into the air worthlessly: the arm holding it detached and flopping to the ground. Their bodies crashed against a wall and a table, slumping over.

"Michael!" Callista screamed at me, and her voice broke me from my reverie.

A string of explosions went off beside me. I'd seen the motion in the corner of my eyes and my hands moved at once. I felt the strikes but they were like punches thrown against thick padding, hands darting up and down and then back again to deflect the bullets. The armor held against them and I spun just in time to see Wyck falling from the air, heels aimed for my head.

I dove out of the way, the gun continuing to fire in rapid pops. Callista hadn't been ready as Wyck landed in front of her, slamming the butt of the gun into the back of her leg. She fell backward in pain as Wyck calmly dropped the now-empty rifle, picking up the pistol from the ground and aiming it at Thad.

I moved to block the shot, but Wyck slung his claws around the other way, catching the edge of mine with his, causing them to clash like swords and become caught in each other. His other hand came around my side but I deflected his slash. Suddenly I was flipped around in a tall circle like a windmill, slamming down on the other side of Wyck. I hit the side of the machine feeding the I/V into Thad, breaking the tubes and sending the tall rack rolling.

I writhed, trying to pull myself back to my feet. Across the ground I could see Callista also crawling up, nudging the petrified Alli to encourage her to run. Wyck spotted her though, and I saw his shoes chasing after Alli as she tried to dive behind the truck for protection.

No! I groaned, my back feeling like it was broken in a hundred places, even my impenetrable scales feeling like they were cracked. But somehow I forced myself up, to crawl on all fours and then to kneel. Alli screamed my name.

Wyck had gotten her. In one hand was the gun, under his arm was my sister. He stopped for only a second, looking from Thad to Callista and then to me all in one sweep. Seeing his motionless followers, he must have realized that he was far too outnumbered.

He gritted his teeth and took off, crushing glass shards one moment and hovering in the air the next. He made a mad dash for the skylight with Alli still in his arms.

Hearing her screams brought me back. Wyck was not going to escape with her—I wasn't going to lose her again. Using my desperation as power, I pushed myself to my feet, ignoring the pain as I launched into the air after him, the Blade held between both my hands.

I yelled at him in challenge but he was far too smart to take me on, the wake of the air behind him threatening to knock me off course. But nothing could throw me off. Nothing would make me stop: not the weakness I felt behind my adrenaline, not the pain from being slammed into the ground. I only flew faster.

Wyck dangled the gun behind him, shooting backward, but I easily dodged the wild bullets until he gave up. The roof grew closer and closer, and Wyck—burdened by the weight of Alli—neared the Blade I held outstretched like the tip of a missile.

All of a sudden, I was right behind him.

I slashed the Blade forward.

It caught Wyck by the back of his heel. The effect was instant. The claws that had been so dangerously close to Alli's throat vanished into silver dust, raining back like powder onto my shirt. Wyck was no longer held aloft, and he tumbled through the air, slamming into one of the large metal supports that held the building up. The roof reverberated with a massive clang.

I dashed through the air to grab Alli from him but he was quicker, spinning over and pulling her into his lap, arm enclosing around her tightly with the pistol into her ear.

"Don't move!" he shrieked, tipping back and forth with the reddened face and wild eyes of a madman. He dug the end of the pistol into her head so deeply that she cried out in pain, her voice muffled beneath his arm that was clamped over her mouth. He sweat wildly, not believing what had just happened even as the blood dripped from his heel and hit the floor far below us.

"We will kill *all* of the worthless eaters!" he said, spit flying as he screamed, the former cruelty in his voice now turned into a blistering rage. "We will harvest through *every* human until there isn't a single weed left!"

He was barely able to keep his balance, unaccustomed to only having hands and legs. If he so much as twitched his finger, there'd be no time for me to reach Alli before the bullet hit her skull.

"You intend to be the *bringer of the dawn*?" he continued at me through his teeth, heaving breaths in and out. "So bring the dawn, then! Your planet's dawn will fall only upon the corpses we leave behind."

Wyck's unbalanced swaying only made his lack of flight all the more obvious—I could see in his face that he'd been shattered inside. He'd been torn from his victory over me—he was on the brink of suicide, preferring death over what he'd become. He could shoot Alli and then himself and not even care.

Wyck winced in pain, fingers flaring out, and from his right hand slipped his red ring. He moved to catch it, but the ring fell out of his reach and struck the ground like a raindrop, bouncing across the concrete. Wyck's jaw fell in anguish.

Through his startled cry, I saw a Glimpse.

Like I was swimming through murky water, I was forced to read past the emotions that first bubbled to the surface. I passed terror, sadness, insignificance, hope for his own death and also fear of what death meant.

But there was one other thing, one lingering revelation that I grasped onto.

"There are no bullets in that gun," I read.

Wyck's face jerked up to look at mine, barely breathing, his pale neck soaked with sweat. *I was right.* He was bluffing.

One push of power sent me hovering toward him but he reacted at the same time, pushing both Alli and the emptied pistol over the edge. I swept my arms out, grabbing her into mine as Wyck gave a gurgling, murderous scream, jumping to seize me in midair. But I was already floating backward, Alli wrapped in my arms, feeling such a rush of relief that it was as if Wyck didn't even exist anymore.

He fell.

With no powers to hold him up anymore, Wyck was like a bag of grain, plummeting straight down, down, down, toward the rolling I/V unit that stood below us.

With a sickening crunch, the tall arm that had held the bag of sedative impaled him through his chest, silencing his cry at once.

The momentum carried it to roll, where his body stopped in front of the camera and the television screens.

The Guardians on the monitors had been wildly speaking into telephones and unable to see most of the action. Their heads all snapped up at once. Their mouths stopped moving, eyes staring in horror. Morgan straightened like a rod. She looked away from the grotesque sight, as the other screens started to click off one by one.

I floated to the ground with Alli still clinging tightly to my neck, dropping her lightly then falling over to kneel, to breathe. Morgan saw me, and with widened eyes, she reached forward to switch her screen off.

Suddenly, the room was quiet again. I was too weak to lift my head, to see how many were still alive. So I counted the sounds of their breathing:

One.

Two.

Three.

And mine made four.

24

ARLETA

There are some places in the world that time seems to have no hold over, like an immortal paradise gated away from ruin or corruption. Wars might have raged and secret battles might have been fought in its very midst, but Arleta continued to stand like a beacon to me, a lighthouse even in the glaring sun of midday.

My feet brushed against the familiar grass of my old backyard as my flight came to a stop. Tall weeds had popped up since the last time I'd mowed it—back when I'd lived there, not so long ago. There was no silence here, always a car struggling to start or a garage door rumbling open or a dog barking at a passerby. All the sounds blended together like a song, like a soundtrack to my life. My former life.

As if to signal how far away my old life really was, the silver Blade in my hands caught the sunlight, its sheath glimmering into my eyes. I couldn't bring myself to let it out of my sight—rarely even risking putting it down. I knew the Guardians were scrambling to regroup and would not attack, at least not now. Still, I held on to it tightly.

My heart pounded a little heavier. I stared across the yard at what remained of my house. With the sun's rays glowing around its edges, my house stood in the form of three remaining walls leaning in on each other precariously, the wooden porch caved in on itself and brick pieces scattered all over. All the windows were busted and the back door was mangled in three pieces, our roof having crumbled into splintery boards. Yellow police tape waved around the parameter.

I drew closer, stepping lightly on the circular pieces of concrete that my mom had put out as decoration between the porch and her tomato garden. *How are you feeling?* I asked myself. I was puzzled by my reactions: calm, composed, not at all what I'd feared to see from myself on the flight back to this place. Perhaps in the days that had passed between Wyck's death and our escape, I'd finally come to terms with how much my life had changed.

But now wasn't the time to think about that. Now, I was standing in front of the broken door, peering in as the stubborn smell of smoke wafted into my nostrils, propelled by the ashes that flew in every gust of wind. The breeze whistled through the windows and the hole in the ceiling. Our old wallpaper and sheetrock was blackened in most places. Everything became eerily calm, in contrast to the blazing madness I'd faced the last time I'd been there.

I pressed on. What remained of the furniture was lit by the newly added skylight. The couches and chairs were tattered down to their springs and stuffing, pillows littering the floor and picture frames fallen from the walls. Our chimney had fallen through the hole in the ceiling and was sitting in the center of the living room television.

It was like walking through a mausoleum, everything around me already dead.

The pile of wood and sheetrock that had once covered my mom's body was moved and gone. I figured that the city had already arranged for her burial. I tried to not look toward the last spot I'd seen her in. As my courage grew, I started to climb the stairs, cautious for any moment that they might break. I inched my way around the holes on the balcony. Light streamed in through every opening in this shattered structure, appearing as golden beams against floating bits of black paper and cinders that my steps stirred up.

My bedroom door was ajar. Floorboards creaked under my shoes as my hands brushed down the wall and the still-embedded nails that'd once held up our framed family portraits. Was I ready for this? I'd been preparing myself for days. I pushed the door in.

It creaked with a familiar sound, coming to a stop when the handle hit the wall. I entered, holding on to my dresser for support as my shoes slipped against the mess of papers on the ground. I looked down and saw that I had stepped onto one of my faces, one of the photographs that had been my Great Work: a Glimpse from the Joy wall.

I let my eyes run along what remained: the desk that was broken through the middle. The plastic and metal camera lenses all in a great pile of ruin. The tall photo lights toppled and looking almost like a pair of dead praying mantises. My bed, its mattress struck through the middle by a ceiling beam with its downy filling drifting across the sheets.

And pictures. Dozens and dozens of photographs of faces on paper half burned and half remaining, still stuck to the walls like the friendly ghosts of my past. Some of them had half a face, others were missing their necks or scalps, but my old friends seemed to all look up at once, to grin or scowl or beam at me like they had for so many years.

They were ruined and disfigured, but they were still alive to me. It made me smile.

Suddenly, I spotted an object that had fallen beneath my bed, shielded under where the mattress and rail had broken. It was my tiny pocket camera. I had a habit of setting it beside my bed some nights, and somehow—by glorious chance—it had managed to hide from the fire and the police and everything else that had raged against this house.

I hurried to the bed and sat down on it as best I could, sweeping the camera up. Its outside was scratched but luckily the lens was retracted into the shell. I wiped soot off its surface with the fold of my shirt and reached for the power button. The camera gave a click and at first I thought it was dead, but then the lens whirred and popped out.

I lifted it up and to test it, snapped one picture. The flash lit up my room and sent another thrill of joy through me. I pressed the review button. The screen immediately changed to show the most recent photograph on the hard drive—it still worked!

Then, at a sudden urge, I clicked the button to go back. The photo unexpectedly changed to one of my sister.

Alli was standing at the corner of a street, head turned away slightly like she had whirled to avoid my lens. But the exposed half of her face was covered in a smile, because she had been laughing as I had struggled to get a snapshot of her. I remembered this scene perfectly—this was the last walk home from school that I had gotten to have with her before…everything. My sister's face was untainted by fear. This photograph was purity.

I looked around the room at the tatters of the photos on the walls, at everything that remained of my Great Work. I could replace it. I was certain that this was not the end.

There was a creak from the doorway and I looked up quickly. When Callista leaned her head in, I relaxed.

"How's Alli?" I asked her. She held rolled up papers in the crook of her arm, already studying the walls with astonishment as she stepped inside. She'd never been here before, never seen my Great Work, and I guessed that my description of it had paled in comparison to the real thing. She stammered before she managed to answer me.

"She's alright," Callista replied. "Thad called and said she'll be fine. He'll probably break her out of there tonight."

I grinned slightly. Thad's idea was to take Alli to a small town hospital many miles from Los Angeles. They'd treat her first before asking who she was, or any of the other questions that would follow upon her identification: like how the girl that Michael Asher had supposedly burned to death was, in fact, still alive. We'd be long gone before anyone discovered who Alli was, and she'd have been treated by then.

Callista was enthralled by my photos. She stepped in so that she could see them better, turning in a circle to take it all in. She shook her head and didn't even try to disguise the wonder in her eyes.

"That's a lot of pictures," she said. I nodded.

"I need to get started on a new one," I told her with a grin. I lifted my camera, snapping a flash at her, but she was quicker. Her hands blocked her eyes and face from view, even though she laughed behind them, until I gave up. She fell to sit next to me with a sigh, dropping the papers into my lap.

"These were outside," she told me with a lifted eyebrow.

One was a newspaper with my photo on the front page. In the picture, I was being shoved into the armored truck, bloodied and handcuffed with my eyes half-closed and my mouth dangling open grossly. Half of my face was covered by an uplifted microphone from one of the other reporters.

"They call this photography?" I said with disgust. "They couldn't snap a single one where you can see all of my face?" I fluffed the paper open dramatically. "Methinks they should have hired Michael Asher for this."

Callista let out a light groan of apathy. The headline of the paper read: *TEENAGE TERRORIST MICHAEL ASHER LABELED PSYCHOPATH, ESCAPES DURING TRANSPORT.* I was really getting a lot of prefixes and suffixes to my name now: Teenager, Terrorist, Psychopath…Ninja Turtle, next? I read the first few lines of the article—the chief of investigation vowed to find me, to avenge their horribly mutilated officers found in an (unusually empty) airplane hangar, to hunt me down until I was brought to justice. There was a new crime, too: I was being accused of an electrical fire that'd burned down a mansion in Beverly Hills.

The rest didn't seem too interesting so I tossed the paper aside. It was hard to take the media seriously when I knew the truth and how far from it they allowed themselves to venture. It made me wonder how many others had been falsely vilified like me.

There was something else underneath the newspaper. A white envelope.

I glanced up at Callista, doubting what I first believed. The expression on her face nudged me to go on. So I flipped it over and saw my name in bold letters on its front.

The envelope was torn apart in a moment, a single page fluttering into my lap. I spread it open with shaking hands:

To: Mr. Asher,

By the mere fact of you reading this, you have proven that I misjudged you in many ways. It is an error I happily welcome.

You have taken a step down a path from which you cannot turn back, an irreversible decision to remove the coat of one life and take on the armor of another. I will admit to believing you were not strong enough. But you have reminded me of a simple truth: not all things can be judged by appearances. Sometimes behind the mask of a normal person hides the face of a hero.

You have caused a stir where one has never been felt before. Perhaps it is time for the next step in the Grand Design.

Prepare yourself. Don't trust anyone.

My hands fell slowly, letting the letter slide into my lap. I couldn't avoid the thrill that burst from deep inside me, so much that my cheeks felt warm and my fingertips felt electrified. Anon, in his own sparing words, had voiced his renewed support of me, and all at once my failures seemed to be wiped away.

"You know, for the longest time I was sure we weren't going to make it," I told Callista, shrugging in an attempt to summarize all the near-deaths we'd faced, and to disguise my excitement. She saw right through me and gave another of her half-grins in return.

"Then Michael, it's a good thing you're hardly ever right," she said.

My first reaction was to counter her, but I didn't. Not long ago, such a reply would have been an insult to me, but now it was merely a reminder of all the things we'd been through, all the times that I'd thought I was in control and wasn't. Somehow, we'd ended up all right.

"What else was I not right about?" I asked her suddenly. She looked up to meet my eyes. A burning question in the back of my mind returned, one that I'd barely realized was there until that moment. She waited for me to embellish and continue, and I almost didn't.

"When you kissed me on the cliff," I blurted. "Was that really just to make you feel better, or did you mean it?"

She gave that same enthralling, ambiguous smile. For a few moments, we stared at each other across the four or five inches again, the cavern between us almost bridged, if only she would drop her final piece into the center. I wasn't sure what I wanted her to do, how I wished she would react. Did I want a yes? A no? I couldn't figure my own hopes out. So I waited for her.

Instead, with a shrug, she gathered her fallen hair back behind her shoulders.

"What do you think, Mr. Eye Guy?" she said elusively. Then she reached across to my hand and took the camera out of it. She turned away, holding it at arm's length to snap a photo of her face, then dropped it back into my lap.

She pushed up from the bed and walked across my room. Gone again.

The moment she disappeared, my gaze shifted down to the camera, to read the ever-unpredictable truth that hid behind her eyes.

THE END OF BOOK ONE

ABOUT THE AUTHOR

KALEB NATION is an entertainment host and online personality. His blogs and videos have received over 50 million hits online, and he has been featured on NPR, Entertainment Weekly, The Huffington Post, and more.

While writing Harken, Kaleb documented his progress through video blogs at YouTube.com/KalebNation. A black belt in taekwondo, Kaleb lives in California with his chinchilla. Harken is his first novel for teens.

Kaleb regularly posts on Twitter ((@KalebNation) and blogs at KalebNation.com.

KALEBNATION.COM
Official Website

TWITTER.COM/KALEBNATION
Follow Kaleb Nation on Twitter

YOUTUBE.COM/KALEBNATION
Watch Kaleb Nation's Video Blogs

FACEBOOK.COM/KALEBNATION
Like Kaleb Nation on Facebook

ACKNOWLEDGEMENTS

LOUIE PINTO, RANDY HANCOCK, STEPHEN HALL,
PENG JOON, LAURENCE OLIVIERO,
KARSTEN AREND & SAM MIKHAIL
*for believing in me and making this book far bigger
than I could have made it alone.*

MY LOS ANGELES YOUTUBE FAMILY
for Maggiano's and Hollywood Sign nights away from my desk.

THE FTW CREW
*for poking through my Skype invisibility cloak and making me communicate
with people who are not imaginary.*

RACHUL GENSBURG
*for dragging me outside to get
food that was not cooked by microwave.*

KIM FULLER
*for suffering through the first draft, the second draft, and all the others,
swearing to never let that awful stuff leak out (you did, right?).*

ILANA ZACKON
*for daily manuscript critiques across two countries,
from my office to your bedroom closet.*

KAREN HANSEN
for knowing far more about how moms think than I ever will.

ARI CORSETTI AND RIE GOLDIE
*for being unrelenting, and never letting me
slide when you knew I could do better.*

ZANE SPRAGGINS, JACKIE ASBURY, ROBYN SCHNEIDER,
LAUREN SUERO & CASSIDY TUCKER
for pre-reading this book and helping me get it ready for the world.

THE BENNINGS
*for letting me ride in your magnificent Shelby GT500
Mustang, all in the name of research (of course).*

LOUIS BECKETT & FERRARI MASERATI BEVERLY HILLS
*for letting me take photos of your dealership's
Maserati even though I couldn't buy it (yet).*

ELANA ROTH
*for gently telling me what needed to be changed
in my first draft, which turned out to be everything.*

TAYLOR
for making the book sparkle more.

AND THE NATIONEERS
for watching from the very beginning as this story came to life.

SPECIAL ACKNOWLEDGMENTS

The author would like to thank the early online fans of HARKEN

AAKANKSHA PATIL
AARON BRAUN
AARON LYNCH
AARON MULER
AARON WILLIAMS
AASTHA SHARMA
ABBIE FOULKE
ABBIE WALKER
ABBY HANSEN
ABBY HANSSEN
ABBY NEAL
ABBY PEDERSEN
ABBY SHAW
ABBY TRECARTIN
ABHIRAM SATHASIVAM
ABIGAIL BALDWIN
ABIGAIL BRANUM
ABIGAIL DUFTY
ABIGAIL JEFFERY
ABIGAIL LYNCH
ABIGAIL MAERKEL
ABIGAIL MILLER
ABIN VARGHESE
ADAEZE OGBUNIGWE
ADAM ANTAR
ADAM GEISWEIT
ADAM PERRY
ADAM STONER
ADAM SULLIVAN
ADAM TURNER
ADAM WILSON
ADDISON MERCER
ADIA RUMELL
ADRIAN KNOBLOCH
ADRIANA BARBADO
ADRIANA CASTRO
ADRIANA CONSTANTINESCU
ADRIANA HENRICHS
ADRIANNA DUBRAWSKA
ADRIANNE ARNOLD
ADRIENNE ENG
ADRIENNE FRAILEY
ADRIENNE WIENS
AFE IYORAH
AFNAN ISHAQ
AFTON MATTHEWS
AGNESE GURECKA
AGNESE LPSK
AGUSTIN GIL
AGUSTINA COTONAT
AHMED BOLAND
AIDAN BOUDREAU
AILISH O'LEARY AUSTIN
AISHA MAGSI
AISLING O'CONNOR
AJ UTKE
AKEEA FOX
AKICE AGWA
ALANA BELL
ALANA HAY
ALANA WEAFER
ALANA WIGLEY
ALANNA HATHCOCK
ALAYNA RILEY
ALBIN MYHRMAN
ALBIN NILSSON
ALEJANDRA MARTINEZ
ALEJANDRA ROMERO FONZ
ALEJANDRA TABARANZA
ALEJANDRO PINTOR
ALEKSANDER ALMBAKK
ALESSIA RICCI
ALEX BENNETT
ALEX COUTTS
ALEX GROVE

ALEX JUNG
ALEX KINSMAN
ALEX NEAGU
ALEX SOUKIS
ALEX TELLEZ
ALEX TRESA
ALEX WHITE
ALEXA GOLDSTEIN
ALEXA NICOLE GARCIA-SIGUENAS
ALEXA REYES
ALEXANDER KING
ALEXANDER OLADOKUN
ALEXANDRA ABNEY
ALEXANDRA CRUZ
ALEXANDRA DE LA ROCHA
ALEXANDRA GLANS
ALEXANDRA HADDAD
ALEXANDRA JARRIEL
ALEXANDRA LICATA
ALEXANDRA MARDIROSIAN
ALEXANDRA MARTIN
ALEXANDRA ROSEART
ALEXANDRA SCOTT
ALEXANDRA ST-GERMAIN
ALEXANDRIA BATTLE
ALEXANDRIA GOUDY
ALEXANDRIA MIDDLETON
ALEXANDRIA RODRIGUEZ
ALEXE BANKS
ALEXIS GRAVES
ALEXIS KILBURN
ALEXIS MAKIN
ALEXIS MCGOVERN
ALEXIS METCALF
ALEXIS PIHL
ALEXIS SIMONS
ALEXIS VIJ
ALEXIS WARD
ALEXXA ORDONEZ
ALFONSO AGUIRRE
ALFREDO HINOJOSA
ALI GREER
ALI HASAN
ALI MILLER
ALI YORDAN
ALICE DWYER
ALICE VAN DUUREN
ALICIA DESANTIS
ALICIA DYOGI
ALICIA MUELLER
ALICJA BUCHOWICZ
ALINA BIELAK
ALINA MEYER
ALISA CLARKE
ALISA MOORE
ALISHA BLANCHARD
ALISHA GILL
ALISHA PILKINGTON
ALISHA SOMMERVILLE
ALISON HAINES
ALISON HOE
ALISON HOMAN
ALISON PITMAN
ALISON SUTTON
ALISSA CARON
ALISSA RABIDEAU
ALISSE SAUNDERS
ALIVIA GARANT
ALIX NAICKER
ALLI MOORE
ALLI SERENCKO

ALLIE JESTER
ALLIE MARCOULLIER
ALLISON ALLAIN
ALLISON DUCLOS
ALLISON GRIMSTED
ALLISON JOHNSON
ALLISON KIBBE
ALLISON LAMPE
ALLISON LUONGO
ALLISON MARSHALL
ALLISON MOSBECK
ALLISON N.
ALLISON WEEKS
ALLISON WILDER
ALLY BURGETT
ALLY H.
ALLY STROUP
ALLYSON JORDAN
ALYCIA GILLASPIE
ALYSON BELLYBEAR
ALYSON HACHEY
ALYSON WANG
ALYSSA DAMN
ALYSSA DURRSTEIN
ALYSSA GRAY
ALYSSA GUYLL
ALYSSA HEWITT
ALYSSA JELLENIK
ALYSSA JOHNSON
ALYSSA LUNZ
ALYSSA MEIKLE
ALYSSA SOLDANO
ALYSSA ULIBARRI
ALYSSIA BUNTS
AMAL IMTIAZ
AMAN SHARMA
AMANA ABDURREZAK
AMANDA ALLEMYR
AMANDA BEADLESCOMB
AMANDA BRADSHAW
AMANDA BRENNAN
AMANDA BRENSEL
AMANDA BRINSON
AMANDA CUMMINGS
AMANDA DRAKE
AMANDA FRYE
AMANDA HOLMBERG
AMANDA JANKOWSKI
AMANDA JONES
AMANDA LAZAR
AMANDA LEMKE
AMANDA MERRITT
AMANDA MILLER
AMANDA NOVAK
AMANDA PARAMORE
AMANDA PUFALL
AMANDA REED
AMANDA ROBERTSON
AMANDA ROSS
AMANDA ROSSETTI
AMANDA ROUGEAU
AMANDA SARINANA
AMANDA SAVIG
AMANDA SPOOLSTRA
AMANDA TILLMAN
AMANDA WARD
AMANDA WAY
AMANDA WEBER
AMANTHA C. WAGNER
AMATHERA HERATO
AMBER DEWITT
AMBER GILLEY
AMBER HARDIN
AMBER MORRIS
AMBER VAN DE KERKHOF
AMEER LAHRIM

AMELIA BREWSTER
AMELIA LEISER
AMELIA RODRIGUEZ
AMELIA WALCEK
AMELIA WILLCOX
AMELIE BROOKS-HOCHHEIMER
AMI POWELL
AMIEE BELANGER
AMINA GOPALA-RAO
AMINA KERCHI
AMIRA GREGORY
AMREEN SALMA
AMY CALLAND
AMY DICKINSON
AMY EARLE
AMY EDWARDS-KNIGHT
AMY GREENBLATT
AMY GUNN BRIGGS
AMY HARRIS
AMY HOLLIDAY
AMY KIEHL
AMY LAWRENCEH
AMY LIU
AMY MATA
AMY MELLING
AMY PHILP
AMY RIES
AMY RILEY
AMY SMITH
AMY WILLIS
ANA CARMEN MARTINEZ SALINAS
ANA NIETO
ANA NOTARBARTOLO
ANA RUIZ
ANA SOLIS
ANA TOMAS
ANALISA ALLEN
ANARRA WHITCHER
ANASTASIA BOLINDER
ANASTASIA FOMICHEVA
ANASTASIYA HOLENCHUK
ANASTASIYA SERNETSKAYA
ANAYA FERREIRA
ANBIYA SALEEM
ANDERS BREGENDAHL
ANDEY WALLEN KEYREW
ANDRE AMPUERO
ANDREA CARON
ANDREA DRAGON
ANDREA HORVE
ANDREA SARPI
ANDREAS ZAKHARI
ANDREEA IONESCU
ANDRES REYNA
ANDREW BELLOMO
ANDREW BLASKOVICH
ANDREW DUNN
ANDREW HALL
ANDREW KELLEY
ANDREW PALACIOS
ANDREW VILLALPANDO
ANDREW WARREN
ANGELA BRITT
ANGELA FERGUSON
ANGELA FUNK
ANGELA WEBER
ANGELICA MARIN
ANGELINA LARSON
ANGELY RINCON
ANH LE
ANIKA SCHULTZ
ANITA JEGARL

ANITA METODIEVA
ANJA LISBET
ANNA BIEWER
ANNA BLADES
ANNA CHO
ANNA GRAY BUCKLEY
ANNA ISON
ANNA LEONARD
ANNA MCGUFFIE
ANNA MURNAGAHAN
ANNA NAVARRETE
ANNA PARKER
ANNA ROBBINS
ANNA WAGHORN
ANNA WESTERBEKE
ANNA WINGARD
ANNA WOOD-GAINES
ANNA ZIETKIEWICZ
ANNABELL SHAW
ANNABELLA PRINX
ANNABELLE OSBORNE
ANNALEISE LOXTON
ANNE BOBIS
ANNE BOSMAN
ANNE CAVOTO
ANNE CRUTCHLEY
ANNE KING
ANNE LESOURD
ANNE STEWART
ANNE-MARIE ELLE
ANNEJET KLEISSEN
ANNELISE DRAWBAUGH
ANNICK SMITH
ANNIE FAROOQ
ANNIE GRIGGS
ANNIE JOHANSSON
ANNIE KUEBLER
ANNIEK GRUNDY
ANNY SABINE MADER
ANOUK TUIJNMAN
ANTHONEE
EKTNITPHONG
ANTHONY CLARK
ANTHONY GIANCOLA
ANTHONY KNOTH
ANTHONY RODRIGUEZ
ANTHONY SCALISE
ANTONELLA AVOGADRO
ANUSHA RAJWANI
ANYA AMIN
ANYA MALTSBERGER
APPOLLO LOVELACE
APRIL JEANETTE MILLAN
APRIL XU
ARI KUEHN
ARIA LOPEZ
ARIA TRUJILLO
ARIADNA SANTOS
ARIAN MASON
ARIANA PENNO
ARIANAH REPP
ARIEL BLEDSOE
ARIEL KLINGHOFFER
ARIEL LAXO
ARIEL RUSSELL
ARIELLE FEHER
ARIELLE STEWART
ARIELLE VISHNY
ARINA CHUNG
ARIQUA FURSE
ARIS SEAMUS
ARJAV SHAH
ARLISSE LIM
ARNOLD BALTAZAR
ASAD SHABBIR
ASE GJEFSEN
ASHA ABRAMS
ASHLEE KEANE
ASHLEE WHITE
ASHLEIGH BROUGHILL-DOWLING
ASHLEIGH POOLE
ASHLEIGH WILSON
ASHLEY BENNING
ASHLEY BROUILLETTE
ASHLEY DYKES
ASHLEY GILBERT
ASHLEY GONZALES

ASHLEY GOODWIN
ASHLEY HORNER
ASHLEY LEONARD
ASHLEY LOMBARDO
ASHLEY MANUEL
ASHLEY MOORE
ASHLEY MORRISON
ASHLEY PANKNIN
ASHLEY RODRIGUEZ
ASHLEY ROSTEK
ASHLEY SEHATTI
ASHLEY SUMPTER
ASHLEY TURNER
ASHLEY WEGENER
ASHLIE BAIRE
ASHLIE HOLECEK
ASHLY NICOLE
ASHLYN WARDROP
ASHWIN SRIDHAR
ASIA AIRELLE LACSON
ASIA PRUCHNIEWSKA
ASMITA BISWAS
ASTRID HERMANS
ASZYA SUMMERS
ATHENA O'GORMAN
ATHENA YE
AUBREY KILL
AUBREY WONG
AUDRA WEIGAND
AUDREY LAFRANCE
AURORA PROVOOST
AUSTIN CROSS
AUSTIN FEEHAN
AUSTIN GRAY
AUSTIN KING
AUTUMN MCLEAN
AV ROBLES
AVA CHARD
AVA CHENOK
AVELINE WATSON
AWLIYA SAGULLO
AYA TAMIR-REGEV
AYELET KAPLAN
AYUMI KOIZUMI
BAILEY DUBBS
BAILEY EASSON
BAILEY HERRMANN
BAILEY MIREHOUSE
BAILEY PIGEAU
BAILEY SALICOS
BAILEY STEWART
BAILEY THOMPSON
BAILIE FISCHER
BAILLIE GRAVES
BARBARA SANCHEZ
BATSI S
BAUNNEE MARTINEZ
BAYAN ABUDAHAB
BAYAN OH
BE'LANNA MARTIN
BEATRICE H.
BEATRIZ CERNY
BEBE BENTLEY
BECCA FANTALIS
BECCA RUSSELL
BECCA TATUM
BECCA WILLIAMS
BECKY DYE
BECKY MCMORROW
BECKY ROGERS
BECKY ROPER
BEKAH LESSMANN
BEKI LILLIE
BELL GIACOMINI
BELLA GREY
BELLA MEANS
BEN DORSEY
BEN GROOT
BEN HUGHES
BEN KELLEY
BENJAMIN PARKIN
BERNADETTE RICO
BES ASHDEUSO
BETH DURI
BETH HELMS
BETH HOWARD
BETH KEITH
BETH RAYWOOD CROSS

BETH REVIS
BETHANY BROWN
BETHANY HART
BHAIRAVY S.
BIANCA BALAZHI
BIANCA CAVALLARI
BIANCA DUARTE
BIANCA GRAD
BIANCA GUTIERREZ
BIANCA SAN LUIS
BIANCA VELA
BIANCA VILLAMOR
BINALI PATEL
BING LAROUCHE
BLAIN SMITH
BLAZE SPIKER
BOBBY KENNEDY
BOBBY SCOTT
BONNIE SHIKLES
BONNIE WELLS
BRAD SELLS
BRADDY RAYES
BRADY TYBURSKI
BRANDI HOFFMAN
BRANDI ROBINSON
BRANDON BOOCKS
BRANDON BURCL
BRANDON CARBERRY
BRANDON HORNER
BRANDON SCOTT
BRAYAN ZAVALA
BREANNA ANGUS
BREANNA BACKSTROM
BREANNA LAWELLIN
BREE MANUS
BREN HOFFMANN
BRENDAN MCPHERSON
BRENNAH ANN
BRETT NEWMAN
BRI FAIRMAN
BRIA MANTHORNE
BRIAN BYRNE
BRIAN MCQUAID
BRIAN ROUNDS
BRIANA DYRNESS
BRIANA HARDY
BRIANA THOMPSON
BRIANNA BUTLER
BRIANNA GITTOS
BRIANNA IVY
BRIANNA MUNN
BRIANNA RYAN
BRIANNA SANDERS
BRIANNE SIMON
BRIAR HECKMAN
BRICE KIMBLE
BRIDGET COULTER
BRIDGET LORENZ
BRIDGET RAYMUNDO
BRIE TRUELOVE
BRITNEY WALLACE
BRITNIE JENKINS
BRITTANY BLAIR
BRITTANY CASSELMAN
BRITTANY GOODNIGHT
BRITTANY HOLLINGSWORTH
BRITTANY JONES
BRITTANY KOONTZ
BRITTANY MAY GARRETT
BRITTANY MENDOZA
BRITTANY MYRVIK
BRITTANY PICKETT
BRITTANY VAN DYKE
BRITTNEE MCQUARRIE
BRITTNEY B
BRITTNEY BEHYMER
BRITTNEY BLEVINS
BRITTNEY MAYS
BROOK BIGNELL
BROOKE DOLEGA
BROOKE HICKS
BROOKE MITCHELL
BROOKE R. BUSSE
BROOKE SCHMIDT
BRUNA ROCHA
BRUNO SALTAO

BRYAN HERMANO
BRYAN TRUSSLER
BRYCE LEW
BRYCE SMITH
BRYNN HENDERSON
BRYNNAN TIMMERMAN
BRYTNEY ANHORN
CAILET LATHAM
CAILLIN HOPKINS
CAITLIN BURRELL
CAITLIN DENNIS
CAITLIN DUERINCK
CAITLIN EHREN
CAITLIN GLIDEWELL
CAITLIN HANSON
CAITLIN HARVEY
CAITLIN LEWELLYN
CAITLIN LOGUE
CAITLIN MARIE
CAITLIN POWERS
CAITLIN SCHULTZ
CAITLIN WILLSEA
CAITLIN WOMACK
CAITLYN HAMMOND
CALEB BELL
CALEB KOPP
CALEB SEBORA
CALEB SILVERS
CALEB WILSON
CALLIE MCINERNEY
CALLIE SWARTZ
CALVIN FRANKLIN
CAMERON BUCHANAN
CAMERON CHEEK
CAMERON CONTE
CAMILA CALDERON
CAMILA PEREZ SAN MARTIN
CAMILA TOSCANO
CAMILLA HAWKER
CAMILLE CASTRO
CAMILLE DEVINE
CAMILLE LE BARON
CAMMIE RICHARDS
CARA CASTO
CARA HANCOCK
CARA MASON
CARA SWITALSKI
CARA WOOD
CARER LAGOW
CAREY FLANAGAN
CARIANN SAUNDERS
CARIE CLARK
CARINA HAMAM
CARINA KOBERL
CARL ARGABRITE
CARLEIGH IRBY
CARLIEN VAN DER STRAETEN
CARLY WILLIAMS
CARMEN GONZALEZ
CAROLINA CORTES
CAROLINA MOGOLLON
CAROLINA THIELL
CAROLINA YNG
CAROLINE AHLBERG
CAROLINE BILLARD
CAROLINE DUNN
CAROLINE IBARRA
CAROLINE LANCASTER
CAROLINE MALONE
CAROLINE SARDA
CAROLYN BONACCORSI
CARYN CHU
CARYN MCGRENRA
CARYS N
CASEY CASSIDY
CASEY NARANJO
CASEY NEALY
CASI BJORGAARD
CASIE GRIFFIS
CASSANDRA DEFALCO
CASSANDRA EKMAN
CASSIDY HOLBROOK
CASSIDY M
CASSIE NUNEZ
CASSIE SANTELLA
CAT VOGEL

287

CATALINA RADU
CATARINA CHAVES
CATE NEUHAUSER
CATHERINE BIEWER
CATHERINE CONNORS
CATHERINE NGUYEN
CATHERINE RIVAS
CATHERINE ROHRMANN
CATHY NGUYEN
CATHY PEAKE
CATIE BORDONARO
CATIE SCHAFER
CATRINA MAXWELL
CATRIONA FEENEY
CEARA SCOTT
CECELIA GEORGE
CECILIA SIBONA
CECILIA SOBRAL
CECILIE BJÄ,RNSKOV
CECILIE SABROE
CELESTE SOLORIO
CELIA RAMSAY
CELINE FERNANDES
SOUSA
CERAH MACINTYRE
CHALSE OKOROM
CHANA EDWARDS
CHANCE YOUNG
CHANDELLE DUMOND
CHANDLER MEAKINS
CHANEE HILL
CHANTEL GILES
CHANTEL KROON
CHANTELL MENESES
CHARISS CREAMER
CHARLES BLACKBURN
CHARLETTE CAMILLERI
CHARLI BALL
CHARLIE HERRERA
CHARLIE WILDISH
CHARLINE JANAUDY
CHARLOTTE FREARS
CHARLOTTE GRANSTAD
ERIKSSON
CHARLOTTE H
CHARLOTTE HYDE
CHARLOTTE WOODCOCK
CHARMAIN HUANG
CHAUNCY CRUZ
CHELCEE MILLER
CHELSEA BLANCO
CHELSEA CONNER
CHELSEA LINN
CHELSEA NICHOLS
CHELSEA RIMEL
CHELSEA RUDE
CHELSIE ROUT
CHERIE PATRICK
CHERISSE YAO
CHLOE BEESON
CHLOE BROBST
CHLOE HOFF
CHLOE LANDAU
CHLOE MEYER
CHLOE NOBLE
CHLOE PALKA
CHLOE PINER
CHLOE SCHMIDT
CHLOE-LYNNE SLATER
CHRIS BAILEY
CHRIS MADDOX
CHRISSY COE
CHRISSY ROBINS
CHRISTIAN GALANO
CHRISTIAN MARSHALL
CHRISTIAN NIXON
CHRISTIAN PHILLIPS
CHRISTIANA MUNOZ
CHRISTIE WHITE
CHRISTINA CROUCH
CHRISTINA GEMINO
CHRISTINA HAYES
CHRISTINA KOURAKOS
CHRISTINA LU
CHRISTINA MAROTTI
CHRISTINA RELAK
CHRISTINA TORNELLO
CHRISTINE CANAVAN

CHRISTINE ENNIS
CHRISTINE GOODELL
CHRISTINE GUTIERREZ
CHRISTINE MURPHY
CHRISTINE PIRANI
CHRISTINE POESKE
CHRISTINE SCHNOOR
CHRISTINE SOMMERS
CHRISTOPHER MILLS
CHRISTOPHER MOONEY
CHRISTOPHER NAVA
CHRISTYN HOPE
CIARA BREWITT
CIARA O'LOUGHLIN
CIARA RAKEL
CIARAN LETT
CINDY DONG
CINDY VOLDSETH
CIOFIRDEL IZABELA
CLAIRE AYOTTE
CLAIRE LATANE
CLAIRE MELIA
CLAIRE MURPHY
CLAIRE WEIS
CLAIRE WYNNE
CLARA JANE
CLARE BOURKE
CLARE MROZ
CLARENCE FLETCHER
CLARINE CHAN
CLARISSE HELOU
CLAUDIA COCHRAN
CLAUDIA COMPIAN
CLAUDIA DE WITH
CLAUDIA GUINANSACA
CLAUDIA LAHTI
CLAUDIA ZOBEL
CLAUDINE MARIE LEE
CLAY HODGE
CLODAGH GRIBBEN
CLOE NEWTON-ADE
COBUS OOSTHUIZEN
COCO XX
CODY ALSIP
CODY ANDRE
CODY HOPPWOOD
CODY TURPLE
COLBI APPLEBY
COLBY MARTINEZ
COLLEEN H
COLLEEN WEST
COLLEEN WILLIAMS
COLLEEN ZANDER
COLTON SMITH
COLTON VANDEGRIFT
CONNIE SEELYE
CONNOR M.
CONNOR MANNING
CONNOR ROGGIE
CONOR BODDY
CONOR DUNWORTH
CONOR O'LEARY
CORALIE BEDARD
CORBAN CAUSEY
COREY DAVIS
COREY DYSON
COREY OLIVER
COREY PARSLEY
CORI DOWELL
CORINTHIA RIDER
COURTNEY BICKER
COURTNEY CHANDLER
COURTNEY CONLEY
COURTNEY HELEN
THOMPSON
COURTNEY JORGENSEN
COURTNEY LANAGAN
COURTNEY LEWIS
COURTNEY PERSONS
COURTNEY ROBB
COURTNEY RUSHING
CRISTINA GONZALEZ
CRISTINA MARTINEZ
CRISTINA ORLOWSKI
CRUCE GRAMMATICO
CRYSTAL BEVAN
CRYSTAL DURANT
CRYSTAL PEREA

CRYSTAL REGALADO
CYN HORCASITAS
CYNTHIA BIERNESSER
CYNTHIA DONG
CYNTHIA WADI
D.J. SMALLEN
DAKOTA BALDWIN
DALLAS GAGE
DALTON GLENN
DAN SMITH
DANA BLACKWELL
DANA CARLO
DANA CUADRADO
DANA LATHAM
DANA STODDART
DANI SPRINGER
DANIEL CANEDO
DANIEL CROTHERS
DANIEL FAIRCLOUGH
DANIEL PRATTLEY
DANIELA CASALINO
DANIELA GARCIA
DANIELA PILLEMER
DANIELA VEGA
DANIELLA RANA
DANIELLE CLOUTIER
DANIELLE DAVIS
DANIELLE DURST
DANIELLE GARVIN
DANIELLE HOLMES
DANIELLE HOLTZ
DANIELLE HUNT
DANIELLE KELLY
DANIELLE MORGAN
DANIELLE SMITH
DANIELLE STUART
DANIELLE VILLAERA
DANIELLE WOODCOCK
DANNIELLE MORIONDO
DANNY MEGILL
DANNY WEE
DARA WAXELBAUM
DAREN SIA
DARINKA THIJS
DARION PALM
DARITH LY
DARREN PERSAD
DASHA BADIKOVA
DASHIELL GRACI
DAVE QUIGLEY
DAVID ANDRADE
DAVID BEDWARD
DAVID ENGELAND
DAVID MASON
DAVID MATHESON
DAVID O'KEEFE
DAVID TREJO
DAY HOLLOWAY
DAYLIN SPROULE
DAYNA BICKHAM
DEANNA JOHNSON
DEANNA MORIN
DEANNA SKAGGS
DEBORAH JOHNSON
DEBORAH KLEBANSKY
DEENA EDWARDS
DEEPTHI ACHARYA
DEIVIDAS AKSOMAITIS
DELOBEL AURORE
DENI BUDMAN
DENIZ KIRCI
DENNISE PELLOT
DEREK BLOOM
DESERAE MCGLOTHEN
DESIRAE CAMPBELL
DESIREE CARO
DESIREE CONLEY
DESTINY BURNETT
DEVAN DEVORE
DEVYN MCCLAY
DEWAYNE HASLETT
DHRUV PRASAD
DIANA ALONSO
DIANA AMPUDIA
DIANA JIMENEZ
DIANA SEBASTIAN
DIANA VERDE
DIANNE DUNCAN

DILLON SPIRO
DIM MANG
DINA YOUNG
DJ NELSON
DJ WISELY
DOMINIC POTRATZ
DOMINIQUE GEORGE
DOMINIQUE LOZANO
DON HUGHES
DONNIE MANGINO
DONOVAN CONVERY
DONOVAN TIMMINS
DRAKE HETH
DREW DUBINSKY
DUCKY PALMER
DUSTIN WISE
DYL GOODWIN
DYLAN EARLES
DYLAN GIRARD
DYLAN HIRSCHBEIN
DYLAN WAHLSTROM
EBONNY LAWRENCE
EDEN ELASH
EDEN HAIN
EDEN ZAKOUSKII
EDUARDO CAMELIO
EDUARDO CHAVEZ
EDVINAS VAKARIS
EDWARD JUAREZ
EILEEN CRINNION
EILISH NEWCOMB
EIMY FERNANDEZ
EIRYN GRIEST
SCHWARTZMAN
EKS SANGHA
ELAINE RU
ELEANOR QUINLIVAN
ELEANOR SCOTT-ALLEN
ELENA SPERONIS
ELENI SAGREDOS
ELENI VASSILIOU
ELIEL LAM
ELIJAH BARBER
ELIN BREND BJORHEI
ELIN SVENSSON
TOLLEHED
ELINA MIHEJEVA
ELIORA HORST
ELISABETH STRASSER
ELISAR HAYDAR
ELISE EVANS
ELISE MADELEINE
ELISE NETHERCOTT
ELISE VIOLA
ELIZABEH LOPEZ
ELIZABETH CHENEY
ELIZABETH COOK
ELIZABETH DIAZ
ELIZABETH EARHART
ELIZABETH ESCOBAR
ELIZABETH FRIDMAN
ELIZABETH GODINEZ
ELIZABETH GROSVENOR
ELIZABETH HAMMONS
ELIZABETH HOLLAR
ELIZABETH HOWARD
ELIZABETH JENNER
ELIZABETH LEE
ELIZABETH MAGLIO
ELIZABETH RAMIREZ
ELIZABETH SAUER
ELIZABETH SHEWAN
ELIZABETH TINDALL
ELIZABETH VILLARREAL
ELIZABETH WEIS
ELIZABETH WILLIAMSON
ELKIN SCOTT
ELLE EPHANT
ELLE FLYNN
ELLEN LUNDSTROM
ELLEN SVENONIUS
ELLI KAMPE
ELLIE BIEBESHEIMER
ELLIE CHAVEZ
ELLIE CORDER
ELLIE HANSEN
ELLIE PUGH
ELLIE ROSIA

288

ELLINOR BERNINGE
ELLY MANHOLLAN
ELLY MCCORNACK
ELSEBETH VANG
ELYANA AMIR
EMERY BOWMAN
EMILEE KUIPHOFF
EMILIE ROCHETTE
EMILY BAGNALL
EMILY BASTIAN
EMILY BAUDER
EMILY BELL
EMILY BOYD
EMILY BURROUGHS
EMILY CARTER
EMILY CASEBOLT
EMILY COSMI
EMILY DENTON
EMILY DEPPERMANN
EMILY DREW
EMILY FOX
EMILY GERETY
EMILY HAN
EMILY HATFIELD
EMILY HULL
EMILY JOHANNES
EMILY LOUDENBACK
EMILY LYON
EMILY LYON
EMILY MACINTYRE
EMILY MCDONALD
EMILY MOHAN
EMILY NANADJANIANS
EMILY NASH
EMILY NETHERCOTT
EMILY PEARCE
EMILY PESTELLO
EMILY RISTAU
EMILY SCHLOEDER
EMILY SHEEHAN
EMILY STEELE
EMILY STRAND
EMILY THOMAS
EMILY WALLACE-SIBERT
EMILY WALLEY
EMILY WHEELER
EMILY WILLIAMS
EMILY WILSON
EMILY WRIGHT
EMILY YOUNG
EMMA BROWN
EMMA DENK
EMMA JOURNAGAN
EMMA LAKE
EMMA MALINS
EMMA MURPHY
EMMA PETFIELD
EMMA PIOLI
EMMA ROBERTSON
EMMA ROWLANDS
EMMA SCHRAM
EMMA SILVER
EMMA TIEDENS
EMMA WASHBURN
EMMA YOUNG
EMMI VARIS
EMMY EGBERT
EMMYLOU BARDEN
ERIC AMI
ERICA D'ANDREA
ERICA MARRS
ERICA MARTIN
ERICK BERGSTROM
ERIKA ARTEAGA
ERIKA CHRISTENSON
ERIKA KREYMEYER
ERIKA OLESEN
ERIKA THOMPSON
ERIN BALLANTYNE
ERIN CARTON
ERIN HEALY
ERIN KOTAS
ERIN LONG
ERIN MALIS
ERIN MCBRIDE
ERIN MISIALEK
ERIN NEWMAN
ERIN RAND

ERIN REGAN
ERIN RENFROE
ERIN RUSSELL
ERIN SCHUHRKE
ERNESTAS VASCENKA
ERWIN SANCHEZ
ESTEE KALINA
ESTELLE TAYLOR
ESTHER AVILA
ESTHER WADE
ESZTER CSUTORA
ETHAN HANSEN
ETHAN PARISEAU
EUGENIO CONTI
EUGENIO PARAMO
EULALEE LUMSDEN
EVA CORTES
EVA DUE
EVA WIND
EVAN JONES
EVAN THOMPSON
EVANGELINE C.H.
EVIE JOHNSON
FAAKHRA CHOUDHRY
FABIO SCITA
FAISAL ALGHANNAM
FAITH MACHUCA
FAITH MIRE
FALETIA STOWELL
FARAH ALBANI
FARAH HANISA
FARAH J
FARIS AL AMOUDI
FATIMA SAGULLO
FATMA ALBANNAI
FAVIOLA TORRES
FEE BROWN
FERDOSA ABDI
FERGUS HALLIDAY
FERNANDA SILVEIRA
CARDOSO
FERNANDO SANTOS
FFION LEWIS
FIONA WALKER
FLO STANLEY
FLORENCE VON
UNGERN-STERNBERG
FLORENCIA GONZALEZ
GRIFFERO
FLORENCIA MESA
FRANCESCA BATTIATO
FRANCIELLE VILLACA
FRANCISCO PIRES
FRANCOIS ASHUN
FRANK FREEMAN
FRANSHESCA MARIE-
GRANT
FRED SHORT
FREDRIKA LINDWALL
FRIDA RICHARDS
GABBY DELFORGE
GABBY GILLESPIE
GABBY LENNON
GABBY MARIE
GABBY MCMANUS
GABBY WINGER
GABE MURPHY
GABI VANBUSKIRK
GABRIEL BELARMINO
GABRIEL CYWINSKI
GABRIELA CARDENAS
GABRIELE LASAITE
GABRIELLE LEFEBVRE
GABRIELLE S.
GABRIELLE STAGATHE
GABY HALE
GABY RAMOS
GAIA CHURCH
GARRETT GREGG
GAVIN TELLER
GEENA JOSEPH
GEM MAGNUSDOTTIR
GEMMA GLANCEY
GEMMA O'REILLY
GENA FRANCZAK
GENEVA CASEBOLT
GENEVA PAULK
GEORGIA CRANSTON

GEORGIA GOOD
GEORGIA HARRIS
GEORGIA HO
GEORGIA WALLER
GEORGIA WARD
GEORGINA PHELPS
GETTER TRUMSI
GIGI WINGEL
GIJS RAAIJMAKERS
GINA BEAUCHEF
GINA TAMBELLINI
GINA-VICTORIA MYHRE
GINNY HAYES
GISELLA CARRASCO
GISELLE ABREU
GISELLE MONTGOMERY
GIULIA DEL'LABON
GIULIANA GAROFALO
GIULIANA RIEDEL
GLADYS BARBOSA
GLORIA RODRIGUEZ
GOKSU SEVIM
GRACE ALSTON
GRACE BERRILL
GRACE BRUMBY
GRACE ELLIS
GRACE HAILEY
GRACE HAUSER
GRACE MUIR
GRACE MURPHY
GRACE PARSONS
GRACE SAWYER
GRACIELA COLIN
GRACIELLA LLAGAS
GRANDON BROWN
GRANT EARLE
GRANT FLORENCE
GRECIA GOMEZ
GRETTA HUNNEKENS
GUNNHILD SKJOLD
GUSTAVO CARO
GWINDALYN HARRISON
GWYN CAREY
HAILEY AUDFROID
HAILEY BRAMHALL
HAILEY BROCK
HAILEY WINDSOR
HAJIRAH OMAR
HALEA DICKINSON
HALEA MONIGAN
HALEY CONATSER
HALEY FARRAR
HALEY GLIDDEN
HALEY HAGEN
HALEY HARBIN
HALEY HEITZ
HALEY KROES
HALEY LAWSON
HALEY LAWYER
HALEY SANDERS
HALI WILSON
HALLEY HAM
HANAE FAYETTE
HANH TRAN
HANNA HOLM
HANNA JUHOLA
HANNA MILLER
HANNA SCHEHAK
HANNAH ANDERSON
HANNAH AUNGST
HANNAH BABCOCK
HANNAH BEVERLEY
HANNAH BLATTER
HANNAH BLOSSER
HANNAH BRIDWELL
HANNAH BROOKS
HANNAH CULLERTON
HANNAH DAYE
HANNAH EARL
HANNAH FREDERICK
HANNAH GRAY
HANNAH HALL
HANNAH HARTLINE
HANNAH HARVEY
HANNAH HASSAN
HANNAH HUNT
HANNAH JENKINS
HANNAH JONES

HANNAH JOY
HANNAH LEE
HANNAH LORENC
HANNAH MARKLIN
HANNAH MARTIN
HANNAH MILLER
HANNAH MILLIGAN
HANNAH PEREIRA
HANNAH PHIPPS
HANNAH S
HANNAH SALLA
HANNAH SCHMICK
HANNAH SCOTT
HANNAH SIMPSON
HANNAH STEVENS
HANNAH SWAFFORD
HANNAH WARNES
HANNAH WITTHANS
HANS HAUPT
HAR LUC
HAREEM ABBASI
HARLEE MILLER
HARRISON HITCHCOCK
HARRY MICHAEL
HARRY ROBERTS
HARRY STYLES
HAYDEN KRISELL
HAYLEY FIELD
HEATH MCCONNELL
HEATHER BARNES
HEATHER GEBHARDT
HEATHER M.
HEATHER MAY
HEATHER MCNAIR
HEATHER ROBERTS
HEATHER TYMMS
HEATHER WARD
HEATHER ZIEMBA
HEIDI PADDOCK
HEIDI TANNER
HELEN MACH
HELEN MARINES
HELEN ROBERTSON
HELENE BENDIKSEN
HELLENA MIDDLETON
HERMIONE GRANGER
HETA NIKULA
HIMAJA MOTHERAM
HO JING EN
HOLDEN BRIMHALL
HOLLY FERNANCE
HOLLY GOODING
HOLLY LUFT
HOLLY MEINL
HOLLY THOMAS
HOLLY YARASKAVITCH
HONEY ROSE
HOPE FELTS
HUGO BURNS
HUNTER BOSS
HUNTER JONES
IAN BROWN
IAN DOKIE
IAN HERMOGENES
IAN KEIERLEBER
IANA MURRAY
ICYE KELLEY
ILEANA FALZOLGHER
ILONA SIIRILA
IMANI CELESTIN
IMRAN ASHRAFF
INA INSANITY
INDI PATERSON
INDIA SLOAN
INDIGO WAYWORTH
INES KASEMIR
INGELA ASP
INGRID HARRIS
INGRID NICKELSEN
INGRID NIXIE
IOLANDA PALMA
IRAM SHAFIQ
IRMAIDA BAERGA
IRVING PALOMINO
IRYNA NIKITENKO
ISAAC BUDDE
ISABEL CORDERO
ISABEL FEN

ISABEL GAURANO
ISABEL NAKONIECZNY
ISABEL VAZQUEZ
ISABELLA
SPIRIDIGLIOZZI
ISABELLE CUMMING
ISABELLE HAYDEN
ISABELLE SIMIONESCU
ISABELLE SJO HANSSON
IVANA LJUBEJ
IVO FERNANDES
IVY ACASIO
IVY ENGWALL
JAAP VAN DER WEL
JAC GRIMM
JACE HOLMES
JACK BAILEY
JACK LOTZ
JACKIE ASBURY
JACKIE CRILLEY
JACKIE LOUISE
JACKLYN HANSON
JACKQULYN
STEPHENSON
JACKSON AMADIO
JACKSON PORTER
JACLYN ALSTON
JACOB ALBRIGHT
JACOB ARNOULD
JACOB CABELL
JACOB JOHNSON
JACOB KEANE
JACOB MCCABE
JACOB SIMMS
JACOB WHITFIELD
JACOB WILLS
JACQUELINE ABELA
JACQUI SILVA
JACY-ERIN GRAY-
DAVIDSON
JADE GARDNER
JADE KIES
JADE LATHAM
JADEN COTTORONE
JAIME GRAHAM
JAIMIE POMARES
JAKLYN LABINE
JAKOB LEWIS
JAKUB MURAWSKI
JAMES CAIN
JAMES HAWORTH
JAMES HOLDER
JAMES HOYLE
JAMES KUEHL
JAMES LECLAIR
JAMIE CHAU
JAMIE GIRARD
JAMIE MAULT
JAMIE STITES
JAMIE TURK
JAMIE WOLFISH
JAMILA YOUNG
JAN ZIPFLER
JANA JAUNBERZINA
JANA MIHALIC
JANA SCHWEIGERT
JANELLE LEYBA
JANELLE PATTERSON
JANET MENDEZ
JANINE MIGGE
JANNA HECKATHORN
JANNIA BERNDTSSON
JARED DURON
JARED FIORI
JARED HANSEN
JASDIN DEUBEL
JASIU RAJCA
JASMIN JAHANDAR
JASMIN KLIEMANN
JASMINA CUBELIC
JASMINE ARMAS
JASMINE GARLAND
JASMINE HOANG
JASON LALLJEE
JASON ST. CLAIR
JASPER SMITH
JAVONIEL TROWERS
JAY ABELLANOSA

JAY MAHARATH
JAY MICHAEL
JAY SHENOY
JAYCEE BRADFORD
JAYDEN BONAR
JAYJAY ATANACIO
JAYME FINN
JAYME RILEY
JAYMIN BECK
JAYNA GOMEZ
JAZMINE SILVA
JAZMYNE BERRY
JC RIDDLE
JEAN PAUL COLLET
RIANCHO
JEAN ZHANG
JEANETTE MENDIOLA
JEANNA MICHEL
JEANNIE LIN
JEANNIE SANDEFER
JEFF DODGE
JEFF FREYSZ
JEFFREY PIZARRO
JEFFREY WEST
JELENA GLISIC
JEMMA SIMPSON
JEN FELIX
JEN GAMBALE
JENA LEPLA
JENI HOLLAND
JENICE CARRASQUILLO
JENIFER BLAIR
JENIFER TEWART
JENN ZYMNIS
JENNA MOSILLAMI
JENNA MULLIGAN
JENNA YOCUM
JENNESSA LANZA
JENNIE BERNHARDSSON
JENNIFER BAILEY
JENNIFER BEEBE
JENNIFER BONDARCHUK
JENNIFER CURRIE
JENNIFER FLACK
JENNIFER KERGOURLAY
JENNIFER LIU
JENNIFER MARIA
JENNIFER MARSHALL
JENNIFER PASQUILL
JENNIFER PAYNE
JENNIFER PLYLER
JENNIFER RODRIGUEZ
JENNIFER STEELE
JENNIFER THORNTON
JENNIFER TRAN
JENNIFER VISCHER
JENNY BUG
JENNY BULL
JENNY GLASSCOCK
JENNY HILL
JENNY POPE
JENNY ROOT
JENNY TRAN
JENNYFER CRUZ
JEREMY BIRD
JEREMY HOLLEY
JEREMY WEST
JERRY HART
JERRY HIX
JESS CLARK
JESS KINSLOW
JESS LISTER
JESS SALDIERNA
JESS WESTERMAN
JESSE EVANS-JENKINS
JESSE MARTIN
JESSE TIMMER
JESSE WILKINSON
JESSICA ALLEN
JESSICA ANDERSON
JESSICA BUKAS
JESSICA CARPENTER
JESSICA CHANDLER
JESSICA DEMETRIOS
JESSICA GARCIA
JESSICA GARZA-SAENZ
JESSICA HALL
JESSICA HIRSH

JESSICA HOLBROOK
JESSICA INGLE
JESSICA KEDDY
JESSICA KWAN
JESSICA LOGAN
JESSICA LOOMIS
JESSICA LOUDERMILK
JESSICA MARTIN
JESSICA OLIVEIRA
JESSICA PLASCENCIA
JESSICA REED
JESSICA REID
JESSICA REINKE
JESSICA RUSSELL
JESSICA SCHMIDT
JESSICA SPENCER
JESSICA STOPERA
JESSICA YANAVITCH
JESSICA YOWELL
JESSICAH HOOPER
JESSIE EDELMAN
JESSIE GALLO
JESSIE LIU
JESSIE LYLE
JEWEL LONG
JHANNA RAMIREZ
JIAN MANGANTI
JIE YU FONG
JILISA GUTHRO
JILL BARCENA
JILL KAPLAN
JILL TALIAFERRO
JILLIAN BATEMAN
JILLIAN WARD
JING WANG
JIZZELLE SAN LUIS
JOAN JAVIER
JOANIE WAELTI
JOANNA SCATASTI
JOANNA WOLNY
JOANNE E
JOCELYN CURLEY
JOCELYN ESTRADA
MONTES
JOCELYN GAITSKELL
JOCELYN HOMMES
JOCELYN HUOT
JOCELYNE LABERGE
JODI VAN
JOE MINAGLIA
JOE VELAZQUEZ
JOEL BURGESS
JOEY HUYNH
JOEY NAREZ
JOHANNA BORMAN
JOHANNE THOMSEN
JOHANNES RYYNANEN
JOHN DAVIS
JOHN FORNER
JOHN HAWKINS
JOHN KEARNS
JOHN KESSLING
JOHN LYNCH
JOHN PERINE
JOHN PHILIP SALALIMA
JOHNATHAN DAINSBERG
JON ALLEN
JON GOLDHIRSCH
JON KITAGAWA
JONATHAN ALICEA
JONATHAN FORD
JONATHAN TANGUAY
JONNA NAMERFORS
JONNY TETLEY
JORDAN CLINE
JORDAN EVANS
JORDAN GRENIER
JORDAN HINCHCLIFFE
JORDAN KEITH
JORDAN KELM
JORDAN MAR
JORDAN MONROE
JORDAN SCHMIDT
JORDAN SHEETS
JORDAY DAWN
JORDIN OVERTON
JORDON KEAR
JORGE AGUILERA

JORGE GAYTAN
JOSE PENA
JOSE TORRES
JOSELIN APARICIO
JOSEPH EASTWOOD
JOSEPH JACO
JOSEPH JENNER
JOSEPH MADLANGBAYAN
JOSEPH MCCARTHY
JOSEPH QUINTON
JOSEPH TOLLE
JOSEPH WILLS
JOSEPHINE EDER
JOSEPHINE TEE
JOSH FOTI
JOSH JAMES
JOSH LEE
JOSH WARD
JOSHUA REYNOLDS
JOSHWA HALL
JOSIAH CLARK
JOSIE BAKER
JOSIE EPPING
JOVANA DJOKIC
JOY COLEMAN
JOY SUMMNER
JOY WANG
JOYCE VAN HERCK
JOYCELYN DOWNS
JULES COURTINE
JULIA FONTE
JULIA GALLOWAY
JULIA HOANG
JULIA HORAN
JULIA LANE
JULIA LOF
JULIA MILLE
JULIA PESCE
JULIA POOL
JULIA POPPELMANN
JULIA STANGL
JULIA TALLEY
JULIA ZALMANOFF
JULIAN GARCIA-KWAN
JULIAN GOMEZ
JULIANA COELHO
JULIANNA HELMS
JULIE ERENST
JULIE LOVENBERG
JULIE MONTGOMERY
JULIE NUNLEY
JULIET DE GOEDE
JULIO QUINTANILLA
JULISSA MARTINEZ
JULIUS ADVINCULA
JUNE HEARTYE
JUNIOR MELO
JUSTIN DEJESUS
JUSTIN KYLE DEJESUS
JUSTIN MCCRORY
JUSTIN UTZ
JUSTIN WASHBURN
JUSTIN WILKS
JUSTINE BEANS
JUSTINE NUNEZ
JUSTINE RAQUEL NUNEZ
JYOTHSNA
MURALIDHARAN
KADEN LACROSS
KADY JONES
KAEJAUNY TUFTS
KAELAH PIKELLE
KAI LING CHONG
KAILEA CONLEY
KAILEY CARRINGTON
KAILEY THOMPSON
KAILYN MAXWELL
KAIQUE STORCK
KAITLIN MACLEOD
KAITLIN ULBRICH
KAITLYN ADAMS
KAITLYN BLEAU
KAITLYN CAPUTO
KAITLYN HEINDEL
KAITLYN SHEHEE
KAITLYN TROWBRIDGE
KAITLYNN BROOKINS
KAITY BRAYMORE

KAITY SHEPPARD
KALEB ASKEW
KALEE MERCER
KALEIGH WHITE
KALEY SHEEHAN
KALI CRIDER
KALINA HILL
KALLY BRUMFIELD
KAMARA HOFFMAN
KAMERON MCCLINTON
KANDICE CHANDLER
KANG JUN LEONG
KARA CHATHAM
KARA KILLINGER
KARA LOPEZ
KARA MAGILL
KARA REDD
KARA SALGADO
KARALINE STAMPER
KAREN HANSEN
KAREN HAUBERT
KAREN MANZONE
KAREN MELLARK
KAREN NG
KAREN RIVAS
KAREN YANG
KARENNA ONER
KARI THOMPSON
KARINA ALEGRE
KARINA DIAZ
KARINA EMERIC
KARINA MURRIETA
KARINA NIED
KARLEY BEAUDETTE
KARLIE CALHOUN
KARLIJN HERFORTH
KARY SHAW
KARYN PEARSON
KARYSSA WHITTON
KASAUNDRA PULLAN
KASEY CASTLE
KASPER CHRISTENSEN
KASSEY ROCHA
KASSIA NECKLES
KASSIE BROWN
KAT GREY
KAT NICOLE
KAT SKAFIDAS
KAT TRNKA
KATARINA WEX
KATE (SUNGLASSES)
KATE DOLAN
KATE FENTON
KATE NEWSOME
KATE SHAFFER
KATE TONGE
KATELYN BARNETT
KATELYN RAWLINGS
KATERYN BUESO
KATEY KOCH
KATHARINA SLOMINSKI
KATHARYN VELA
KATHERINE BOUFFORD
KATHERINE CAMACHO
KATHERINE GOMEZ
KATHERINE MACPHAIL
KATHERINE MEEKER
KATHERINE PALMER
KATHERINE PURVIS
KATHERINE STONE
KATHERINE WRIGHT
KATHLEEN BURKE
KATHLEEN HARKINS
KATHLEEN MCGROARTY
KATHLEEN RICKARD
KATHRYN ADAMS
KATHRYN MILLAR
KATHRYN NOYES
KATHRYN OKADA
KATHY RUSSO
KATIA MARTINEZ
KATIE ANNEAR
KATIE BUNT
KATIE CROSS
KATIE DEO
KATIE DURRETT
KATIE EDWARDS
KATIE FERRY

KATIE FITZGERALD
KATIE GARNETT
KATIE HANSEN
KATIE LECH
KATIE LEE
KATIE LETEXIER
KATIE LINFIELD
KATIE MARSHALL
KATIE MURNANE
KATIE MUSULIN
KATIE OLACH
KATIE REIS
KATIE ROBERTS
KATIE ROELLCHEN
KATIE ROWLAND
KATIE SOKOL
KATIE STOMPS
KATIE STONICH
KATIE TEMBY
KATIE TERRY
KATIE VALAIKE
KATIE VALLEM
KATIE WALSH
KATIE WARREN
KATIE WILLIAMS
KATIE-ANN DRYDEN
KATO DE BOCK
KATRIN PAGEL
KATRINA CLEMENTS
KATRINA THOMSON
KATSA STERLING
KATY KAY
KATY NAGY
KATY PADDOCK
KATY ROSE
KAY POWER
KAYAN PATEL
KAYCE FELDKAMP
KAYLA ABRAMOWSKI
KAYLA BENSON
KAYLA CLARK
KAYLA GEORGE
KAYLA GUBOV
KAYLA MASUR
KAYLA MYERS
KAYLA NELSON
KAYLA NOBLE
KAYLA OTERO
KAYLA PETERSEN
KAYLA WHITTLE
KAYLA ZAGRAY
KAYLA ZYNEL
KAYLEE GAINES-MCGEE
KAYLEIGH COLBOURN
KAYLEIGH GADES
KAYLYN ROBARDS
KC SHUAIGE
KEAGAN MILITANTE
KEATON WESTMORELAND
KEELAN BRYDON
KEENA GEORGE
KEIRSTIN SKINNER
KELCI LEGG
KELLEN NG
KELLI THOMPSON
KELLI TILFORD
KELLIE GROLLE
KELLIE HENEY
KELLY BILENKIS
KELLY CARLSON
KELLY JENKINS
KELLY LEMASTER
KELLY LO-A-FOE
KELLY MORRISSEY
KELLY N
KELLY ROSS
KELLY SHOULDICE
KELLY TOWNSEND
KELSEY AKIN
KELSEY BECKER
KELSEY DICKSON
KELSEY FARRAR
KELSEY GLASS
KELSEY GREEN
KELSEY HANSEN
KELSEY NAVARRO
KELSEY QUINN

KELSI MCCABE
KELSIE SMITH
KENDALL LIPPSTREU
KENDALL MURPHY
KENDRA JOHNSON
KENNEDY ENNS
KENNEDY JOSEPH
KENNEDY LAFFOON
KENNEDY PASAY
KERRIE RITCHIE
KERRY GRAZIANO
KETKI JERE
KEVIN HU
KEVIN LEWIS
KEYLA ALEMAN
KHALISAH WAN
KHANH HUYN
KIAHRA MONK
KIERA HOGGAN
KIERRA WEATHERHEAD
KIERSTEN JOHNSON
KIKO BLAKE
KIM ANDRIC
KIM ELENOR CUASAY
KIM LE
KIM VAN WAAYENBURG
KIM ZENKER
KIMBERLY COMBS
KIMBERLY HO
KIMBERLY KALINEC
KIMBERLY METZGER
KIMBERLY THORNTON
KINSEY VAVRUSKA
KINZEE P.
KIRA BRIST
KIRA ROBBINS
KIRBY CALLAN
KIRK TORNGA
KIRKLAND GRANDSTAFF
KIRSTEN BRUNELLE
KIRSTEN RENFROE
KIRSTIN DALEY
KIRSTIN MORRIS
KIRSTY AITCHISON
KIRSTY DINHAM
KIRSTY WONG
KIRTI NUTHI
KITTY SCHEPKENS
KORTNEY BURPEE
KOURTNEY CINTRON
KOURTNEY SUSZKO
KRISITNA CROMWELL
KRISTA W
KRISTAN ALEXANDER
KRISTAN SHUFORD
KRISTEE COPLEY
KRISTEN CHERNEY
KRISTEN COWGILL
KRISTEN GABRIEL
KRISTEN JOY DIZON
KRISTEN KEIBEL
KRISTEN MOORE
KRISTEN SIMMONS
KRISTEN TOLSTRUP
KRISTI DEL GUIDICE
KRISTIE MATHESON
KRISTIN CHANG
KRISTIN SCHULTZ
KRISTINA KRASNY
KRISTINA MATTHEWS
KRISTINA WALDEN
KRISTINE ILJINA
KRISTINE ZABALA
KRISTY HOSKINS
KRISTY POISSANT
KRISTY ZAVORKA
KRISTYN PATTON
KRITIKA GOVIL
KRYSTAL RODRIQUEZ
KRYSTOL GRAYSON
KWAKU SEFA
KYAH LEWIS
KYE HANDELMAN
KYLA QI
KYLA-MARIE GOODHEW
KYLE BRITTAIN
KYLE PEARCE
KYLE SCHWARTZ

KYLE SHEHAN
KYLEE CRAVEN
KYLEE RATH
KYLEEN SORENSEN
KYLEIGH DAVIS
KYLIE GRIFFIS
KYLIE JANE KUDRAVY
KYLIE SACAPANO
KYNAN DOCKSSTADER
KYR ELIESON
KYRA ODWARKA
LAINIE BEAUCHEMIN
LAIS BAPTISTA
LANDON SHULTZ
LANE MCDONALD
LANEY DAVIS
LARKYN TIMMERMAN
LARRY BOLTOVSKOI
LARS SANDNES
LAURA ALEXANDER
LAURA ARIAS
LAURA BENNING
LAURA BUTLER
LAURA CHATHAM
LAURA DINN
LAURA DONOHUE
LAURA ESCOBAR
LAURA FERNANDEZ
LAURA FLEIG-CARTA
LAURA FLEURY
LAURA HEIT
LAURA MORALES
LAURA MURPHY
LAURA NIDAY
LAURA S
LAURA SIGMUND
LAURA THEALL
LAUREL CLARK
LAUREN ANDERSON
LAUREN BAKER
LAUREN BARCLAY
LAUREN BEDNAR
LAUREN BINLEY
LAUREN BLANCHARD
LAUREN DARBY
LAUREN GOFF
LAUREN JESSUP
LAUREN JONES
LAUREN LANSEIGNE
LAUREN LINDQUIST
LAUREN MCCALL
LAUREN MCCAW
LAUREN MORALES
LAUREN PILEGGI
LAUREN SKY JENKINS
LAUREN STOOKEY
LAUREN TIMOTHY
LAUREN WEINTRAUB
LAUREN WILSON
LAUREN YATES
LAURIE MCLEAN
LAVENIA ALICE SCOTT
LEA HUBNER
LEA WALKER
LEAH CARTER
LEAH HELLO
LEAH LOWRY
LEAH MERRITT
LEAH MOSS
LEAH RILEY
LEAH SECORD
LEAH TAYLOR
LEAH WOONTON
LEANNA MCCORD
LEANNE MUEHLEISEN
LEE CHU YEM
LEENA MOMONIAT
LEIGH ZINSKI
LEIGHANNA LEASK
LEILA GROSSMARK
LEILANI REYES
LEILANY LOPEZ
LENA MARTINOVIC
LENA SCHWARZ
LENKA KOTALIKOVA
LEO COLLINS
LESLEY DEWAR
LESLI RANSOM

291

LESLIE YATES
LETISHA MEADOWS
LEVI MOORE
LEXI MCCAIN
LEXI RAPHAEL
LEXI REEVES
LEXY BURROUGHS
LEXY LYONS
LIA RUDD
LIAM FISHER
LIAM MONTAGNE
LIAM ROBSON
LIANA MERK
LIBERTY JUSTICE
LILIAN CHENG
LILIBETH RAMOS
LILLI MOHLER
LILLIAN MAGERS
LILLIAN WHITHAUS
LILY FORSMAN
LILY JACOBS
LILY MEDVICK
LILY MEVAN
LILY PERRY
LILYANNE EATON
LINA ASTROM
LINA EL-SAIEH
LINA SABBOULA
LINAE LEWTER
LINCOLN LAW
LINDA BRAUS
LINDA KOHLSTOCK
LINDA REYNOSO
LINDA SHERMAN
LINDEN JOHN
LINDSAY MEAD
LINDSEY AMES
LINDSEY COKER
LINDSEY DAVIS
LINDSEY HEMMING
LINDSEY KENYON
LINN BERGKVIST
LINNEA SVENSSON
LISA BLACKWELL
LISA BLAINE
LISA COURTNEY
LISA GIBSON
LISA HANSON
LISA HORDIJK
LISA JONES
LISA LOWDERMILK
LISA SANDNER
LISA STRAUSZ
LIZ ANDERSON
LIZ BROENE
LIZ COMFORT
LIZ VALLISH
LIZBETH GAMA
LIZETH RODRIGUEZ
LOES KIP
LOGAN BLACK
LOGAN MEDNICK
LOIS BILBREY
LOLA VICTOR-PUJEBET
LORALEAH FELEY
LOREN NICOL
LORENA EL-KADRE
LORETO V
LORI FRAY
LORNA LEE
LORUAMA ESPINOSA
LOUIS FEVOLA
LOUISE KENDALL
LOUISE PANAYE
LOUISE SOUZA
LOURDES BUSTILLO
LOVIISA SCHULTZ
LOW PEIQI
LUCAS FIDELIS
LUCAS TABISI
LUCI DELPILAR
LUCIA MOLINA
LUCIANO SPANTO
LUCIE CARMIN
LUCIE PHILPOTT
LUCINDA GARCIA
LUCY COOKE
LUCY KING

LUCY TAYLOR
LUCY WICKHAM
LUELLE JINGCO
LUIS RUBIO
LUISA BIE
LUKAS HUDA
LUKE BARTLETT
LUKE MORONEY
LUKE SMITH
LUKE STEWART
LUNA AMI
LUPA LATIF
LUPITA CAMPOS
LYDIA BUNTIN
LYDIA HALL
LYDIA MARGARET
LYNDEE PAXMAN
LYNLEE ANDERSON
LYNN PHILLIPS
MACAYLA HOPE
MACKENZIE LYND
MACKENZIE PROVOST
MADARA SPRUDE
MADDIE DOWDEN
MADDIE MOULIN
MADDIE ROSEVEAR
MADDY B
MADELEINE STERN
MADELINE PIPPIN
MADI CONNOLLY
MADIE FARRIS
MADISON CHO
MADISON HODGE
MADISON HOPE-
TATNELL
MADISON HUGHS
MADISON LEAP
MADISON LOVE
MADISON MILHOUS
MADISON MILLER
MADISON WABER
MADISON WOCKNER
MAFALDA WILTON
MAGDALENA NEUBAUER
MAGGIE BARDIS
MAGGIE CAMPBELL
MAGGIE KOLF
MAGGIE LAMPL
MAGGIE MARTIN
MAGGIE MCAULEY
MAGGIE MORGANS
MAHA ROSALES
MAIAN DUNDAS
MALACHI ALLEN
MALCOLM DAVIS
MALENE MAINS
MALINA BRATAON
MALLORY ALLAIN
MANDI STRZELEWICZ
MANDI TUCKER
MANON VAN DER MAAS
MANUEL GIGLIO
MARANDA VOMUND
MARC CROSS
MARC ROUBE
MARCELENE SUTTER
MARCELLA ANJOS
MARCIA MANZONE
MARCO LOCATELLI
MARCO MEYER
MARCUS HOWELL
MARCUS LEE
MARCUS WALTON
MARGALY MONELUS
MARGARET DUNCAN
MARGARET STAUNTON
MARGARET TAVENNER
MARGIT KIENZL
MARGRETHE KOFOED
MARIA BALLESTEROS
MARIA CASKEY
MARIA FERNANDA
GONZALEZ
MARIA KEANE
MARIA MORALES
MARIA STANICA
MARIAH BOONE
MARIAH CARTER

MARIAH LOPEZ
MARIAH LYONS
MARIAM SAGULLO
MARIAN TRUDEAU
MARIANA AMADO
MARIANA GARCIA
MARIANA MILHOLO
MARIANA REIS
MARIANA SOUSA
MARIANA TABIN
MARIANNE VINAS
MARIE DOR
MARIE ENZMANN
MARIE OLIVA
MARIEL TISHMA
MARIELA ESPINOZA-
LEON
MARIELA SHULEY
MARIETT ROMTVEDT
MARILEN GONZALEZ
RUBIO
MARILYN SUTER
MARINA GREGO
MARINELLA ROSE
MARINN CEDILLO
MARIO POPOCA
MARIO ROMERO
MARIS-JOHANNA TAHK
MARISA BRADEN
MARISOL GUERRA
MARISSA DAVIDSON
MARISSA HERNANDEZ
MARISSA JOHNSON
MARISSA RAMSEY
MARISSA WALKER
MARK ALI
MARK BARON
MARK MARINER
MARK RAYSKI
MARLAYNE
BONDARCHUK
MARLENE GARCIA
MARLEY BOURKE-
O'NEALE
MARLEY PRATT
MARTHA WINSLOW
MARTIN KRISTJANSEN
MARTINA IANEV
MARTINA WEIL
MARVIN RADDING
MARY ALINE FERTIN
MARY CALNAN
MARY CAPOLUPO
MARY DOWD
MARY G
MARY GARAVAGLIA
MARY HEALY
MARY JO HERNANDEZ
MARY KRZYZEWSKI
MARY NYE
MARY PEARSON
MARY WAHLSTROM
MARY WATTS
MARYAM ALI
MARYAM EL MOKHTARI
MARYANN DARLINGTON
MASHA BARYCHEVA
MASI DEHDAR
MASOOMA BATOOL
MATEY CATHY
MATISON HALL
MATT ANDERSEN
MATT OAK
MATTEO PULLICINO
MATTHEW BEATTIE
MATTHEW EPPARD
MATTHEW HAYES
MATTHEW KING
MATTHEW STENNES
MATTHEW TSVETKOV
MATTHIAS THACKRAY
MAUREEN GRAHAM
MAURICE REED
MAX MASTERSON
MAX PRYBYLA
MAXINE DOUGLAS
MAYA MASLOVSKA
MAYS AL-KHAWAJA

MAYTE NORIEGA
MCKELVY LAW
MCKENNA ROSE
MCLAREN BOYD
MEAGAN FUNCK
MEAGEN DURRANT
MEDEEA ANTON
MEDINA MIFTARI
MEENA NACHIAPPAN
MEG CORNELIUS
MEGAN BARTLEY
MEGAN CODLING
MEGAN CONWAY
MEGAN DAVIES
MEGAN GRANDAS
MEGAN HALE
MEGAN HALL
MEGAN HILLS
MEGAN HULEN
MEGAN JANETSKY
MEGAN JARRELL
MEGAN KORTMANN
MEGAN MCCULLOH
MEGAN PAYNE
MEGAN SHIPMAN
MEGAN VANDERMOLEN
MEGANNE HULSEY
MEGAYN RAY
MEGHAN GURLEY
MEGHAN KEMP
MEGHANN HORST
MEGS WRIGHT
MEKIAH HALL
MELANI DOS SANTOS
MELANIE BAXTER
MELANIE CHRISTENSEN
MELANIE GRECH
MELANIE
KONSTANTINOU
MELANIE KRESS
MELANIE LAMEIRO
MELANIE LEHNEN
MELANIE SKIDMORE
MELANIE YODER
MELI MAZO
MELINDA C
MELINDA HARRIS
MELINDA MEGINNESS
MELISSA CARMONA
MELISSA JOYCE
MELISSA NOGUES
MELISSA ORLANDI
MELISSA ROMO
MELISSA SAWATZKY
MELISSA SIGNORE
MELISSA STUBBINGS
MELISSA TAYLOR
MELISSA WALSH
MELISSA WASHBURN
MELISSA ZOON
MELODY GUILLEN
MELODY MALONE
MEMO TERRAZA
MENDY STAD
MERCEDES OHLEN
MEREDITH KAGY
MEREDITH KRESIC
MEREDITH SAUNDERS
MERSEDIEZ SZABO
MERVYN GRAHAM
METTE JENSEN
MEYLA SATIN
MIA APOLLONIO
MIA CAMPION CURTIS
MIA CRACKNELL
MIA MANNS
MIA TURNER
MIAH WINTON
MICAH DELIN
MICHAEL ANGELO
BOLIDO
MICHAEL BURNS
MICHAEL CLAXON
MICHAEL COURTNEY
MICHAEL DEELY
MICHAEL FIGUEROA
MICHAEL HERNANDEZ
MICHAEL J HELTON

MICHAEL MATHIEU
MICHAEL MIDNIGHT
MICHAEL NATELLI
MICHAELA BLEDSOE
MICHAELA CAROLAN
MICHAELA HANSON
MICHAELA HOFINGER
MICHAELA HOUGH
MICHAELA LONG
MICHAELA NASH
MICHAELA WHATNALL
MICHAL GREINER
MICHAYLA WICKER
MICHELINA MURRAY
MICHELLE ARIAS
MICHELLE BACZKOWSKI
MICHELLE BROCK
MICHELLE CHESTER
MICHELLE DE NOIA
MICHELLE GARCIA
MICHELLE GRAY
MICHELLE HUYNH
MICHELLE JUDY
MICHELLE LAI
MICHELLE LAVOIE
MICHELLE LEE
MICHELLE MORAN
MICHELLE POTO
MICHELLE ROSS
MICHELLE SIMPSON
MICHELLE SOARES
MICHELLE SUGIARTO
MICHELLE SWOLFS
MICHELLE WANG
MICHELLE WU
MICKI ANDREWS
MIKAYLA BENNETT
MIKAYLA BERLINGERI
MIKAYLA PIERCE
MIKE DOLAN
MIKE MESSNIA
MIKE ROTH
MIKE SCIMECA
MILENA BUKOEVA
MILES ARELLANO
MILES MCGUINNESS
MILES REBEIRO
MILIANAH TOSHA
MILLE KNUDSEN
MILLIE SHENTON
MINA ROSE
MIRANDA JAMES
MIRANDA LANZA
MIRANDA SCHUCH
MIRANDA SHERRELL
MIRANDA UNDERWOOD
MIRIAM BURROUGHS
MIRIAM HERNANDEZ
MIRIAM JENKINS
MIRIAM MCGOVERN
MIRIAM WAINWRIGHT
MIRJAM VAN DEN
HOORN
MISBA KHAN
MISSY SMITH
MITCHELL BARTLETT
ML WHITAKER
MOA LYTH BRAND
MOE ALABDULLATIF
MOHAMMAD SHAH
MOHAMMED MOUSAWI
MOIRA MCCARDELL
MOLLIE WASSER
MOLLY EASTOL
MOLLY GAUMER
MOLLY KING
MOLLY LEAVES
MOLLY RUNYON
MOMEN ADAS
MONA OLSEN
MONET ST. LOUIS
MONICA IBRAHIM
MONICA LOPEZ
MONICA RIVERA
MONICA VLAD
MONIEK VAN
WAAYENBURG
MONIKA HAJDECKI

MONIKA TANAKA
MONSE ZAMORA
MONTANA MCKEOWN
MONTSE DEL BOSQUE
MORGAINE PAYSON
MORGAN BELANGER
MORGAN HOBDAY
MORGAN MCGRATH
MORGAN OLLER
MORGAN PARKER
MORGEN EGESDAL
MORGYN GILLIS
MORRIGAN PROUDE
MUSKAAN DUDEJA
MYA FRAPPIER
NAARA SILVA
NABILA ANUAR
NADGEE FLORES
NAIMA GUHAD
NAIMA MEBCHOUR
NALIYAH GRANT
NANNA ANDERSEN
NAOMI GROSS
NAOMI LEMIRE
NAOMI SPICER
NARAYANA SAUCEDA
NARDEEN AL-GAITAR
NASTASSJA CHAN
NATALEA MARTIN
NATALIA MENDONCA
NATALIE DINA
NATALIE CASABONNE
NATALIE
CHETVERIKOVA
NATALIE CURTIS
NATALIE FREER
NATALIE HARWOOD
NATALIE HISHMEH
NATALIE JONES
NATALIE KLEIN
NATALIE PARKER
NATALY CALDERON
NATASHA BONNICI
NATASHA FRANCIS
NATASHA SANDILANDS
NATHALIE LARSON
NATHAN KERWOOD
NATHANIEL BRILLIANT
NAVI SURESH
NAVNEESH BATH
NAYBETH ROMERO
NEARY HOK
NEIL CATHRO
NELLIE WEY
NG ZAC
NIA CARTER
NIA NAVAL
NIA NIGHT
NIA PICKERING
NICHOLAS CLARK
NICHOLAS
PAPADOPOULOS
NICHOLAS PHAM
NICHOLAS SANDERS
NICHOLE MCCANN
NICK HERNANDEZ
NICK HIGHT
NICK PENNER
NICK YEE
NICKI COLLETT
NICOLA SAMPAIR
NICOLE ABBOTT
NICOLE ARMSTRONG
NICOLE BARTA
NICOLE BOGDAN
NICOLE BRYANT
NICOLE DAN
NICOLE GRIGSON
NICOLE KRASON
NICOLE LANAGHAN
NICOLE LANGDON
NICOLE MINER
NICOLE SANDLER
NICOLE SMO
NICOLE STABILE
NICOLE SWISTACK
NICOLE WOLKING
NIDI GHOSH

NIKAYLA SPRIGGS
NIKI KAE REDMON
NIKI ROMEO
NIKKI BELSCHES
NIKKI INGWEILLER
NIKKI RITA
NIKKI-LEE PIGOTT
NINA KAHN
NINA ROEBBERS
NINA WAGNER
NIRMALI SHAH
NISHA RAO
NOAH HALMRAST
NOELLE GEORGE
NOELLE SAWYER
NOOR ANWAR
NOOR KOUKI
NOOR-UL-AIN ALAMGIR
NORA K
NUMRA TARIQ
NUR AMIRA ZULKIFLI
NURAZLIN KHALIT
NYSSA KUDRAVY
ODA RAMSDAL
ODA SELVIK
ODYSSEY RIOS
OFEK GOLDREICH
OHAILA KHAN
OLGA-ERENIA
KONTOLATOU
OLINDA SAENZ
OLISA ONWUALU
OLIVIA AARONS
OLIVIA AGAR
OLIVIA ASBURY
OLIVIA BOYD
OLIVIA CRAKER
OLIVIA HAHN
OLIVIA HILL
OLIVIA HUMPHREY
OLIVIA HUPALOWSKY
OLIVIA JONES
OLIVIA KALPAKIS
OLIVIA MALDONADO
OLIVIA MORALES
OLIVIA NIDAY
OLIVIA PAPADOPOULOS
OLIVIA REBOLD
OLIVIA SYNAN
OLIVIA WILLIAMS
OMAR OVERMAN
OMEGA BETTS
ORIEL SANCHEZ
ORIENE SHIEL
ORRIN BERTRAND
OTIS CARTER
OWEN WALTER
PAIGE OWENS
PAIGE WHITNEY
PAIGE WIADUCK
PAITYN GAGE
PAM WOLFE
PAMELA PINTO
PAMELA WISE
PAMMY BRUTZKUS
PAMODA RUPASINGHE
PAN DANIELS
PAOLA BENAVIDES
PARIS COLLINS
PARIS PHILLIPS
PARKER WEST
PATRICIA CLAUDIO
PATRICIA HORVATH
PATRICIA HUFFMAN
PATRICIA SCNEAR
PATRICIO TORRES
PATRICK BESLER
PATRICK BICALDO
PATRICK BRAUE
PATTI BUTLER
PATTY GONZALEZ
PAUL BISHOP
PAUL BUTLER
PAUL DECKER
PAUL PETTY
PAUL VIGIL
PAULI ALAMAKI
PAULINE SOHN

PAYTON CHAPLEY
PEDRO CAETANO
CARVALHO
PEDRO PAIS
PEDRO RIVERA
PEDRO VALA
PEGAH HAZARY
PEOGO SMYTH
PETER MCPHERSON
PETER PALSKI
PETER TRAN
PHILIP HURST
PHILLIP DUONG
PHOEBE HEATH BROWN
PHOEBE KALID
PHOEBE TAM
PHOEBE TANG
PHOENIX BAUDELARIE
PHOENIX CABILING
PIA OLOFSSON
PILAR CASARES
PIPER LANE
POLINA LASTOCHKINA
POPPY WILLIAMS
PRESLIE STEVENSON
PRESTON
BAUMGARDNER
PRISCILLA ROSAS
PRISCILLA RUIZ
PUANANI HORNER
QUINLAN HARP
RACHAEL BIRRI
RACHAEL COLLINS
RACHAEL MOGCK
RACHAEL THARP
RACHAEL VELLA
RACHAUD SMITH
RACHEL BARROCAS
RACHEL BASS
RACHEL BATEMAN
RACHEL BELL
RACHEL BENESH
RACHEL BRADSHAW
RACHEL BRANSON
RACHEL BROOKS
RACHEL BUSKEY
RACHEL CANNON
RACHEL CARTER
RACHEL COUSINS
RACHEL DULA
RACHEL HUSSEY
RACHEL JACKSON
RACHEL JONES
RACHEL KIMMEL
RACHEL KIRBY
RACHEL KNIGHT
RACHEL KOH WOON SIM
RACHEL KOSTRZEWA
RACHEL LOPEZ
RACHEL MACRAE
RACHEL MARSH
RACHEL MAYBERRY
RACHEL MCATEE
RACHEL MCCARTHY
RACHEL MCINTOSH
RACHEL MIKKAY
RACHEL PATRICK
RACHEL PIETREWICZ
RACHEL PORTING
RACHEL RACICOT
RACHEL RYAN
RACHEL SCALES
RACHEL SEAS
RACHEL SKIDMORE
RACHEL TARVER
RACHEL VENEZIANO
RACHEL WEASE
RACHEL WEIMAR
RACHELLE LEBLANC
RACHYL ELLIOTT
RADVILE LIRIKAITE
RAE ULRICH
RAELEEN LEMAY
RAFAEL MARTINS
RAFAEL PINHEIRO
RAFAEL PORRAS
RAINN HEPBURN
RAISSA MORAES

RAKEY ZUROFF
RAMON CHIRATHEEP
RANE SALAZAR
RANI STREFF
RAPH GAIL
RASHMI YADAV
RAVEENA REUBEN
RAVEN PRATT
RAYA BOGARD
REBECCA BUTLER
REBECCA CONGI
REBECCA DESNOYERS
REBECCA GOULDMAN
REBECCA
JEYAMANOHARAN
REBECCA LANGLEY
REBECCA LAW
REBECCA MILLIGAN
REBECCA MURPHY
REBECCA PERNA
REBECCA PRUITT
REBECCA SWAINE
REBECCA THOMPSON
REBECCA TRY
REBECCA VERONA
REBECCA WALL
REBECCA WHEELER
REBECCA WOODWARD
REBEKAH CARROLL
REBEKAH HANDLEY
REBEKAH JASWA
REBEKAH MYERS
REBEKAH QUIXANO
HENRIQUES
REBEKAH ROMANI
REBEKAH WILLIAMS
REBEKKAH GRANT
RECEL WYNSLEY
TONELADA
REECE GHERARDI
REEDHIMA MANDLIK
REGAN MAHONEY
REGAN SANDERS
REGGIE BROOKS
REGINA BIRDS
REGINA FAYE
REGINA GONZALEZ
REHANN RHEEL
REILLY SCHEFFING
REINE FRESCO
RENE M RODRIGUEZ
RESUL CEYLAN
REYNA VILLA
RHIANNE SUCKLING
RHONA WELDON
RIA REIS
RICHARD HEALY
RICHMOND LARTEY
RIGOBERTO SANTANA
RIIKKA SARKELA
RILEY BOYES
RILEY SADLER
RINIEL CALAELEN
RISCHA HERSCHEL
RIYA SHAH
ROBBIE RACINE
ROBERT BROWNSELL
ROBERT JOSEPH ISLES
ROBERT MARTINEZ
ROBERT VENNE
ROBERTO GUERRERO
ROBIN DE BRUIJN
ROBIN WESTERLUND
ROBYN JANSEN
ROBYN POTTER
ROBYN POTTINGER
ROBYN SCHNEIDER
ROCIO TEMPONE
RODNEY FLEMING
ROGER CREE
ROGIER CAPRINO
ROMAN KALEI
ROMESSA MIRZA
ROMI FOSTER
ROMY DINGLE
RONNIE HARRIS
RONNIE SAWYER
ROOSA KOLI

ROSA WESTFALL
ROSALBA GAMBOA
ROSE AL-KAHILI
ROSE ARMSTRONG
ROSE DICKINSON
ROSE GRUBB
ROSE HATAWAY
ROSEMARY GUERRERO
ROSIE CASSARA
ROSIE LOPEZ
ROSIE SYMES
ROXANA CASTANEDA
ROXANNE BALZANA
ROXY MOURE
ROXY TRASK
RU BEE NG
RUBY REPLOGLE
RUOLE XIA
RUTH BROEKEMA
RUTH COOPER
RUTH DAY
RYAN LANE
RYAN MOUNTFORD
SABINA ATAMOVA
SABRINA CHIODO
SABRINA GARDNER
SABRINA HOSSAIN
SABRINA JOHNSON
SABRINA KHAN
SABRINA KOCK
SABRINA LEUNG
SABRINA PAVAO
SABRINA TUNLEY
SAFA A
SAFIRE STAR
SAIF ALMAMARI
SALAM ORFALY
SALEM YOHANNES
SALLY ANN
CUNNINGBIRD
SALLY MILLS
SALMA DEERA
SAM BLACK
SAM KOH
SAM MCKIBBIN
SAM SMITH
SAM W
SAM WORMAN
SAMA AMGAD
SAMANTHA BARRETT
SAMANTHA CANTOR
SAMANTHA COSGROVE
SAMANTHA DENNIS
SAMANTHA FINAMORE
SAMANTHA GARRETT
SAMANTHA
HENGESBACH
SAMANTHA JOY GO
SAMANTHA LOZANO
SAMANTHA MARTIN
SAMANTHA MARY
CRONIN
SAMANTHA PETERSON
SAMANTHA ROSS
SAMANTHA SEELBACH
SAMANTHA SMITH
SAMANTHA TOTHE
SAMANTHA
WHITTINGTON
SAMEER USMAN
SAMI MCLAREN
SAMMY STRUNK
SAMMY TYSON
SAMPRATI PRASAD
SAMPRIT BAINS
SAMUEL CAPRI
SAMUEL HARDIN
SANDER DE LEEUW
SANDI GAMMON
SANDRA MARI MILLER
SANDRA RODRIGUEZ
SANDY HINES
SANIA ELSHORBGY
SANIYA NAIEEM
SANNE
DUIVENVOORDEN
SANTA SUDNIKA
SANTANA STOUT

SAPPHIRE SMITH
SARA ANDERSON
SARA CHURCH
SARA DUNN
SARA GRIGSBY
SARA HEALEY
SARA JOHNSON
SARA LIDSTONE
SARA LOMBARDI
SARA PANNELL
SARA PRATT
SARA RAZIULLAH
SARA SHREVE
SARA THIESSEN
SARA WALECKI
SARA ZEROF
SARAH BELK
SARAH BILGASEM
SARAH BRADSHAW
SARAH CARNICELLA
SARAH CHANG
SARAH CHAU
SARAH CHIMOFF
SARAH CLARK
SARAH CLEMENT
SARAH CRAGGS
SARAH DEFRANCESCO
SARAH GAITAN
SARAH GARZON
SARAH HOLMEN
SARAH JENSEN
SARAH JESSICA
SARAH KEBIRE
SARAH LINARES
SARAH MARCH
SARAH MCCABE
SARAH MCCALL
SARAH MOHR
SARAH MORGAN
SARAH MORI
SARAH NOELLE
SARAH RAE
SARAH THEALL
SARAH THOMAS
SARAH TRAYNHAM
SARAH VANROYE
SARAH VORHERR
SARAH WACKER
SARAH WEISE
SARAH WILKOWSKE
SARAH WILLIAMSON
SARAH WRAY
SARAH YEO
SARAH-JEANNE
SARAH-MAE LIEVERSE
SAREMA SHORR
SASHA SODEN
SASKIA KARSEN FERRER
SATU BERGMANN
SAVANNA GARDNER
SCARLETT MIJATOVICH
SCOTT SAUNDERS
SEAMUS FLYNN
SEAN EMERY
SEAN MCGUIRE
SEAN-ELIZABETH
TAKAOKA
SEAONNA KELLY
SEBASTIAN FIGUEROA
SEBASTIAN SABIR
SEBASTIAN THERIOT
SEHRINUR SUCU
SELBE DITTMAN
SELINA CHONG
SELMA ALAHMAD
SEMINA PEKMEZOVIC
SENELA YURDAKUL
SENIA SIKKINK
SERA JAY
SERA L
SERENA CRONIN
SERGIO VELASQUEZ
SERGIO ZARATE
SEWEY WILOMAS
SHAINA CONNELL
SHAMIAH BECK
SHANA SLAVIN
SHANNAH TENIO

SHANNEN MICHAELSEN
SHANNON BROOKS
SHANNON COLLINS
SHANNON COOK
SHANNON LONGFELLOW
SHANNON MCBRIDE
SHANNON MCNAIR
SHANNON SMITH
SHANNON WOOD
SHANNON WOZNICKI
SHANNON YARDLEY
SHANNON ZUCCARELLI
SHARA CHOWDHURY
SHARMIN PIANCCA
SHARNABELLE REILLY
SHARON MCINTOSH
SHAUKI AL-GAREEB
SHAUN GOULET
SHAUN MCALISTER
SHAUNA CASKIE
SHAWN FITZGERALD, JR.
SHAWNA DURBIN
SHAWNAH MITCHISON
SHAWNYA PETERSON
SHAY NEWELL
SHAYNA JOHNSTON
SHAYNE DUFF
SHEA HAVILAND
SHEENA KNUDSTRUP
SHELBIE CANALES
SHELBY BALDWIN
SHELBY CORTEZ
SHELBY GRASSO
SHELBY KRENN
SHELBY LARSON
SHELBY METCALFF
SHELBY VARNER
SHELBY WALLACE
SHENDIVA KIMIORA
SHERRY FARR
SHERYL DOUGLAS
SHEYENNE ROWE
SHIRA MILLER
SHONA MALONE
SHULA BRONNER
SHUMAILA KIDWAI
SIDNEY BIRCHFIELD
SIDNEY DEBIE
SIENIE VAN GEERTERUY
SIERRA EHLINGER
SIERRA HOY
SIERRA SANGER
SIGRID UNDERLID
SIGRUN ZASCHE
SILAINE THORDARSON
SIMON DEAN
SIMON TORFFVIT
SIMONE CEDOTAL
SIOBHAN HUDSON
SIOBHAN MORONEY
SIV HEGE BERG FORNES
SIVA O'NEILL
SKY PTAGA
SKYE RUSE
SKYLAR WATSON
SOETKIN CHARLIER
SOFIA MATIAS
SOFIA RODRIGUEZ
SOFIA ROSENBERG-
KLAINBERG
SOFIE GEITHUS
SONNY FRANCO
SOPHIA BEATRICE DELOS
SANTOS
SOPHIA HONICKA
SOPHIA LIM
SOPHIA MENCONI
SOPHIE BARRY
SOPHIE BEER
SOPHIE BIGNELL
SOPHIE CREIGHTON
SOPHIE EIKLI
SOPHIE JANSSEN
SOPHIE KING
SOPHIE MACKAY
SOPHIE MCADAM
SOPHIE MCALLEN
SOPHIE ROGERS

SOROUSH ABTAHI
SOUMIA BEKKA
SPARKY TREEMIGHT
SPIRYT MCMAHON
STACEY RUDGE
STAFANI ALMANZA
STANISLAV SHESTEL
STATON ELISABET
JOHNSON
STEELE SCHIMMING
STEFANIA RUSSO
STEFANIE MCNEAL
STEFANY SOTO
STEPH JURY
STEPHANIE ASHBY
STEPHANIE BENT
STEPHANIE BOWEN
STEPHANIE COHEN
STEPHANIE COUILLARD
STEPHANIE COWLEY
STEPHANIE CRAIG
STEPHANIE DIMOVSKI
STEPHANIE DOUGHTY
STEPHANIE HAYES
STEPHANIE HOOVER
STEPHANIE LINDT
STEPHANIE MCCONNELL
STEPHANIE OSTERHUS
STEPHANIE SCOTT
STEPHANIE SPICE
STEPHANIE TEJADA
STEPHANIE TUBBS
STEPHANIE VAN LAERE
STEPHEN KELLER
STEPHEN-MARSHAL
BOVE
STEPHENIE THORNE
STERLING V HILLMAN
STEVE HARDY
STEVE OJA
STEVE TAYLOR
STEVEN AUSTIN
STEVEN FORTIER
STEVEN HILL
STEVEN UNDERWOOD
STINE B
STORM ST JACQUES
STORMI REAGAN
STORMY ASKEW
STUART WILSON
SUMMER FEALLY
SUMMER SPIKER
SUMMER THURMAN
SUSAN DE BRUIN
SUSAN MESLER-EVANS
SUSAN SOARES
SUSANA FRAGA
SUSANNA DE LA PENA
SUSU RAWWAGAH
SUZANNE BORSJE
SVETA SLOBODYAN
SWONTER ONCEST
SYAFIQ WAHAB
SYDNEY BRINKDOEPKE
SYDNEY ERIN TAYLOR
SYDNEY LEVINE
SYDNEY LEWIS
SYDNEY MELNYK
SYDNEY PENA
SYDNEY SANFORD
ZOE ROBINSON
ZOE WILLEY
ZOIE KUJAWA

SYDNEY SAVAUGE
SYDNEY YALOWSKY
SYDNEY-MICHELLE SOTO
SYMONE GRIFFIN
T-JAE MULLINGS
T.J. KEANE
TABATHA OUTLER
TABITHA QUALLS
TAI JOHNSON
TALIA ANDREA
TALIAH HERRERA
TALOR ROBARE
TAMARA CARSON
TAMARA WARDHANA
TAMARA YU
TAMBRILYNNE OLSON
TAMMY MOSCOSO
TAMMY SPARKS
TANIA JARAMILLO
TANISHA TAYLOR
TANJA RUSTAND
TANJE VAN LINGEN
TANNER MCMAHON
TANNIA RODRIGUEZ
TANYA BRYAN
TANYA VERNOIA
TARA ANAND
TARA MELKI
TARA NGUYEN
TASHA DION
TASHYA WILSON
TASNEEM BOOTWALA
TATIANA BARRIENTOS
TATIANA TAPASCO
TATUM JAMES
TAYLA MALLOW-SPEARS
TAYLOR CASH
TAYLOR CLARK
TAYLOR CLIFTON
TAYLOR DAVIS
TAYLOR ELIZABETH
TAYLOR G.
TAYLOR GODBY
TAYLOR HANSARUK
TAYLOR LOTT
TAYLOR MARZALEN
TAYLOR PIPES
TAYLOR ROSEBERRY
TAYLOR SPARLING
TAYLOR SWAN
TEDDY CHRUPCALA
TEGAN CLEVELAND
TEGAN ROBERTSON
TEGAN WILLIAMS
TERESA HOANG
TERESA MEJIA
TERIZA MIR
TERRA DAO
TESS CYR
TESS PIERCE
TESSA CHURCHILL
TESSA JONES
THE DOCTOR
THEO WRIGHT
THERESSA GOLDBERG
THIANNA NOORDZIJ
THOMAS REID
TIA BEARDEN
TIA STILL
TIANA KATE

TIERNAN BERTRAND-
ESSINGTON
TIERRA JOHNSON
TIFFANY CROUCHER
TIFFANY DAINS
TIFFANY JOHNSON
TIFFANY MCARTHUR
TIFFANY NABORS
TIFFANY NG
TIFFANY TYREE
TIMOTHY THOMPSON
TIMOTHY WATSON
TINA GAO
TINA ROSETTE
TJ GRUNFELDER
TOBEY MAHONEY
TOM CLEMENTS
TOM JOYCE
TOMI TUNRAREBI
TOMMY CROFT
TOMMY WIADUCK
TONI-JAYNE WOOD
TONIA MARIN
TORI JARRETT
TORIANO LACOSTA
TRACIE FOWLER
TRACY DAWSON
TRAVIS CURTIS
TRAVIS MOYE
TRENT CRAIG
TREVOR DOS
TREVOR WHALEN
TREY ROGERS
TREY TOBIAS
TRICIA HUGHES
TRINA YU
TRINE JOHNSEN
TRINITY CAUDLE
TRISHA KICK
TRISTAN CURTIS
TROY HARRISON
TUSHAR PRASAD
TYE CARTER
TYLER ALFORD
TYLER HAGAN
TYLER JEREMIAH
TYLER MCGINNIS
TYLER WARNER
TZUF LIFSHITZ
UDYAN AIONO
UGNE DERESKEVICIUTE
UNAL YUCEL
URBANA ARA
VAL GARCINI
VALENTINA
VALDERRAMA
VALERIA DE LA ROCHA
VALERIA IBARRA
VALERIA RAMOS
VALERIA VALDIVIA
VALIA LIND
VANESSA CORDOVA
VANESSA LAM
VANESSA MARIE FLORES
VANESSA PHILLIPS
VERA RULISON
VERENICE
ANTOMMARCHI
VERONCIA SHEANODA
VERONICA CRUZ

VERONICA GAMON
VERONICA JAMES
VERONICA LEE
VERONICA LI
VI NGUYEN
VICKI LIPTROT
VICTOR DANIEL VERA
VICTOR REIS
VICTOR VO
VICTORIA BOZDECK
VICTORIA BRO
VICTORIA BROWNLEE
VICTORIA FLORENZANO
VICTORIA HUDGEONS
VICTORIA KENNEDY
VICTORIA LEPINE
VICTORIA MEZA
VICTORIA MITCHELL
VICTORIA NG
VICTORIA RODGER
VICTORIA STAMP
VIDYA THAKOORDEEN
VIOLET REBELO
VIRGINIA RAMIREZ
VITA JAUNBERZINA
VIVIAN MAI
VIVIEN T
VY LE
WEISHI YANG
WENDI SUN
WENDY STAPLES
WENNIE VAN
GEERTERUY
WHYTNEE SHATTUCK
WILLIAM JACKSON
WILLIAM MOSIER
WILLIAM ROZARIO
WILLOW GRACE
WINONA FLAY
WINSTON BOLLINGER
XIN XIN SHU
YAMAN ALAWA
YASEMIN FEY
YASHITH FERNANDO
YASMEEN MCCREADY
YASMINE GLUECK
YEN DAU
YSRAEL YUGAN
YUEN LING TSUI
YUKO HARA
YZABELLE BOSTYN
ZACH FULLER
ZACH WADE
ZACHARY GIBSON
ZACK MORRIS
ZAHIN MOHAMMAD
ZANDRINA MCGOWAN
ZELIA CHAN
ZENDELL CRICHLOW
ZEYNEP IREM EREZ
ZHARMAINE ZAFRA
ZINA BROWN
ZOE ALBERTS
ZOE ANDERSON
ZOE BUTTERWORTH
ZOE GENDEREN
ZOE GIANDUZZO
ZOE GONZALEZ
ZOE NIXON

COMING SOON

THE NEXT BOOK IN THE *Harken* SERIES

READHARVEST.COM

Made in the USA
Lexington, KY
02 October 2013